Last Wish

Helen Harper

Chapter One

'What do you get when you cross a goose with a mouse?'

I frowned. As much fun as cheesy jokes were, I was trying to concentrate. 'This isn't really the time, Bob.'

'Ohhhh,' he flounced. 'So it's alright for *you* to force your poor excuse for humour in our faces but when one of us tries to do it…'

A passing troll halted and glared at him. 'Chieftain. If you wish the imp to be disposed of, then I would be more than happy to oblige.'

Bob gasped in outrage. 'How dare you! You great lump! I'm a genie, not an imp.'

The troll's gaze grew even more disparaging. 'You all look the same to me.'

Flitting up to the troll's face, Bob reached inside his tiny jacket pocket and drew out an even tinier glove. He reached out and slapped the troll across the nose with it. 'I challenge you to a duel, sirrah.'

The troll swung his heavy head towards me. 'Chieftain, shall I…?'

I rubbed my forehead. 'No.'

He nodded once. 'Very well.'

Bob and I watched him amble off, shuffling with a heavy gait towards the mansion. 'Yeah! Run away like the coward you are!' the little genie shouted.

'Bob,' I said tiredly, 'give it a rest.'

'S'not my fault,' he mumbled.

I shook out my hair. Effectively trapped here within the Adair lands, we were all going stir crazy but it didn't change the fact that there was still work to be done. I had to gain control over my magic; the fate of thousands of people across the Veil might depend upon it, not to mention everyone here behind the Adair borders.

I refocused on the patch of ground. I was getting there. Faint threads of power snaked through my veins and I felt rather light-headed. There was a hiss and the hard ground began to crack. Green shoots pushed their way upwards all along the largest fissure. Yahtzee.

'You've still not answered me, you know,' Bob said. 'What do you get when you cross a goose with a mouse?'

I bit the inside of my cheek. Just a little bit more … beside my toe, a bud was already beginning to emerge.

'A moose!' Bob started to cackle, the sound penetrating my skull to the exclusion of anything else.

I exhaled loudly and straightened up. 'I don't get it.'

'Duh!' He spun up and twanged me between my eyebrows with his fingers. 'Goose combined with mouse makes moose. It's all about blending the letters.'

'I understand that part,' I said through gritted teeth. 'But where's the funny?'

His brow furrowed. 'What do you mean?'

'It's not funny, Bob. Jokes have to make people laugh.'

He stared at me, still not understanding. 'Nobody laughs at your jokes.'

'Sorley does.'

Bob snorted. 'Sorley is an idiot.'

I opened my mouth to reply but I was interrupted by Morna stamping over. She gazed at my growth efforts with what could only be described as disgust. 'Integrity Adair!' she scolded. 'I did not permit you to take more of my Gift so you could fritter away your time. Is that all you've managed to accomplish?'

Suddenly I felt like a small child caught with her hand in the cookie jar instead of Chieftain of my very own Clan. Albeit a remarkably odd Clan. 'I've been distracted,' I protested. 'It's Bob's fault.'

'A good Chieftain takes responsibility for herself and for her Clan. You're the one in charge.'

'Ha ha!' Bob jabbed his finger at me. 'Stop blaming me! A bad workman always blames his tools.'

I raised my eyebrows. 'And we all know that you're a tool.' Bob's mouth dropped open in mock outrage.

'Robert,' Morna said, fixing her steely gaze on him, 'aren't you supposed to helping inside?'

'I'm on a break.' Morna simply looked at him. His head dropped. 'Going back to work now,' he muttered. He floated off. One day I'd like to exercise that kind of control but it didn't matter what I did; I'd never achieve Morna Carnegie's iron power.

'Felled by a mere glance,' I said to myself. I looked at Morna. 'When will you let me take *that* Gift?'

'Being Chieftain is more than the title, Integrity. It's a state of mind.'

'The job's yours if you want it. The pay is shite and there aren't any holidays. But you get to pretend to be dead and that really cuts down on your junk mail. Plus, I've not had a bill to pay for months.'

Her expression didn't change. 'You can't play dead forever.'

My attempt at humour faded away. 'I know.'

'I have to get back to my own Clan soon. My Chieftain is starting to think I've been abducted. I'm running out of excuses to explain my absence.'

I swallowed. 'I do appreciate what you've done for us.'

'It's not for you. The prophecy has yet to be fulfilled.'

'It *has* been fulfilled. I saved the Foinse. In return, I saved the country.'

Morna raised her hand dismissively. 'You and several others. Besides, that wasn't the prophecy.'

'You don't know that.'

She smiled serenely. 'Yes, I do. It's all in the wording.'

'One Adair will save Alba. Yeah, yeah. That's what I was told. I saved the Foinse, therefore I saved Alba.'

Morna patted my shoulder. 'Alba doesn't just mean the Highlands. It means all of Scotland.'

I wrinkled my nose, my scepticism palpable. Scotland hadn't been a whole country since the Fissure – and that was almost three centuries ago. Scotland, in the sense that Morna meant, no longer existed. 'There are a hundred thousand Fomori demons in the Lowlands. At least. Even if I weren't a pacifist, there's not a single thing I could do that would change that.'

Despite my dismissive reply, the thought of all those demons and the people they'd effectively enslaved – and conditioned not to question their enslavement – continued to gnaw at me. I wasn't about to abandon them to their fate but, even with an army of trolls at my back, I couldn't see a way to help them. Yet. I clung onto that word every night when my churning thoughts refused to let me sleep: yet.

Morna shrugged. 'I didn't say I had all the answers. But with the Foinse here, I'm now more inclined to believe in the prophecy than to discard it out of hand.' She pointed at the patch of green by our feet. 'Now come on. Before you save anyone, I'd like to see you rescue yourself. Bring this land back to life.'

'You're a real pain in the arse, Morna.'

Her smile spread. 'I know, dear.'

I returned my gaze to the signs of growth. It was slow going but, thus far, I was rather impressed with my efforts. Aifric Moncrieffe had ordered this ground salted after the massacre which took place on the day of my birth. Normally that would mean many generations' worth of unusable land. With the help of Morna's Gift, however, I was reversing the effects. From what had once been the sacred Adair grove to down here by the old mansion, there was now a swathe of green. Morna was a hard taskmaster though; she expected more.

I reached down inside myself and concentrated. Her Gift buzzed through my blood, my veins and my very soul. I had to admit that it was getting easier, although I could still feel the queasy light-headedness. I had little choice but to embrace it.

'Good,' the older woman said. 'Search for the power in the earth and draw it out.'

I swayed. When you knew what you were looking for, it was quite remarkable. I could feel the throb of life from Mother Nature calling out to me, asking to be restored in much the same way that a desert flower will stay dormant for months and even years, waiting for the rain that finally brings it to blossom. I was the rain. Here, at least, I was life.

Lights exploded behind my eyes and I gasped. My body fizzed with the sudden surge of magic. Goosebumps rose across my skin, pricking me with their intensity.

'Not too much,' Morna warned.

As more blades of grass and green shoots sprang up, I yanked on the threads of power inside me before carefully dampening them down. I might have Morna's Sidhe-given magic but, unless I ripped it all from her, it was a finite source. I had to use it sparingly. Breathing hard, I struggled for control while the ground continued to transform into a blanket of spring. I staggered.

'You're getting there,' she said approvingly.

I clutched at my chest, my heart hammering against my ribcage. 'I don't suppose you'd like to take over,' I enquired when I could finally speak again.

'I could,' she answered. 'But then you'd never learn anything.' She looked at me searchingly. 'Your magic is running out. You need to take more.'

'No, I have enough.'

'Not for the whole Adair lands, you don't.' She took my hands in hers and squeezed. 'Take,' she ordered. 'You have enough control.'

She had considerably more faith in my abilities than I did. I was tempted to refuse but her eyes were hard and insistent. I swallowed and focused on the glow inside her. It wasn't that I could see it, as such, more that I could sense it. Like all acts of thievery, the more often I drew from the Gifts of other Sidhe, the better I became at it. I tugged at wisps of her magic, pulling them gently into myself as if by osmosis. I had to be careful – the last thing I wanted to do was to take too much. My soul hungered to grab and guzzle but I pushed down my primal urges and sucked in a breath, stopping when I felt the nausea.

'You should take more,' Morna chided gently.

I pressed my lips together and shook my head. 'No. You need it. It's yours.'

She let out a bark of laughter. 'I'm an old woman. There's a whole wellspring of magic inside me which is untouched. Better that it gets used than it seeps away into the ether when I finally quit this body.'

I glanced at her, alarmed. Surely she didn't think she was at death's door? Her expression was calm and placid. 'How long till you go?' I asked. Then I realised how that sounded and said quickly, 'I mean how long till you go back home?'

She frowned as she considered my question. 'Soon,' she said eventually. 'But we should conduct a field test first and see how adept you've really become at stealing.'

There was a certain irony in that, given what I used to do for a living and how good I'd been at it. I rubbed my chin. 'I can't be seen. And we should wait until after the next visit.'

Although Morna knew exactly what I meant, 'visit' was something of a euphemism. Delegations from the Clans had been appearing with increasing regularity at the Adair border. So far they'd given the trolls a whole lot of pleading mixed with some grandiose promises. They'd been little more than an annoyance up till now but, when the Sidhe finally realised the carrot was never going to work, they were going to switch to the stick.

'They're not going to stop, you know. The Clans want their security details back.'

I let out an unladylike snort. 'I can't see why it's such a big deal. The Fomori have retreated back beyond the Veil. There haven't been any attacks since Aberdeen.'

'It's about more than the illusion of safety, dear.' Morna's eyes were sad. 'It's about power.'

There was a sudden screech from above. I twisted round in panic, only to see the shining orb of the Foinse fly out from one of the higher windows, followed almost immediately by Tipsania's scowling face. 'You bastard!' she shrieked after it. 'You numbskull ball of idiocy!'

The Foinse somersaulted in a manner that could only be described as taunting and sped away. Morna raised an eyebrow. 'Does the Scrymgeour lass know that she's screeching at the source of all magic?'

'Oh, yes,' I nodded. 'She has no qualms about who she yells at.'

Morna bent down and cupped a daisy. Its petals were white and delicate with just the hint of blush at their tips.

—

8

I had helped to bring that to life. If I thought about it for too long, I was completely staggered by what I'd done. 'It proves my point,' Morna said.

'You mean that by yelling and throwing insults, Tipsania feels like she's more powerful?' Tipsania had bullied me when we were kids so I was well aware that she had a history of wanting to feel strong.

'Well, yes,' Morna said. 'But I was actually referring to the Foinse. The Clans locked it away. They hampered its power and clipped its wings. Look at what it's capable of now that it's free.'

I knew what she meant. As a warlock, Speck had access to some magic. Sure, it was unreliable and weak and had almost killed us on more than one occasion back in our good old thievery days, but it had always been there. The longer he spent near the Foinse, the stronger his magic grew. And, unlike the Sidhe, he wasn't limited to whatever Gift he'd been granted at puberty. We had access to clean, running water as a result of Speck's abilities – not mine.

The only person who didn't seem happy with his burgeoning magic was Lexie. I suspected that was out of fear that she would no longer be good enough for him rather than jealousy. We were complex beings indeed.

I pointed at the ground and the now-verdant carpet. 'How much of that is down to the Foinse?'

A trace of a smile crossed Morna's lips. 'I suppose we'll never know.'

I muttered something under my breath. She looked at me expectantly and I shrugged. 'The Fomori,' I explained. 'I can't help wondering about their magic.'

'You mean the *draoidheachd* you were told about,' said Morna, pronouncing the word *dreeocht* and with a far better Gaelic accent than mine.

I nodded. 'The Foinse is supposed to be the source of all Scottish magic. But if the Fomori have their own version locked away in Edinburgh Castle, someone's screwed up. And if they have it, why don't they do more with it?'

'Their skies are black and their earth is scorched, Integrity. I'm not sure they care.'

'May cares. She came outside last night and spent several hours rolling around in the grass like a puppy.'

'I think we all agree that May is different.'

I couldn't argue with that. Everyone treated the mute Fomori demon who'd tailed me back from beyond the Veil as if she were made of glass. Even Lexie and Bob, initially the most reluctant to befriend her, were now going out of their way to help her. Having her around was proving to be a welcome distraction and the busier we kept, the less we worried about the outside world. And the less I thought of Byron and the look on his face when he realised I was apparently dead. I could still taste him on my tongue. It was a ridiculous notion; I had brushed my teeth many, many times since we'd last kissed. And yet...

I sighed. No. Keeping busy was definitely important.

Taylor popped his head out from the mansion entrance. 'Grub's up,' he said cheerfully. 'Some tasty looking game birds which made the mistake of wandering across the border. Last one to the table is a rotten egg.'

'Your old mentor has no doubt laid a bet with one of the trolls as to which one of us will get there first,' Morna muttered in a disgusted undertone. 'The man is incorrigible.'

Taylor twinkled at us. 'Brochan will snarf it all down if you don't hurry. And Lexie's pissed off at waiting. That's not to mention some very hungry-looking trolls who—'

I held up my hand. 'I got it, Taylor.' I glanced at Morna. 'What did the gamekeeper say to the Lady of the Manor?' She responded with a long suffering sigh. I grinned. 'The pheasants are revolting.'

Bob winked back into existence by my shoulder. 'I don't get it, Uh Integrity. Where's the funny?'

I narrowed my eyes at him. He grinned and spun up to my shoulder, perching next to my ear. 'It's not all bad, is it?' he whispered.

I smiled. 'I guess not.'

***

Taylor was right about one thing – dinner was indeed very tasty. It was just a shame I didn't get to eat more than a few bites before we were interrupted.

Lyle burst through the doors when I was mid-chew. 'Chieftain!' he gasped, doubling over, his sweat-sodden hair straggling against his bulbous forehead. 'The border! Someone's there!'

I muttered a curse. I'd been sure we'd have another few days before the next Clan contingent arrived. I pushed back my chair and stood up. 'How many?'

He held up a single finger. I frowned. One? That was unusual enough to merit notice. One interloper was more intimidating than several; it suggested a diversion – or an ambush.

'The other lookouts?' I asked.

'They've been alerted. Nothing as yet.'

'Is our visitor Sidhe?'

Lyle dropped his shoulders. 'I couldn't tell.'

I grimaced. Disguised, then. That didn't do a damned thing to assuage my concern. Someone friendly would have no need to conceal their identity.

Brochan was already on his feet and handing me my jacket. Tipsania waved her hand. 'Do you want…?'

I nodded. 'If you wouldn't mind.' I hated having to resort to magic all the time but I had to be careful for all our sakes. She flicked her fingers towards me while I squeezed my eyes shut, reminding myself that I didn't want to steal her Gift. She'd give it all to me if I demanded it.

The only indication that she'd finished was the faintest prickle across my skin. I opened my eyes and glanced down. The strangeness of not being able to see my own body encouraged a rush of nausea. These days I felt sick more often than a pregnant woman in her first trimester. I gave her a hasty thanks and darted for the door. 'Anyone who's not a troll stays put,' I yelled behind me.

Lexie's plaintive complaint rang out across the dining hall. 'Aw, Tegs, come on.'

'The only ones who are supposed to be here are trolls, Lex. Everyone else needs to stay hidden.' What I didn't say was that if the border had been breached I'd also need people I could count on to stay back here and hold the mansion. We had to be prepared for every eventuality. Even with his knowledge of my apparent death, I could never be sure what Aifric was planning.

I sensed the blue-haired pixie pouting but she fell quiet. I barrelled out of the door and sped towards the border, doing everything I could to avoid looking down again at my own body. One of these days I was going to get the trolls to build a giant slide from the mansion down to the bottom of the hill. Either that or learn how to roller-skate.

The only light visible by the border was cast by old-fashioned torches which used flame rather than electricity to illuminate the area. The flagpole remained in place but, in order to keep to the fiction that the Adair Clan was finally gone for good, Sorley had taken down the flag.

Instead he'd concealed some stitched Adair colours into the flat top of the pole to maintain the border magic but to keep my presence secret from prying eyes.

I scanned the area and spotted a small army of trolls glaring at the lone figure who stood across the border and who was, incongruously, holding a bicycle. The nearest settlement was miles away; it was a long way to cycle, especially in the dark.

Whoever our visitor was, he was wearing a hooded top and keeping his face shadowed. Sorley was closest to him and was gesticulating wildly. 'Show yourself!' he hissed.

The hooded man crossed his arms. 'Not until I see Chieftain Adair.' His voice was hoarse. I frowned. I recognised the accent.

'I've already told you. She's dead. We own these lands now.'

'I don't believe she's dead at all,' the man – or rather the Bauchan – said huskily.

My eyes narrowed. Fergus might have proved knowledgeable on the few occasions we'd met in the past but that didn't mean he should not believe I was dead. Had someone talked?

I stepped forward, inadvertently brushing against one of the trolls. He flinched, a movement so brief that I barely caught it.

Irritatingly, Fergus noticed it too. 'Chieftain Adair!' he called out. 'How good of you to come and greet me!'

Sorley spun round, searching for me. 'You're seeing things,' he growled. 'Because unless Integrity Adair's ghost is haunting these parts, she's not here.'

'It's alright, Sorley,' I said softly.

He stiffened, rage at his security measures being discounted lighting up his eyes. He took his job very seriously. I skirted through the trolls until I was by his side. 'I know this guy,' I told him in a half whisper. 'He's helped us out before and—'

'And you made me a promise,' Fergus said. 'Tell me, did you steal Invisibility from Tipsania Scrymgeour? Or did she give it to you?'

I hissed. He had better sources than the Nile, the Amazon and the damned Mississippi combined. First things first, though. 'Are you alone?'

He pushed back his hood, displaying his face for the first time. His good looks were marred by several ugly bruises. I couldn't be sure but it also looked as if his nose was broken. The dark shadows round his neck suggested that his croaky voice wasn't down to an overly energetic karaoke session. 'Yes,' he said pleasantly, 'I am.'

Truth. I relaxed slightly. During the Sidhe Games the previous year, I'd inadvertently stolen all of Kirsty Kincaid's Truth-Seeking Gift. The action had almost killed her, although she was relieved when she discovered what had happened because she'd found being able to separate truth from lies too onerous a burden. So far, I was finding her Gift very useful. All the same, I wasn't about to let my guard down entirely.

'How did you know?' I asked. 'How did you know that I was still alive?'

Fergus's mouth lifted into a half-smile, revealing two chipped front teeth. He had indeed been in the wars. Curiouser and curiouser. 'A certain green-eyed assassin,' he said. I stiffened. There was no way that Chandra had given me up. 'She undertook a perilous job to kill a certain Sidhe and yet, despite the obvious dangers, she abandoned her team to complete the murder alone.' He shifted his weight. 'She could have killed this Sidhe on a previous occasion but she chose not to because they were old friends. However, weeks later, she changed her mind and suddenly assassinated her bestie in full view of the

Moncrieffe heir and his mate.' His smile grew. 'And a couple of Fomori demons. I'm told this assassin still has no trouble sleeping.' Fergus shrugged. 'I like puzzles. And this one was easy to solve.'

I tried to breathe normally. 'Who else knows?'

'I've not told anyone, if that's what you mean. As to who else is as intelligent as I am and has managed to work it out, I couldn't say.'

It was difficult to intimidate someone when they couldn't see you but I still tried. I hardened my voice and crossed my arms. 'Yes, you can. You've proved you're intelligent enough.'

Fergus nodded smugly. 'Yeah, alright, you've got me there. I don't believe anyone else has put two and two together. Not with the state Byron Moncrieffe has been in. He's been marching up and down the Highlands and growling at anyone who so much as glances in his direction.' He smirked. 'Your boy is hurting.'

Pain stabbed at my heart. The urge to leap through the border and grab Fergus by his blood-stained lapels and demand he tell me everything he knew about Byron was almost overwhelming but I had to act responsibly. My role demanded it. 'You've been in a fight,' I observed, glad that my voice remained tremor-free. 'Tell me about it.'

'I'd love to. But, *Chieftain*, why don't you let me inside first? You promised me sanctuary.'

'I promised sanctuary in the event of more Fomori attacks,' I pointed out. 'I don't believe they've ventured across the Veil since I died.'

'You're nit-picking.' Fergus stepped forward, letting the bike drop to the ground. His features were clearer now that he was closer to the flickering torches and I realised how pale he was. He was in considerable pain. 'I need asylum.' He swayed slightly.

Alarmed as I was by his condition, I still needed to know more. I couldn't afford to be soft-hearted. 'Why?'

'I might have slightly irritated the Innes Chieftain.'

'Go on.'

Fergus's eyes were growing unfocused. 'I might have met his only daughter in a Dundee nightclub. And I might have taken her back to my place.' He paused and shrugged ruefully. 'She had fun but Daddy Dearest is less than impressed. Our Sidhe overlords don't like the idea of their bloodlines being tainted.'

Tiring of the conversation, Sorley waggled his spear. 'I suggest we keep him outside the border until we can be sure, Chieftain.'

'Let him in,' I said. 'He's telling the truth.'

Sorley's heavy bottom lip jutted out. He did as I bade, however, gesturing to two other trolls who took hold of Fergus by the arms to help him.

'Bring him up to the mansion,' I said. 'At least Taylor will be kept busy for a while.' My old mentor was no surgeon but he did possess some sterling first-aid skills.

'Wait,' Fergus whispered. 'There's something else.' His eyes fixed on a patch of ground to my right; I was, after all, still invisible. 'I was right before, wasn't I? Tipsania Scrymgeour is here.'

I took a leap of faith. 'She is.'

Fergus chuckled softly. 'Is her dress ready?'

Confused, I asked, 'What do you mean?' His jaw worked in response. Judging by his pupils, he was on the verge of passing out. 'Fergus!' I demanded. 'What do you mean?'

'The invitations have gone out,' he said. 'Her wedding to Byron Moncrieffe is happening in thirteen days' time.'

I drew back. What? That didn't make any sense. I opened my mouth to question Fergus some more but his head dropped forward. He was already out for the count. Shite.

Chapter Two

'He's still unconscious,' Taylor informed me. 'I don't think he's in any real danger but he's travelled a long way and he's lost quite a bit of blood. There's probably mild concussion too.'

Tipsania flounced towards him, hands on hips. She was the perfect modern-day representation of Scarlett O'Hara. 'Can't you throw water in his face or something? I need to know what's going on!'

As ridiculous as her statement was, I sympathised with her. Even her father, the Bull, wasn't thick-headed enough not to have noticed that she'd been missing for months. How on earth he planned to hold a wedding without the actual bride was beyond me. Tipsania wasn't concerned with logistics, however; despite the appearance she maintained in public, she had no interest in Byron. Not these days, anyway. Her heart belonged to a rather intimidating Wild Man by the name of Candy.

'He needs to sleep,' Taylor said.

Tipsania gave a frustrated growl. May, who'd been watching the proceedings wide-eyed, shuffled over and put her head on Tipsania's shoulder. It was a measure of how far my old adversary had come that she didn't shake off the demon and start throwing things.

'It could be,' Brochan rumbled, his gills twitching with the tension, 'that it's just smoke and mirrors and the wedding will be cancelled at the last moment.'

I scratched my head. 'But to what end? The marriage is supposed to cement the alliance between the Moncrieffes and the Scrymgeours. Leaving Byron standing at the altar isn't going to achieve that. In fact, it'll do the opposite.' What I didn't ask was why Byron was apparently going ahead with the charade. I shouldn't feel hurt – after all, he thought I was dead. And even if I wasn't dead, I had no claim on him. But rationality has no place when it comes to affairs of the heart; I could still feel a dull ache in the centre of my chest.

Lexie piped up. 'Maybe they think the wedding is still going ahead.'

'It can't go ahead without the bride,' Speck said. He paused. 'Can it?'

'Of course not,' I dismissed. A niggle of worry gnawed away at me. I wouldn't put anything past Aifric Moncrieffe; he might change the law to suit his own purposes, although I couldn't imagine that he'd get away with marrying someone off in absentia. Even he wasn't that crazy. But the Moncrieffes were still in debt and they'd been counting on the Scrymgeour gold.

Morna laughed without much humour. 'The other Clans would never let him do that. We're living in the twenty-first century, not the first. And Byron is a decent boy. He wouldn't permit it.'

'He hasn't seen or heard from his supposed fiancée in weeks and yet he's apparently letting the wedding proceed,' I pointed out, disgust in my voice.

'He knows I'm here,' Tipsania said dully. 'My father knows I'm here and he's going to force me to leave.'

Taylor shook his head. 'He can't. He couldn't get past the border.'

I swung my head towards her. '*Does* he know you're here?' I asked sharply.

She sank down, her shoulders dropping in defeat. 'I don't know. It's not like I left a note. I wasn't followed here, I made sure of that.'

'Did you tell anyone you were coming?'

Her face was completely miserable. 'Only Candy. And Byron knew as well, of course, because he brought me.'

I exchanged glances with the others. 'When was the last time you spoke to Candy?'

'Last month.' She gave me an icy glare. 'If the phone signal was better…'

Exasperated, I pushed back my hair. I couldn't solve all the problems in the world, regardless of what everyone thought. If all we had to worry about was the lack of a mobile phone mast, we'd be laughing. 'Would Candy have confided in anyone else?'

She scowled. 'If you're asking whether he'd betray me then the answer is no.'

I hoped she was right. 'Who else knows that the pair of you are together?'

'Only Byron.'

I blinked in surprise. 'Really?'

'Byron wouldn't know but for the fact that he walked in on us a while back. He didn't care. He wasn't interested in me in the first place and, unlike most Sidhe, he's not against inter-species relationships.'

My heartstrings twanged with joy. It had been a long time since I'd believed that his relationship with Tipsania was anything but a farce but knowing for certain still made me feel like dancing on the ceiling. Lexie gave me a knowing glance and I immediately sobered up.

'We should find out what's going on,' I said decisively. 'I'll investigate.' I rather liked the idea of being Hercule Poirot; maybe I could invest in a moustache to twirl at appropriate moments. Hot pink, of course.

Taylor blew air through pursed lips. 'It's far too dangerous. What if someone sees you?'

It probably wouldn't be wise to suggest my Poirot disguise idea. I pointed at Tipsania. 'Hello? Invisibility?'

'It won't last for more than a few hours. That won't even get you past Perth.'

Tipsania's mouth flattened. 'She can take my Gift from me. As much as she needs.'

'You might regret that later,' Brochan rumbled. He had a point. I didn't want to draw on Tipsania's Gift unless it was absolutely necessary. I'd already taken more from her than I probably should have when I ventured across the Veil to retrieve Matthew MacBain's bones. 'Besides,' he continued, 'a wedding is not that big a deal. It's certainly not worth risking discovery over.'

'You green-skinned oaf! It's my wedding we're talking about here! *My* life!' Tipsania yelled.

'But you're here,' he said calmly. 'You can't marry Byron Moncrieffe if you're not at your own ceremony.' His heavy shoulders rolled in a shrug. 'So who cares?'

Even without the narrow glance he shot me, Brochan's meaning was clear. *I* cared – whether anyone else wanted me to or not.

'It's not going to be difficult. All I have to do is get far enough north to get a signal and call the Bull. He'll tell me what's what.' I smiled at Tipsania. 'I can make sure he cancels the wedding.' I had his true name, after all; I could make him dance the merengue with a stoor worm if I so wished.

'You can't compel him unless you're face to face, and you can't do that without him realising that you're still alive.'

True. 'Then I'll meet him face to face. I'll command him to keep my resurrection a secret.'

Taylor shook his head. 'You're putting too much faith in your ability to bend the Bull to your will. There are ways around those sorts of things. He could still drop enough hints to Aifric to make him doubt your death.'

'I'm not sure the Bull is that intelligent.' I realised I was casting aspersions on Tipsania's father but she wasn't listening. She was too wrapped up in her own panic and worry, pacing up and down and causing various haggis to flee out of her path with alarmed squeaks.

Brochan folded his arms. 'You can't take that chance.'

'Much as I hate to say it, Tegs,' Speck interjected, 'I think he's right. And we all know that you're not concerned because of Tipsania. You should let Byron go.'

Lexie frowned. 'Why should she?'

'Well, for one thing he thinks she's dead.'

'That can be easily solved,' she scoffed.

Somehow I doubted that. Even if I told Byron the truth, he'd probably never speak to me again. 'This is about more than Byron,' I said, not sure whether I was being honest with myself or not. 'Something must be up for the wedding to be going ahead in Tipsania's absence. We can't allow Aifric's machinations to continue and we need to know exactly what he's up to. Knowledge is power, people.'

Bob beamed. 'Indeed it is! I am a supremely knowledgeable being. It's only natural that you'd want to be as wise and knowing as I am.' Nobody acknowledged him but it didn't seem to matter. He snapped his fingers, magicking up a pair of horn-rimmed spectacles and a mortar board.

'Much as I hate to say it,' Morna said, 'I think this is worth investigating. Aifric Moncrieffe never does anything without good reason. Something worrying is going on here and it would pay to know what. It would be nice to think that you can hide here for the rest of your days but it's completely unrealistic.' She nodded. 'We can kill two birds with one stone: find out what's going on with the wedding, and make sure you have a decent enough handle on your Thievery Gift.'

Before the others could protest again, I said, 'So it's settled. And who knows? Maybe we'll find what we need to bring Aifric down for good. We can get in touch with Angus, too. He might have other insights we can use.' Suddenly, I felt buoyant with optimism. I clapped my hands. 'Now all we need is a plan.'

Taylor looked as if he wanted to argue some more but in the end he just sighed. 'We need to be sensible and make sure the odds are in our favour. The longer everyone believes in your death, the better.' He jerked his chin at Brochan. 'I think that has to include the Bull, too.'

May squeaked, no doubt sensing my excitement and I grinned in response. This could end up being a lot more fun than leaving the safety of the Adair Lands just to make a phone call. 'No problem.'

***

It felt like a lifetime since I'd last been in Aberdeen. It was like returning to an old friend – albeit one who'd been in the wars since I'd last seen them. From the foot of the main parade at Union Street the evidence of the Fomori demon attacks was still painfully visible. Many of the grey granite buildings were scarred and there appeared to be a healthy trade in scaffolding. All the same, a deep satisfaction uncurled within my chest; it really was good to be back.

For the time being, we'd gone the old-fashioned route. Not for nothing had I spent my formative teenage years practising the art of thievery on the streets. I'd learnt how to blend in. It wasn't about wearing a hat and big sunglasses, it was about attitude. So while my long white hair was completely covered, my skin was temporarily darkened and my face was in shadow, I also held myself differently. Rather than projecting the image of an all-powerful Sidhe Chieftain who cared nothing for the opinion of others, I'd chosen to take on the persona of a slick trophy wife.

Anyone who's never had to disguise themselves won't get it. Amateurs always believe that the best way to conceal yourself is to hunch over and fade into the background. The truth is that there are very few people capable of successfully pulling off that kind of feat. Even my years of slinking around the corridors of the Bull's mansion and trying to avoid being noticed hadn't made me an expert at it. Misdirection is far easier. As far as anyone who saw me knew, I was a rich woman who cared far too much about her appearance. My tight, expensive clothes and showy designer headscarf were as much about creating a picture as providing a disguise. With the obvious strut in my step and the way I thrust out my chest, even people I knew would be hard pressed to believe I was anything other than what I presented. Although my posture meant that my lower back was beginning to twinge, the high heels I was wearing made me feel rather sexy. It was a real shame they weren't pink. Even with my supposed demise, pink would have been too dangerous.

'Admit it, Uh Integrity,' Bob murmured in my ear, 'right now you think you're pretty hot.'

Just then a car passed by with a scruffy-looking warlock in the passenger seat. He leaned out and leered at me. I smiled. 'I don't *think*, Bob,' I murmured. 'I *know*.' It was true; looking like this was about self-belief. As Bob himself could attest if he were introspective enough, ego was vital to any façade.

I lifted my chin and strutted down the long street. From time to time I paused and glanced in shop windows to check who was behind me as well as to maintain my cover as a woman hell-bent on shopping. So far so good. I hummed to myself and crossed the street. As Tipsania had said, there was only one store in town worth visiting if you were planning upscale nuptials. I grinned as MacKay's Marriage Emporium came into view. Bring on the meringues.

The door jangled as I entered, not with a bell-like noise but with the opening bars of Wagner's bridal march. Neat.

'I think I just vomited in my mouth,' Bob whispered.

I avoided rolling my eyes as a shop assistant gave me the once over. Apparently deciding I was a fish worth reeling in, she strolled over and thrust out a perfectly manicured hand. 'Good afternoon,' she purred. 'My name is Shona and I'm a bridal consultant here at the wonderful MacKay's Emporium.' Her smile grew to a blinding intensity. 'We can make all of your wishes come true.'

Bob choked. I returned Shona's smile and took her hand. 'Thank you so much,' I responded breathily in my best Italian accent. 'I have heard you are the best in Scotland and, as I cannot be home in Milano for my wedding, I am looking for a shop which can meet my expectations.' I leaned in slightly. 'They are very high. One only gets married once – or perhaps twice.' I paused and gave a self-deprecating laugh. 'Maybe three times. It's very important that the wedding is perfect.'

Shona didn't even blink. 'Of course! And you're Italian, you say? *Benvenuto al nostro meraviglioso negozio.*'

Shite. I should have opted for Greek. I clapped my hands as if in wild applause. 'You Scots are so charming!' I replied in English, adding just the faintest patronising tone to keep her away from any more attempts at my 'native' language.

A consummate professional, Shona's smile didn't waver. 'Is this your first visit here?' she enquired.

Playing dumb was fun. I smiled prettily to mask my smirk. 'To the Granite City? Why no.'

'Uh, great.' Shona's expression didn't flicker. 'And is it your first visit to our little store?'

I looked around. Calling MacKay's Marriage Emporium 'little' was hardly apt. The place might look rather nondescript from outside but I could see that inside it stretched back in a cavernous confection of lace, frills and wedding joy.

'It is,' I replied. 'I'm just shopping around for now. The truth is that I don't even have a date yet. My fiancé, Byr...' I shook myself. Where the hell had that come from? 'My fiancé,' I repeated, 'wants a spring wedding but I'm not sure I can wait that long.' I added a simper. Considering I was already blushing, it looked very natural.

Shona raised an eyebrow. I couldn't be sure whether my Freudian slip had caught her attention or not. 'Oh, spring is simply the best time,' she said. 'Let me show you what we have on offer.'

I allowed Shona to lead me round, pausing every so often to gush over a particular piece of tulle or laced frippery. When we reached the display of wedding cakes and her head was turned the other way, Bob zipped out from underneath my headscarf. In one fell swoop he knocked both the miniature bride and groom off the top of the largest tiered monstrosity. Then he posed this way and that while I tried – with some difficulty – to keep a straight face. When he dropped onto his back and began to wave his arms and legs up and down to make an icing angel, I had to blink rapidly and swallow.

'Your collections are beautiful,' I said, taking Shona and leading her away from the cake before she noticed him. I spoke with a fair degree of honesty; there was a tad too much virginal white for my taste, and my eyes were beginning to swim from all the delicate lace, but there was no denying that MacKay's took great care over its offerings. I bit my lip. 'I wonder, though, whether you can produce what I require. I anticipate my wedding will be very large scale.' I smiled innocently and pretended not to notice the flash of avarice in Shona's expression.

'Oh,' she said reassuringly, 'we deal with large weddings all the time. How many guests were you thinking of?'

I plucked a figure out of the air. 'I've only just started the list,' I answered, 'and I'm already at more than a thousand. It's so important in this day and age to ensure that no one is left out in the cold or offended because they're not included. Perhaps if you could tell me of any large weddings you're currently planning I would have a better idea about whether you could manage *mine*. I want it to be the best.' I sounded like the worst kind of bridezilla. Considering Shona didn't blink, however, I guessed that in this industry it was par for the course.

Fortunately it worked. She glanced round as if wary of being overheard and then dropped her voice. 'You didn't hear this from me,' she said conspiratorially, 'but we've been engaged to arrange the upcoming nuptials of Byron Moncrieffe and Tipsania Scrymgeour. It's going to be the wedding of the century, and not just because it's Sidhe. Byron is son to the Steward himself and the Scrymgeours are incredibly wealthy. No expense will be spared.'

My eyes lit up while I quashed the desperate sinking feeling in my stomach. 'How wonderful!' I cooed. 'I imagine Ms Scrymgeour has been in regularly for dress fittings. She'll want to make sure everything is perfect for such a high-profile ceremony.'

This time Shona couldn't prevent her mask from slipping. Her face dropped in genuine dismay, although she did her best to provide Tipsania with excuses. 'She's been far too busy to come in. We are some distance from the Scrymgeour Clan Lands here. We have precise information of her measurements, though, and we're confident her dress will be perfect.'

I looked from side to side. 'I don't suppose I could see it? I promise I won't tell a soul.' Her expression immediately closed up. Uh oh. She opened her mouth to speak but I forestalled her. 'Of course, I understand if you can't. Confidentiality is important and if the dress isn't ready yet...' I paused. 'When did you say the wedding will be?'

Shona began to fidget. 'A week on Saturday.'

'That's cutting it fine.'

'The dress *is* ready. In fact we're to deliver to Miss Scrymgeour tomorrow.'

I smiled, making it obvious that I didn't believe her. 'Mmm.'

My prevarication did the trick. Shona took me by the elbow. 'You can't tell anyone.'

Only just managing to keep the grin off my face, I nodded fervently. 'Of course.'

We veered through the shop, side-stepping a few wide-eyed women, and headed into a back room. There, in the centre, was a massive white ... thing. My jaw dropped and I wasn't even faking. 'That's, er, that's big.' My gaze drifted over the white monstrosity. There were bows everywhere. The skirt was so large that I doubted Tipsania would fit through the massive doors at the Cruaich. It was also surprisingly demure, with a high sweetheart neckline. In fact, it looked like the kind of dress a girl dreamed of when she was about six years old. Or the kind of dress a father might imagine his princess wearing.

I scratched my head. 'So, this is what Tipsania Scrymgeour wanted?'

'Oh yes.' Shona nodded proudly.

'She told you that?' I asked, circling it. It took a good ten seconds to work my way around, even at a brisk pace.

'She was very explicit in her emails.'

Sure she was. Asking to see those emails would be a step too far, even for the compliant Shona. Anyway, I had everything I needed from her. Whatever was going on, the Bull was fully complicit. I smiled my thanks, retrieved Bob from underneath a scrap of veil that he was admiring himself in and made my escape.

Chapter Three

'The wedding's not taking place at the Cruaich,' Angus MacQuarrie informed me. He joined us as we regrouped down by the windswept dunes of Balmedie beach, where the granite grey city of Aberdeen met the stormy grey North Sea.

That was a surprise. Given Byron's status as the Steward's son, I'd assumed the Sidhe seat of power would be the natural choice for a venue. 'Really?'

'The invites have only just gone out or I could have come and told you about it in person. It appears that both Clans have decided on neutral ground. It's happening on Muck.'

'I take it that you're referring to the Hebridean island and not that this entire charade is a piece of shite and everyone's just mucking around?' I asked drily.

His mouth flattened into a grim line. 'Tegs,' he said, sounding worried, 'word is that Byron wants it to happen there because it's where his mother was from. He wants to marry the woman he loves there in a homage to his mother.'

I shook my head. 'Nope. This whole thing has been cooked up between the Bull and Aifric. They probably want it to happen there because it's the most isolated damn place you're likely to get. That way neither Tipsy nor Byron is going to run away at the last minute.'

Taylor placed a heavy hand on my shoulder. 'Tipsania's already run away.'

I ignored that part. 'What we still don't have is motive,' I mused. 'Aifric needs the money the Scrymgeours can offer but there must be a reason why he still wants the ceremony to go ahead even though he doesn't have the bride. And we still don't know what that reason is.' I toed at the soft sand. 'Something's afoot.'

Taylor remained impassive. 'Are you sure you're not getting involved in this because of what's between you and Byron?'

I ignored Angus's raised eyebrow. 'Nothing's going on between me and Byron. He thinks I'm dead. And it's not just me who thinks this is worth the risk. Morna reckons it should be investigated.' I paused. 'And Tipsania is my guest. It's my duty to protect her.' I didn't meet his eyes; I was starting to feel that I was protesting too much.

Taylor gazed at me, our decade and a half long relationship reflected in the knowing wisdom in his eyes. 'Don't kid a kidder, Tegs. And don't kid yourself either.'

'Okay,' I conceded. 'Maybe part of this is to do with Byron. But,' I held up my hand, 'more of it is to do with Aifric.' Taylor huffed in disbelief. 'I mean it. We know that Aifric is the bastard here, Taylor. He's the one who murdered my parents and destroyed my Clan. He's the one who was desperate to see me cold in the ground. What if he knows that Tipsania is missing and is going to use her absence and the way that absence snubs Byron to attack the Scrymgeours? It could be some kind of power grab. Now he thinks he doesn't have to worry about me any more, he could be going after the rest of his competition.'

Taylor eyed me. 'What do you care? You've lived most of your life without giving a hoot about any Sidhe, living or dead.'

Angus nodded in agreement. 'The Clans have always ignored you. Leave them to their machinations.'

I glanced from one to the other and sighed. 'I can't pretend that I'm that person any more,' I said quietly.

'And one way or another I'm going to bring down Aifric Moncrieffe.'

'Even if it means destroying his son in the process?'

I looked down. 'I'll cross that bridge when I come to it.' I was hoping I wouldn't. Unfortunately, there's no fool like an optimistic fool.

'Three to one this is going to end in disaster,' Taylor said. My head shot back up and I glared at him. 'Those are pretty good odds given the circumstances.'

I tutted in disgust, although I appreciated that he was doing what he could to lighten the mood. 'Let's stay focused, shall we?' I pulled off my headscarf and let the wind do its worst to my hair, whipping it round my face in white tangles. 'Maybe we should concentrate on the Bull. He's the weak link in all this and not just because I have his true name. He must know that his daughter is missing. I mean, she's been with us for months.'

'He's telling everyone that she's sick and is staying at home.'

'Obviously she's not though,' I persisted. 'Why hasn't he done something to stop the wedding?'

'That's easy,' Lexie said, appearing from behind the nearest dune and holding hands with Speck. 'He's afraid of Aifric.'

'He'll have more cause to be afraid when Aifric's only son gets jilted at the altar. We need to find out for sure,' I said decisively. 'They could be in cahoots and he could lead us to Aifric's true motives. The Scrymgeour borders are weak because of the lack of trolls guarding them. We can slip through.'

Speck frowned. 'There's no *we*,' he chided. 'You don't have enough of Tipsania's Invisibility Gift left and you can't afford to let Aifric see you and realise you're still alive.'

'Except,' I grinned, 'I'm the only one who knows the layout of his castle. It's too complicated to map out for you. I *have* to go. I can conceal myself well enough without magic.'

'Brochan won't like it.'

I shrugged.

Lexie tilted her chin, her blue hair ruffled by the wind. 'Speaking of the grumpy merman, where is Brochan? Did he find Candy?'

'No trace of the Wild Man. They're a law unto themselves at the best of times.' I smirked. 'Brochan is hiding back there, away from the sea. Bob is keeping him company.'

We exchanged glances. I pushed myself onto my tiptoes and looked over the bank of sand. Bob was wearing a rather startling mankini and tugging at the finger of a glowering and sneezing Brochan as he tried to get him to move closer to the sea.

'I think Brochan will be happy we're going to the Bull. At least we'll be inland,' Lexie mused.

Speck still appeared troubled. 'This castle. We're not going to have to scale any walls, are we? And it doesn't have any mice or bats or anything, right? Or cramped spaces?'

My smile widened. 'You're the most powerful warlock in Scotland now, Specky. All you have to do is cast a spell.'

'I'd rather stay here by the sea,' he muttered.

'What do you call a warlock who hangs out on the beach?' I received nothing but sighs of irritation in response. 'A surfer druid!'

'I have to say it, Tegs,' Lexie interjected. 'That's truly the worst one you've told us for a long time.'

'Yeah. I'm under a lot of pressure these days, though,' I admitted. 'Stick with me and I'll do better soon.'

She raised her eyes to the heavens. 'That's what I'm afraid of.'

***

We left Angus to return to the MacQuarries. It was no secret that he'd sworn fealty to me on their behalf and, even with my alleged death, it was important that he didn't do anything out of the ordinary which might raise suspicion. Having him – and the rest of his Clan – on our side made me feel considerably better. Despite my jokey bravado, however, I had mixed feelings about coming back to the Bull's corner of Scotland.

Taylor pulled up in the same layby where we'd first met all those years before and I couldn't prevent a shiver rattling down my spine as I stared at the familiar spot. With the wedding less than two weeks away, time was of the essence. We couldn't afford to run back to the Adair Lands so that I could nab some more of Tipsania's Gift. Even so, I was starting to regret not taking a couple of hours to find a Sidhe in Aberdeen whose Gifts I could steal. I was being brave, not foolhardy, I told myself. This was necessary.

Lexie, Speck, Brochan and Bob were oblivious to the historical nature of our surroundings but Taylor and I got out of the car and stayed silent, looking around then looking at each other. 'It makes you wonder, doesn't it?' I asked him eventually. 'If you'd left five minutes earlier…'

'Or if you'd come out at a different spot…'

I smiled at him. 'You'd probably have been arrested. You'd have ended up in the clink as the buddy of some hulking Bauchan with wobbly tattoos and a penchant for ginger-haired humans.'

'There's not much ginger going on these days. My hair's almost as white as yours.'

'Aren't you the lucky one?'

Bob buzzed over and peered at us. 'What's with you two? We're in a godforsaken layby in a scrap of land. It's hardly a romantic setting and yet the pair of you are making googly eyes at each other.' He narrowed his eyes in suspicion. 'Is there something you're not telling us? I know there's a bit of an age difference but did you come here and...' He made a rude gesture with his fingers.

'Ewww! Bob, get out of my face!' I flicked him away. 'This is where Taylor and I met.'

Bob's bottom lip jutted out. 'Here? I will never understand humans. Why would you come here? I mean, I'm an all-knowing supreme being with...'

'...powers you can only dream of,' the rest of us chorused for him.

'Exactly,' he huffed. 'But why would you come here?'

I shrugged. 'Fate?'

'Luck?' Taylor suggested.

Bob regarded us both. 'I met Lady Luck once.' He lowered his voice. 'Between you and me, she's not all there.' He tapped his temple.

Taylor stared at him. 'Lady Luck? She's a real person?'

'Well, duh.'

'Is she still around? Because I've got to tell you I could really do with—'

'Bob's having you on,' I said, glaring at the genie. 'And we've got more important things to do than shoot the breeze and discuss how you can gamble away more of your life.' I pointed at a clump of bushes. 'Come on. The Scrymgeour border is over this way. Single file and stay frosty.'

'This is just like old times,' Lexie sighed happily as she fell into place.

My skin prickled in a familiar frisson of anticipation. All I had to do was to focus on the fact that this was a heist of sorts – and forget that I was returning to the place where I'd spent my deeply unhappy formative years – and I'd be fine.

Bob aside, we all knew exactly what we were doing. We were dressed in black from head to toe, camouflaged for the night and against prying eyes. I kept my body low as I wove my way through the foliage, avoiding the thorns and brambles which barred the route. Soon we emerged onto a thin path which snaked upwards. If I squinted, I could just make out the glimmer of lights up ahead. I hoped the Bull hadn't done any drastic renovations in the years since I'd run away. Despite his wealth, he was a tight-fisted bastard so chances were that everything remained the same and I'd have no trouble finding my way around. I crossed my fingers just in case.

We skirted silently through the woods. It had rained recently, so each of us left distinct tracks in the mud of the path. It didn't matter; it's not as if we were actually stealing anything. It was unlikely that anyone would discover our footprints and think that a gang of highly skilled thieves had wandered up this way in the dead of night. All the same, we'd have to take care that we didn't track mud into the castle. That would be a sure-fire giveaway that something was up.

It was a good twenty minutes before the border finally came into view. Just as with the Adair Lands, there was a massive flagpole with the Scrymgeour colours hanging loosely at the top. The flag was there for more than just show; the magic that kept the border in place stemmed from it, bolstered by ancient spells and wisdom lost to almost all Sidhe. The trolls who normally maintained these borders were well aware of it, though. Sorley had given me a detailed – and rather unnecessary – history, as well as bestowing on Speck the means to unlock the magic to permit entry.

If the trolls had still been in place, I doubt we'd have managed to sneak in but the trolls were now at Clan Adair. All we had to deal with were a few dozing Scrymgeour servants. The presence of the Scrymgeour Sidhe inside the border helped bolster the magic but Speck was strong enough now to beat it.

I counted four border guards: a warlock, two humans and – surprise, surprise – a Sidhe. I wondered what he'd done to piss off the Bull and end up here on guard duty. He was the only one of the four who seemed fully alert. He scowled at his companions from time to time, especially when the warlock let out a loud snore. As I stayed low and watched, he strode towards the warlock's slumped body and raised his foot, as if preparing for a sharp kick. Then he grimaced and seemed to think better of it – though he still looked distinctly unhappy.

I considered. It was imperative that we slip through unnoticed and it didn't appear as if the Sidhe boy was going to drift off any time soon.

'You're going to have to do it, Tegs,' Brochan murmured in my ear. 'It's the best way.' Unfortunately, Brochan was right. Short of waltzing up to the Scrymgeour Sidhe and clocking him on the nose before he managed to raise the alarm, I couldn't see an alternative. I wasn't convinced that this course of action fitted with my pacifist morality but I'd brought us here and I had to step up to the proverbial plate.

Taking a deep breath and holding the air in my lungs, I concentrated just like Morna had taught me. If I focused hard enough and used the meditation techniques I'd been practising, I could almost visualise the swirl of magic within the Sidhe's soul. I had no idea what his Gift was and I wasn't stealing from him because I wanted it for myself – there was another method to my madness.

Bit by bit, I tugged, grasping first at a single thread of his Gift and pulling it inside me as if my body were a magnet. As his power left him and filled me, I gasped inadvertently. The Sidhe would have heard me if he hadn't already started to feel woozy. He clutched at his stomach, then at his head and groaned faintly. I slammed on my magic brakes; I didn't want to seriously hurt the poor bugger and neither did I want to steal his Gift in its entirety. He might be a Scrymgeour but he was a stranger to me and I couldn't completely destroy him.

'He's gonna chuck,' Bob said knowingly.

I gestured to him to keep quiet. He huffed in irritation but did as I asked. We watched from the shadows as the Sidhe staggered backwards then spun round and began retching violently. I winced. Shite. So much for all that pacifism.

The sound was enough to wake his dozing companions. The warlock muttered in alarm and scrambled to his feet. The two humans looked groggier but they got up and stumbled over to check on the Sidhe.

'Now. Speck,' I hissed.

He slipped forward, moving soundlessly past Brochan and me and up to the flagpole. Even through the darkness I saw him gulp. It was rare that Speck was our point man but, given how much his recent proximity to the Foinse had affected his magic, he needed to get used to it. All the same, I watched him with my heart in my mouth. If any of the Scrymgeour sentries turned round, he'd be done for.

The Sidhe continued to retch, falling forward onto his knees. I was starting to suspect he was making a bigger deal out of his nausea than was absolutely necessary. I'd stolen partial Gifts from others and they'd not reacted this badly. I gnawed at my bottom lip and prayed I was right. The humans were hunkered down, one on either side of him and both facing away from the border. The pesky warlock, however, was kneeling in front of him. All he had to do was lift his head and he'd catch sight of Speck pulling the scrap of Adair fabric from his pocket and pinning it to the base of the Scrymgeour pole.

'Go, Bob,' I said urgently.

For once the genie chose not to argue. He spun in the air, transformed himself into a large bluebottle and zipped forward. As Speck murmured out the words to let us pass the border, Bob landed on the Scrymgeour warlock's ear and buzzed loudly enough to be an irritation. Scowling, the warlock stood up and batted him away but Bob wasn't about to quit and shot towards his ear again. The warlock cursed and waved his hands around, shaking his head like a dog emerging from a dip in the sea.

The tightness in my stomach eased slightly as Speck signalled. I sprang forward, angling my body to the left to veer round the Scrymgeour group. With the others on my heels, I wasted no more time; I acknowledged Speck with a bob of my head as he joined us and we pushed past the border.

My skin tingled, traces of the magic that held the border in place still trying to hold me back. I'd been through far worse than this; let's face it, if I could pass through the damned Veil several times, then I could skip through the Bull's weakened border. As the Sidhe finally stopped being sick and wobbled back to his feet, pushing his companions away in irritation, our small group sped towards the nearest copse of trees on the Scrymgeour side. By the time we reached them, the sentries had turned back to their original posts. The Sidhe was still rubbing his stomach and looking confused while the other three settled down again to return to their doze. Excitement over.

I breathed out. Speck, visibly shaking, let a large grin spread across his face. 'Did you see me?' he whispered in delight, punching the air. 'I was awesome!'

Lexie shifted her weight and stretched up on her tiptoes to plant a sloppy kiss on his lips. When she pulled away, they both looked flustered. Speck pulled off his glasses and began hastily to rub them.

'Steaming up?' I asked with an arched eyebrow.

Brochan choked. Bob, now back to normal, looked unimpressed. 'Don't I get a kiss?' he complained. 'I'm the one who had to get up close and personal with those guys.' He licked his finger, an expression of utter pleasure crossing his face.

'What are you eating?' Taylor asked.

Bob blinked. 'Mm? Oh, ear wax.' He held his finger out. 'Want some?'

Taylor looked almost as ill as the Sidhe had. 'I'll pass.'

The genie shrugged and licked it again. 'Your loss.'

Rolling his eyes, Brochan turned to me. 'What did you steal?' he asked. 'What was his Gift?'

I reached down inside myself, feeling for the magic. It was definitely there – and it was definitely unfamiliar. 'I have no idea,' I admitted. 'And we're still too close to those guards for me to experiment and find out.' I glanced up at the night sky. 'We've got a good four hours before dawn. Let's make the most of it and see what we can learn from my old friend the Bull.' I pointed upwards. 'This way will take us round to the back of his castle. We can enter through the kitchens but we'll have to hurry. When I lived here there was always someone up early baking bread. We need to get inside before they start work.'

'Are you alright, Tegs?' Taylor asked.

I smiled. Now that we'd overcome the first hurdle, I could concentrate on the matter in hand. The rattling memories inside my head were just ghosts from another life; I wasn't that scared little kid any more. 'I'm good,' I told him. I meant it. 'Now let's move.'

We were lucky that it was a cloudy night because the moon was almost obscured, making it easy to slip unnoticed to the main buildings. I spotted a couple of others wandering about the grounds, no doubt under orders to keep the Bull safe, but they didn't glance in our direction.

Buoyed up by our success so far, I sped up, knowing that the others would keep pace. Before long, I was standing in front of the old oak door leading into the Scrymgeour kitchens. Taylor was breathing heavily – it was a long time since he'd participated physically in any heists – but there was no denying the gleam in his eyes. He'd missed this. Perhaps we all had.

The door was locked and bolted from the other side. Opening it wasn't impossible but there were easier ways to gain entry than to waste time fiddling around and trying to pick the lock. I spotted a grimy window high up in the right corner of the wall. If the Bull had been re-modelling, he hadn't done anything to change the exterior. Not that the comfort of his servants had ever been his concern; he'd always demanded that the kitchen door be kept closed so the grounds staff couldn't wander in to nab some food whenever they wanted. It could get mightily hot when the kitchen was in full swing, however, so back in my day that little window was always left open to provide ventilation. It appeared that nothing had changed.

I jerked my chin and the others understood instantly. Brochan strode over and pressed his back against the wall before cupping his hands. I lifted my foot onto his makeshift step and pushed myself upwards until my heels were on his shoulders. Then Speck shunted Lexie upwards. His hands lingered on her arse – that was definitely a new development since we'd last done this manoeuvre – until she gained enough purchase to clamber up both Brochan and myself to reach the little gap. The pixie shimmied inside head first. There was a faint clatter as she landed on something metal on the other side. I froze for a moment, waiting to see if the noise had alerted anyone. When the silence continued, I dropped down and dusted off my palms.

Unbolting the door to let us in, Lexie gave us a little curtsey and an apologetic glance. She pointed at a large saucepan which she must have knocked down during her descent. No harm, no foul; I shrugged and patted her shoulder. From here on in, however, we had to be as silent as the grave.

Leading the way, I padded through the tiled kitchen, noting the differences since I'd last been here. A sudden image of the head cook slapping me for tardiness rose unbidden in my head but I choked it back down. I could reminisce later.

Using memory rather than sight, I went to the interior door and nudged it open with my toe to reveal the long, dimly lit corridor ahead. I paused, head cocked, but I couldn't hear a thing beyond the faint buzzing from one of the wall sconces. With a quick signal to the others, I made a beeline for the Bull's study. No one was allowed inside – even Tipsania had been roundly scolded one day for daring to snoop while her father was away – and at this hour the Bull himself would be in his quarters snoring like a foghorn. It was the place where we were least likely to risk discovery and also where he would keep any information about the upcoming wedding.

I turned right then left and right again before emerging into the main hall. There was a sudden *eep* from behind me. Alarmed, I spun round; Speck was clasping his heart and staring, stricken, at an ancient suit of armour. I frowned at him and he looked embarrassed. Bob, taking every opportunity to assert himself, flew into Speck's face and put his finger to his lips in overly dramatic outrage. At least he did it quietly.

Apart from the occasional creak of a floorboard and the heavy tick from the grandfather clock next to the armour, everything was silent. This was proving to be a piece of cake.

Our mute train continued, twisting down corridors until we reached the room I needed. Just to be on the safe side, I leaned towards it and cupped my ear against its reassuringly solid door. No one was inside. I tried the handle, delighted that the Bull relied on his Clan's obedience and had left it unlocked, and pushed it open. We shuffled in and closed it behind us. Yahtzee. We were finally inside.

As it was one of the few rooms I'd never entered during my time here, I was curious to see what secrets it held. The reality was disappointing; it looked like any other study anywhere in the world. There were bookshelves containing row upon row of leather-bound tomes, none of which, I noted sardonically, had cracked spines. It was no surprise that the Bull wasn't much of a reader. He also wasn't very clean or tidy. Despite the lack of a lock, he guarded the interior of this study too carefully to allow anyone inside to dust or sweep up and the results were obvious. There was a thick layer of grime along the windowsill, making me glad that we'd not entered that way, and several messy piles of papers on the desk. And, in the far corner and in plain sight, an old-fashioned safe.

Taylor cracked a grin and stepped over to it. He ran his hand across its top in admiration. 'I've not seen one of these models for years,' he whispered. 'What a beauty.'

Lexie scrunched up her face. 'It's ancient,' she said with a note of disgust. 'I'd been hoping for a challenge.'

Taylor wagged his finger at her. 'Now, now,' he warned. 'Just because it's old, doesn't mean it's weak.'

'Are you talking about yourself, old man, or about the safe?'

He jabbed a mock punch in her direction. 'Have some respect for your elders. One must wait until evening to see how glorious the day has been.'

I opened my mouth but Brochan reached over and clamped his hand over it. 'I love you, Tegs, but no.'

'Mmmmph.'

'You have to promise.'

I glared at him then nodded. He released me. Stepping away, I pouted. 'It was a really good joke. Now you'll never know just how funny it was.'

'I'll live.' He pointed at the safe. 'Open sesame.'

Bob, who'd been snoring on my shoulder, jerked his head up abruptly. 'You called?'

'Figure of speech, Bob. We've got this.'

He frowned. 'Are you sure? Because you could just wish…'

'No wishing.' I glanced at Taylor. 'Do you want to do the honours?'

He swept a bow. 'I'd be delighted.' He grinned at Lexie. 'Watch and learn, young one. Watch and learn.'

He knelt by the safe, one hand on the dial at the front and the other resting on the side. A look of intense concentration crossed his face as he began to turn the dial. It clicked round, Taylor muttering to himself as he listened for the tell-tale changes in sound that would indicate the correct numbers for the combination. I left him to it and flicked through the papers on the Bull's desk. There was little here of interest, just letters from tenants and old bills. Interestingly, there was a photo of Tipsania hidden behind one pile of envelopes. She looked about twelve years old and she was wearing a dress that wasn't a million miles away from the one I'd seen in MacKay's Marriage Emporium. So that was where the Bull had got his inspiration from. I picked it up to examine it more closely and realised as I did so that the photo didn't quite fit the frame. There was something underneath it. Biting my lip, I unclipped it to reveal another picture. When I drew it out, my mouth dropped open.

Brochan edged up and peered over my shoulder. 'Is that…?'

I nodded. 'My mother. I knew they'd had a relationship but I thought it hadn't meant much because the Bull cheated on her.' I stared down at her smiling face, itching to take the photo with me. I didn't have any images of her; whatever was left in the Adair mansion had been destroyed. I'd really liked to have had this one but if I took it would be like leaving the Bull a great big note saying 'Integrity was here!'. I cursed aloud and put the photograph back inside the frame. Desire for just one photo of my mother warred with common sense. Damn him. I returned the frame to the desk but my eyes lingered on it.

'Ta da!' Taylor stood up and cricked his neck. He checked his watch and gave Lexie a cheesy grin. 'And in record time, I might add.'

'Yeah, yeah. Is there anything useful inside?'

Speck knelt down and rummaged through the contents. 'Deeds to some land up north. Some cash, a few bearer bonds and stock certificates…' He whistled. 'This Bull guy really is loaded, you know.'

'Leave the money,' I instructed.

'Aw, Tegs…'

'It's not what we're here for. Is there anything about the wedding? Anything about Aifric?'

Speck rifled some more. 'Not that I can see.'

'Shite. Are you sure? Because—'

Bob piped up. 'I think I should tell you guys that we're about to be interrupted.'

We all swung our heads towards him. Bob held up his hands. 'I can feel the Bull's presence. Ommmmmm…'

Double shite. 'Everyone out. Now!'

They didn't need telling twice. Lexie wrenched open the door, darting out and away with the others hot on her heels. I went to join them but realised at the last moment that the sodding safe was gaping open. Gritting my teeth, I dashed back and tried to slam it shut. A piece of paper jammed in the opening. Feeling my pulse speed up, I fumbled to yank it free and toss it back inside so I could close the safe door. It was lucky that the Bull was a messy boy or he'd immediately have realised someone had been going through his papers.

I got back to my feet. Making a hasty and knowingly foolish decision, I grabbed the photo frame off the desk and ran for the door but it was too late. The Bull was only steps away.

I pulled back inside. There had to be somewhere to hide. Behind the curtains perhaps? They were too flimsy. Under the desk? No, that was stupid. I could wedge myself between the bookshelf and the wall. I leapt towards the gap just as the Bull's shadow fell into the room. Too late.

The Bull stared at the open study door, his expression thunderous. Then his eyes landed on me, catching me red-handed in the middle of his room. So much for my supposed death. Oh well.

Chapter Four

The Bull's expression immediately changed from anger to what I could only describe as terror. 'Integrity Adair,' he breathed. He snapped his arm upwards.

Convinced he was going to attack, I did the first thing I could think of: I reached inside myself for the Gift I'd stolen from the retching Sidhe at the border and drew on it, desperately hoping it would be something I could use to defend myself. Magic flashed through me but, instead of anything useful, the photo frame in my hands suddenly felt heavier. I glanced at it; it had turned into gleaming gold. My heart sank. A useful Gift in most circumstances but not in these ones.

'Don't, Cul-chain' I commanded, using his true name to compel him. I really should have done that at the start.

His arm dropped to his side like a heavy weight. 'B–b–begone, spirit,' he stammered.

I blinked. Eh?

'I cast you out,' he intoned, his voice still shaking. 'I cast you out!'

I tucked the frame into my waistband and relaxed. So the Bull was superstitious. Brilliant. 'That's not going to work, Cul-chain.' I hummed, trying to make my voice sound mysterious and ghostly. 'I'm haunting you for a reason.' I suppressed the temptation to add a *woooo* for effect.

'It's not my fault you died! I didn't know Aifric was going to kill you!'

The Gift I'd stolen from Kirsty Kincaid buzzed in my veins. 'You're lying. I can see everything and I know the truth.'

He dropped to his knees. 'I'm sorry.' He covered his face with his hands. 'I'm so sorry.'

Pathetic. I folded my arms across my chest and tilted my head. 'You *have* been getting yourself into trouble, haven't you?' He murmured something. 'Take your hands away from your face and say that again.'

'Go ahead,' he said miserably, lifting his face. 'Go ahead and curse me. I deserve it. And you can't do anything worse to me than what's already been done. Why do you think I'm awake at three o'clock in the morning?' His eyes turned baleful. 'Did you murder my daughter?'

Er… I cleared my throat. 'She is beyond your reach now.'

He choked out a sob. 'Tipsy. My Tipsy…'

'You know she's gone and yet you persist with this wedding,' I said, watching him closely.

'It's not me who wants it to go ahead!' the Bull babbled. 'The Steward will kill me when she doesn't show up! Do you think I want to die?'

I stepped forward. 'Do you think *I* wanted to die?'

He blanched, going paler than I would have thought possible. 'It wasn't me! It was him! It was the Steward. Aifric Moncrieffe did it all. I'm innocent!'

'The last thing you are is innocent, Cul-chain,' I scoffed. 'Why don't you tell Aifric that she's missing?'

'He already knows! Of course he knows! Do you think I could keep something like that a secret from him? The man has eyes and ears everywhere.'

I rocked back on my heels. 'So why is he going ahead with the wedding?'

'He's got Farsensers out scouring for her. He thinks he can find her.'

I managed – just – to remain expressionless. 'But he won't.'

The Bull moaned. 'If Byron wasn't in love with her there wouldn't be a problem.'

For some reason my tongue stopped working. I stared at him, dumbstruck.

'It's all that boy's fault. Aifric is trying to make up for the fact that he left his son for dead across the Veil. He'll give him whatever he wants.'

I licked my lips and swallowed. 'And … and what Byron Moncrieffe wants is to marry Tipsania?' Even though Kirsty's Gift told me the Bull was telling the truth, I didn't want to believe it. Every other piece of evidence I'd had was to the contrary but doubt was starting to creep in. Actually 'creep' was the wrong word; it was more like a vicious assault.

The Bull's head dropped again. 'Tipsania was such a beautiful girl. She wasn't perfect and I know she was spoilt but she didn't deserve to die so young. Byron will be heartbroken. He wouldn't listen to me when I tried to delay the wedding. He wants it done as soon as possible.' He moaned again.

I barely heard him. I was still absorbing the revelation that Byron was pushing for the ceremony. I'd been such an idiot. The others were right: this had nothing to do with Aifric's machinations. Byron was in love with Tipsania and wanted to wed her – or worse, he wanted her money to maintain his Clan's ascendancy, regardless of anyone's feelings.

I knew the Bull was telling the truth and I knew that I was the worst kind of idiot. I wasn't denying that Byron had felt something for me but it obviously hadn't run very deep. Sharp pain stabbed at my heart. My alleged corpse was barely cold. I understood that I'd betrayed him by faking my death in front of his eyes but I hadn't had any choice – it had been pretend to die or, well, die.

My knuckles tightened around the picture frame and the hurt in my chest expanded. How could one man make me feel like this? A hard knot rose in my throat. I wasn't going to cry. There was no way I was going to cry.

'What else is he planning?' I asked once I could form words again. 'What else does Aifric Moncrieffe have up his sleeve?'

The Bull's eyes were wild. 'How the hell should I know? I'm not exactly his confidante, am I? You put paid to that when you told him you had my true name.' He paused, his expression suggesting he'd suddenly had a revelation. 'Hang on. If you know everything then why don't you know what Aifric is up to?'

I thought quickly. 'I have your true name. That is why I know of your dealings, Cul-chain,' I intoned.

The Bull was only mildly appeased. He looked me up and down, taking in my dark clothing. His stance shifted and, as he put his weight onto his toes, I saw suspicion in his eyes. Without further warning, he lunged for me. 'You're no ghost,' he spat.

I dodged the blow just as the study was abruptly illuminated with a glowing white light. An odd sensation flitted through my stomach and I felt myself rise into the air, as if my system still had traces of the Levitation Gift I'd once stolen from a Fomori demon. If it hadn't been for the glimpse I caught of Speck in the open doorway, his hands raised and a look of intense concentration on his face, I'd have believed that's what it was.

I swallowed and went with the flow while the Bull staggered back a step, slack-jawed. 'Oh you fool,' I told him.

He cowered. 'I'm sorry! I'm sorry! Just don't hurt me!' His hands covered his head as if he were trying to protect himself from a blow.

My lip curled. 'You have been punished already. You will suffer to the end of your days knowing that your daughter is gone as a result of your actions. Tell anyone of this encounter and you will be considered nothing more than a demented old man, turned mad by grief.'

He shook his head violently. 'I won't tell anyone!'

'Promise me, Cul-chain.'

'I promise!'

I watched him. He was telling the absolute truth; given that my use of his true name compelled him to do what I said, that was hardly surprising. But truth was rarely absolute. Just because he believed he'd stay quiet now didn't mean he wouldn't change his mind later. As Brochan had pointed out, he could find ways around the compulsion.

There was little I could do about it. I'd just have to enjoy the relative safety of my death for as long as I could and be prepared for things not remaining that way. I wondered what Byron would think. Would he regret jumping to Tipsania so quickly or had he been in love with her all along? It felt like there was a gaping hole in my chest, exactly where my heart used to be.

Behind the Bull, Speck was starting to tremble. A bead of sweat ran down his forehead; he couldn't hold out for long. I gave him a brisk nod and, with relief, he released the spell and dropped me back to the ground with an unghostlike thump. The Bull started to look up but I growled at him.

'I'm taking this,' I told him, pointing at the photo frame. He flinched then both Speck and I were in the corridor and sprinting away soundlessly.

***

Morning was well under way by the time we arrived back at the Adair border. I remained silent for most of the journey, lost in my thoughts and assailed by a sense of grief for something I'd once almost had and now lost forever. The others had the sense not to press me. Unfortunately, that same sense didn't apply to Sorley, on duty out by the flagpole with a few other trolls who were standing rigidly upright. Unlike his compatriots, Sorley was kneeling down and murmuring something, his squat fingers running over the fur of a nearby haggis. When he saw us approach he stood up and aimed an irritable kick in the little animal's direction. I noticed that his foot wasn't close to connecting with it.

'You're not supposed to be back yet,' Sorley sniped when Speck rolled down the window. The troll was holding a clipboard in his hands; he tapped it with a gnarled fingernail and glared. 'I'm responsible for everyone's safety. If you don't stick to the schedule, you make my life almost impossible.'

'Sorley,' Taylor groaned, leaning across to speak to him, 'this really isn't the time for your complaints.'

'Oh yeah, dunderhead? Then when is the time? There was another contingent of Sidhe here while you were gone. This time they said that if all the trolls didn't return to their posts within the next seventy-two hours, they'd come down here and make us.' He glared and pointed to some scorch marks on the ground on this side of the border. 'Look at what they did!' he spat. 'They said it was a warning.'

I grimaced. Wonderful. 'How many of them were there?' I asked. As much as I might want to go up to my bedroom with a bottle of wine, a ton of chocolate and Joni Mitchell on repeat, I couldn't abandon my duties as Chieftain. And one of those was making sure that all of my Clan members were safe.

Somewhat mollified at being taken seriously, Sorley's hold on his spear relaxed. 'Seven,' he grunted. 'All from Clan Moncrieffe.'

I cursed. That wasn't good; anything that the Moncrieffes did was a worry. Still, I reasoned, in a half-arsed attempt to be logical, at least concentrating on the wedding and trying to find Tipsania would distract Aifric from the trolls for a while.

'One of them was a Farsenser,' Sorley added, destroying any silver lining I thought I'd found.

'Shite!' I exploded, causing everyone – even the trolls – to turn and gape at me. I sighed. 'Sorry. But the Bull told me that Aifric has got Farsensers out searching for Tipsania.'

'They don't have much reach though, do they?' Brochan said. 'A mile or two?'

I ran a hand through my hair, teasing out the tangles and trying to stay calm. 'Based on what I know from stealing farsensing, yeah. Some will be better at it than others, of course. There was no reason for them to come down this close to the Veil to look for her so I didn't worry about it before, but now…' My voice trailed off.

'They'd be trying to work out how many trolls are here. Or to search for weak spots in the border,' Taylor said, in an attempt to ease my worry, 'not Farsense for her.'

I gritted my teeth. 'It doesn't really matter why they came here to begin with. They'd have been on the alert for her presence so we have to assume that they know now that she's here. They can't pass through the border and drag her out because of the trolls, so they're going to try something else.'

We exchanged glances. 'The Wild Man,' Lexie said. 'Candy. He's missing. The Moncrieffes must know about his relationship with Tipsania and they'll use him to force her out of hiding. It's the only thing I can think of that would make her give herself up.'

'How can they know about him?' Taylor asked.

'Byron,' I said grimly. I didn't want to believe it of him but Tipsania had been adamant that no one else knew about her and Candy. And Byron knew that Tipsania had been here on my land because he brought her himself. Maybe he'd even sent the Farsenser to see if she was still here.

Nobody looked at me. I bunched my hands into fists. 'We need to think quickly. Right now we have the edge because we know what they're up to. That's not going to last for long.'

Taylor licked his lips. 'I hate to be the one to say it, Tegs…'

I crossed my arms. 'But you're going to anyway.'

He gave me a disarming smile which didn't fool me for a second. 'You don't owe Tipsania anything. I can understand why you're concerned about the trolls. They've sworn fealty and they're Clan Adair now. Tipsania Scrymgeour isn't.'

'She offered fealty,' I pointed out.

'But she didn't actually give it.'

Speck sniffed. 'Taylor is right. We all know she's a bitch—'

'A reformed bitch.'

'Ha! She's not there yet,' he replied. 'She treated you like shit when you were kids. If Byron Moncrieffe wants to marry her then let him marry her. It's no longer your concern.'

For once even Lexie didn't stand up for the Moncrieffe princeling. I tried to make the hurt I felt inside coalesce into anger but it didn't work. I still just felt hurt. 'Aifric and Byron have probably banded together to kidnap, or maybe even kill, Candy for falling in love with the wrong person. They'll get away with it because they're the rulers of this stupid country. Not only that, they're going to force a woman who's currently under my protection to marry someone else, as if we're living in the Middle Ages instead of the twenty-first century.' I looked at them. 'I can't just let that lie.'

Brochan's mouth turned down. 'When you put it like that…'

I shrugged. 'I have to do what I can.' I lifted my chin and gazed at the horizon – and the dark cloud of the Veil. 'It'll be another good opportunity to practise stealing Gifts and prepare us for what's to come. Sooner or later I'm going to have to deal with the Fomori demons.'

'The Lowlands of Scotland are not your responsibility, prophecy or no prophecy,' Taylor said.

There didn't seem much point in responding. We all knew we couldn't let the situation in the Lowlands continue forever; someone had to do something. And if that someone was going to be me, whether I had a clue about what to do or not – well, so be it. Before that, however, I was going to rescue a damsel in distress and her boyfriend. And I was not going to waste any time being heartsick over any bastard of a Moncrieffe. Screw the lot of them.

***

I showered quickly before grabbing my bag and stuffing everything I could think of inside it. I had no idea when there would be another gang of Sidhe at our door but I had to assume it wouldn't be long. Time was of the essence.

With wet hair still dripping down my back, I went off in search of Morna and found her at the edge of the Adair grove. New saplings were already springing up, pushing their way towards the sky with an optimism that gave me hope for the future. If they could grow here, on this land that was once so desolate and destroyed, then anything could happen. I brushed the nearby leaves, which might look tiny and delicate but were imbued with considerable strength, and cleared my throat.

'What is it, dear?' Morna asked, half-turning towards me.

'Hi,' I said, the epitome of awkwardness. 'The trees are looking good.'

Morna smiled. 'They are, aren't they? You've done a good job. They're still small but they're all healthy.'

'What type of tree fits in your hand?' She looked at me patiently. 'A palm tree.'

I received another polite smile in response. 'Very good, dear. You're not here because you want me to laugh at your jokes, though.'

'No.' I smoothed my hands down my jeans and took a deep breath. 'You were right. It's time for you to go.'

Morna looked at me questioningly. 'Are you strong enough to manage on your own?'

'I'll have to be.' I looked away. 'It's too dangerous for you to stay any longer. Aifric is virtually at the gates.'

'Does he know you're alive?'

'Not yet but it's just a matter of time. There are … other matters to deal with.'

'The boy? Byron?'

'No.' I scratched my neck. 'Yes. Sort of.'

She tutted. 'You should just find him, tell him you're alive and that you're in love with him.'

I swallowed. 'He doesn't want me.'

'I doubt that very much.'

'It's true. It doesn't matter anyway,' I said dismissively. 'It was never going to happen. I'm going to help Tipsania then go across the Veil and try to help the people there.'

Morna's gaze was sharp. 'How?'

'I don't know yet,' I answered honestly. 'I'm still making all this up as I go along.' Every avenue I thought of ended up in abject failure and my own tortured death but where there was a will…

'It pays to be prepared.'

I nodded. 'I know. And I will be. I'll steal everything I could possibly need until I'm the most powerful damn Sidhe this country has ever seen.'

Morna smiled faintly. 'You're already that, dear.' She put her hand on my arm. 'Have you been practising while you were away?'

'A little bit. I stole part of the Gift from a Scrymgeour Sidhe. I didn't even know what it was and yet I managed to take it. Not all of it – he's still okay. He still has some magic but…' I shrugged again.

'Good. You're learning self-control. I'm proud of you. Your parents would be proud of you.'

I was both taken aback and embarrassed. Unsure of how to respond, I murmured, 'Thank you.'

'When would you like me to leave?'

It was starting to sound like I was kicking her out. I suppose I was. 'Er … as soon as possible. And I have a favour to ask.' I winced; I'd already asked so much of her. 'Can you take Tipsania with you? Drop her off at the MacQuarries' Land? They'll keep her hidden for a little while, at least until her wedding date has been and gone.' I explained briefly about Candy and what I thought was going on.

For a moment I thought Morna would refuse. Eventually, however, she sighed. 'Yes, I suppose I can do that. You're not going to tell her the truth?'

'She'll do something stupid like fly off to try and rescue Candy and mess everything up. She's a lot stronger than she looks but I'll feel better if she's out of the way. If she goes after Candy she'll walk into a trap.'

'She's not going to like it when she finds out the truth,' Morna warned.

I sighed. 'The truth makes fools of us all.'

Morna watched me closely but chose not to pursue the line of conversation. 'Well,' she said, 'if that girl is coming with me, I'd better stay at the MacQuarries for a few days until she settles down. If she's on her own she's liable to open her mouth and cause offence. Even with their sworn oath to you, that won't go down well. She really has to learn some manners. I've had enough spoilt Sidhe brats in my time. I'm getting too old to deal with many more of them.'

I breathed out. 'You'd do that?'

She nodded. 'But only until I convince her to think before she speaks and the MacQuarries to grant her some leeway.'

'Thank you,' I said wholeheartedly. 'You're the perfect person to teach her the error of her ways.'

'If you say so.' Morna raised her eyebrows. 'And speak of the devil.'

I glanced over my shoulder to see Tipsania flouncing up the hill towards us. 'Integrity!' she yelled.

How did she manage to make her voice so piercing? I pasted on a grin. 'Hi, Tipsy!'

She marched up, hands on her hips. 'What's going on? Nobody is telling me a thing. I'd like to remind you that this is *my* wedding we're talking about. Is it just a farce or is it really going ahead?' I opened my mouth to answer but she didn't give me the chance. 'Well?' she demanded. 'Come on! *Tell* me. I insist that you do.'

'There's nothing to worry about.'

'Pah! That's easy for you to say!'

'Everything's under control. I want you to go away with Morna for a few days. Just until things have died down.'

Tipsania's mouth fell open. 'Why?'

'You'll be safer with her.'

A fleeting expression of hurt crossed her face. 'Sure. I understand. You don't want me around.' She turned away.

I reached out and grabbed her arm. 'It's not like that. It really is for your own safety. You're welcome back here after the wedding.'

'The wedding that's not going to happen.'

'Yeah.' Hopefully.

'I want to see Candy. I think a Wild Man will be able to protect me better than a geriatric.' She glanced at Morna. 'No offence.'

Morna gave a tight smile.

'Candy wants you to go with her,' I lied.

Tipsania frowned, her delicate brows snapping together. 'Why? He's never met her.'

'I spoke to him and he agreed it was for the best,' I said, crossing my fingers behind my back.

Her expression immediately brightened. 'You saw him? Is he alright?'

'Great,' I lied again. 'Now go grab your stuff. You're leaving in an hour.'

'What?' she shrieked. 'It'll take me longer than that to pack. And what about May? I can't just leave her here with that … that … Bauchan.' Her voice dripped with disdain.

I tilted my head, confused. 'Fergus?'

'Never mind, dear,' Morna interjected. 'You go get your bags.'

Tipsania sniffed haughtily. 'Someone will need to carry them for me.' She didn't wait for a response but twirled round and stomped back towards the mansion.

'I think half the time she just wants to get a reaction out of people,' I said hastily to Morna.

'Mmm.'

'And what did she mean about Fergus and May?'

Her face wreathed in sudden smiles. 'You should go and see for yourself.'

***

I found Fergus and May in a newly sprouted meadow near the back of the mansion. They were sitting together, surrounded by long-stemmed flowers; a few bees buzzed close to them and the Foinse was lazily making figures-of-eight in the air. A gigantic umbrella which appeared to have been fashioned out of an old bedsheet and some branches was shielding May's delicate skin from the sun. Even with their backs to me, I could see how relaxed they were. Standing watching them made me feel like a voyeur and I almost turned away to leave them to it but then May's head turned, as if she sensed my presence. She grinned at me and waved. Caught out, I felt I had no choice but to join them.

'Hey,' I said. Feeling awkward was starting to become my natural state.

Fergus leaned back on his hands and grinned. 'Hey yourself. You're back.'

'And you're awake.'

He gestured nonchalantly. 'You can't keep a good Bauchan down.'

'Mm,' I said. 'Anyway, I'm not here for long. I'm just heading back out again.'

He frowned. 'Is that a good idea? You're safe here.'

'Fergus,' I said, not unkindly, 'unless you want to swear fealty, right now you're effectively an asylum seeker. What I do and where I go is my business.'

He held up his palms. 'I wouldn't dream of telling Chieftain Adair what she should do,' he said easily. Then his expression sobered. 'Thank you for taking me in. You didn't have to do that. I'll swear in if you want me to.'

'God, no. I don't need more warm bodies on my conscience. But you're welcome to be here. I'm glad to see you're on the mend.'

'The blue-haired pixie told me something about what happened up north. You should have waited until I woke up. I could have told you that it was Byron who wanted the wedding to go ahead.'

Damn it. I'd managed to stop thinking about Byron for at least a minute. 'You were out for the count. And there's more going on than just Byron Moncrieffe.'

The Foinse stopped its swirling and spun round, zipping towards me with such velocity that I thought for a moment it was going to smack me in the forehead. It stopped inches away from my face, however, and nuzzled in towards me. The warmth exuding from it was rather comforting.

'Did you ever consider why the Clans were so keen to keep the Foinse locked away?' Fergus asked.

I reached up and stroked it tentatively. It buzzed happily in response. 'They wanted control of the magic.'

He nodded. 'I hear your warlock friend is suddenly growing remarkably adept.'

I raised my eyebrows. 'Lexie has been telling a lot of tales.'

'Oh,' he grinned, 'that part wasn't the pixie. May told me that.'

I blinked. 'May doesn't have a tongue.'

I smiled at her and she gave an uncertain smile in return. Fergus turned to her, his hands fluttering. May watched them carefully and responded. My jaw fell open. 'Sign language?'

'Yep.'

'But she doesn't speak English.'

'Gaelic.'

'Wow.'

Fergus's eyes softened. 'Yeah. She's pretty amazing.'

I stared at him. There was an odd flush rising up in his cheeks. I looked at May; she was peeking up at him from beneath her eyelashes. I took a step back. No wonder I'd felt like I was intruding.

'Er, Fergus?'

He didn't take his attention away from May. 'Mmm?'

'What about the Innes girl?'

'Pardon?'

'You're here because you shagged some Sidhe girl and her dad was pissed off.'

'Oh yeah.' He registered what I was saying and turned to meet my gaze. 'You want to know what my intentions are.'

'Don't lead May on.'

His expression was serious. 'That's not what this is about.'

I bloody well hoped not.

'Uh. Eh. Ee.' May got to her feet and grinned. She braved the weak Scottish sunlight for a few moments and wrapped her arms around me. Not long ago, those arms had been little more than twigs but now I could feel flesh beneath her skin. She was definitely looking healthier. It was amazing how quickly things could change. She leaned her head on my shoulder while the Foinse buried itself between the pair of us. I hugged her back.

There was no mistaking the warning in the look I gave Fergus. He bowed. Oddly enough, I didn't think he was being facetious or flippant this time. Eventually I drew away and led May gently back to the safety of the shade. Hugs were all well and good but I had business to attend to. 'Where would Aifric Moncrieffe keep a prisoner?'

Fergus gave me a confused look. 'In prison.'

I shook my head. 'No, I don't mean a murderer or...'

'A thief?'

'Funny. Where would he keep someone he wants to hide?'

A spark gleamed in his eyes. 'Now who would the Steward want to hide?' he mused. 'You're here. Your friends are here. The trolls are here. Your assassin buddy is busy opening up a dress shop. Byron Moncrieffe is getting measured for his new wedding kilt.' I tried not to flinch. 'So who are you asking about?'

'That's on a need-to-know basis.'

'You can trust me.'

I snorted. 'You know it's been bugging me for a while about who you remind me of. I've finally got it. You think you're like Q. From Star Trek.'

For possibly the first time since I'd met him, Fergus didn't know what I was talking about. 'Is that a television programme?'

I smirked. 'Yeah. Sci-fi. Q is an omnipotent being who knows everything.'

From out of nowhere, Bob zapped into existence. 'Hey!' he complained. 'I'm the only all-knowing being around here, Uh Integrity!' He glared at Fergus as if the Bauchan were stealing his very soul.

I laughed. 'In the end, Q has to keep going to the *Enterprise* crew for help. He's not as all-knowing as he thinks he is.'

Bob frowned suspiciously. 'Are you alluding to me or to him' – he nodded at Fergus – 'with this pathetic comparison?'

I shrugged. 'You're the clever ones. You tell me.'

There was a shout from behind us. Taylor and Brochan were near the mansion and waving at me. I checked my watch; yeah, it was time to go.

'Look after May,' I said to Fergus.

He put his arm round her. I couldn't be sure but it looked as if she blushed. 'I will,' he said quietly.

I nibbled on a hangnail. 'Could you ask her about what things are like beyond the Veil? The more information we have about life there…' I shrugged.

Fergus's eyes were sharp. 'You're planning an expedition?'

'Not exactly but we can't just pretend it's not there. People are suffering. Sooner or later, I'm going to have to do something.'

May's shoulders shrank as if she knew what we were talking about. Fergus edged even closer to her. 'I can do that,' he said finally. 'If she's willing to tell me. But,' he added in a rush, 'if you go, then I'm coming with you.'

'Why?' I asked suspiciously.

'I deal in knowledge, Chieftain. Just think what I could do if that knowledge extended to the Lowlands.'

'I couldn't guarantee your safety,' I said honestly.

He gave me a lopsided grin. 'No one ever can.' I nodded in agreement and turned to leave. 'Integrity?' he called out after me.

'Yeah?'

'The Cruaich has a series of dungeons underground. They can be reached from a closed-off staircase next to the library. That's where I'd keep someone if I were the Steward.'

I grinned my gratitude. Excellent; I'd been aiming for the Cruaich all along.

'I could have told you that, Uh Integrity,' Bob complained. He folded his arms and pouted. 'In fact, if you make a wish to free Candy, I can show you just how impotent I really am.'

'I think you mean omnipotent,' I said drily as I started walking away.

———

'Candy?' Fergus asked from behind. 'The Wild Man who works for Byron Moncrieffe?'

'Nice going,' I muttered to Bob.

'It's not my fault Bauchans have big ears.'

'A right ear, a left ear and a final front ear?'

'Uh Integrity?'

'Yes?'

Bob shoved the Foinse out of the way and scooted up to my neck, settling himself above my collarbone with a happy sigh. 'I really hate you sometimes.'

Chapter Five

It wasn't easy to persuade the others to stay behind, even though I knew it was the sensible thing for them to do. The Cruaich wasn't like the Bull's castle and, even if the Moncrieffes worked out that Tipsania was no longer here, the trolls were in increasing danger and might need help. Unfortunately, my surrogate family was all packed and ready to go and gazing at me with expectant faces.

'I need people here,' I explained. 'We don't know for sure what the Clans are going to try next.'

Brochan glowered. 'There are hundreds of trolls.'

'Yep,' I nodded, 'there are. But they're no match against Sidhe Gifts. You can control the weather – you could call up a storm and delay anyone who tries to get in.'

Brochan's gills flapped in irritation. 'I can't control the weather. And I can't create storms.'

'You can make it rain.'

'It's not the same thing.'

I shrugged. 'It's going to be easier for one person to slip in and out of the Cruaich. Especially a Sidhe. You're better placed here.'

Speck stepped up as if he were tag-teaming the merman. 'We've done it before. And now I've got magic,' he said. 'Real magic. You saw how strong I'm getting. I just proved it by helping you get away from the Bull.'

'Which is why I need you here too. That magic might be needed.' I crossed my arms. 'Anyway, if you stay close to the Foinse your magic will get stronger.'

'The Adair border is strong, Tegs. It'll hold against anyone who tries to breach it.'

There was a stubborn set to my jaw. 'We don't know what else Aifric might have up his sleeve. The Adair Lands need to remain unbreached.'

'Well, I don't have magic,' Lexie interrupted. 'I can come.'

'You need to stay and keep Speck grounded.' I pushed back my hair. 'This is the most sensible course of action.'

'What about me?' Taylor asked.

I glanced at my old mentor. As much as I'd like to have him along, even just for reassurance, I couldn't live with myself if he got hurt. 'No,' I said flatly. 'You have a good relationship with the trolls. They'll listen to you if everything goes tits up.'

He sighed. 'You're supposed to be dead. If anyone who's not as stupid as the Bull sees you then…'

'Then, as I keep saying, we'll deal with it. I've taken some threads of Tipsania's Gift for emergencies and I'll steal more Gifts when I'm at the Cruaich. I'll need them for later when I venture across the Veil again.'

Bob beamed. 'Excellent. Uh Integrity can go and save Sweetie and we'll all stay here. I'd been hoping for a holiday. Some relaxation time will do me good.'

'His name is Candy. And you're coming with me.'

'But…'

'I might need that last wish from you, Bob.'

He opened his mouth to argue then thought better of it. I turned to look at the bits of rubbish near my feet just as he leaned in towards Taylor and whispered loudly, 'Reverse psychology.' He grinned. 'Works every time. You'd know that if you were as powerful as I am.'

'What's with the rubbish?' Taylor asked, ignoring the genie.

My eyes danced. 'Has no one ever wondered why the Scrymgeours are so wealthy?'

'They're canny bastards.'

'Oh, they are that,' I said. 'But they've also got some particular Clanlings who help them out from time to time.'

Taylor's brow furrowed. 'Eh?'

I smirked. 'Watch.' I pulled on the Gift I'd stolen and directed it at the mess on the ground. As everyone gaped, the tins, empty crisp packets and various bits of shite began to transform.

'Is that...?'

I nodded smugly. 'Gold. That Scrymgeour Sidhe's Gift was Alchemy.'

Taylor swallowed. 'No way.' He knelt down and picked up a twig, holding it up to examine it more closely. Its golden edge gleamed in the sunlight. 'Do you know what this means?'

'I do. It means you have no need to gamble ever again because we have all the wealth we could ever need right here.'

His face immediately fell. 'That's not what I...'

'I know.' I pointed at pile of gold. 'But there's enough there to bribe anyone. And enough to at least make a decent effort to sort out this place. The trolls have done well but we're lacking in raw materials. I'll take a bit of gold with me for emergencies but you can keep the rest.' My gaze turned hard. 'So even if I don't return, there's enough to set you and everyone else up for life.'

Lexie tossed her head. 'You'll return.' She jabbed Speck's ribs.

He coughed. 'Yeah. You'll return because no one else can do anything about the Lowlands.'

'You're too damned stubborn,' Brochan agreed.

Taylor scratched his chin. 'And we're going to need more gold so you'll need to come back and make us even richer.'

I laughed. 'That's the last of it. I needed to make room for other more useful Gifts.'

He stared at me. 'More useful Gifts than Alchemy?'

'Au, is that all you want me for?'

Taylor frowned. 'Pardon?'

'Au? A U?'

Lexie shook her head in dismay. 'Yeah, you're right. We'll stay here and Bob can go with you. I've heard enough, thank you very much.'

I jabbed a finger at her. 'If I die, you'll end up with a gilt complex.'

She put her hands over ears. 'Just go.' She paused. 'No, wait.' She ran up and gave me a tight hug. 'Now, go. And if you see Byron Moncrieffe, turn invisible and give him a good kick in the balls for me.'

I ignored the lurch in my stomach. I was going to make sure I kept well away from him. It was doubtful he'd even be at the Cruaich – he had a wedding to prepare for, after all. 'I have no claim on Byron. I never did.' I was speaking the truth. I couldn't help feeling wounded by his sudden desire to marry Tipsania but I couldn't keep moaning about it.

'We all know that's not true,' Lexie scoffed.

'I'm also a pacifist,' I pointed out.

'There are exceptions to every rule, Tegs. Stay safe. And,' she added with a wink, 'guard that heart of gold of yours.'

Speck nodded. 'He only wants Tipsania because he's a gold digger.'

'Rescuing Candy could prove to be incredibly useful,' Brochan said. 'He's probably a gold mine of information about the Moncrieffes.'

Taylor gave me a fatherly grin. 'We'll stay here and be as good as gold, Tegs.'

I straightened up. 'Don't try to beat me at my own game.' I waved goodbye to them all. 'Remember,' I called out over my shoulder as I got into the car, 'I'm going to be interrupting Aifric and Byron's plans so when I get back, be sure to have my gold *meddle* ready for me.'

Bob just groaned.

***

As it was the seat of power of the Highlands, the Cruaich borders were simple to cross. All Sidhe were granted admittance automatically and there were simply too many people of all backgrounds and ethnicities passing back and forth for strict rules to be maintained. Perhaps it was arrogance, too; except for the Fomori demons' incursion earlier in the year, no one had attacked the Cruaich for decades. If they had done, they'd have found themselves up against a considerable number of Gifted Sidhe – and no wanted those sorts of hordes after them. The Sidhe Clans were adept at keeping everyone else in their place.

All the same, I wanted to stay hidden. Long before I reached the border, I abandoned the car in favour of walking, skulking around like a shadow, flitting in and out of the trees that led towards the main Cruaich driveway. While I couldn't expect the Bull to maintain his silence forever, I didn't think he would have already passed on tales of my 'ghost'. It would take him a while to realise that what he'd seen was wholly corporeal and alive. At least for now, I could count on being unexpected and I had to make as much use of that as I could.

The first group of people who passed me were humans heading up towards the main castle. They looked nervous and their heads were bowed in conversation as they walked. No doubt they were petitioning the council on some matter. I wished them well but they weren't the sort of people I needed.

I hung back until they were out of sight then kept on going and eventually crossed the border itself. My skin buzzed faintly with the magic but my Sidhe blood kept it at bay easily. Staying alert, I skirted away from the drive, continuing to use the trees as cover but staying near enough to the road to see who was on it.

I'd barely gone a hundred feet when a lone Sidhe came wandering down, hands in pockets and expression distant. A Labrador trotted by his side, which immediately made me warm to him. Then I reminded myself why I was here and concentrated on stealing whatever Gift he had.

Nothing happened. I kept pace with him and concentrated harder. I could see the magic inside him but, when I called to it, it refused to come. The first vestiges of panic swirled inside me. I'd always been confused by my strange Gift of theft, even if it made sense considering what I used to do for my day job. I'd come to rely on it and to expect it to work at my bidding; the thought that it might have deserted me was worrying. I focused, feeling pressure behind my skull. Still nothing happened. What was going on?

I reached into the sheath which hung at my waist and carefully drew out Bob's letter opener. He spent more time out of it than inside it these days but he was prepared to hide in there to avoid listening to any more of my quips. I waited until I was completely alone again and then rubbed the blade with my sleeve.

There was a familiar flash of light and Bob blinked into existence. 'I need your help,' I hissed.

'You want your last wish?' He drew himself up with quivering excitement. 'Well, that's worth abandoning *Buffy the Vampire Slayer* for.' He clapped his hands. 'Do you want Byron to suffocate in his sleep? Or something a little more violent? I can arrange for castration…'

I winced. 'No. Listen, it's—'

'Massacre everyone in the Cruaich?'

'Jeez, Bob. How many times do I have to tell you that I won't resort to that kind of thing? I'm not psychotic.'

He pursed his lips. 'It'd be fair retribution for what happened to your Clan. Revenge isn't psychotic, Uh Integrity, it's noble. This world has been built on the pillars of revenge.' He snapped his fingers, creating a miniature floating pulpit that he climbed on to. 'Think Caesar,' he intoned with a grandiose flourish. 'Think Charles IX, the forty-seven Ronin, Operation Wrath of God.' His eyes gleamed. 'Think Lorena Bobbit.' He lowered his voice in a knowing aside. 'Guess which one of those I had a hand in!'

'Bob!' I snapped. 'Pay attention!'

The miniature pulpit vanished. 'Go on then.'

'I just tried to steal the Gift from a passing Sidhe. It didn't work.' I tried not to sound too anxious. 'Is something wrong with me?'

Bob regarded me seriously. 'I wouldn't even know where to begin, Uh Integrity. We've had words already about your dress sense. Then there are those jokes…'

I ground my teeth. 'Bob.'

He grinned. 'No, you are the same as always.'

'Then why couldn't I steal from him?'

'As you keep saying, you abhor violence regardless of how sensible and fulfilling it can be. The Sidhe probably had a violent Gift. Thus proving that if you concentrated harder, you could probably tell what each person's Gift was. Your subconscious knows, so you just need to tap into that.'

Could Bob be right? 'Okay,' I said slowly. 'Let's try that theory. Point me in the direction of more Sidhe.'

He cocked his head. 'Is that your wish?'

'Call it a favour.'

'In return I would like…' He fell silent at the expression on my face. 'Fine,' he muttered. He jerked his head to the right. 'There's a group about two hundred metres away.'

'That wasn't so difficult now, was it?'

He stuck out his tongue.

Following Bob's directions, I carefully wound my way towards the oblivious Sidhe. I doubted whether I could work out what Gifts each one had; it wasn't something I'd been capable of before now. If I couldn't achieve that kind of knowledge with Morna's help, there was little chance I could do it with Bob's. It would make life considerably easier, though. If I could pick and choose which magic to steal, I could end up with an array of Gifts as part of my arsenal. That thought spurred me on and I moved faster.

'They're in a clearing just up ahead,' Bob whispered in my ear.

I cast around. Just in front of me there was a large oak tree with some low-lying branches and heavy foliage that might do the trick. Grinning, I began to climb. When I thought I was high enough, I shimmied out across one of the far-reaching branches and peered through the leaves. Bob was right: there were more than a dozen male Sidhe milling around for no apparent reason.

I looked from one to another. Their clothing signalled they were from different Clans – Moncrieffe, Kincaid, Darroch, MacGillivray and Riddell. I didn't recognise any of them. Focusing my attention on the closest one – a youngish guy with red hair – I furrowed my brow. As before, I could see the magic inside him but I had no clue as to what it was. I emptied my mind of all my turbulent thoughts, blocked out the Sidhe's chatter and my arboreal-induced discomfort, until the two of us might have been the only people in the entire world. His Gift called to me. Desire to take it ran through my veins as if I were being seduced into stealing. I held my breath, only aware of the thrumming of my heartbeat and the twisting magic within the Sidhe.

'Huh, that's interesting,' Bob said.

I just managed to avoid yelping. 'Goddamnit, Bob!' I hissed, my fingers gripping the branch harder so I could remain in place. 'I'm trying to concentrate!'

'Well,' he huffed, 'I'd have thought you of all people would be interested in their conversation. D'you think Byron would invite me?'

'What?'

He tsked and poked my cheek. 'He thinks you're dead. I have no reason not to be here. I could pretend to bump into him and then maybe he'd invite me along. I like parties.'

'Bob, what on earth are you on about?'

He sighed as if I were incredibly dim-witted. 'Listen.'

I widened my focus so that instead of being wholly absorbed in one man, I was paying attention to them all.

'What about strippers?' asked one swarthy Sidhe, who was Moncrieffe judging by the tartan he was wearing.

'I know this girl,' another answered, 'who is able to shoot ping-pong balls…'

I gagged and made a face. Fortunately, I wasn't the only one.

'Mate, this is Byron we're talking about. He's classier than that.'

'But this girl is classy! You need to meet her. She's got legs that go on for miles.'

'I've got a company lined up. They're going to give us their most talented girl for the evening.'

'Which company?'

The speaker consulted his phone. 'Tartan Exotica. I know Mark, the owner, and he's giving me a good deal.'

'Grand.'

There was a rustle of leaves. All the Sidhe turned guiltily, relaxing only when they saw who had joined them. 'So,' Jamie Moncrieffe said. 'How are the preparations going? Have you managed to book the Haven?'

'Done and dusted, mate.'

He smiled. 'Good. Byron has no clue about what's going on. I'll tell the band to show up around 7pm but it's up to you guys to make sure everything's a surprise.'

'No problem.'

'And the entertainment is sorted? No strippers, right?'

The others all nodded vigorously. 'Right.'

'Damn,' Bob whispered. 'If it's a surprise, I'll need to talk to Jamie about my invite. He doesn't really know me, though.'

'You're not going to Byron's bloody stag do, Bob.'

He pouted. 'I might find out some serious intel. Maybe Aifric will be there.'

'Yes, because I'm sure that the Steward wants to spend his evening with strippers and young Sidhe blokes getting off their faces.' I snorted in disgust. 'This is a waste of time.' I started slithering back down the branch. I had zero interest in this.

'Oi! Where are you going? What about their Gifts?'

'I'll find some others instead. Anyway, it'll be safer to nick their magic when they're alone.' As to what that magic might be, I'd just have to hope I managed to get some worthwhile Gifts. A lucky dip rather than a selection box. No problem.

***

Obviously, wandering in through the Cruaich's main doors was a big no-no. I took inspiration from our jaunt to the Bull's lair and headed round the back of the massive castle. I shoved all my hair inside my trusty baseball cap and kept my head down. It was unlikely that any Sidhe would be hanging around the servants' quarters so all I had to do was avoid looking anyone in the eye and I could skate by without suspicion. If the worst came to the worst, I had enough of Tipsania's Gift to vanish.

I smiled humourlessly. If word got round that Integrity Adair's ghost was haunting the Cruaich, at least I'd have something new to laugh about.

I found a small door leading in to the staff quarters. Having used one of the guest rooms at the Cruaich on a previous occasion, I was shocked at how shabby these rooms were. They were cramped and small, they didn't look particularly clean and the sheets on the dorm-room beds were threadbare. Another black mark against the Moncrieffes, I thought sourly.

A couple of people wearing the Cruaich livery brushed by me, obviously on their way to work. I angled my face away and murmured greetings. As I'd suspected, everyone was too busy to pay me much attention.

Towards the end of the first corridor, I came to a bank of old-fashioned bells, the sort once used in grand houses to summon servants. The signs beneath these bells were new, however. When the one marked 'Boss' began to ring, I almost jumped out of my skin. Aifric really was an old-fashioned kind of guy. I was tempted to remove the ringer so that he would sit for hours waiting for someone to bring him a cup of tea but it would be a petty thing to do – and it would get the servants into trouble. Instead I moved smoothly past, happy in the knowledge that he was tucked out of the way, and set off for the library.

This was going to be the most dangerous part of the expedition. I hissed at Bob to remind him to keep out of sight and debated for a moment whether I could afford to use Tipsania's Gift. I wanted to be sparing with it; it was a finite resource and, if I took too much from her, she might end up with none. Ripping away someone's Gift in its entirety seemed to be the only way for me to keep hold of it for good but that was too high a price to pay for more power.

I cast my gaze across the wide space, taking in the different people milling around. I couldn't see the library from here and all I knew from Fergus was that there was a door nearby leading to the dungeons. I'd have to hope that I found the right one without too much bother. Waiting for an appropriate break in the crowd, I took a deep breath and strode out.

I'd barely gone ten metres when a well-dressed woman who I vaguely recognised from the Sidhe Games strolled in my direction. Attempting to look casual, I stayed on my path for a few steps then moved to my right. I craned my neck up as if examining the large painting hanging on the wall. When the woman stopped at my side and also glanced up at the giant picture, my stomach dropped.

'It's not often you see people stopping to take in their surroundings,' she said approvingly.

'It's a beautiful piece,' I murmured, praying she'd keep her attention on the painting rather than look at me. My tell-tale white hair was hidden and I was wearing contact lenses to mask my violet eyes but my weak disguise wouldn't stand up to close scrutiny. All she had to do was look me in the face to discover the truth. I might have to use Tipsania's Gift and make like a ghost again after all.

'Yes. I'm told it was acquired from the Adair Clan after they— Well, you know.'

I stiffened. Shite. She must have recognised me. I tensed, ready for action. Run or hide?

'I suppose,' she continued, 'they're going to be consigned to history now.'

I almost snorted, despite my panic. Aifric controlled history like everything else. I'd seen what was missing from the library with my own eyes; he had effectively rubbed out the Adair Clan's existence. Until I came along.

'Still,' she said, as if reading my thoughts, 'the Steward knows best.' She paused. 'And what's your name? Are you Clan Moncrieffe?'

I licked my dry lips, trying to find my voice. 'You don't know?'

'No,' she replied pleasantly as my veins buzzed with the truth of her answer. Her comment about the Adairs was nothing more than coincidence. I almost sagged to the floor in a puddle of relief. She glanced at me curiously as I angled my face away. 'Have we met?'

I opened my mouth to answer but fortunately I was interrupted by someone calling to her from across the room. She turned, her arm brushing against my body and her Gift – whatever it was – immediately spoke to me. Like a pickpocket with invisible hands, I responded.

I gasped faintly while she stalled and pressed her hand to her forehead. 'Goodness,' she said, 'I suddenly feel rather light-headed. Do excuse me. I think I'd better sit down.' She walked away with small, uncertain steps, leaving me and the painting alone.

Bob whistled in my ear. 'That was close, Uh Integrity.'

Yeah. It really had been. I reminded myself of everything I'd learnt while growing up with Taylor. People saw what they were expecting to see – and she wasn't expecting to see Integrity Adair because Integrity was dead. Therefore she saw a stranger rather than me. I'd do well to remember that.

I turned slowly. If I could steal that woman's Gift in plain view of everyone else then I could certainly steal more. Buoyed up, I got to work.

I avoided the elderly male Sidhe crossing my path, unsure what stealing from someone so advanced in age might do, and picked on a simpering man who was giving detailed instructions to a servant. 'I want a glass of water,' he ordered. 'Room temperature, no ice. A slice of lemon cut diagonally and placed on the rim so that…'

I closed my eyes momentarily and snatched a fistful of his magic. He staggered as I turned away.

Wandering in from a nearby door were three giggling girls. 'Did you see her face?' the middle one cackled.

I stole from her first, pulling at the threads of her magic and drawing them into me. When she froze mid-step and her two companions stopped to check on her, I stole from them too.

My soul stretched and settled, as if altering itself to accommodate the new Gifts. I had to be careful not to overdo it – I'd already made that mistake once before and too much magic could finish me. As long as I took small amounts from each person, however, I didn't think I'd be over-burdened and they would recover quickly from my actions.

I wove my way to the library, grabbing a pinch here and a saucerful there. I was beginning to feel heady from the power surging through me. The magic mixed and coalesced. These Sidhe with their airs and graces, they had no idea what real power felt like. I wanted more. I *needed* more.

'Uh Integrity…' Bob began.

I brushed him away, lifting my hand as if I were flicking away an irritating fly. In the far corner a man was flirting, turning a simple stick into an elaborate bunch of flowers through what must be his Gift of Illusion. Amongst the Sidhe, Illusion was considered a lesser Gift, something with which to amuse children. No one could make use of it quite like me, though.

I drew on it, sucking it inside me and feeling delight course through me. The hapless Sidhe fell against the wall while Bob pinched me. 'What are you doing? You're taking too much!'

I barely heard him. Right now I felt strong enough to fly. I could take down Aifric with one swoop; I could storm into the Cruaich dungeons and free Candy with a blink of my eye. I could twitch my little finger and every scrap of Scottish magic would be mine. I could … oh shite. I twirled round and faced away from Byron as he strode in from the hall to the right.

'I was going to warn you,' Bob murmured. 'But you seemed kind of preoccupied.'

Suddenly, I felt woozy and nauseous. I wasn't the only one. Several of the Sidhe from whom I'd stolen also looked distinctly unwell. I paid them scant attention. It was the knowledge that Byron was at my back that made me tremble all over.

I shuffled to the nearest wall, as far away from him as I could without drawing attention to myself. I'd allowed my over-confidence, along with the adrenaline of theft and the vertigo-inducing nature of magic, to make me almost lose control. If I wasn't more careful it wouldn't matter how many Gifts I managed to steal; I'd end up in the cell next to Candy. Or worse. And I'd hurt a lot of people in the process.

I gulped in air as Byron swept past me. He didn't feel my eyes on him because everyone else was watching him too. I couldn't see his face but that didn't stop me fixating on him. The way his hair curled into the nape of his neck and the tantalizing glimpse of tanned skin where he'd pushed up his sleeves. I frowned. Had he lost weight?

I shook myself. He was probably on a damned wedding diet. It was no business of mine and I wasn't here to gaze after him like a love-struck puppy. I was a Highland Chieftain who was far, far better than that – whether anyone here was aware of me or not.

As soon as there was enough distance between us, I scooted back to the other end of the room. Seeing Byron had been helpful in the sense that it brought me back to full awareness, like having a bucket of icy water poured over my head. I passed the library. Spotting a plain unvarnished door next to it, which I hoped led to the staircase Fergus had mentioned, I made a beeline in that direction.

'Uh Integrity! Byron's turning round!' Bob squealed. 'He's looking this way. He seems…'

I wrenched the door open and ran inside to the welcoming darkness.

'Uh Integrity? Why are we in a cupboard?'

I twisted round, knocking over a mop. When I tried to pick it up, I hit my head against a low shelf. I cursed loudly as pain exploded in my skull and lights danced in front of my eyes. I didn't need to worry about Aifric or Byron or anyone else; at this rate, I would inadvertently kill myself.

'As unpleasant as it is in here,' Bob remarked, 'it's no spooky dungeon.'

'Gee,' I said sarcastically. 'Thanks, Bob. I hadn't noticed.'

'Just trying to be helpful.' He waited for a beat. 'Byron looked really bad.'

I stiffened. 'In what way?'

'Tired. Great big expensive Louis Vuitton bags under his eyes. Awful skin. He must be stressed out because his fiancée has disappeared.'

'Yeah,' I said sourly, 'he must be.' Whatever. 'Any chance you saw another door when you were gawping at Byron? One that might lead to the dungeons we're supposed to be heading for?'

'Ooooh!' Bob flounced. 'Get you! I'm not the one who was getting drunk on magic and flitting around like the Artful Dodger on speed.'

'Sorry. I messed up,' I muttered. I could hardly pretend otherwise.

'What?' he screeched. 'No, no, no, no, no! A Chieftain does not apologise. Have you ever heard me apologise?'

I sighed. 'I'm not infallible just because I've got a poncey title.'

'Of course you're not. But you don't ever let other people know that.' He paused. 'Are you making a face at me?'

'No.'

'You are, aren't you?'

'I already said no, Bob.'

'Honestly,' he huffed. 'This is what I get for working with amateurs.'

Chapter Six

Although I hadn't intended to hide in a bloody broom cupboard, in the end it proved rather useful. It gave me time to sort through the different Gifts I'd taken and work out what each one was. Together with Illusion – and I was already well aware of how useful that particular Gift could be – I'd taken Electrosurge, Dowsing, Animal Summoning and Apportation. I sent out tiny bolts of each one, tugging tentatively to test them and identify them while Bob crowed out the different magical names. An ancient lightbulb, long since blown, zapped back to life and illuminated the tiny cupboard until I released the magic. I sensed a string of jewels round an elegant Sidhe lady's neck less than twenty feet away which called seductively to my inner thief. A cat meowed outside the cupboard door and scratched the wood until I hastily sent it away. I sent a mop head up to the top turret and brought it back. I flexed my magic muscles until I was satisfied that I could control each one. Candy's life might depend on it.

When I eventually edged out of the cupboard, the large hall was as busy as before. Fortunately there was no longer any sign of Byron and no one paid me any further attention. The giggly Sidhe girls from whom I'd stolen were still hovering around, no longer looking worse for wear. As long as I hadn't done any permanent damage, I could ignore my temporary loss of control.

My eyes landed on another door that was almost identical to the one to the cupboard. Hoping that this time I'd found the correct route to the dungeons, I slipped over and turned the knob. When I saw a narrow stone staircase leading downwards, I expelled the air I'd been holding and quickly entered, making sure to close the door behind me.

'Now we're getting somewhere!' Bob squeaked, freeing himself from his hiding spot and flying in front of my face. 'But if it turns out these dungeons are empty and Sweetie isn't here, you're going to feel pretty foolish.'

'His name is Candy, as I keep telling you. And keep your voice down. We're not out of the woods yet.'

'Yes, we are. We left the woods ages ago. Now we're in the castle.'

I tutted. 'Come on, let's find out if I'm right and Candy is here.' Part of me hoped he wasn't then I could still pretend that Byron wasn't culpable.

Apart from the dilapidated staff quarters, the parts of the Cruaich I'd seen had all been well maintained. Here, however, the air was stale and there was more than one cobweb looping across the cracked ceiling. I wound my way downwards. Apart from the occasional clunk of hot-water pipes, there was nothing to be heard. I felt as if I were descending into the very belly of the beast itself, as if the Cruaich were a living, breathing monster rather than an ancient castle made out of nothing more dangerous than stone.

By the time we reached the bottom, I'd counted almost two hundred steps. That placed us at least five floors underground. Despite the fusty odour and the depth, the basement level was well lit. I guessed there was nothing like fluorescent strip lights for highlighting every facet of fear on your captives' faces.

A long corridor stretched out, with branches off in various directions. I started walking down it, resisting the temptation to whistle to fill the silence. The first few turns seemed to lead to dead-ends. I peered round each one, using my SAS-style navigational skills from my thieving days. My caution seemed to be unwarranted; this place was dead.

Just as I was wondering if I'd been mistaken about Candy's whereabouts, Bob flapped his arms and gesticulated wildly to the right. I peered across. The light down there was dimmer – and there was a Sidhe woman leaning against the wall, gnawing at her fingernails.

I pulled back out of sight and considered. I had numerous options and I didn't want to rush into doing the wrong thing. Neither did I want to hurt her, even if her job was some sort of black-ops guard duty. If I played my cards right, I could turn this into a fact-finding mission as well as a covert rescue. I grinned.

Because I'd been high on magic and not worried about the consequences, I'd stolen more of the last Gift than any of the others so there was a fair amount of Illusion swirling around inside me. Concentrating hard, I pulled on it, letting the Gift envelop me completely. When I saw Bob's look of horror, I knew that it had worked.

'What do you think?' I asked quietly. I pirouetted. 'Close enough to the real thing?'

He stared then jabbed a finger at me. 'Steward Moncrieffe?' he asked, his voice wavering.

I smirked. 'Call me Aifric.'

Bob shook his head in a mixture of giddy fear and delight. 'Awesome,' he breathed.

'Glad you like it.'

He pointed at my newly acquired paunch. 'How does it feel to carry around that extra weight?'

'It's an illusion. I'm not actually Aifric Moncrieffe.'

'You certainly look like him.' His gaze turned wary. 'How do I know you're still Uh Integrity under all that?'

'I might look like him but I don't sound like him, do I?'

Bob still seemed doubtful. 'What's your favourite colour?'

'Hot pink.'

'Ha! Everyone knows that's your favourite colour.'

There was a shuffling noise round the corner; the Sidhe guard had probably heard something and was coming to investigate. I glared in warning but the genie wasn't done yet. 'Who is the smartest person you know?' he asked.

'Fergus.'

He glared. I grinned. There was no further time for Bob to interrogate me as the guard was upon us. 'Who …' her voice faltered. 'Steward. I apologise. I didn't realise it was you.'

I reminded myself that Aifric presented a benign, kindly face to the world and twinkled at the Sidhe. I coughed to disguise my voice. 'No problem.'

Luckily she was still surprised by my appearance or she might have questioned why 'Aifric' sounded so strange. I would have to limit my words if I wanted to pull this off. I jerked my head in the direction of the corridor, a question in my eyes. The Sidhe understood. 'He's sleeping,' she said. 'He had some food at midday.'

'Hm,' I nodded. I waited, still looking at her expectantly and hoping my silence would encourage her to fill the void with helpful chatter.

'It's good he's sleeping,' she said anxiously, as if desperate to please. 'It means that when you get him down to the Adair Lands, he'll be more alert.' I pursed my lips to encourage her to continue. 'I still can't believe that a Wild Man is working with those trolls. Traitors,' she spat. 'And abducting Byron's fiancée.' She shook her head. 'It beggars belief. He deserves to be hung, drawn and quartered.' I frowned and she quickly backtracked. 'I know you're trying to be lenient, Steward, because of the pressure everyone's been under. It's not a criticism. Obviously you have the full picture and I'm just a lowly guard.'

I patted her on the shoulder. Aifric had been spinning quite a yarn to his minions. What were the odds that if he managed to get Candy down to my border to dangle him in front of Tipsania, the Wild Man would then die in some horrific 'accident'?

Byron wasn't that kind of bastard; maybe he wasn't involved in this at all. Not that it mattered either way. I'd had my suspicions confirmed and I now knew for sure that Candy was going to be used as bait to drag Tipsania back for her impending nuptials. Once I got Candy out of here, Aifric's plans would be scuppered. There was a lot of satisfaction in knowing that.

I smiled at the Sidhe and pointed behind me. 'You may go,' I croaked.

Her brow furrowed. Desperate to get rid of her before she started to question my hoarse voice, I folded my arms and tried an expression of vague impatience. She was obviously still confused but she bowed her head and marched past me, snapping out a salute as she passed. Maybe it would be a good thing if she came down to my place; she'd get on with Sorley like a house on fire.

As soon as the Sidhe had disappeared, I dropped the illusion in order to conserve my magic and hurried down the corridor.

'You weren't very convincing,' Bob told me.

'I only need five minutes. Keep watch in case she comes back.'

He saluted as well, although it was a considerably sloppier version. I checked my watch, took a deep breath and looked around.

There were six cells. Three didn't look as if they'd been used since the days of Robert the Bruce, given the rusting manacles and the thick layer of dust in each one. Two were spick and span but empty; there was a spatter of dried blood in the corner of one which made me shudder and reminded me that Aifric Moncrieffe really was a bastard. The last cell held a sleeping occupant.

I looked at Candy's inert form. His cheeks were ruddy and a lock of long, straggly hair, which fell across his forehead, gently lifted every time he exhaled. So he was here and he was alive. I watched him for a moment. This was where love got you: thrown into a deep, dark dungeon with only damned spiders for company.

I shook myself. As insane as it might appear to those on the outside, I was going to do my best to give Candy and Tipsania their happy ending. Someone had to come out all of this with a smile on their face otherwise what was the point?

I checked the corridor again then, satisfied that it was clear, I ran to the cell door and knelt, making short work of its lock. This was not a state-of-the-art system. I frowned and touched one of the bars. Candy was a Wild Man; I didn't know much about them but their strength and size were legendary. Candy had once bopped me lightly on the head and knocked me unconscious. I couldn't understand why he hadn't tried to bend these bars. Surely he had the power to do so? Surely he wasn't scared of one little Sidhe guard?

Biting the inside of my cheek, I swung open the door. It creaked, making me wince and Candy stir. He grunted softly then, as if realising someone was standing and staring at him, suddenly bolted upright.

'Wh–what?' His jaw dropped as he stared at me. 'Integrity Adair. What in bejesus are you doing here? I thought you were dead.'

Huh. 'Tipsania didn't tell you I was alive?' She was more circumspect than I'd given her credit for. Or maybe the world didn't revolve around me after all and when she'd spoken to him on the phone they'd been talking about other things. The thought of them murmuring sweet nothings was kind of cute.

'Tip?' Panic flared in his eyes. 'Is she alright? Has she been hurt?' He leapt to his feet. Given the way he was looking at me, I suddenly understood why they were called Wild Men.

Now that I could see him properly, I could see several painful-looking bruises on his face and body. I gestured at him awkwardly. 'She's fine.'

He glanced from side to side, his pupils dilated and his muscles bunched up. 'Is she here?'

'No,' I soothed. 'She's away. She's safe. They can't get to her.'

Candy's attention returned to me and, as he fixed on my face, he appeared to calm down. I wasn't fooled though; he was still panicking. He was just doing a better job of hiding it. 'They?'

'Aifric. Byron. Whoever. Let's concentrate on getting you out of here.'

Candy didn't move. 'Does Byron know you're alive?'

'No. Let's go.'

'Does Byron know where Tip is?'

'No. Come on, Candy. I'll answer your questions properly once we're out of here.'

He stepped backwards. 'He needs her.'

I blinked. Er... 'Byron needs her? But don't you need her too?' I asked stupidly.

Candy crossed his arms across his massive chest. I swear he had the girth of a bloody oak tree. 'I have her.'

I tilted my head to the side. 'I hate to point out the obvious but you're stuck in a medieval dungeon while she's wandering around in the free, fresh air of the Highlands.'

He regarded me impassively. 'You should tell Byron you're alive. He'll be very happy.'

Yeah, yeah. 'Look, Candy,' I said, trying again, 'I understand this is all a surprise to you but we probably don't have very long. We need to get out of here before the alarm is raised.'

He turned round and settled back on his narrow bed. I gaped at him. 'I have to stay here,' he rumbled. 'I promised Byron.'

'Byron is planning to marry the love of your life!' I shrieked. 'You can't trust him!'

'He is very honourable.'

Good grief! 'Candy…'

'I am staying here.'

'Aifric is going to drag you down to the Adair border – *my* border – and use you to lure Tipsania out.'

He shrugged, rolling his massive shoulders. 'I know.'

'What do you mean you know? Don't you care?'

'Is Tip safe?'

'Yes. For now. But—'

'Then I am staying here. You should tell her to give herself up.'

I threw my hands up in the air. 'What is going on?' I turned and looked again at the bars which were ostensibly holding the Wild Man here. 'You could have escaped at any time,' I whispered. 'But you're choosing to stay. Why?'

He opened his mouth to answer. Before he could, there was a shout from Bob. 'Someone's coming!'

Shite. 'Candy,' I pleaded. 'This is our last chance. We need to get out of here.'

He turned his head away. I balled up my fists, at a complete loss. I couldn't force him to come. Bob zipped towards me, his arms akimbo and his expression panicked. 'There are at least six of them. We need to get out of here! I don't want to end up as the Steward's slave.'

If there were so many, my Illusion ruse as Aifric had probably been discovered. Maybe the guard had bumped into him when she left or she'd realised how wrong our conversation had been. Either way, I couldn't use that deception any more.

I reached into myself, grabbing Bob with one hand and slamming the cell door with the other. With one last baleful glance, I yanked on Tipsania's Gift and turned both myself and Bob invisible. I heard Candy gasp but there was little I could do about him now. The posse of Moncrieffe guards was already here.

They ran down the corridor, their boots hammering on the hard floor. I pressed against the wall, hoping that Candy wasn't about to give me up. The guards stared into his cell as I sidled past and jogged away, keeping my steps as light as I could.

'What's going on?' I heard one of them demand. 'Has anyone been here?'

'I've been sleeping,' Candy said, his voice coloured with confusion. I exhaled the air I'd been holding in my lungs. He hadn't completely gone over to the dark side then and he was covering for me. I spun away, twisting back to the staircase, my thoughts racing and tripping over each other as I flew towards the main hall. I didn't understand what was going on and, no matter how hard I tried, I couldn't make sense of it. The best I could do right now was to get out of this place.

I rounded the last corner, my heart dropping into my stomach when I spotted the large figure looming in the doorway ahead. His features were in shadow but there was no mistaking that silhouette. Aifric. And he was completely blocking my path. I might be invisible but I was still solid. I came to a halt, holding my breath and trying to decide what to do next.

His legs were spread; I could barrel forward and push myself through the gap – he might never notice. Then he shifted his weight, pulling one leg closer to the other. I wasn't so petite that I could slide through now. I clenched my teeth. All I had to do was wait. He wouldn't stand there forever.

Barely any time passed before I heard the booted feet pounding back up the staircase towards me. Now I was caught between the bloody guards and Aifric. None of the Gifts I'd stolen would work here. I tiptoed another few steps until I was so close to the Steward that I could feel his hot breath on my skin. My heart was hammering so loudly that I was sure he could hear it.

'Steward!' gasped the first Sidhe guard. 'There's no one there. The Wild Man is still in his cell.'

'Did you talk to him?' Aifric demanded. 'Touch him? Are you sure he's not an illusion?'

Arse. Damn Aifric for being such a canny wanker.

'It's him alright.'

Aifric turned and, for the first time, I saw his expression; in fact, I could almost hear the cogs turning in his head. If he wasn't sure that I was dead, he'd know immediately that all this commotion was down to me.

'Someone is here. Someone is playing with us and I want to know who.' His eyes narrowed. 'Set guards around the perimeter. No one is to get in or out unless I know about it. And release the dogs. Maybe they'll pick up this intruder's scent. Whoever they are, they're going to rue the day they picked a fight with me.'

I was tempted to open my mouth and tell him that there hadn't been any fighting and he should look to his own actions before he pinned the blame on others but I was more concerned about the mention of dogs. Neither Invisibility nor Illusion would work against the nose of a hound. And if the Cruaich border was going to be teeming with guards on the lookout for the slightest thing, I couldn't count on escape in that direction.

'Do we have any Farsensers on the grounds?' Aifric asked.

I squeezed my eyes shut. Just when I'd thought things couldn't get any worse...

'Most of them are off scouting for the Scrymgeour lass. But I think Stephen McGillivray is a Farsenser. He's here for the stag party.'

Aifric nodded. 'Find him. No one rests until every inch of this place has been checked.' He pivoted and marched away.

Without waiting for the guards to pass me, I leapt up and darted left towards the main doors, away from Aifric.

'This is bad, Uh Integrity,' Bob hissed. 'What are we going to do?'

I was rather touched that he said we. 'I don't know,' I muttered tightly. I could already feel the invisibility draining away; I wouldn't be able to use it for much longer before I started becoming less invisible and more opaque. I had to find somewhere to hide, somewhere out of reach of a Farsenser.

I ran outside and tried to think. I could always go to the old Games grounds. That cabin where we'd been made to stay would work as a hiding place if it weren't for the Farsenser. I had to find a way of disguising my trail. Something that would fool the magic... 'I've got it,' I whispered. If this didn't work, nothing would.

I ran as fast as my legs could carry me, glad that there was a cement path leading down to the grounds. 'I used to have a hobby pouring cement,' I told Bob. 'But then it became too hard.'

'You're telling jokes?' he howled in my ear. 'We're about to become dogfood and you're telling jokes?' As if on cue, I heard barking in the distance.

'Chillax, Bob. I've got this.' The wind whipped past, making my baseball cap fly off and my hair stream out behind me. Crapadoodle. I stopped, prepared to run back and get it, then I saw Byron's stag mates appearing around the corner of the castle. I grimaced and left the cap where it was. I had to hustle.

The towering trees and dark shadows of the Cruaich grove soon came into sight. When Bob saw that was where I was heading I felt him relax against me. 'Clever girl,' he murmured.

'I hope so.' I crossed my fingers on both hands for luck. The grove was sacred – no way would a pack of hounds be allowed to tear through it after an intruder who hadn't actually done any damage. If my plan worked the magic bound into the land would stop anyone, regardless of how skilled they were, from being able to farsense through it. As long as no one thought to come and comb through the grove, both Bob and I would be safe.

I ran through the first fringe of trees, keeping to the path until I was deep enough inside to slow down. The sunlight disappeared almost immediately above the canopy as I was swallowed into the grove's interior. The sounds of the dogs and the shouting faded away but I didn't slow down. Even when strands of my hair caught in outstretched twigs and it felt as if my scalp were being pulled from my skull, I didn't stop. I was not going to let Aifric win. I was *never* going to let Aifric win.

Gasping for breath, I pounded ahead. I only realised that I'd arrived at the central clearing – the place where I'd seen fleeting images of my ancestors and received my true name – when I felt a frisson of electricity shoot through me. I sloughed off the invisibility and came to a halt.

Bob was awestruck. 'Uh Integrity,' he breathed. 'This is amazing.' He stretched out his arms, spreading his fingers wide. 'I can feel the power. I can even hear it.'

So could I. Already a chorus of indecipherable whispers was rising in my ears. I swallowed. It was probably alright for me to be here. Unlike the individual Clan groves, this one at the Cruaich was open to all Sidhe. In essence, it was the central point for all of us.

I put my hands on my hips, trying to slow down my breathing. Regardless of right or wrong, it would be wise to stay away from the clearing. I didn't need to be haunted by angry Sidhe spirits of yore.

I turned round, planning to leave the path and plunge into the trees in case a search party did come through here. Before I could take a step, a word rang out and made me freeze. 'Layoch.'

My true name. I thought I was nervous before, trapped on that staircase between Aifric and his guards, but it was nothing compared to this. I slowly turned around.

'Layoch.'

My mouth was dry. I swung my head from left to right but, unlike the last time I was here, there was nothing to see. There was the only the voice, accented with a gentle Scottish lilt which I couldn't distinguish as male or female.

'Uh Integrity,' Bob quavered. 'This is scary.'

'I know. Don't worry. We'll be fine.' I wished I could be sure of that.

'Join them,' the voice whispered.

My spine went rigid. Join who?

'Join them,' the disembodied voice repeated.

I folded my arms. Now hang on a bloody minute. 'If you're telling me to join the damn Moncrieffes, you've got another thing coming,' I said aloud. 'I don't care who you are. I'm not doing that.'

Something icy cold brushed against my cheek and I leapt about three feet in the air.

'Join them, Layoch. Join them and Alba will be saved.'

The whispers rose in a tide, encircling me, getting louder and louder. I cupped my hands over my ears. 'Stop it!' I yelled. 'Stop it!' I twirled round and sprinted out of the clearing until I was surrounded again by nothing more than trees. Then my knees buckled underneath me and I collapsed.

Chapter Seven

Dusk was falling when I finally felt safe enough to pick myself up and leave the grove. Bob and I skulked towards the edge and peered out. The search for me had been abandoned for now; I could hear no dogs and see no people. Aifric had had a good four hours to search the Cruaich and its grounds and with Stephen McGillivray, or whoever the Farsenser was, it would have taken much less time than that. All the same I remained cautious in case we were walking into a trap down by the border.

I slipped across the main thoroughfare to the line of trees beside the long, snaking driveway. All the while Bob crowed in my ear, 'Ha ha! We showed them, didn't we, Uh Integrity! We are the masters. All those Sidhe against us and every single one of them was clueless while we are free and in the wind.'

Much as I appreciated that I wasn't now facing an executioner's axe, I felt that Bob was viewing our expedition as more of a success than it actually was. 'We came to rescue Candy,' I pointed out, 'and he didn't want to be rescued. I wouldn't get over excited. In effect, we've accomplished nothing.'

'But just look at what we've learned, Uh Integrity. Now you're getting a glimpse of what it's like to be as all-knowing as me.'

I wasn't sure we'd learned anything useful. 'Candy has made some mysterious promise to Byron which makes no sense.' I sighed. 'And the Sidhe ancestors think I should join up with my enemies.'

'Technically that's not what they said.'

I shrugged. 'So what do you think they meant?'

Bob stroked his chin. 'I could tell you,' he said slowly, 'because of course I know.'

'Of course.'

'But you need to come up with the answer yourself to achieve true enlightenment.'

'Right. So what you're actually saying is that you don't have a scooby what they were on about.'

He sniffed. 'I'm not even going to deign to answer that.'

I gave up on debating further as we approached the border. There were more guards in place than before but I reckoned I had just enough of Tipsania's Gift left inside me to slip across without being noticed. I brought it up, vanished from sight and darted towards the car.

'The good thing,' Bob said, once the last of the danger had passed, 'is that we get to go home and sleep in our own beds.'

I pointed at the letter opener, still hanging from the belt around my waist. 'You can go to your own bed whenever you want.'

'I don't tend to sleep in there any more.'

I was surprised. 'Really?'

'Yeah. It's much more comfortable snuggling up to Brochan. Do you know he talks in his sleep?'

I wondered if the merman was aware that he had a sleeping companion. Deciding it was probably better not to know, I kept my mouth shut and jogged to the car, got into the front seat and started the engine. The sense of failure still hung over me like a cloud.

I checked my watch; it had just gone half past six. The night was still very young. 'You know, Bob,' I said, as casually as I could, 'it's been quite a stressful day. And you really were fabulous – you were a great lookout. We might not have rescued Candy but I did pick up lots of shiny new Gifts which I can use in all sorts of situations.'

'I was magnificent, wasn't I?' Bob beamed, bouncing up and down on the dashboard.

'We should have a drink to celebrate,' I said. 'You know, wind down and prepare for the journey home.'

Bob considered. 'I'm not sure that drink-driving is a good idea, Uh Integrity.'

'I'll have a Coke but you don't need to abstain.'

'Hmm. There's a great place in Dundee that does the most amazing mango daiquiris.'

'Yum,' I said unconvincingly. 'I was thinking Perth would be a better idea. It's closer to home.'

'Last time we went to Perth you streaked naked down the high street. I'm not sure the good people of that fair city want to see you again.'

'I didn't streak. I just happened to be in my underwear when a Fomori demon showed up.'

'One and the same. Byron Moncrieffe might find your jiggly bits attractive but you need a good personal trainer to…' He paused. 'Hang on a minute,' he said suspiciously. 'Where exactly in Perth were you thinking of going?'

I smiled innocently. 'I've heard some nice things about the Haven.'

He put his hands on hips. 'And I have it on good authority that the Haven is closed for a private party tonight. Byron Moncrieffe's stag party.'

The corners of my mouth lifted. 'Well, now that he's taken, I need to find a new bachelor, don't I?'

Bob shook his head dismally. 'This is going to end in tears.'

***

I'd never been inside the Haven but the place was much as I expected. Loud music thumped and I swore I could taste the tinge of tequila in the air.

A burly Bauchan was on the door, no doubt to prevent anyone who wasn't on the stag party list from getting in. I had more wiles than that, however. Rather than approach the front, I skirted round the side of the building, weaving in and out of empty beer barrels until I found the back entrance. There, inhaling deeply on a glowing cigarette was a young, pretty human woman wearing a large coat. Handy. I'd even put a bet on with Taylor at this point that she wasn't wearing much underneath.

I loped up to her, nodding in greeting. She nodded and took another drag. Despite my lack of disguise, there was no flicker of recognition in her greeting. It helped that it was now dark; in this light I could pass for a blonde.

'Hey,' I said cheerfully, 'I was hoping you could help me. I'm looking for a friend of mine. Chandra. She's…'

The woman blanched slightly. 'I've heard of Chandra. If you know her, then you'll know where to find her.'

My mention of my ex-assassin buddy did the trick, placing me at an advantage. I kept my tone casual and continued. 'Yeah. She's not at her shop though, so I thought she might have gone out for the night.'

'She wouldn't be here. The Haven is off limits tonight.'

I nodded. 'So I hear. You're working inside?'

'Yeah. What of it?' She eyed me, the unspoken challenge obvious, but I wasn't about to comment on her job. As long as being a stripper was her choice, it wasn't my place to say anything.

'Nothing. It's a stag party, I take it?'

She shrugged. 'So I'm told. My boss wouldn't say who it's for.' She stubbed out her cigarette and tossed it into a bucket. 'Like I care. Just another bunch of spoilt Sidhe wankers.'

I coughed slightly. She tilted her head and looked at me more closely. 'Oh. You're Sidhe too. Sorry, I didn't mean any offence.' She gave me a pretty smile but there was no denying that she was suddenly scared. She clenched her fists and there was a faint wobble to her voice. Personally I was thrilled. She wouldn't have any qualms about abandoning her job for the night if she didn't care that the Steward's son was the party boy.

'Don't worry about it,' I said. 'I might be Sidhe but I'm still a nobody. I have a useless Gift and I'm from a useless Clan. I think the lot of us are wankers.' I smiled slightly. 'I'm on your side, not mine.' The woman relaxed a little but she was still very wary. I had to make sure she stayed here until I got what I wanted.

Before she could vanish inside the club, I forced my eyes to well up with unshed tears. Unless she had a heart of lead, she'd feel compelled to stick around for at least a bit longer. I sniffed and bit my bottom lip. 'Maybe it's just as well that Chandra's not around. I was going to ask her to…' I shot the woman a look and faltered, as if I'd just realised I was talking to a complete stranger and was about to reveal that I wanted someone killed. 'Never mind.'

She raised a knowing eyebrow. 'Let me guess. Ex-boyfriend?'

'Ex-fiancée.'

The woman winced. 'Ouch.'

'Yeah. Between you and me, he's the one getting hitched.' I laughed humourlessly. 'I should just let bygones be bygones. It bloody hurts though.' Unfortunately, I wasn't lying.

'I don't think Chandra is the answer.'

Yeah, she definitely knew all about Chandra's old job. 'You're probably right. I'd still love to get my revenge on him.'

'I hear you.'

I took out the gold I'd carried with me for emergencies. 'I was going to give this to her as payment.' I gazed at it ruefully. 'I'm not sure what to do with it now. I'm tempted to throw it at him. Maybe I'll get lucky and hit an eye.'

The stripper stared. 'That's a shitload of money.' Her expression soured and I immediately knew what she was thinking. I was Sidhe; to me this was probably small change.

I bit my lip. 'I'd give it all away if I could just confront him. Let him see what he's given up for that bitch. I don't really want to hurt him but I'd love to bring him down a peg or two.' I sighed loudly. The best way for this to work would be for her to make the suggestion but I could only lead her so far. 'He's got a bunch of minders with him though. They'd never let me get near him.'

I could see her mind working through the possibilities. I was holding the equivalent of more money than she'd probably ever seen in her life; she had to weigh up the chance that she would get fired versus the chance that she could be set up for years to come. I held my breath. Come on, love. You want to do this.

'Well,' she said slowly, 'you could always take my place.'

Yahtzee. 'What do you mean?' I asked, looking surprised.

She dug into her coat pocket and pulled out a pretty feathered mask. 'I usually wear this when I go in to these kind of parties. Some men like imagining you could be anyone, you know? I wasn't going to bother because of today's outfit.' She opened her coat and I caught a glimpse of a fake police uniform. 'But it'd let you get in and close to him and then you could say your piece.' Her eyes drifted back to the gold in my hand. 'I'm all for the sisterhood.'

I threw back my head and laughed. 'I'd just love to see the look on his face. But won't you get in trouble with your boss?'

She shrugged. 'I've been thinking of finding something else to do with my life. These hours suck and there are only so many times you can let men paw at you before it becomes tired.'

I nodded. 'I hear you.' I thrust out my hand before she could think about it any further. 'Here, take this in return. You're doing me a massive favour and I won't forget it.'

She took the gold and hefted it before it disappeared into her coat. 'You're really not going to hurt him?'

I met her eyes, hoping she could see the truth; I didn't want her to feel bad about this in any way. 'No,' I said. 'I really won't. I just want to say my piece then maybe I can get on with the rest of my life.'

'Amen to that,' she murmured. 'Well, good luck to you. Someone will come out soon and tell you when it's time.' She smiled slightly. 'Don't get hurt.' With that, she whirled round and took off into the night.

I grinned. That was easier than I thought.

There was a flash of light and Bob appeared, two points of colour high on his cheeks. He was absolutely furious. 'What on earth do you think you're doing, Uh Integrity? This is not part of the plan! I thought you were going to hide in the corner and watch him. Do this and you'll get caught and everything we've done up to now will have been a complete waste.' He threw up his hands. 'If you want your revenge on Byron so badly then ask for your last wish. I'll do what I can to minimise the damage. But you can't throw everything away because you're feeling hurt that he's moved on.'

I was touched by his concern. 'Chill, Bob. I'm not going to get caught. And I'm not looking for revenge.'

'Then what are you after?' he demanded.

The truth was that I wasn't entirely sure. The glimpse I'd caught of him back at the Cruaich had started up a strange, yearning itch, one that I'd never be able to scratch again. Maybe this was my last chance to get my kicks with Byron before all hell broke loose. Maybe I thought I could find out what he and his father were up to. Or maybe I was just a fool. I suspected it was the latter but it didn't matter now; I was set on my course.

'Never mind,' I said dismissively. 'But if I can use Illusion to pretend to be Aifric and get away with it—'

'*Almost* get away with it.'

'Then,' I continued, ignoring his interruption, 'I can use it to pretend to be that woman.'

He stared at me. 'You're going to pretend to be a stripper? Do you even know how to strip?'

'Ha!' I scoffed. 'It's taking your clothes off, Bob. I do that every single day.'

I concentrated, pulling out the magic and telling myself to mimic every part of the stripper, seen and unseen, until I was transformed. It couldn't just be coincidence that I'd ended up with more Illusion than any other Gift. This was meant to be.

I examined myself. Instead of my usual pale, milk-bottle skin, I had an all-over tan. I whistled. Damn, I looked good. I checked underneath the coat. Hmm. I was also dressed as a policewoman as the stripper had been. Talk about stereotypes. I glanced at the mask she'd given me and, deciding the Illusion was more than good enough, discarded it.

I gave Bob a twirl. He huffed and looked away. 'Stay out here,' I told him. 'It'll be safer for you that way.'

'Don't come crying to me when you end up in a real grave instead of an imaginary one.'

'Everything will be fine.'

He sniffed loudly and vanished just as the back door opened and a rush of noise greeted my ears. A face peered out. 'Chardonnay? Is that you? Are you ready?'

Chardonnay? Good grief. I smiled and nodded. At least my voice would be less of a concern this time around. I pitched my tone slightly higher to match the real Chardonnay's. 'Who am I looking for?'

'You don't know? The stag is Byron Moncrieffe.' He said it as if there should be a drum roll.

'Oh.' I tried to look impressed and I felt the Illusion ripple to mimic the thought. 'Okay, then.'

He looked me up and down sleazily. 'He's a lucky boy.'

Yeah, yeah. I smiled daintily and dropped a curtsey. 'Then let's get this show on the road.'

I followed the man inside, past cardboard boxes filled with pork scratchings and crisps which made my stomach grumble loudly. He turned and frowned at me. I giggled. 'I've not eaten yet,' I said. 'I find I've got more of an edge on an empty stomach.'

He waggled his eyebrows. 'Well,' he said in a voice that was more of a growl than a purr, 'I can fill you up when you've finished with those Sidhe.'

I tried – and probably failed – not to look nauseated.

He gestured at me to wait behind the door. I took off my coat, and he smirked at my police outfit then popped his head out front to check that everything was ready. All of a sudden, I felt the tumble of butterflies in my belly overtaking my pangs of hunger. Bob was right: this was a mistake. All I was doing was torturing myself.

I took a step backwards, ready to run away, but the man wasn't having any of it. When he saw me hesitate, he shoved me onto the main club floor. Shite. I couldn't change my mind now.

The music, which had been pumping out a loud staccato beat, abruptly faltered. I strode into the centre of the floor as at least forty pairs of eyes turned in my direction. Licking my dry lips, I lifted my chin – and almost had a mini heart attack when I saw that Aifric was here after all. I reasoned that he'd have no reason to suspect that the Illusion ruse from earlier was being carried on here but all the same, I was suddenly more terrified than before.

Forcing myself to play the game, I completed a slow half turn. Byron was looking distinctly ill at ease in a chair in front of me. I cleared my throat. How was this supposed to go?

'Er… You're all making too much noise,' I said.

A chorus of jeers immediately answered me. I scowled and raised my hand. 'The borough of Perth takes noise pollution very seriously.'

Out of the corner of my eye, I saw Aifric frown and jerk forward. One of the men from the Cruaich clearing grabbed hold of him and murmured in his ear. He relaxed and settled back, with a leer on his face. Ick.

'Who is in charge of this gathering?' I demanded.

Jamie, believing I was the real thing, opened his mouth, his brow knotted with tension but several others smirked and pointed at Byron. Keeping my expression severe, I looked straight at him. He wasn't as naïve as his Moncrieffe friend and I could already see the angry recognition in his eyes that his buddies had hired a stripper to make the evening more entertaining. His reaction sent him up a notch in my estimation – a tiny notch, anyway.

Bob was right: Byron looked painfully tired. He might be dressed to the nines but the shadows under his eyes were very heavy and there was a pallor to his skin that I'd never seen before. I quashed my worries and glared, still in my role as angry policewoman. 'You're going to have to explain yourself,' I said loudly.

Byron, still looking irritated, got to his feet. 'I don't want this.'

'Oh,' I answered, injecting the tiniest amount of breathiness into my words, 'you're going to have to try *harder* than that.' I deliberately dropped my gaze to his crotch. 'The borough of Perth doesn't enjoy limp responses.'

Laughter rose amongst Byron's friends. He rolled his eyes. 'Look,' he said, in a way that almost made me feel sorry for him, 'I'll pay you if you just…'

I walked up to him. 'Did you just try to bribe a police officer?' I pulled the handcuffs from by my belt and dangled them in front of him. 'I think that's a very serious offence.'

He raised his hands to try to get me to back off and in one swift movement, I snapped the cuffs round his wrists. Now he was even more pissed off. I gave him a tiny shove, forcing back onto his chair, then I lifted my foot, nudged his legs apart and rested my shoe on the edge of the seat, right in front of his groin.

Catcalls rose all around us but this time I barely heard them. Byron was *mine*. 'You've been a naughty boy,' I purred. 'But I've lost my truncheon. I don't suppose I could borrow yours? It looks … big.'

The shouts got louder. Byron, glancing around at the crowd, realised that he'd get out of this faster if he just played along. He sagged back, irritation still flickering in the emerald green depths of his eyes. I flicked a hand at the DJ and the music started up again. This tune was much slower than before.

I took three steps backwards and the men formed a circle round me. I wouldn't have been surprised if the lot of them had started drooling and I'd ended up drowned in puddles of spit. Bleurgh. I played along, however, reaching up and loosening my hair from its tight constraints. I shook out the dark waves that were so unlike my own tresses.

I spotted Jamie in the corner, shrugging to himself then turning away to line up shot glasses. As I started unbuttoning my blouse, he poured vodka, moving up the line until every glass except one was full. I threw back my head and laughed while he surreptitiously sneaked a bottle of water from his pocket and used that to fill the final glass. Now that was interesting.

I spun round, wiggling my arse, all the while unfastening buttons until I reached my waist. It appeared that I was wearing a very lacy bra that left little to the imagination. I swayed in time to the music, backing up until I was almost sitting on Byron's lap. I started rubbing against him, half wishing I could see the expression on his face and half hoping the ground would swallow me whole.

I pulled the blouse off my shoulders, intending to slide it down my back, but it caught on the bra strap. I tried to tug it free while still looking sexy; maybe this was going to be harder than I'd realised. I wiggled this way and that; when that didn't work, I tried to yank the blouse away even if it meant ripping the fabric. From the expressions on a few of the watching faces, my contortions were more like those of a beached whale than a sexy stripper.

I turned my face to Byron's. 'You'll have to use your teeth,' I breathed.

'Good grief,' he muttered. He sighed and then I felt the fabric free itself. He must have used his Telekinesis Gift instead of his mouth. Oh well.

I twisted round until I was facing him, then hovered over his hips and raised my hands, lifting my hair and running my fingers through it. His gaze remained stony cold.

'Here,' Jamie said, thrusting a shot glass in between us. He held it to Byron's lips and the princeling downed it in one as everyone cheered. Suspiciously, I leaned forward and nipped at Byron's bottom lip with my teeth, my tongue darting out to brush across his mouth. He hissed in annoyance. Taking the hint, I leaned forward to his ear instead, using my curtain of hair to conceal my expression. It was Byron who was sneaking water, not Jamie. I hadn't been able to taste alcohol on his lips at all – which begged the question why he was supposedly getting pissed.

I moved back slightly, trailing kisses along his neck and back up towards his mouth. Byron didn't relax; his body was stiff and unyielding and there was no doubt he was hating every second of this. I smirked. I could rise to that challenge.

I twined my arms round his neck, swaying slightly. Jamie pushed another shot at Byron and he dutifully drank it before glaring at his friend and muttering, 'Get me the hell out of here.'

I pretended to push Jamie away, affording him a saucy wink which inflamed the watching crowd. I wondered what Aifric made of all this. But then, as Byron's eyes narrowed in disgust and I moved my head down, drawing in his musky scent, I forgot to care. My head dipped and my lips brushed against his once more. I deepened the kiss and pressed against him. With his hands still cuffed, there was little he could do to stop me.

Even with our audience, I felt my pulse speed up but he was determined not to respond.

I ran my hands down his arms, resting them briefly on his biceps. My mouth was insistent and continued to press against his. I trailed one hand down his body and he groaned suddenly, his lips parting. My tongue darted inside his mouth and the catcalls and whoops faded into background noise. It was just me and Byron. A moment later, he gave in and began kissing me back. He raised his arms, looping them over my head, and pulled me closer to him. Blood roared in my ears. God, he tasted good. I moaned slightly – and then I was blinking as something wet splattered my face.

Drawing back, I saw Jamie looking overly contrite, holding a glass and apologising. 'I'm so sorry! I tripped!'

Byron yanked his arms back and stared at me, confusion clouding his gaze. His eyes swept across my features and for a moment I was assailed with panic that the Illusion was fading. Then he shook himself slightly. 'Get up,' he muttered.

I paused, unsure whether to obey or not but my body was lifted as his Gift pushed me to my feet. Byron got up as well, swaying from side to side. 'Thish lovely policewoman wantsh to take me in for questioning,' he said aloud. I tilted my head. He should be careful, he was overdoing the slurring. And what on earth was he up to? 'We're going to go upshtairsh to a more private room.'

His friends' response was a mixture of disappointed boos and encouraging shouts. Byron jerked his head at Jamie who nodded and led the way. 'I'll show you where you can go,' he said, half smiling. Close up, there was no denying that he was worried.

Jamie led the way as the yells behind us got louder. Someone muttered that they should have hired more than one stripper. I tried not to shudder and allowed myself a sneaky look at Aifric. He wasn't watching me; he grinned in amusement at his son then turned away to talk to an older man.

The three of us tripped up the stairs and into a room on the left. Jamie closed the door behind us and locked it, while I told myself I wasn't nervous.

Byron dropped the act immediately. He flicked his magic towards his bound wrists and the handcuffs fell off and clattered to the floor. He ran a hand through his hair. 'Who are you?' he hissed.

I smiled. 'Who would you like me to be?'

He snarled and whirled away. 'Pay her,' he snapped at Jamie.

'We can't just let her walk away,' Jamie answered. 'Not now you're supposed to be up here and…'

Jeez. Even with everything else that was going on, I really hadn't thought that Byron was this sleazy. He cursed under his breath.

I found my voice, only just remembering in time to alter it so I didn't sound like myself. 'I'm a stripper,' I said, 'not a hooker.'

'Relax. Nothing's going to happen.' Byron looked at Jamie. 'This could work in our favour. She's the perfect diversion.' He bunched his fists. He seemed unable to look me directly in the eye. Was that because I'd ignited his desire and he was embarrassed about it? If only I'd not set my own lust alight at the same time. 'We'll pay you triple,' he said, 'if you stay up here and don't tell anyone.'

'I think everyone already knows,' I said, forcing myself to smirk.

He glared. 'We're leaving.' He pointed at Jamie. 'Me and him.' He ran a hand through his hair and I watched as it flopped down against his forehead, one golden curl standing out against his perfect skin. 'You will stay here until morning. If you keep quiet and don't answer the door, you'll get three times your usual fee.'

What the *hell* was going on here? What were they up to? 'I guess I can do that,' I said hesitantly.

All business now, Byron nodded. 'Jamie, we'll stick to the rest of the plan. You stay downstairs in case anyone gets suspicious. If you need to, you can come up here and pretend to check on me from time to time.'

'Where are you going?' I asked.

'None of your business,' Byron said sharply.

Jamie touched my arm. 'He's sneaking off to see his fiancée,' he said. Well, I knew that was a lie even without my Truth-Seeking Gift. 'It's nothing against you. He's just not that into the whole stag night thing.'

'Yeah,' Byron muttered unconvincingly.

I moved past him and perched on a sofa. 'Sounds like easy money to me.'

'Do up your shirt.'

'Huh?' I glanced down and realised I was still proudly displaying my – or rather Chardonnay's – rather bounteous assets to the world. I licked my lips. 'Don't you like what you see?'

'I'm not interested,' Byron growled. There was an edge of anger in his words that I'd ever heard before, not even when he'd discovered I could steal magic.

If Jamie hadn't been present, I might have played around some more. Instead, I nodded and fastened the buttons. 'So where is your lovely bride?' I asked casually.

He ignored me. 'I'll be back before dawn.'

'See that you are,' Jamie said. 'You know what could happen if this gets screwed up.'

Byron's answer was flat. 'I'd better not screw up then.' With that, he walked to the sash window, yanked it up and disappeared into the night.

Jamie looked at me. I held up my hands. 'I'll be good.'

'Can I get you a drink or something while you're waiting?'

I shook my head. 'I'm absolutely fine. You go and enjoy the rest of the party.'

'Thank you for this.' He was being honest. Jamie Moncrieffe really was a nicer guy than anyone gave him credit for.

I shrugged. 'I'd hate to stand in the way of true love.'

He scratched his chin. 'Have we met before? I'm sure we haven't but there's something about you that's incredibly familiar.'

Er... 'I get around,' I purred. 'Maybe you've been to one of *my* parties before.'

For a moment, he looked absolutely terrified. 'I don't think so.' He opened the door and stepped out. 'Thanks again.'

The second the door shut behind him, I sprang into action. I grabbed a chair and propped it underneath the doorknob – that would keep him out for a short while if he felt the need to come up and check. Then I dashed to the window and peered out. Byron was already on the ground, running towards a parked car. I flipped over the edge of the window sill, dropping cat-like. I had no idea what he was up to but I was going to find out.

Chapter Eight

'Well?' Bob grunted, flashing back into existence when I called softly to him. 'Have you finished making a complete idiot of yourself? Have you been killed yet? Because black is not my colour so don't expect me to go to your funeral and mourn.'

'Come on!' I hissed. 'We need to move. Byron's already driving away.'

'What do you mean?'

'I mean, that he's pretending to be drunk, pretending to be in a room shagging Chardonnay and is actually driving away on some secret mission. We need to get to the car and follow him.'

Bob blinked, as surprised as I had been. 'Are you sure?'

I grabbed him by the scruff of his neck, pinched him between my finger and thumb and began to run. 'There's no time to delay!'

'Is he like James Bond, do you think?'

I snorted. 'Hardly.'

'Or maybe he's the Milk Tray man. He knows where Tipsania is and he's going after her with a box of chocolates.'

I didn't deign to answer. Instead, I vaulted over the wall to my left and dashed for our car with Bob flitting behind me. Maybe I'd get lucky and catch up with Byron at the first intersection. I bit my lip, remembering that one of my stolen Gifts was Electrosurge. I squeezed my eyes shut and focused, silently telling all of the nearest traffic lights to flicker to red. From the distance, there was a squeal of tyres and some loud beeping of horns. Shite, I hoped I'd not just hurt anyone. More haste less speed, I reminded myself. I wasn't in the business of causing car accidents.

I flung open the car door and jumped in, before gunning the engine and taking off. I swerved round the corner and completed an illegal U-turn to head the car in the same direction as Byron's. When I spotted it up ahead, waiting in a growing queue, I exhaled in relief and released my hold on the traffic lights.

There were four cars between me and Byron. That was good; I didn't want to get too close. Many aeons ago, not long after I'd passed my driving test, Taylor had schooled me in the art of evasion whilst in control of a car. Despite his dire warnings about how difficult it would be to avoid the police if they ever tailed me, it had been more fun than anything else. Unfortunately I'd never had any practice at being predator rather than prey.

The lights changed back to green. As soon as I started driving again I winced, noting with a sinking heart the fender-bender between two cars that had stopped on the side of the road to my left. Bob, perched on the steering wheel, made a point of highlighting it too. 'You're a pacifist, Uh Integrity. Or is it that you're a pacifist except when you're chasing down the hot, sexy man of your dreams?'

I craned my neck, breathing out in relief when I saw the two drivers getting out of their stalled vehicles. They were obviously unharmed. 'No one got hurt.'

'That's not the point.'

Bob was right. I was determined to follow Byron but I wasn't going to put anyone else in harm's way. I braked slightly, staying back from the car in front, and forced my shoulders to relax.

'Go back and get their number plates, Bob,' I said. 'I'll make things right later.' I could track them down and send them some kind of compensation. Frankly, compensation was the least I could do. The last day or two I'd been getting ridiculously reckless. I needed to remember who I really was.

Bob threw me a scowl but did as I asked and zapped away. When he returned, he sniffed grudgingly. 'They're fine. The damage is minor.'

I smiled. 'That's not the point.'

Appeased, he shrugged and patted my finger then turned to the front. 'Let's not waste all our efforts and lose Byron now. Look, he's indicating left up ahead.'

Bob was right. Two of the cars in front drove straight on, leaving only two between Byron and me. That was cool. I followed them, keeping strictly to the speed limit as we continued through the streets of Perth.

'Where do you think he's going?' Bob asked.

'I don't have a clue. Neither do I understand why he's sneaking away from his own stag party.'

'Maybe he's doing a runner. He's going to head for the sea and swim across to Europe.'

'Right now we're going west,' I pointed out.

'So he's going to America then.' Bob began to hum the 'Star Spangled Banner'.

I had no idea how I managed to get into these conversations. 'You think he's going to swim across the Atlantic Ocean? What is that? Three thousand miles?'

'Fine,' Bob said, obviously stung. 'What's your suggestion?'

'I told you, I don't know where he's going or what he's doing. That's why we're following him.' We were reaching the city limits now and I still couldn't work out where we were heading. The Cruaich was in the other direction and The Veil – and my own lands – were more southerly.

'You're no fun.'

I huffed. 'Bob, we're tailing Aifric Moncrieffe's son. He's obviously on some secret mission and we're the only ones who know about it. What kind of fun do you want?'

Bob considered this. The last of the street lights vanished in the rear view window and another car pulled off the main road, leaving just one vehicle between Byron and us.

There was a blinding flash and I cursed, swerving across the centre of the road briefly before righting the car again. 'What the hell are you doing?' I glared at Bob. He'd changed into a tuxedo and was sipping what looked like a martini.

'Mish Moneypenny, you ought to calm down.' His accent was a good approximation of Sean Connery's but I still rolled my eyes. 'If Byron Moncrieffe isn't going to be James Bond, then I will be.'

'No more of that,' I hissed. 'Any further flashes of light and Byron will know something's up. If we're going to be spies, then act like one.'

'Don't worry, Uh Integrity,' Bob said, more cheerful now. 'This isn't my first secret mission. I worked with Kim Philby, you know. If it wasn't for me, he'd never have been a double agent for the KGB.'

I drummed my fingers against the steering wheel. There wasn't much petrol left in the tank so I hoped Byron wasn't planning a long expedition. 'So what you're saying is that you aided and abetted a traitor.'

Bob pursed his lips. 'I'm helping you. *You're* a traitor too.'

'It's hardly the same thing.'

'Depends whose point of view you're looking from.'

I was liable to toss Bob out of the window if he didn't stop talking soon. I did the only thing I could think of to shut him up. 'What do you call a traitor with a lisp?'

'Is this a joke?' he asked suspiciously.

'Judith.' I grinned.

'Uh Integrity…'

'What do spies do when they get cold?'

He dropped the martini in favour of putting his hands over his ears. 'Stop it,' he moaned. 'I'll tell you whatever state secrets you want to know. Just please stop the torture.'

'Then I'm going to need you to be quiet. Not one word out of your mouth unless I ask for it. Got that?'

He nodded vigorously. 'Sure. Sure. Sure.' He drew his finger across his lips.

I beamed. 'Great.'

Bob dropped his hands and sighed – but at least he didn't say anything.

'Oh, one more thing,' I added casually. 'Cold spies go undercover.'

His cheeks went bright red. It was quite possible that Bob was about to explode.

***

We tracked Byron for several miles. He wasn't speeding and he didn't seem in any hurry, though he wasn't driving at snail's pace either. It wasn't until we passed a road sign that I got an inkling of where he might be heading. It made even less sense than Bob's theory about Byron swimming across the Atlantic so I kept my mouth shut and continued, grimacing when the last car between us turned off the road and away. The only saving grace was that it was dark and the glare from my headlights would prevent Byron from seeing inside the car. All the same, I slowed down slightly and let him pull away from us.

When we reached the next turn off, I swung towards it. Bob opened his mouth to question my action then remembered his promise and snapped it shut again.

I brought the car to a stop and waited until Byron's headlights were little more than pinpricks in the distance. Then I killed my lights, did another U-turn and headed after him again, making sure that this time I didn't even begin to get close. From this distance we'd be all but invisible. I smiled. Who needed magic when you had a bit of nous?

It wasn't long before Byron's car also turned – and when I saw where he was going, I realised that my suspicions were correct. Bob gazed round, his expression as flummoxed as mine, as we tailed Byron down the first part of the driveway which led to the Moncrieffe Lands.

Aifric spent most of his time at the Cruaich, as befitted the Steward of the Highlands, but this was still his ancestral home. That meant it was Byron's home too – so why was he was sneaking away from Perth simply to return to his own damned house?

I was forced to stop again after Byron paused at the border. It was too dark to tell for sure but this time he seemed to get out of his car. I watched, worried that new guards had been posted there now that all the trolls had vamoosed. If that were the case, I'd have to be more than careful – I'd have to be the luckiest damn woman alive to tail him up to the main building. There was nothing obvious, however, other than a flare of light which was extinguished quickly. A torch, perhaps?

Unwilling to drive right through the Moncrieffe border – or even close to it now that there might be prying eyes scanning the landscape – I parked near a copse of trees and walked the last part. The driveway wasn't as long as those at the Adair or the Scrymgeour Lands and I could see the lights of Byron's car as he continued on his way. He didn't go to the Moncrieffe castle but halted halfway. Maybe that was where everyone was supposed to park.

Aware that we were now some way back, I hurried towards the border with Bob on my shoulder. Unfortunately, this time we were without Speck. Although I understood how passing through individual Sidhe Clan borders worked in theory, I wasn't convinced that I could manage it in practice, not without preparation. I couldn't even call my warlock buddy for help; the signal at the Adair Lands was too weak to receive calls. All the same, I wanted to give crossing the border a shot. My curiosity was too great to turn back now.

When we were less than fifty feet away, I slid towards the bushes at the side of the road. We were in the middle of nowhere so there was little light, something that was working in my favour. I hunched and tiptoed forward. I couldn't see any flickering shadows but that didn't mean there wasn't anyone there and it didn't ease my tension. I moved faster and gradually got closer to the border. There weren't any people – but there was *something* there.

I stopped at the edge of the border, remaining still for a long moment, as I scanned up and down for any sign of life. I knew from the puddle of fabric at my feet that I wasn't going to see anyone; Byron hadn't stopped and got out of his car for a chat with a family servant, he'd got out to bring down the Moncrieffe flag. No doubt he'd done so by sending up a pyrokinetic bolt so the flag fell to the ground without Byron putting a single foot across the border. That was the little flare I'd seen. And he hadn't stopped there; Byron had apparently made use of his second Gift as well, lifting up the flagpole to remove it entirely from the spot that controlled the border itself. It now lay uselessly on its side.

I rocked back on my heels. Byron could never have managed a feat like this if the trolls were still in place.

Their presence helped maintain the magic of the Sidhe borders, together with the flagpoles, the Clan colours and the incumbent Moncrieffe Sidhe, most of whom were back at the stag party. The majority of Sidhe didn't understand how the borders worked but it was obvious that Byron did. What wasn't obvious was why he had sneaked away from his own party and was skipping unseen into his own Clan Lands. He should have been able to pass them without consequence.

I glanced at Bob. He raised his eyebrows at me and I jabbed a finger at him. 'Speak.' He crossed his arms and pouted. 'Bob,' I said, 'you may speak. I won't tell any jokes.' I gestured at the fallen flag and horizontal flagpole. 'But I need to understand what's going on.'

He shrugged. 'S'easy. Byron knows you're tailing him and he's setting a trap. He's made it easy for you to cross his border. As soon as you do, he'll pounce on you, tie you up and slit your throat.'

I narrowed my eyes.

'Or,' Bob added, 'he doesn't want anyone to know that he's been home. If there's no real heavy magic in place at the border, no one will know that it's been crossed, even by a Moncrieffe Sidhe.'

I rubbed my chin. 'But why? He's the sodding Moncrieffe heir. He can come and go as he pleases.'

'So *now* you want to hear my theories?'

I sighed. 'If we're talking about wild speculation, no. Can I pass through unnoticed now?'

Bob tapped his mouth. 'Probably. There's still magic there but it's pretty faint. What remains is less likely to be activated against another Sidhe than it is against, say, a Fomori demon.' He paused. 'However, as an all-knowing magnificent being with powers you can only dream of, I would say it's still too dangerous. You're far better abandoning this entire project so we can go back home.'

I nodded. 'Yeah.' He beamed in glee but I wasn't done. 'You stay here. If I'm not back in three hours, head back to the Adair Lands and tell the others what's happened.'

Bob's smile vanished. 'If you're dead, I'm no longer beholden to you in any way, shape or form. I don't want you to be dead. Despite your irritating nature, you're my friend.' I didn't imagine the pleading note in his voice. 'Leave it be. I understand how you feel about Byron Moncrieffe but this isn't worth it. You've got more important things to do. You're supposed to save Scotland.'

'If that prophecy is real,' I said with an arch grin, 'then I'll save Scotland regardless of what happens. So there's nothing to worry about.'

'Uh Integrity!' Bob howled. 'You know prophecies don't work that way!'

'Then don't bring it up.' I smiled reassuringly. 'I'll be back before you know it.' Before he could protest any further, I ducked my head and passed across what little remained of the Moncrieffe border.

***

I sprinted up the driveway, no longer attempting to conceal myself. The darkness was enough of a shroud, although it also worked against me as the road here was almost as badly maintained as the Adair one. On at least one occasion I narrowly avoided landing in a deep pothole. When I reached the spot where Byron had parked his car, I wondered if he'd left it there to avoid damaging its suspension on the uneven ground. Given what I'd seen at the border, however, he could well have parked there because he wanted to disguise his approach to the castle.

I paused to peer through the windows. The car was spick and span; I'd find no clues there.

I started running again. I'd never been here – at least, not that I could remember – so I was travelling blind. Taylor had always maintained the importance of preparation when making an incursion and I'd always stuck to that rule but these were special circumstances. I pushed away the voice that told me I was being reckless and acting out of character and kept on going.

The Moncrieffe castle was lit by two flickering torches near the heavy, studded main door. I couldn't see any other lights in the windows; with their crappy finances, the Moncrieffes were probably trying to cut back on the electricity bill. Perhaps Aifric considered financial fraud beneath him, even if mass murder was acceptable.

I debated whether to open the door, slip inside and take on whatever came my way but it was too much of a risk. And there was always another way in. Always.

I darted to my left. There was a bank of windows along the eastern side, all firmly closed. It didn't matter; Scottish architecture always included a handy back door. I'd nip in through there.

I ran softly round the outskirts of the castle, taking care to duck and roll every time I passed a window in case someone happened to spot me flying past. I zipped round the corner, my confidence growing when I saw a small door built into the back wall. Easy-peasy.

I tugged on the handle. Nothing happened so I tugged again. Arse. I couldn't even find a suitable lock to pick; the bloody door was bolted on the other side in several places. Not insurmountable, but it would take time I didn't have. Maybe it was locked because Aifric knew someone could finagle their way in past the border and massacre everyone inside. After all, he'd done that himself to my Clan. Then I reminded myself that the

Bull's back door had been locked too. I was over-thinking.

I pulled back, looking around for another entrance. If Byron had sneaked in here, he had to have entered the castle somehow. It was his childhood home so he'd be well aware of every nook and cranny, unlike a stranger like me. I was, however, a gifted thief; if there was another entrance through which I could slip in unnoticed, I'd find it.

I abandoned the far side of the castle in favour of the western-facing wall. This structure was simple, little more than a square. That narrowed down my options and meant I wouldn't waste time wandering around exterior alcoves. When I rounded the last corner and spied a window which was ajar on the first floor, I finally smiled. Good enough.

I positioned myself directly underneath, bending my knees slightly before springing up. The walls were smooth and there were no helpful footholds. I managed to curve my fingers over the sill and used sheer strength and will power to pull myself up, nudging the window open further with my elbow so I could slip inside. I flipped over in an unnecessary somersault – but one which I felt the situation called for – and landed on my feet facing the room. A second later, a hand slammed across my mouth and a muscled arm tightened across my chest, holding me in place.

'What the hell are you doing here?' Byron growled in my ear.

Shite.

Chapter Nine

I struggled against his grip but, when it was clear he was far too strong and I was never going to get clear, I let my body relax. He was a lot more tense than I was. I might have fallen for the oldest trick in the book and wandered in through the only entrance to the castle because it had been left open for me to do just that, but my one advantage was that he didn't want anyone to know he was here. He was on his own and wanted things to remain that way, which gave me some breathing room. Anyway, he'd probably have learned sooner or later that I was still alive; at least this way I might get some answers about what was really going on.

Unable to speak with his hand clamped over my mouth, and confident that he'd realise that soon enough, I waited for him to release me. As soon as he did, I spun round to face him. The expression on his face wasn't the stunned epiphany that I'd been expecting; instead he was glaring at me with a malevolence that shone from every pore of his body. 'Who hired you?' he demanded. 'Was it my father?'

For a moment I was totally confused. Why would Aifric hire me? I was his sworn enemy and, anyway, he thought I was dead. Then I realised that I'd been so focused on Byron and what he was up to that the Illusion I was Chardonnay was still in place. Byron thought I was the stripper. Well, wasn't I a prize idiot? I'd needlessly wasted almost all that magic.

'No,' I said softly, 'he didn't.' I stepped forward until I was inches away from him. 'Byron…'

He snarled something under his breath and side-stepped as if he were afraid of me. He flexed his fingers. 'I could snap your neck like a twig,' he spat. 'So start talking before I do you some damage.'

I almost grinned. I could believe a great deal of Byron: I could believe he wanted to marry Tipsania to get the money his Clan needed so badly; I could believe he was now working with his father against Candy; I could even believe he was sneaking into his own house even though I didn't know why. But I couldn't believe he was that kind of violent person. He'd threaten and bluster but he wouldn't physically hurt me. Not to that extent anyway.

His voice was low and dangerous. 'Are you amused?' His fury seemed to grow. 'Do I amuse you?' He flicked his wrist, sending out a stream of magic in my direction that bound itself round my chest and lifted me into the air. I hovered there, still wearing the ridiculous police uniform. 'I don't have time for this,' he muttered, as much to himself as to me.

'You're very angry,' I told him.

He glared at me in disbelief. 'Angry? You have no idea. Angry doesn't even begin to cover it.'

I continued to watch him. I didn't want to play games but I had to ease my way in. Right now, he looked as if he were about to have an aneurysm. 'You wanted me back at the Haven,' I said carefully. 'You were … turned on.'

The magic binding me tightened slightly. Careful, Byron.

'I was not,' he said through gritted teeth.

My veins buzzed with the lie. I licked my lips. 'Does Tipsania make you feel that way?'

His eyes hardened even more. 'No one makes me feel that way.' There was an edge to his voice I'd never heard before.

'Someone must have rocked your world once,' I said softly.

He stared at me, something indefinable in his expression. Come on, Byron, you can puzzle this out. 'The only person who ever made me feel anything,' he said, 'is dead. And that's what will happen to you if you don't start answering my questions.'

'You desired me,' I told him, my heart in my mouth. 'You wanted me. Maybe you still do. Byron…'

'Shut up,' he ground out. 'Shut the hell up.'

My stomach churned. He was too focused on the Illusion to work out what was going on. There was no other way around this – it was time for the truth. *All* the truth. I took a deep breath, reached down into myself and extinguished the Illusion. My long dark hair transformed into pure white. The tan I'd so admired disappeared back into my milk-pale skin and my body shifted. There, I was Integrity again. I'd miss those breasts though.

Byron blinked. 'What the fuck?' He peered at me and blinked again. He took a step back, swallowed and balled up his fists. 'What is this?' he snarled. 'You think you can taunt me? You're obviously a Sidhe. Which Clan are you?'

'It's me, Byron. It's Integrity.'

His emerald eyes flashed. 'Integrity is dead. Just because you have powerful Illusion magic doesn't mean I'm an idiot.' His neck muscles were straining as he held himself back. Held himself back from what, I wasn't entirely sure.

'I'm Integrity, Byron,' I repeated. 'I stole Illusion from someone back at the Cruaich earlier today. I pretended to be that stripper because I wanted to know what you were up to.' And I wanted to see you again, I added silently. I wanted to press myself against you and have your arms round me so I could pretend that everything was alright between us. 'I faked my death because if I hadn't, your father wouldn't have stopped coming after me. Neither would the Fomori demons.' My voice faltered slightly. 'I wanted to tell you the truth. But I didn't have any choice.'

He took another step back then a step forward. Then he went back again. If this situation weren't so serious, I'd have made some quip about his dancing but he still looked as if he were barely controlling himself. His jaw tightened and he flicked his wrist again, bringing me towards him so my face was directly in front of his. He reached up as if about to touch me and drew back again. 'This isn't real,' he whispered. 'You aren't real.'

'I am.' I scanned his features, willing him to see the truth. 'I can prove it. Ask me anything Integrity would know.'

His nostrils flared. I knew he was scenting me, doing everything he could to ascertain the truth. 'Where did we first meet?'

'In a hotel bar. We drank pink champagne.' My mouth curved into a smile. 'Well,' I amended, 'I drank pink champagne. I'd been trying to avoid alcohol but you didn't give me much choice. You were avoiding alcohol tonight, too. Why don't you tell me what you're up to?'

He ignored my question. A muscle in his cheek pulsated but he'd schooled the rest of his face into an impassive mask. 'During the Games, I went to see you in your competitors' accommodation. You were wearing a fancy outfit. What was it?'

'Princess Leia,' I answered easily. 'But only because I'd made a deal with Bob.' Byron's eyes narrowed. I countered with another of my own questions. 'Why are you holding Candy captive? Isn't he supposed to be your friend?'

He didn't answer, just kept staring at me unable to believe the evidence of his own eyes. That was understandable. My tongue darted out, wetting my lips. He followed the movement. 'We almost made love under the only remaining tree in the Adair grove,' I told him quietly. 'There are more trees there now. They're saplings really but they're growing. When I went across the Veil, I found you on top of Arthur's Seat in Edinburgh, shackled to a post. I used Illusion to help us escape so it shouldn't be too hard to believe that I've used it for other things. You told me I smelled bad.'

Byron seemed to stop breathing.

I leaned forward, pushing against the constraints of his magic as best as I could. 'I wouldn't know any of these things unless I really was Integrity.'

Even with the darkness surrounding us, his skin seemed leeched of all colour. 'You're a ghost.'

'Oh for goodness' sake!' I said, without thinking. 'What is it with you Sidhe and ghosts? The Bull thought I was a bloody ghost, too. I thought you were smarter than that.'

Something changed in Byron's eyes. All at once he released me, dropping the Telekinesis that had been holding me in place. Before I fell to the ground, however, he grabbed me, wrapped his arms round and pulled me to him. His hand cupped my face and his thumb stroked my skin while he gazed into my eyes. 'You're alive,' he said simply.

I opened my mouth to reply but he didn't give me the chance. His lips descended, pressing into mine with hot urgency and a demanding possessiveness that was almost painful. We stumbled backwards until I was pressed against the wall. Byron ran his hands down my body. His legs pinned me in place while he explored every clothed part of me, as if double-checking that I really did exist. All the time, his mouth didn't leave mine. The air was being pushed out of my lungs but, despite the violent embrace, I didn't want him to stop. He couldn't ever stop. Then, whether by accident or design, he bit my bottom lip.

I yanked my head away, my yell of pain loud and sharp. Now it wasn't just Byron I could taste in my mouth. There was also the bitter tang of blood.

He drew back, panting, and giving us both the breathing space we needed. My tongue darted out to the tiny cut while Byron's green eyes followed the movement. He closed his eyes briefly as if in agony, his fists curling and uncurling as he calmed himself. I reached out and touched his jaw and he relaxed.

Rather than apologise, he tilted his head and planted a soft kiss on the wound. He gently brushed my hair away from my face before starting to trail butterfly kisses from my temple down to my neck. On the way he pulled back – once, twice, three times. Every time, he stared hard at me, as if checking it was still me. Every time it just made the ache inside me grow. Neither of us spoke because neither of us needed to; we were saying all we needed to without a single word.

More carefully now, he helped me out of my jacket and tossed it to one side. He lifted my hand and stroked upwards towards my shoulder with the lightest of touches. I couldn't stop myself from shivering. His fingers danced across my collarbone and then down my other arm before venturing to my waist where they twitched at the hem of my T-shirt. Together, we pulled it over my head. As soon as it was out of the way, his stroking began again, feather-light movements down my chest. I groaned. He brushed against the lace of my bra then swept further down over my belly. Then he crouched down and I felt his hot breath against my skin as, instead of his fingers, he used his tongue. When he reached my belly button, he circled it exquisitely slowly.

I unhooked my bra and he watched me take it off, his greedy eyes fixed on me. He stood up, his thumbs brushing against my painfully erect nipples then he used his tongue to circle them slowly while I clumsily tried to unfasten the buttons on his shirt. As my fingers grazed his skin, he gave a guttural growl and pulled away, taking it off himself. As soon as it was discarded, he moved onto his trousers, kicking them away. And enjoyable as it was letting my eyes travel across the tight bulge in his perfect white underpants, he wasted no time in divesting himself of those too. He stretched out his arms, inviting my gaze to take in every inch of him. Despite the obvious fatigue lining his face and the visible weight loss, he still possessed a taut washboard stomach. The sight of him standing in front of me like some kind of sacrifice made my heart skip a beat.

He gestured at my jeans, his meaning clear. I smirked and shook my head, pointing down at his feet. He frowned then, realising I wanted him to take off his socks, did just that. Only then did I unbutton my jeans and slide out of them. I hooked my fingers teasingly into the waistband of my panties, threatening to wriggle them down over my hips but not quite seeing it through. Byron's eyes narrowed enough to make me quit playing the flirt. A moment later, the pants joined the pile of clothing on the floor. Forget Chardonnay – this was much more my kind of striptease.

He tugged at my hand, leading me over to an elegant chaise longue. I draped myself across it, the very image of lady of the manor – apart from the fact I was stark naked. He smiled slowly and lifted his foot, gently nudging my legs apart until he was satisfied I was completely exposed to his hot gaze.

He knelt down, turning his attention to my feet and using the same feathery light strokes to caress my skin. He swept upwards with his fingers before going back to the beginning and doing the same with his tongue, inch by inch, centimetre by centimetre, gradually getting closer and closer to the top of my thighs. I shuddered and moaned with both the sensation of now and the expectation of soon.

Just as he reached my inner thigh and I could bear it no longer, he shifted and moved onto the chaise. He blew gently and I almost fainted. His head lowered, his tongue darting down my clitoris, mimicking the same circular motion he'd used everywhere else. I let out a ragged sob, my fingers clutching the crushed velvet of the chaise. At the sound, Byron stiffened and lifted his head. His eyes met mine with an odd note of regret that I didn't understand at first. When I focused on the tension of his body and the flaring desire in those emerald depths, however, I realised what it was. He wanted this to be perfect. He wanted it to be slow and sensual and to last for hours. The trouble was that he couldn't wait.

Recognising this because I felt the same, I smiled and pulled him upwards until the length of his body hovered over mine. I grabbed his hips, positioning myself. We shared one mutual glance of fire and desperate need before we met each other halfway and he plunged inside me, filling every inch of me.

He withdrew more slowly, teasing out the sensations, his eyes fixed on mine. I could feel his body trembling and I shook my head. Enough of slow – I wanted fast and hard. I twisted, forcing him to move with me, flipping round until I was on top of him. I had to take charge or he'd feel guilty for losing control. His hands curved round my waist while I set the tempo, sliding up and down, almost purring as I built up to the inevitable crescendo. I'd never felt connected like this before, not just physically but on an almost telepathic level. I could feel him clinging on, still wanting to draw this out. No. I wanted it now. I increased the strokes and he rose to meet me every time, our bodies pounding together. Byron moaned, his eyes boring into mine one last time. Then I nodded, crying out as he thrust upwards in one final, fluid movement and we collapsed into each other, his heart hammering against mine as wave after wave of orgasm racked us both and the rest of the world fell away into meaningless ether.

I dropped my head against his chest. This was the way it was meant to be. This was what the poets wrote about. For one long moment, we lay together, my skin burning and my mind at rest.

I felt it the instant the atmosphere changed. Still slick with sweat, Byron yanked himself away from me and stood up, tension rolling across his shoulders. There was still passion in his eyes but now it was passion of a different sort. 'You bitch,' he said quietly.

I propped myself up on my elbows. 'Excuse me?'

'You let me believe you were dead.'

Uh-oh. I guessed the celebration was well and truly over. Bites aside, I'd known he was going to get angry sooner or later but I'd kind of hoped that what had just passed between us might delay it. I got to my feet, not bothering to cover myself. We faced each other, both as naked as the day we were born. 'I had good reason,' I said calmly.

'After everything we'd been through, you really thought that the best way forward was to fake your own death?' His voice remained low but there was a tremble to his words. If I thought he'd been angry before when he'd caught me flipping through the window, I was sadly mistaken. This muted rage was far scarier than any shouted admonition.

He wasn't done yet. 'Who else knows you're alive?' he demanded.

'Hardly anyone. Taylor, of course. And Bob, Brochan, Speck, Lexie, the trolls…'

'Angus MacQuarrie,' he ground out. 'He was there when you supposedly died. Does he know the truth?'

Shite. I was getting the impression that there was little I could say to appease him. Maybe I should just jump on him again and kiss him. That would shut him up. I sighed. It would also only delay the inevitable.

'How many times,' I asked, 'did I try to get you to see the truth about your father? I even tried again, right before the entire charade. I had no choice.'

'There is always a choice, Integrity. Always.'

I drew myself up. 'Yes, there is. I'm a Clan Chieftain, Byron. I have to make decisions and choices not just for myself but for the people under my care. If I hadn't pretended to die, those demons would have kept after me until I really was a cold corpse. They would have hurt the people I loved, too.'

'That doesn't justify lying to me. Do you have any idea what that did to me? What the last few months have been like?'

'I'm sorry. But you don't seem to have been all that upset.'

He glowered. 'What the hell is that supposed to mean?'

I crossed my arms over my chest. 'Your wedding to Tipsania,' I said pointedly. 'You don't know where she is and yet you're still going ahead with it. You've kidnapped the love of her life and you're going to use him as bait to draw her out. And for what, Byron?' I demanded. 'So the Moncrieffes can have a bit more money to spend on blackmail and murder and…'

He stepped towards me with such a look in his eyes that I lost track of my words. 'I am not my father.'

I barely heard him. 'Yeah? But you've defended him enough bloody times! I told you again and again and you wouldn't believe me! How was I supposed to trust you?'

'Don't you get it?' his voice was strangled. 'Don't you understand how I feel about you? Your supposed death almost destroyed me, Integrity.'

'Why are you still marrying Tipsania?'

'I'm not.' The magic inside me told me he was telling the truth. Confused, I shook my head while Byron clenched his jaw. 'Why couldn't you see how much your death would hurt me?'

'It was a necessary evil.' I glared at him. 'Why is your friend rotting away in a damn dungeon?'

'He's perfectly comfortable and he's there because I asked him to be there. I have a plan and he's part of it. What the hell have *you* been doing all this time? Laughing at me?'

'No. I've been getting stronger and sorting out my damned ancestral Lands. You know, the ones your fucking father effectively destroyed. And what's your plan? What's so important that it's worth locking up someone for?'

'Bringing down my fucking father.'

My mouth dropped open and I stared at him, stunned into silence. It wouldn't have lasted long, however, if it weren't for the sudden thump from outside. Byron and I looked at each other with wide eyes. He lunged forward, grabbed me and hauled me behind a large chintz-covered chair, effectively barricading me within the cage of his arms. He murmured, 'Stay quiet.'

I raised my head, peered round the corner and spotted the chink of light under the door at the far end of the room. Someone was on their way.

'Byron,' I hissed. 'Our clothes!' They were still strewn all over the floor. He cursed and I felt his body tense then he used his Telekinesis Gift to yank at each discarded item and drag it out of sight. He was just in time – a heartbeat later the doorknob turned and a figure glanced in.

'Hello?'

I tried not to breathe too loudly. I could feel Byron's naked chest against my back, his pulse hammering.

'Hello?'

'There's nothing there,' someone else said. 'Come to bed.'

'I could swear I heard something.'

'Love, no one is going to break into the Moncrieffe castle. If they did, the Steward would hunt them down and set their head on a pike.' There was a yawn. 'Come on. I need to sleep.'

I remained frozen, praying that the first figure would take the advice. Silence stretched out then the door closed and Byron and I were alone again. I exhaled. That was too close.

'I thought you were a skilled thief,' Byron murmured in my ear.

'Usually, I come prepared,' I replied with a hint of snottiness. I waited for a moment but he didn't move. 'You can let me go, you know,' I told him.

For a second, his arms tightened as if he were afraid to let go. Then he released me and I stood up and began searching for my clothing.

'Tell me,' I said, finding my T-shirt underneath a chair and pulling it over my head, 'why are you sneaking into your own house?'

'It's part of my plan.' He tugged on his trousers. 'I meant what I said. When I realised what my father was really doing – what he'd done – I started looking for ways to stop him.'

I paused. 'So you believe me now?'

Byron's answer was grim and he was telling the truth. 'Yes.' Still shirtless, he took my hands. 'My father killed your parents and committed genocide against your entire Clan. He plotted to have you killed as well. And he's probably in league with the Fomori demons.' He drew in a breath. 'I'm sorry I didn't believe you before. And, trite as it sounds, on behalf of Clan Moncrieffe I am sorry for the wrongs done to you.'

Suddenly there was a painful lump in my throat. 'Thank you.' My fingers grazed the rough stubble on his cheek. 'But it's not your fault. Are you … are you okay?'

'I've had a while to get used to the idea.' He laughed harshly. 'For a long time I was more fixated on the fact that you were dead.'

I swallowed. 'How long have you known the truth?'

'Eighty-two days. That's how long you've been gone, Integrity. Eighty-two fucking days. I found out about an hour after you…' He cursed and stared at me with an uncomfortable intensity.

Shite. That long? 'I'm sorry too.' I meant it with every atom of my being but words couldn't compensate for the agony in his eyes. 'I'm sorry I pretended I was dead. It wasn't done to hurt you. I really didn't think I had a choice.' His eyes glittered in the faint light. I frowned. 'Are you crying?'

Byron didn't hesitate. 'Yes.'

For some reason that scared me more than anything else. 'Oh. Okay then.'

'Does that make me less of a man?'

I smiled. 'No.'

We grinned at each other like idiots until Byron glanced at his watch. 'Damn it. We need to get a move on. I've got things to do and I have to get back to Perth before dawn.' He pulled away and finished dressing.

'Why? What exactly is going on?'

'My father's study. He must have papers in there which either incriminate him or provide more information about what he's up to. I've been through what he has in the Cruaich and came up short. It makes sense that he'd hide the important stuff here, where it's less likely there will be any snoopers. Jamie arranged the stag party and invited everyone who might possibly get in my way or find out what I'm up to.'

'The whole party is a ruse?'

'Yeah.' He looked embarrassed for a moment. 'I wasn't expecting a stripper though.'

I smirked. 'You fancied me.'

'You had a great body.'

'Had?'

'That's not what I meant.' Byron coughed while my smile grew. 'She reminded me of you. You reminded me of you.' He shook his head. 'Never mind. Let's not get into this now.'

I nodded but there was one other thing. 'Candy,' I said quietly. 'And Tipsania.'

Byron sighed. 'I know. I needed my father to believe I'd do what he wanted. Candy agreed to help. I knew Tipsania was probably still hiding at your Clan Lands so I was going to wait until the last minute and go down there with him.'

'You'd threaten to hurt him if she didn't come out.'

He looked away. 'Yes. I need everyone to think the wedding is going ahead. I wouldn't have actually *hurt* him.'

It wasn't a very sound plan and I wasn't ready to let him off the hook completely. 'You said you weren't going to marry her.' So that I didn't come over as a whiny sort-of-ex-girlfriend, I added, 'Tipsania doesn't want you.'

'I know. And I'm not. Trust me on this, Integrity, I'm really not going to say any vows. I didn't think I'd ever get married after you...' His voice faded and I watched him carefully. This wasn't the Byron from before, it was an odd, contradictory mix; he was both harder and more vulnerable.

'I need Tipsania there for the ceremony or my father won't believe it's real. He has to think that everything is as he wants it to be.' He ran a hand through his hair. 'All I requested was that the wedding take place on the Isle of Muck. My mother was from there so it was easy. It's isolated and small and every damn Sidhe with an ounce of power in the Highlands will be there for it.' He smiled humourlessly. 'The Steward demands it. I'm going to wait until everyone is in the church and expose my father to the world for what he really is. There will be too many witnesses for him to escape.' He paused while I tried to absorb his words. 'That's why we need to move. If I can find proof in his study of what he's done, everyone will have to believe me. He won't be able to wriggle out of it.'

Byron was either incredibly brilliant or incredibly naïve; until I thought about his plan some more, I had no idea which. For now, however, I'd do whatever I could to help him. 'Then,' I said softly, 'let's get a move on.'

Chapter Ten

As we tiptoed out of the door and headed down a long, dark corridor, Byron insisted on holding of my hand. It was a bit weird and if I thought about it too much I'd probably have been annoyed but it was also oddly reassuring. To be fair, if I'd thought he'd died I might have not wanted to let go of him either. I kept my mouth shut and let him lead me past old portraits of frowning Moncrieffe Clan Chieftains until we reached a set of stairs down to the ground floor.

'His study is that door at the bottom on the right,' Byron whispered. 'He keeps it locked when he's not here and no one ever goes inside. I think I've only been in on six or seven occasions in my entire life.'

I couldn't help being reminded of the Bull and his own special snowflake version. These old men with their secrets. I shook my head. Idiots.

We waited for a moment or two. When Byron was confident that everyone in the castle was either asleep or elsewhere, we padded down to the door. I reached up to my hair for the tiny lock pick I'd concealed there but Byron was prepared. As I watched, open-mouthed, he pulled his own version from his pocket, knelt down and got to work.

'You *have* been busy,' I murmured.

'I've not been twiddling my thumbs for the last few months, Integrity,' he sniped, obviously still not completely over the news of my resurrection.

It took him more time than it would have taken me but he managed to get the door open. Go, Byron. With a swift glance at me, he nodded and we entered. In comparison to the Bull's study, this place was far neater. Other than old books on the shelves, there was little on display. The room possessed a certain shabby chic which, had I not known what Aifric was like, might have made me admire him.

Carefully closing the door behind me, I looked at Byron. 'Do you know where he's likely to keep the most incriminating documents?' I asked.

'One of my earliest memories is when I was a kid,' he said. 'I must have escaped from the nursery and come here to find my father.' His expression soured. 'I don't think I've ever seen him so angry as when he realised I'd sneaked in.'

My heart went out to him. Since he'd discovered the truth about Aifric, he'd probably spent hours – days even – poring over their relationship and everything that had occurred between them. He'd have wanted to know if he could have accepted the truth earlier, or if there had been any clues that his own flesh and blood was a murdering maniac. I'd spent most of my life believing the same of my father and, although the circumstances were very different, I wasn't insensitive to how Byron probably felt.

'Anyway,' he continued, 'from what I remember, there were renovations going on. There wasn't anyone present apart from my father but the place was a mess. There were brushes and tools … it was like he'd been building something. I never thought much of it before but now I'm not so sure. What if he built somewhere to hide the things that no one else should see? Some kind of secret compartment or room?' He gazed at me in mute appeal; he needed me to agree with him even if Aifric really had just been redecorating.

I considered Byron's words and stepped back to get the best vantage point. The study was a perfect oblong and there were no signs of anything out of place. I had to trust his instincts, however. He watched me carefully. 'Do you see anything?'

'Not at this minute,' I said truthfully. 'Despite the age of most of the buildings in the Highlands, you'd be surprised at how few secret rooms there are. Even the ones that do exist are usually easy to find.'

Byron pointed behind himself. 'I've not just been practising the art of lock picking,' he told me. 'I've also been scouting things here. The library is on the other side of this wall and a store cupboard in the opposite direction. The dimensions of the library are wrong. It's cleverly concealed because of the shelving but, if there is a secret room here, it's behind this wall.'

There was an easy way to find out. I edged from one side to the other, thumping the wall at strategic points. Thud. Thud. Thud. Dup. I grinned. Dup. Dup. Thud. 'It looks like plaster but there's definitely something behind here. It's hollow. We need to find a way in.'

Byron's eyes flashed in grim delight as if he were not sure whether to be pleased or dismayed that his suspicions were proving correct. He nodded decisively. 'Step back,' he said.

I did as he asked, thinking that maybe I was blocking his line of vision. As soon as I was out the way, he flicked his wrist and a little fireball coalesced in front of him.

I scratched my head. 'Er…'

The fireball grew in size, hissing and crackling. Within the confines of the small study, the heat was immense and I was forced to turn my head. With one intense glare, Byron sent the fireball smack into the hollow part of the wall. The plaster crumbled almost immediately; it wasn't just the fire but the force of the fireball that did considerable damage.

Dark billowing smoke filled the space. Coughing, I darted to the window and yanked it open. 'If anyone is outside…' I began.

Byron wiped his streaming eyes. 'No one's there. They're all either upstairs or at the stag party. I made sure of it.'

I sighed. 'All the same, I'm not sure wanton destruction was the best way to go.'

As the smoke cleared, I saw him shrug nonchalantly. 'I've been planning this for a long time, Integrity. I wasn't sure anything was here but I covered every eventuality. Trust me. I know what I'm doing.'

I had no choice but to let it go. I mirrored his shrug, grabbed a sheaf of paper and wafted it vigorously to get the rest of the smoke out so we could see what was behind the magical door.

'Bricks,' I said. I peered closer. The fireball had certainly done its job; there was a good-sized hole in the wall. But if this really was Aifric's secret room, where was the door? Maybe one of Aifric's Gifts was the ability to turn himself incorporeal; that would be seriously cool.

Byron glanced inside. 'I can't see anything,' he muttered. He flicked his hand again and sent out a small flame. In an instant the tiny space was flooded with light. I gasped and pulled back.

'What—?' Byron whispered.

I shook myself and checked again but I hadn't imagined it. There were no boxes filled with dodgy documents, no flashing signs indicating that the evidence we needed to put Aifric away for good was here. There were, however, three fully-dressed corpses.

I retched. No wonder the bloody wall was brick and the study's dimensions were odd. Whoever these unfortunate people were, they'd been buried alive. They weren't like the stripped skeleton of Matthew MacBain that I'd come across in the Lowlands; judging by the two quick glimpses I'd had, these bodies were more recent. Not this year, or even this decade, although they appeared more mummified than decomposed. Their clothes were old-fashioned but not ancient.

'They're not Sidhe,' Byron muttered.

I steeled myself for another look. He was right. Nausea roiled across my stomach. 'They're not human or Bauchan or troll. Or anything like that. These three are … were…'

'Fomori,' Byron finished grimly. He looked like someone who thought they'd reached rock bottom and thought there was no way things could get any worse. The trouble was that I knew they always could.

'We should go, Byron. There's nothing else here and you probably woke up everyone when you busted the wall.'

'We're not leaving yet. There has to be something else, some evidence of his culpability.'

A thin layer of dust now covered Aifric's desk. I tugged on the drawers, pulling them open and looking inside before gesturing helplessly. 'See? Nothing. Much as hate to say it, your father is too smart to leave anything lying around, even here. I found evidence at his rooms in the Cruaich that he'd had something to do with Fomori demons.' I pointed at the hole in the wall. 'Now we have more. Those bodies look too recent to be anything other than a result of his work. Maybe that'll be enough.'

'It's not,' Byron growled. He glanced at me balefully. 'You're new to this world, Integrity. I'm not. I know exactly what it will take to get everyone to believe the truth about my father.' He jerked his head at the three dead Fomori demons. 'And this is not going to do it. He's got a silver tongue that can talk him out of anything. Maybe he'll place the blame on some poor builders who were never even here. Maybe he'll even own up to it – they are Fomori demons, after all. Who's going to mourn their deaths? We've got your Clan emblem which Jamie gave to me. Even with his psychometry, that gives us circumstantial evidence against him at best. There's the Fomori trinket you found which my father could dismiss as some kind of artefact. And these three bodies. It's not enough.'

'You're not going to find a smoking gun. But if you can plant enough doubt in the other Chieftains' minds…'

'You don't get it! Half of them will believe any lies he tells them. The other half will either already be colluding with him or will keep quiet because they're too afraid. He's fooled me my entire life! I've been working my way around the other Clans and listening to what's going on and how they think. I need more to get them to pay attention.'

I sighed and pinched the bridge of my nose. 'They're wearing clothes,' I said eventually.

'Huh?'

'The Fomori demons are wearing clothes, probably as much to cover their skin from the sun as anything, but almost all the others I've seen were naked or as good as.'

'The demons who attacked Aberdeen last winter apparently had some kind of gloop all over them. They were virtually naked too,' he said slowly. 'So why would these ones wear formal attire? Look – that one's even got a bloody tie on.'

I squinted. Is that what it was? I hadn't been sure. It solidified my suspicions. 'When in Rome…' I said. 'They're dressed as you would be if you were visiting a foreign country and wanted to appeal to its leader. By matching the fashion of the day.' I considered. 'Check their pockets.'

Byron gave me a sidelong glance then stepped into the nightmarish hole. I heard fumbling and a muffled hiss before everything went silent. 'What is it?' I asked.

He didn't answer. Quelling my squeamishness, I looked into the hole. Byron was staring at a tattered piece of paper. He held it up. 'It was in the middle one's inside pocket.'

I peered at it. Bloody Gaelic again. I tried to translate it. 'Arrive here for all Fomori to ask for…' I frowned. Er… 'A fox?'

'We come here on behalf of all Fomori demons,' Byron corrected, 'to request a peaceful settlement between the Highlands and the Lowlands.'

Oh. 'No foxes?'

'No. But,' he said, in a bid to make me feel better, 'the words are fairly similar. It's an easy mistake to make.' It was unfortunate that the magic inside me assured me he was lying. He offered a half smile and stepped out. 'The demons came here to petition my father for peace. And they ended up dead.'

I gave another quick glance at the three Fomori bodies. Whatever other secrets they'd held, they were never going to reveal them now. This document was all we had. 'When they say peace, what do they mean exactly?'

Byron's expression was cold. 'It's all written down here. In return for the Sidhe dropping the Veil and returning the Lowlands to their former state, the Fomori were prepared to open trade negotiations and make amends for wrongs done in the past.'

I rocked back on my heels. 'Wow. Aifric never mentioned this to you?'

'As far as I know, he never mentioned it to anyone. Maybe he never saw it. He might have killed these three before they got the chance to make the offer.'

I mulled it over. Aifric had mentioned that he'd made a deal with the Fomori but what he'd actually said was that he'd killed my entire Clan at the Fomoris' insistence to stop them from coming to the Highlands and killing many more. He'd told me this over the telephone so I couldn't be sure of the veracity of his words, but it seemed as if they'd had a kernel of truth. All the same, I'd seen nothing from any of the Fomori demons I'd encountered that suggested they wanted to broker a deal with us now. Of course there was May, but she was unique. The Fomori demons were vicious monsters who had annexed half our country. They lived in darkness and, to all intents and purposes, kept other races as slaves. How could we ever come to an agreement with them? Nevertheless, my skin tingled. Something like this really could change the world. A niggling voice at the back of my mind whispered 'prophecy' and every part of me seemed to light up. Don't jump to conclusions, Tegs, I warned myself.

'What was it really like for you?' I asked. 'After the demons grabbed you, I mean.'

Byron grimaced. 'I was unconscious for most of the time. They certainly weren't kind to me.'

I bit my lip. He'd been in a sorry state when I'd found him. A group of demons looking for peace wouldn't have tortured the Steward's son. Something else occurred to me. 'If someone like me was discovered to have infiltrated the Moncrieffe Lands, what do you think your father would do to me?' Byron looked at me impassively. I waved my hand. 'Okay, bad example. How about if it was the MacFie Lands?'

'They'd probably hurt you. Are you trying to make excuses for the Fomori demons? Justifying the fact that they hurt me because I intruded on their turf? Because they've *killed* people here, Integrity. Recently.'

I spoke quietly. 'I know. You killed one of them too.' Byron scowled at my reference to the demon he'd barbecued in Perth and I held up my hand. 'I'm not trying to make excuses for them. I'm just…' I shrugged. 'I don't know. Maybe trying to see things from their point of view. I've been a criminal for most of my life, Byron. I guess that makes me a bad person – but I'm not evil.'

'You've never killed anyone,' he pointed out.

True, and I wasn't planning to do so. I persisted. 'Most of the world believes that my father was a mass murderer. Clan Adair is being wiped from existence. Even the history books mentioning us have been … amended.' I leaned forward, suddenly animated by the idea. 'What if it's not the first time? What if we believe the Fomori are evil for no other reason than we've been told they are? What if history is wrong?'

Byron looked at me for a long moment. It was good that he was no longer dismissing my theories out of hand but he still didn't buy it. 'It's a big leap.'

'Yeah, but it's possible. Maybe they're not the villains, Byron. Maybe we are.'

He sighed and glanced at the three bodies. 'Regardless of what's going on with the demons either now or in the past, we need to get a move on. I wasn't expecting the, er, delay upstairs.'

'Is that what you're calling it?'

Amusement flickered in his eyes. 'Come on.'

'You went to all the trouble of sneaking in past the border,' I told him, 'and yet you've left a great big pyrokinesis-induced hole in your father's study. Isn't that going to be something of a giveaway?'

'I knew I'd have to cover my tracks,' he said. 'Just as I knew that having the library next door was going to be an advantage.'

I was still confused. 'What do you mean?'

He smiled sadly. 'Watch.' He strode out and opened the library door.

I gaped; it was a beautiful space. Say what you like about Aifric, this was magnificent. Even in the gloom of the wee hours, shelves upon shelves stretched out. I couldn't stop myself reaching over to the nearest one and trailing my finger along the leather-bound books. 'This is wonderful,' I breathed.

'Yes.' Byron took a deep breath and flicked his fingers, sending out a plume of fire straight ahead.

I yelped in alarm. 'What the hell are you doing?' I made to run forward but he grabbed my arm and pulled me back. The old books had already caught fire, the smell of burning paper filling the air.

'You might not have come prepared, Integrity, but I did. One of my best friends is in a dungeon because of me; I'm going to blackmail Tipsania to draw her out of hiding; I've broken into my own father's study.' His eyes studied me intently. 'If all that, plus burning down his house, means removing him from power and showing the rest of the world what he's really like, it's more than worth it. Collateral damage.'

Fire rippled along the walls. It wouldn't be long before the whole place was ablaze. 'Just how far are you prepared to go?' I whispered.

He didn't blink. 'I thought he'd killed you,' he replied simply.

'He didn't.'

'Not for want of trying.' He tugged gently on my arm. 'We need to leave.'

'There are people inside here! Sleeping! You can't—' I was interrupted by a loud fire alarm screeching from all corners of the castle.

'My first Gift is Pyrokinesis and I was a precocious child,' Byron said. 'The fire systems here are up to date.

It's about the only thing that is. Now we really need to go.'

We pelted to another room where Byron yanked open the window and all but shoved me out. He dived after me and we began running down towards the driveway, away from the growing inferno that was the Moncrieffe stronghold. Everyone would be too occupied with dealing with the fire to look for anyone scurrying off but I still felt rather sick. Just as with my foolish actions in altering the traffic lights back in Perth, there was still the possibility that someone would get hurt.

Byron, seeming to sense my reluctance, slowed down. 'Trust me, they'll all be fine.'

'You can't be sure of that. And won't someone have called Aifric and told him what's going on? He'll be on his way here.'

'Which,' he said with infinite patience, 'is why we need to hurry.'

We reached his car and jumped in. Byron gunned the engine and careened down the road. 'How did you get here?'

'Car,' I said. 'Bob is waiting with it.' I checked my watch. There were still ten minutes before my deadline to meet him.

Byron nodded, driving past the border and then coming to a halt. He sprang out and began using telekinesis to return both the flagpole and the slightly singed fabric to their original places. From out of nowhere, Bob's tiny shape flew at him. 'What are you doing?' he shrieked.

Nonplussed, Byron batted him away. 'I'm busy,' he said. 'Just hang on.'

Bob's eyes were wild. I walked up behind him and softly murmured his name. He swung round. 'Uh

Integrity! You're…' he glanced at Byron. 'You're alive! It's a miracle!'

Byron grunted as the pole dropped back into place. I smiled at the genie. 'It's alright, Bob. He knows.'

His face screwed up. 'Well so much for that master plan,' he grumbled. 'Isn't he pissed off?'

I opened my mouth to answer but the expression on Bob's face stymied me. 'What?' I asked.

'You – you – you had sex! You shagged him, you dolt!' He put his hands on his hips as if it were a personal affront.

'How do you…?' Oops. I mentally slapped myself.

'How do I know? How do I know?' His voice was getting higher and higher. 'I'm a magnificent being with powers you can only dream of!'

'Bob,' I said tiredly.

'Your T-shirt's on back to front,' he informed me. I glanced down. Ah. 'You'd better pray you used protection,' he continued. 'Who knows what nasty disease you might have caught? And what about Tipsania?'

I reached out, grabbed him and cupped him in both hands to muffle his protests. He banged around, nipping with his teeth at the soft, fleshy part of my palm. I grimaced in pain. Byron, satisfied he'd returned the border to its original state, strolled over and bent down. 'Hi Bob,' he said cheerfully. 'Great to see you too.'

'Won't anyone notice that the Moncrieffe flag is a bit burnt?' I asked anxiously.

Byron shrugged. 'If they do, they'll think it's some old damage from years gone by. I don't think it's been changed since I was in nappies. I only found out that I could gain access this way a couple of weeks ago – although it helps that half the Moncrieffe Sidhe are in Perth for the stag party. Those trolls were good at keeping their mouths shut.' He gave me a sidelong glance. 'They still are.'

Bob yelled something. We both ignored him. 'What now?' I asked.

'I tie you up, shove you into the boot of my car and prevent you from leaving me ever again.' His expression was so deadpan that for a moment I believed him. 'Or you could find Tipsania and tell her what's going on so I don't have to make a show of threatening Candy to draw her out.'

'You still want to go ahead with planning the wedding? I thought you didn't have the evidence against Aifric to pull off your plan.'

'Even with this Fomori letter, I don't think I have. But the stag night was scheduled for tonight so there would be enough time for Plan B if I needed it. There's a fortnight to go before the ceremony. You might not be dead but my father's still a monster who needs to be stopped. You won't be safe until he's dealt with.' He brushed a lock of hair away from my face. 'You wouldn't trust me before but you can trust me on this.'

Worry gnawed at me. Aifric had been prepared to abandon his only son to the Fomori demons beyond the Veil. I dreaded to imagine what he might do if he discovered just how far Byron would go to betray him. But he wasn't my father and I had to let Byron do this. 'Okay,' I whispered. 'Okay. I'll get Tipsania. I'll tell her the plan and take her to her father's to get ready.'

He relaxed and pulled me towards him, one arm wrapped round me while the other cupped the back of my head. 'Despite everything, this might have been the best night of my life,' he said.

He hadn't lied to me; I couldn't lie to him. 'Mine too.'

His head dipped. Bob, still caught in between my hands, zapped me with an electric shock. 'I'm still here!' he yelled. 'And you won't be saying that soppy stuff tomorrow when you realise you have itchy pants!'

I kissed Byron and pulled back, releasing Bob. He spun up into the air, still indignant. Then he stared behind me. 'Fire! There's a fire up there!'

'We should go,' I told Byron.

'Yeah,' he nodded. 'We should.'

Neither of us moved.

'Make a wish, Uh Integrity!' Bob yelled. 'I can put the fire out if you just wish for it!'

I watched Byron. 'I'm not sure this fire will ever go out,' I said quietly. Then I kissed him once more and turned away to my car.

Chapter Eleven

'He wasn't angry?' Speck asked. 'When he realised you were alive?'

'Oh, he was raging,' I said happily. 'He got past it though.'

'He was so furious that he set his own castle on fire,' Bob added with a knowing waggle of his eyebrows. 'But that's confidential. Don't tell anyone.'

Lexie threw herself at me. 'I'm so thrilled for you!' she squealed, wrapping her arms round my chest. 'He's been working against his own father all this time! That's brilliant!'

'I'm not sure that encouraging patricide is a cause for celebration,' Brochan said.

I glared at him. 'Byron's not going to kill Aifric.'

'Are you sure?'

'Of course I am.' I folded my arms. Then I remembered the coldness in Byron's expression whenever he mentioned his father and the way he'd said the words 'collateral damage'. I dropped my arms. 'I think I am.'

Brochan wasn't the only one who was concerned. Taylor rubbed his chin and sat down with a heavy sigh. 'It's a convoluted plan. A fake wedding?'

'Yeah.'

'The best plans are the simplest ones.'

'Yeah.'

'This is not a simple plan.'

'To be fair,' I argued, 'we've not managed to come up with anything to beat Aifric. At least Byron is trying.'

Brochan's gills bristled. 'We've been busy.'

I threw up my hands. 'I know! I wasn't blaming anyone. If anyone should have been working out some way of dealing with the Steward, it should have been me. All I'm saying is that Byron's way might work and we should support it.'

'*Might* work,' Speck said. 'Key word *might*.'

'Yeah,' Taylor drawled in agreement. 'I'm not sure about those odds.'

Lexie wrinkled her nose. 'Tegs is right. Byron Moncrieffe has had nothing but this to think about. He's probably already considered every other avenue. He succeeded in breaking into the Moncrieffe castle, didn't he?'

'Lex, it hardly takes a criminal mastermind to sneak into your own damned home.'

She whirled round, squaring up to Speck. 'Oh yeah? Because last night, I seem to recall that you couldn't even sneak into your own bedroom after doing some midnight magic gallivanting!'

The rest of us exchanged looks. Perhaps it was time to change the subject. 'Just because we don't have a plan yet,' Taylor said, 'doesn't mean that we can't come up with one. Get Byron down here, Tegs, and we can thrash out some ideas.'

'I can't. He has to stay and make sure everything is ready for the wedding. And he's got his Plan B to sort out.'

'You don't even know what Plan B is.'

I sighed and glanced down at my feet. 'I'm not blind to the fact that it's not perfect, I'm really not. But he was right when he said that the Sidhe and the Clans aren't my world. I don't know them like he does. In the absence of any alternatives, I think we need to go with him.'

Taylor ran a hand through his hair. 'We have an alternative.'

There was something about the tone of his voice that I didn't like. 'What?'

He wouldn't meet my eyes. 'We play Aifric at his own game. I've done some research and it wouldn't be too hard to get hold of some kind of poison…'

Bob clapped his hands together in glee. 'Now we're talking!'

I counted to ten. 'I can't believe you're bringing that up as an idea.' Taylor was normally as anti-violence as I was.

'Take a look around, Tegs. We saw exactly the same vision that you did.' He pointed over to the faint patch on the cobbles where my mother and father had breathed their last – and I had breathed my first. 'He ran a sword into your father's back, not to mention murdering your entire Clan. Maybe it's time to put your pacifism to one side.'

'We've been through this before.' My jaw was clenched so tight that it hurt. 'No. Nothing's changed since last time.'

'A lot's changed. Byron is with us now. That bodes well for the future.'

Brochan shook his massive head from side to side. 'I told you not to mention this.'

I glared at them. 'So you've been discussing this while I was away? Behind my back?'

'Stop being so testy. It's a reasonable conversation to have. You wouldn't have to have anything to do with it. One of us could manage it for you.' Taylor finally looked at me directly. 'We need to keep you safe, Tegs. Having this temporary reprieve has made us all realise just how good life could be here when we don't have to keep looking over our shoulders.'

'No. And if any of you try anything like that, we're done. I don't care how good your intentions are, I won't

have it. We are better than that.' I paused. 'Is that clear?'
Everyone nodded. I tried again. 'I said, is that clear?'

This time I received a chorus of replies. 'Yes, Tegs.'

'You do still have one wish left,' Bob began.

I pointed at him. 'Zip it.'

Lexie raised her hand tentatively. 'Are *you* angry
now?'

I exhaled. 'No. I understand where you're coming
from. And you don't have to put up your hand to speak,
Lex.'

'Are you sure you're not angry?'

I narrowed my eyes. 'If you want I'll tell you all a
joke to prove just how un-angry I am.'

Taylor stood up and backed away. 'There's no need
for that.'

Sorley, who'd been sitting silently in the corner and
gnawing impressively on a yellowing toenail, glanced up.
'I'd like a joke.' Everyone groaned loudly and hushed
him. He shrugged his wide shoulders then he seemed to
squeak.

Lexie tilted her head, confused. 'Did your bones just
cheep?'

His eyebrows snapped together. 'I'm not cheap! I
swore fealty. I don't require financial remuneration
because my kind is too honourable to stoop to mere
monetary rewards.'

'No, I meant cheep. Like a bird.'

'No, you blasted pixie! I'm a damned troll.' There
was a momentary pause before there was another squeak.

Lexie stared round at us all. 'I'm not the only one
who heard that, right?'

'Sorley,' I asked, 'are you carrying around a haggis?'

'What?' He got to his feet, his face the picture of
outrage. 'Why would I carry one of those vermin around
with me? It's bad enough that they get into everything

and chomp on all my equipment. I wouldn't want to touch one.' His loose-fitting shirt bulged; poking its way up from the collar was the tiny questing nose of a haggis. Sorley whipped round and fumbled with his shirt.

'If you want the trolls to sort out this mess then we can,' he bellowed, trying to disguise what was now a series of high-pitched haggis complaints. 'We can muster within the hour and march on the Cruaich.'

'This isn't your fight.'

He turned round, the haggis no longer in sight. 'It's Clan Adair's fight and we are Clan Adair,' he said stiffly.

I shook my head and smiled. 'We're not fighting. We're too smart for that.'

The Foinse spun down from a nearby window, nuzzling into Sorley's belly. There was another, much happier, squeak.

Brochan raised his eyebrows. 'I wouldn't count on that.'

***

Taylor and I set off at first light, heading north again, although this time we were heading for the small MacQuarrie Clan Lands near the east coast. This wasn't going to be a particularly dangerous venture and my old mentor's presence effectively killed two birds with one stone. Because of Taylor's age or gender, Tipsania was more likely to listen to him than she was to me – and she'd probably require some persuading to go along with Byron's fake wedding plans. Plus, Taylor's presence appeased the others. Speck, in particular, seemed to think that as soon as I was let loose in the wild blue yonder I wouldn't be able to stop myself from running full pelt back to Byron and conceding my wits, personality and independence to him with one simple kiss. Given his relationship with Lexie, he ought to have known better.

I'd made a half-hearted attempt to get Bob to come along with us but he'd huffed so much about being dragged away from his latest boxset, not to mention about being left to wait around in the dark while I had 'thrilling, dangerous sex' – his words, not mine – that in the end I left him behind. I wasn't going to be gone long and I certainly had no intention of using up that last wish, no matter how often he dropped it into the conversation. It was rather nice to get some time alone with Taylor. I'd missed our chats. All in all, things seemed to be looking up.

Not long after we hit the main road, when I finally managed to get a signal on my phone, I rang Morna. 'How's it going?'

'Well, dear,' she answered, slightly caustic, 'you spend time alone in close proximity with Tipsania Scrymgeour and *you* tell *me* how you think it's going. I swear the MacQuarrie Chieftain almost took his father's sword and lopped off her head the other night.'

I winced. 'Is she being difficult?'

'That girl won't give me a moment's peace. And every time I suggest to her that good manners are a boon, she spits fire.'

'Uh…'

'Things are fine. We've relocated away from the main castle and we're in a cottage near the border. I'm working on placating the MacQuarries, too.'

I took a deep breath. 'That's good of you but you don't have to worry about it now. I'm on my way up. It's kind of complicated but I'm going to take Tipsania back to her father. You won't have to worry about her for more than another hour or two.'

There was a pause. 'Could you perhaps make it three or four hours? She's cleaning the cottage and I'd hate to pull her away from that. If she keeps it up then at least the

160

MacQuarries will get something out of all this besides my flowers.'

I laughed. We all enjoyed the fact that Tipsania was a bit of a neat freak. 'Sorry.'

'Are you quite sure about this, dear? Returning her to the Bull will undo all the progress she's made. The man is a buffoon. He's bound to rub off on her again.'

I grimaced. 'He certainly is a buffoon but it won't be for long. I'll explain what's going on when I get there. It's probably best if you don't mention anything to her in the meantime.'

'Anything for a quiet life,' Morna replied cheerfully. 'Is this going to save Scotland?'

I considered her question. If everything went to plan, it just might. 'Who knows? I still don't think we should put too much credence in the prophecy. No one else does.'

Morna snorted. 'That's because they're too afraid.'

I didn't have anything to say to that. Hanging up, I settled down while Taylor threw me an arch glance and sped up to overtake a trundling tractor that seemed to be dropping more hay than it was actually carrying. 'Is she still harping on about the prophecy?' he asked.

'Yeah.' I nibbled my bottom lip. 'Maybe this plan of Byron's will mean that we stop Aifric and get him locked up. Then Scotland will be saved.'

'Then why isn't Golden Boy named as the one?'

I thought about it. 'Because he'd never have believed the truth about his father if it weren't for me,' I said eventually.

'Right,' Taylor drawled.

'It might not even be me. It says the one Adair will save Alba. That could be my child. Or my grandchild. Or any number of descendants.'

'Do you really want that burden to be on someone else?'

I sighed. 'No.'

'And since when were you planning on children?' His shoulders shot up as a thought struck him. 'You're not pregnant, are you?'

I smirked. I could have a little fun with this. 'We never did have that conversation about the birds and the bees, you know. I'm not sure I know how it all works.'

Taylor's cheeks reddened. 'I asked Bella to talk to you.'

I nodded. 'She did. She told me never to charge less than fifty and to make sure they paid up front.'

He seemed to go even redder. 'She said *what*?'

'Byron did mention something about...' I wrinkled my nose as if trying to remember. 'Con ... dom? I told him I was good enough at conning for the both of us and that I didn't need Dom to help me.'

'Tegs?'

'Mm?'

'You're making fun of me, aren't you?'

I grinned. 'Yep.'

'That boy doesn't know what he's getting himself into,' he muttered.

'He's one of the good guys, Taylor. No matter what happens, remember that.'

Taylor was silent for a long while. 'How often do the good guys win?'

'Sometimes it might take them a while but they always win in the end.'

'How do you know?'

'George Lucas.' Taylor hissed through his teeth. I shrugged. 'What's the bet that the prophecy is actually about rescuing a haggis called Scotland from the clutches of a grumpy troll called Sorley?' Taylor opened his mouth to answer and I realised what I'd said. 'Whoa – no actual bet. It was a figure of speech.'

It was his turn to grin. 'Yeah. You're backtracking because you know the good guys win in the end.'

I laughed again and reached over to give him a quick hug. 'Amen to that.'

***

It was still fairly early when we reached the MacQuarrie border. Taylor parked carefully and we both got out and walked up on foot. 'If you didn't know that Morna was visiting these Lands,' I said wonderingly, 'you could certainly work it out.'

Taylor put an arm round my shoulders and drew me close as we gazed in front of us. 'She's definitely something,' he agreed.

Swathes of multi-coloured heather covered a hilly bank, reaching all the way around it. There wasn't a pattern as such, and the flowers didn't spell out 'MacQuarrie' or anything as twee as that, but the different hues somehow fit – deep reds blending into seductive purples, followed by musky blues then brilliant greens. It was a damned shame Morna hadn't worked out how to make hot-pink heather. All the same, my gratitude to her was immeasurable. She kept going above and beyond our growing friendship. It wasn't just because of the prophecy; she believed in us. All of us. Either that or Tipsania had said some truly heinous things to the MacQuarries that Morna was trying to atone for.

Alongside the flowers there was a winding road leading up, no doubt, to the main MacQuarrie buildings which were currently invisible to the eye. On the other side was a forest. It was an even more stunning copse than the Cruaich grove. Trees of all shapes and sizes grew there, each one perfectly placed to receive the optimum amount of sunlight or shade, depending on the species. Was this a result of nature or of magic? It occurred to me that I could beg, borrow or steal as much of Morna's Gift as I wanted but I'd never have the knowledge to support it so I could achieve something on this scale. The Bull's Gift was the same. I'd stolen Aura Reading from him without realising it but it hadn't done me the slightest good without a key to understand the auras. Admittedly, I wasn't convinced that the Bull had a key either. He'd been convinced that my aura – identical to my father's – meant that I was evil. Slightly wicked, perhaps. Definitely not evil.

'Maybe,' I mused, 'Sidhe are only given one or two Gifts because that's all they can handle. Having a lot doesn't work. You become a jack of all trades instead of a master of one.'

'Tegs,' Taylor said, his voice taut with tension. 'What's that?'

I turned my head, my veins turning ice cold as I saw a plume of dark smoke snaking its way upwards to the clear, blue sky. The MacQuarries wouldn't bother with a bonfire; with Morna visiting, the Gifts they had at their disposal negated the need to burn old crops or garden waste. And it was hardly the weather for an open hearth. Of course, one of the MacQuarries could simply be playing around with their magic. Or it could be something far, far worse.

'Where's the MacQuarrie flagpole?' I asked, whipping my head around.

'I don't see it,' Taylor muttered. 'But it might be round that hill or near another section of the border.'

I ran ahead, feeling the brush of faint magic across my skin. 'There's virtually no border,' I spat. A scream rent the air. That was when I began to sprint.

I paid no more attention to the beautiful field of heather. Instead, heart pounding, I ran as fast as I could.

When I reached the top of the hill, I saw what was wrong. On the other side, less than a hundred feet away, there was a quaint little thatched cottage. Its roof was burning and billowing smoke was pouring from its open door. That was the good news. Outside were two Fomori demons. There was a gap between them but they looked as if they were struggling to hold onto something. Or someone with the Gift of Invisibility.

'Tipsania!' I yelled and ran towards them.

Both demons' heads jerked up and I heard their snarls. One of them fell back and yelped in pain. I smiled grimly to myself; I knew from experience just how sharp Tipsania's kicks could be. Then I caught a glint of sunlight from a long, lethal blade that he was holding and my smile vanished.

I searched deep inside myself, scanning through the different trickles of magic which I'd stolen from the various Sidhe at the Cruaich. I had to have something which would work. Dowsing was useless, as was Animal Summoning. Getting a creature here would take far too long. Apportation, however…

I focused in on the long knife and concentrated. It shimmered for a few seconds before zapping away to drop into the old well back at the Adair Lands. The demon gaped down at his suddenly empty hands, baffled by what had happened. 'You bitch!' he screamed. He charged right for me.

There was a strange cracking sound and the ground beneath our feet trembled. A moment later the demon was sprawled face first, his ankle caught on a root which had appeared from nowhere. Morna. I looked around but I couldn't see her and there wasn't time to seek out her position. There was still another demon to deal with. From the way his arm was being wrenched from one side to another, he still seemed to be wrestling with Tipsania. I was almost out of options.

I drew out the very last of the Illusion magic, using it to make my hands light up as if on fire. 'Release her or I will barbecue you!' I shouted.

The demon turned to me. His expression was an ugly snarl but the distraction was enough. He was yanked to the side and let out a frustrated screech.

'I'm free!' Tipsania's voice screamed. 'End him!'

I swallowed hard and raised my hands. The demon cowered, holding his hands over his head. Then Taylor was by my side, handing me a loop of rope. 'It was in the boot of the car,' he explained. 'It seemed like the sort of thing you might need.'

I nodded gratefully, darted over to the creature before he could change his mind about surrendering and tied his hands and feet together. He lay curled foetal-like in the long grass while I surveyed the damage. 'Where's Morna?' I scanned around. 'Morna!' I called. 'You can come out now. It's safe!'

'How the hell did Fomori demons get the border down and get through here?' Taylor asked.

'They're not demons,' I said tersely. 'Morna!'

'Eh?'

'That one who tripped and knocked himself unconscious called me a bitch.' Where the hell was Morna?

'Some of them must speak English though?'

'Not with Aberdonian accents, they don't.'

Taylor grabbed my arm. 'There.'

I looked at where he was pointing and saw Tipsania materialise. She let out a cry and fell to her knees. Something flickered in my peripheral vision; the main castle inhabitants had apparently realised something was wrong. I dimly registered Angus leading the charge towards us. The MacQuarries weren't my focus though; it was the crumpled figure at Tipsania's feet, almost completely camouflaged by the long grass, which made me forget to breathe.

Time seemed to slow down. It was probably only seconds before I reached Tipsania and collapsed beside her but it felt much longer. When I saw what state Morna was in, things got even worse. She was on her back, her white hands clutching at the hilt of the knife that protruded from her belly. Blood bubbled up from her lips as she tried to breathe. Oh God, oh God, oh God.

'I don't know what to do,' Tipsania yelled, grabbing my sleeve. 'What do we do?'

My jaw worked as I tried to speak. Morna's eyelashes fluttered as she turned her face to me. She opened her mouth to say something but no words came out.

'Integrity!' Tipsania screamed. 'What the fuck do we do?'

I didn't know. I reached down for the knife. Maybe I should pull it out or do something to stem the blood that was seeping out from the edges of the ragged wound. My heart thumped against my ribcage with fear. None of the Gifts I had would work, not a single one. Think, Integrity. Bloody think.

Taylor joined us, taking in the situation in one glance. Deftly he examined the wound. I didn't need to read his expression to know how grave the situation was. I grabbed hold of Morna's hands. 'Let go,' I told her, hoping my voice didn't betray my panic. 'I need you to let go.'

For a moment I wasn't sure she'd heard me then one hand moved away from the lethal blade and flailed upwards. 'Integrity,' Morna whispered.

'Don't talk,' I said. 'Conserve your strength.'

'Integrity,' Taylor said, his voice strained. 'The blade is too deep. There's nothing you can do.'

I paid him no attention. His skills lay in first aid, not mortal wounds; he didn't know everything. I yanked off my jacket then pulled my T-shirt over my head, before bending over to dab at the wound and clear some of the blood so I could get a better look. Maybe the blade wasn't that long. It was possible that none of Morna's vital organs had been hit.

She moaned in response. 'Stop,' she gasped.

I ignored her. 'Blood loss,' I muttered. 'We need to stop her from losing more blood.'

Taylor tried again. 'Integrity…'

I growled at him and pressed down, trying to staunch the flow. Tipsania reached round me to help. A heartbeat later Angus was with us. 'What the hell happened?'

'We need to get her to a hospital.'

He nodded. 'There's already an ambulance on the way.'

'Is there anyone here with the Gift of Healing?' I asked, even though I already knew the answer.

'No.' His was face was pale. 'Why would Fomori demons come here? Why would they do this?'

'Integrity,' Morna whispered again. 'Take it.'

I stared at her face. 'What?'

'Take it,' she repeated. Her pupils were unfocused. A tear rolled from the corner of eye, trickling down her lined cheek.

'I told you to be quiet,' I choked.

'It doesn't hurt any more.'

'Morna…'

'Take it.'

'No.'

Angus shook his head. 'I don't understand. What is she talking about?'

Morna's lips moved again. Tipsania's face was bloodless as she looked at me. 'She says it's her time.'

Morna blinked. 'Do it.'

I couldn't begin to imagine where she got the strength to speak. I clenched my teeth. 'Don't you dare give up, Morna Carnegie. It is *not* your time. The ambulance is on its way and this time tomorrow you're going to be scolding us all from a comfy hospital bed.'

She smiled sadly. 'No, I'm not. Take it, Integrity. You'll need it.'

I heaved in a ragged breath. 'You're too weak. It will kill you.'

'I'm…' Her chest rattled as she struggled to speak. 'Already dead.' She clutched at me. 'Take it now.'

I glanced at Taylor. Sorrowfully, he gave me the tiniest shake of his head and rocked back on his haunches. Tears flowed freely from Tipsania's eyes and Angus had to glance away. Only Morna was calm. She fixed me with a serene gaze. 'Do it.'

My tongue darted out, wetting my dry lips. I rubbed furiously at my own eyes and then focused. I could see the swirl of magic within her. She was right – it was already leaking away, dissipating into the ether. She had only seconds left. My body was racked with uncontrollable shivers while Morna's skin seemed to grow paler by the second.

I released the breath I was holding and did what she asked, pulling her magic inside me. The force of her Gift almost overwhelmed me as it flooded my system. I fell back, dizzy and sick and gulping for air, just as Morna's hand dropped and she went completely still.

Tipsania gave a choked sob. Through blurred vision, I saw Angus reach down and close Morna's eyelids. No. It wasn't going to happen like this. I wasn't going to let it. I threw back my head and screamed. 'Bob!' Then

Angus was by my side and hauling me up to my feet and away from Morna's body.

Taylor rushed round and grabbed my shoulders. 'Don't do it, Tegs.'

'Bob can get here. I still have a wish left. I can…'

He cupped my face and forced me to look at him. 'It's wrong. You know it's wrong.'

I didn't give a toss. Bob had told me before that he didn't have the kind of power to resurrect people but I'd make him do it – no matter what it took. I opened my mouth to yell for him again. This time I'd make damned sure the genie heard me.

Taylor slapped my cheek, stunning me into silence. 'Morna wouldn't want this.' His voice hardened. '*You* don't want this.'

I stared at him for a long moment then I sagged against Angus, barely able to hold my own weight. That's when I really started to cry.

Chapter Twelve

I don't know how much time passed before I finally stood up again. I declined Taylor's offer of help and brushed myself off, then swung my head with bitter malevolence towards the two supposed Fomori demons. They were encircled by a large group of stony-faced MacQuarries. The Chieftain stood to one side, his arms folded and his expression grim. I walked over, forcing my arms to remain loose by my sides.

'Chieftain Adair.' He inclined his head. 'Words cannot express my sorrow. We granted Morna Carnegie sanctuary and failed. This loss is ours to bear.'

'It wasn't your fault,' I said dully. 'I'm the one who sent her here with Tipsania.' I glanced back at my old nemesis who was still kneeling beside Morna's body, her face slack with shock. 'And besides, if we're going to go down that road then Lily's death was down to me.' I tilted up my chin and met his eyes. 'And we both know that's not true.' I knew that the guilt about what had happened here would affect me for the rest of my life but I also knew that I hadn't wielded the blade: *I* hadn't killed Moira. I was going to have to work hard to remember that.

Straightening my shoulders, I walked over to the two captives. 'Who sent you here?'

The nearest one hawked up a ball of phlegm. Before he could spit it in my direction, a MacQuarrie Sidhe cuffed him hard on the side of his head. He reeled down to the ground, making a demon-shaped dent in Morna's pretty heather.

I shook my head. 'Don't.' I hauled him upright and stared into his eyes. They still looked like Fomori eyes.

'They're demons,' Chieftain MacQuarrie said. 'We should execute them and be done with it.'

'They're not demons,' I replied. 'Not that that should make a difference.' I pointed to the brilliantly blue sky, which had only a few fluffy clouds scudding across it. 'The sun is shining.'

If the MacQuarries were confused, they didn't say anything. I ran my tongue across my teeth and took a deep breath then I grasped ahead with the full force of my soul, ripping away the last of the magic that remained there. Morna's killer let out a howl of anguished pain. I just prevented myself from flinching and turned to his companion and did the same to him. Then I stared at them. They weren't demons but neither were they Sidhe. I crouched down by the first one. 'Hey,' I said softly. 'Remember me?'

Ramsay, the surly human who'd been on Chandra's crew when I was ambushed on my way to my Clan Lands, glared at me. 'Thought you were dead,' he grunted.

'Ta dah,' I answered with a grim smile. 'I'm not.'

'Fucking Sidhe.'

'That sentiment would make more sense if you weren't a hypocrite about it. If you really hated all Sidhe, you wouldn't have taken the contract to come here. You wouldn't have let a Sidhe wrap you in their magic so all this could be blamed on demons from beyond the Veil.'

His mouth flattened. The same MacQuarrie as before raised his hand as if to hit him again. I flashed a frown and his fist dropped.

'Who hired you?'

A glint of stubbornness lit his expression. 'Soon as I tell you, you'll kill me.'

I remained calm. 'I'm not the murderer here.'

'Unless reading minds is one of your blasted Sidhe tricks, you'll never find out the truth.'

I considered this before looking at his companion. His head hung low so I reached over and gently put my fingers under his chin to force him to meet my eyes. He still wouldn't do it. I pursed my lips; I could work with this.

Digging out my phone from my back pocket, I found Chandra's number and dialled. She answered almost immediately. 'Designs by Chandra,' she trilled. 'How may we be service of you?'

'It's me.'

She dropped the phone voice almost immediately. 'Hey. What's doing?'

'Chandra,' I said, deliberately using her name so that the two bastards in front of me knew who I was talking to. 'I'm looking at an old buddy of yours. Ramsay.'

There was a moment of silence. 'Did he try to hurt you?'

'Not me.'

She sucked in a breath. 'But someone else.'

'Yep.' I watched Ramsay's companion stare at the phone. He was obviously trying to work out how someone who had a hot-pink mobile had managed to best him. Sucks to him.

'He wasn't working for me, Tegs. I told you, I'm not in that business any more. After what happened with you, I decided it was time to retire for good.'

'I'm sure I could persuade you to do one or two more jobs for me. They wouldn't take long.'

The nameless human stopped caring about the colour of my phone and suddenly paled. He swung alarmed eyes towards Ramsay who looked away, his jaw set.

'Er...' Chandra paused. 'Is that really you, Tegs?'

173

'Ramsay is here with a friend,' I told her. 'Human but looks kind of like a troll. Heavy brow, wiry hair, bad skin.' I looked him over. 'Wearing a silver necklace with a tooth on it.'

'Smack.'

I frowned. 'Smack who?'

'That's his name.'

'Ah.' I raised my eyebrows at him. He was frozen, not even blinking. Somehow I didn't think the innocent puppy-dog look was going to work for him here. 'You must know where he's from.'

'Little town north of Inverness. Some godforsaken hole with nothing more than a post box and a pub to commend it.'

'And he has family there?'

'Tegs, you're not really suggesting…'

'The Bull!' he burst out. 'It was the Bull who hired us!'

Ramsay sighed loudly in disgust.

'Never mind, Chandra,' I said. 'Talk to you later.' She murmured back, obviously confused. I'd explain later. I hung up and crossed my arms. 'What were your instructions?' I asked.

'To retrieve his daughter.'

At his words, Tipsania flung her head up and stared at him with a haunted expression. Her hand curled round her own throat.

'And do what?'

He sighed. 'Bring her back to him. That's all.'

I shook my head. 'No, it's not.'

His nostrils flared. 'We were to dispatch the old woman too.'

'Dispatch?' Taylor growled.

'Send her to Sidhe hell,' Ramsay said, unhelpfully. He received a kick for his effort. This time I didn't complain.

'That's not all, though, is it?'

'We were to get rid of as many MacQuarrie Sidhe as possible.'

There was an audible gasp from the others around me. My chest tightened. 'Why?'

'I don't know.'

'She asked why!' Angus spat.

'He's telling the truth,' I said. 'He doesn't know.'

I turned my back on him, shoving my hands in my pockets and walking away a few metres. It was only a few days since I'd seen Tipsania's father and been assured that he thought she was dead. Something had happened since then to change his mind. Not only had he worked out that she was here but he'd turned vengeful in the process. I gnawed on the inside of my cheek. Something didn't fit.

Tipsania, looking more dishevelled than I'd ever seen her, got to her feet. She pushed her limp hair away from her tear-stained face and cleared her throat. 'No,' she said, her voice ringing out across the meadow. 'He wouldn't do that.' She put her hands on her hips as if daring me to disagree. The trouble was that she was right.

There was no denying that the Bull was a bully and I wouldn't have put it past him to kidnap his own daughter. I wouldn't even have put it past him to suggest that anyone helping her – like Morna – be killed in the process. But to come here? Onto another Clan's Lands with the intention of destroying as many of those Sidhe as possible? That was tantamount to inciting civil war. The MacQuarries were considered the weakest of all Sidhe and the Bull, with his magically enhanced wealth, would probably have no trouble in seeing them off, but others would protest if he moved against the MacQuarries. No one would stand for another's Clan seat being invaded unless…

I sucked in a breath. 'Where's the ambulance?' I whirled round. 'How long has it been?'

Angus blinked and checked his watch. 'Too long,' he admitted. 'I'd forgotten with Morna's … passing. They should have been here ages ago.'

Who had the power to stop the emergency services from getting through? Who had the impunity to cause bloodshed on another's Land? 'We need to get out of here,' I whispered. 'All of us.'

The MacQuarrie Chieftain cocked his head. 'What do you—?' He broke off mid-sentence, his eyes falling on something behind me. A heartbeat later I heard the engine. I closed my eyes briefly. Too late.

It was a stretch limousine. It glided towards us, halting next to where Morna lay. As the door opened, I raised my voice and spread out my arms. 'Everyone get back.' When they didn't immediately do as I said, I repeated it louder.

Tipsania seemed frozen. Taylor, sensing her dismay, grabbed her arm, pulling her back towards the crowd of MacQuarries for safety. The pair of them had only just moved past me when Aifric emerged. 'Try anything,' he smiled at us, 'Invisibility or Teleportation or goddamned flower arranging, and it'll be the last thing you do.'

It was hardly the most inspirational of threats. Then again, when three burly guys stepped out after him, each holding a shit-scary machine gun, it didn't need to be.

I watched them all. The Apportation trick had worked on Ramsay's knife but I wasn't sure how much magic it would take to work simultaneously on three guns and, with no practice, it was a dangerous manoeuvre. If it had just been me standing there, I would have tried it without thinking but there were fifty people at my back.

The last person to get out of the car was the Bull. His eyes landed immediately on Tipsania and he let out a choked cry, throwing out his arms as if to run towards her full of fatherly joy. He hadn't realised that Morna was lying next to him, however, and his foot caught on her outstretched hand. If Aifric hadn't grabbed him, he'd have gone flying. Tipsania snorted in disgust but I could feel her fear.

Aifric smiled at me, the very picture of dictatorial benevolence. 'Integrity,' he boomed. 'I'm so thrilled that you're still alive.' The scariest thing was that I knew he was telling the truth.

'If you want to call for Bob again,' Taylor murmured, 'now would be a really good time.'

If I could have been sure that Bob would hear me and appear in a flash I wouldn't have hesitated but there were too many variables to consider. I told my thumping heart to quieten down. I wasn't even close to waving my white flag – but I wasn't going to rush into anything either.

'I believed you, you know. The whole death shebang. It was very clever.' Aifric smiled again. 'Just not clever enough.' He paused. 'Tell me, does my son know you're alive?'

I prayed that my expression wouldn't give me away. If Aifric remained ignorant of Byron's actions, it could only work to our favour. I supposed there was a certain irony: Byron wouldn't believe that his father was evil and Aifric wouldn't believe that his son could plot against him. All the same, I didn't reply. I wasn't ready yet.

'What's the matter? Cat got your tongue?' he grinned, trying to appear disarming. 'Or are you still pretending to be a ghost? You know it took me some time to work out what my friend the Bull here was referring to when he kept going on about hauntings.'

I cursed inwardly. So the Bull had found a way past the compulsion after all. Maybe I could use his real name to order him to attack Aifric. That was an idea.

The Steward was already five steps ahead of me. 'Unfortunately for him,' he continued, 'your knowledge of his true name makes him too much of a liability these days. Even though he did as I asked in hiring these idiots to mop up things.' Aifric shrugged at the Bull. 'It's not my fault, friend. It's hers.'

He stepped away and flicked a finger at the gunmen. There was a sharp retort and then, as if in slow motion, a blossom of red appeared on the Bull's chest. He seemed puzzled initially and stared down at himself, then he spun and fell, landing in a sprawl next to Morna. Tipsania screamed, her knees buckling beneath her. The rest of us stared in horror. Sickness rose in my gullet, threatening to overwhelm me. Aifric Moncrieffe wasn't just the villain of the piece; he was bloody psychotic.

'It's quite a clever set-up, don't you think?' Aifric murmured. He jerked his thumb at Ramsay and Smack. 'The Bull hired them to get his daughter back then, when he refused to pay them, they took their revenge and gunned him down.' He rubbed his palms together. 'That was the plan I originally had but that was before I realised you were still breathing, Miss Adair. Now I have an even better idea.'

I couldn't help myself. Setting aside my unfeigned disgust at what he'd just done to the Bull, I drew myself up. 'Chieftain,' I growled.

Aifric put his hand up to his ear. 'Pardon?'

'Chieftain Adair, you prick.'

He laughed. 'Not for much longer. And it's not much of a Clan that you're Chieftain of, is it? Although I have to thank you for getting rid of the trolls for me. I'm not sure I'd have managed to broach the MacQuarrie border if it weren't for you.' His eyes narrowed. 'Call it my own petty revenge for you breaching mine. Is Pyrokinesis a Gift of yours or did you simply use a match?'

I breathed out. He definitely didn't know about Byron – that was something. Neither was he aware that I could steal Gifts. There was still some wiggle room.

Tipsania was gulping for air by my side. Any second now, she'd probably do something that would get her killed too.

'Don't worry, my dear,' Aifric said to her, apparently thinking the same thing. 'I need you. You're going to marry my son, after all.' Nonchalantly he inspected his fingernails. 'Your father's untimely death means you inherit more quickly and the Moncrieffes can get those Scrymgeour riches.'

'Never,' she gasped.

Aifric smirked and rolled forward on his toes. 'But I've still got your sweetheart.' He laughed at her expression. 'Tut, tut. Didn't your new best friend tell you? Integrity, I thought more of you than that.' He grinned. 'Candy is enjoying the very best dungeons that the Cruaich has to offer. He'll stay there at my pleasure.' He paused and licked his lips. 'Unless you step out of line, dear Tipsy. I've always known you and he had a thing going on. The truth is, I know just about everything.'

Nope, not everything. My blood was still fizzing with Morna's magic, not to mention the rest that was swirling around my system. If I could get Aifric out of the way, I could steal his. I just had to work out how to do it without his goons shooting everyone first.

'Steward!' the MacQuarrie Chieftain bellowed. 'This is outrageous! You cannot come here and do this. You will answer for your crimes!'

The three gun-toting goons raised their weapons once more. With my heart in my mouth, I yelled, 'No!'

Aifric was amused. 'There's no denying that you have some moves, *Chieftain,* but I don't think you can dodge bullets. What's to stop me from killing everyone right here, right now?'

Morals? Decency? A shred of empathy? None of those was worth mentioning to him. However, the fact that we were still talking and not yet bleeding suggested that Aifric did indeed have something else up his rotten sleeves.

I regarded him calmly. 'What is it that you want?'

His smile grew. 'Oh, there are so many things that I want.' He was determined to eke out this moment.

The bastard was enjoying every minute of this. Well, I wasn't going to give him the satisfaction of looking frightened. I pasted on a bored expression and examined my fingernails. 'Try me,' I drawled.

His mouth twitched and I realised that my nonchalance was irritating him. Good. 'You come with me. You will answer for your crimes.'

'My crimes?' Was he for real?

'You have been a naughty, naughty girl.' His nostrils flared. 'I have a little gathering planned. My son and heir is getting married on the Isle of Muck in a matter of days.' He looked at Tipsania coyly and she all but snarled in response. 'Everyone who's anyone will be there. And not just Sidhe.' Aifric licked his lips. 'I've made sure of that.' He cracked his fingers. 'You see, you were becoming a folk hero. The young orphan who battled against the evil Sidhe empire and who tragically lost her life in the process. People are talking about you on the streets. There are gatherings using your name to galvanise the sheep into action against us. I can't have that.' He made a moue of disgust.

'You can't control everyone,' I told him flatly. 'You're not the respected leader you think you are.'

Aifric laughed. 'Do you think I care about respect? I'm not a school teacher. I'm delivering this country from evil. I'm Scotland's saviour.'

I stared at him. He was telling the truth; he really believed that about himself. Maybe he wasn't just psychotic, maybe he was plain insane.

Aifric stepped towards me. 'Right now you're a martyr. The world will think differently – the Highlands will *know* differently – after I tell them the truth. Instead of being the figurehead that encouraged a bloody coup, you'll be the most reviled name in history. I'll make sure of it. People will soon know who the true hero is.'

'You?' I scoffed.

Aifric didn't even blink. 'Me.' He inhaled deeply and looked around. 'Everyone knows that Clan MacQuarrie has more than a touch of the moon about it. You will all remain here behind your pointless borders. You will not communicate with anyone. You will not come to the wedding and you will not get in my way.'

'And why the hell should we do that?' Chieftain MacQuarrie growled.

Aifric beamed, as if he were delivering wonderful news. 'If you don't, I will raze your Clan to the ground. Do this, keep quiet and you might live to see next year.'

'We'll do no such thing! We could never trust you anyway.'

I turned round and met his eyes. The MacQuarrie Clan had sworn fealty to me and they would do what I asked. Yes, Aifric was lying; he'd find a way to destroy this Clan one way or another, no matter what we decided today. But if they didn't give him at least the illusion of passive agreement, he would destroy them right now. There was no choice to make. 'Agreed,' I said quietly.

Chieftain MacQuarrie opened his mouth. He would have disagreed but something in my expression gave him pause. 'I've got this,' I told him. I looked at Angus. He looked almost as sick as I felt. 'Bob,' I mouthed silently.

Angus swallowed and nodded slightly to show he understood and I relaxed slightly. I knew Angus: there was no way he'd permit Bob or the others to mount a kind of rescue without him. Even if Aifric killed me right now, Angus would make sure that Bob's indenture, such as it was, passed to him or someone on our team. If I didn't live to fight another day, they would.

'There,' I said to Aifric, 'you've got what you wanted after all.'

His lip curled. 'Somehow I don't feel I can trust you.' He pointed at Tipsania. 'I want her too.'

Tipsania was an independent being and I couldn't tell her what to do, I could only hope that she understood there were other factors in play. We weren't giving up entirely, not yet. I swallowed and looked at her, expecting her to flatly refuse. Her eyes drifted from Morna's body to me and then back to Aifric. She tossed her head. 'It would be my pleasure,' she said loudly.

I sensed Taylor stiffen. Hell, even I was taken aback and I knew she was lying.

'I never wanted to be with these dirty outcasts,' she continued. 'I want to be the wife of the next Steward. It's what my father wanted for me.'

Considering her father was lying dead in front of her, she did a damned good job of dissembling. From the expression on Aifric's face, he wasn't buying her act, regardless of how believable she appeared. All the same, I inwardly applauded her for trying. Tipsania understood the machinations required to get what she wanted – she'd had all her life to perfect that attitude. No doubt if all this ended as Aifric wanted it to, she'd find a way to worm herself back into his good books, not because she was a bad person but because she understood what survival took. That thought scratched at me.

She marched ahead, her spine ramrod straight. She didn't glance at me as she passed. When she reached Aifric and his goons, he patted her hand. 'My condolences on the passing of your father.'

For the briefest moment, her eyes widened. Realising that she was on the verge of smacking the Steward in the face, I intervened. 'You've got Tipsy for your son. The MacQuarries will stay here and stay quiet. I will come with you and participate in whatever bullshit farce you've got planned.' My mouth flattened. 'You win.'

Aifric examined me like I was a bug under a microscope. There was an odd light behind his eyes. 'Not quite,' he said eventually. 'I'm still not convinced I know everything that you're capable of and I want to make sure you're not going to stray from my plan.'

'You've got what you came for.' I stepped forward, holding my hands in front of me. 'Go ahead. Tie me up. I'll be good, I promise.'

Aifric held up a finger. 'I'm not sure you will be.' He beckoned and the nearest machine-gun toting goon peeled off, striding over to stand next to me.

'What do you call a man holding a machine gun?' I asked. He gazed back at me impassively. 'Sir.' I managed a smile. 'See? I'm not going to do anything stupid.' I glanced at Aifric.

He smirked. 'I know.' He raised a second finger. This time it wasn't pointing at me, it was pointing at Taylor.

Panic overtook me. 'No, wait!' I dug down into myself, drawing on all the available magic I had left preparing to use it in one go, even if I didn't know how it would work. It was too late. The goon next to me raised his gun and brought it down on my skull just as there was a short burst of gunfire. I heard Taylor scream in agony and the world slid to black.

Chapter Thirteen

My mouth felt like sawdust. Every bone, muscle and sinew in my body was screaming out in agony and it felt like there was a duck-egg sized lump on the back of my head. I moaned and opened my eyes. Even though the light here was dim, it was still painful.

'You're okay,' rumbled a gruff voice.

I winced and slowly turned round. Candy. 'Are we at the Cru…' realising that once I'd begun, I could barely speak.

'No, we're being moved somewhere.'

I sat up and everything swam until I felt like I was on the verge of passing out again. I lay down again hastily, pressing my palms against the large metal bars underneath me for balance. The room continued to sway.

'Boat,' I whispered. Candy grunted in affirmation. We had to be on our way to the Isle of Muck. Everything came flooding back to me in a rush of images. Taylor's scream reverberated round my head. No. Just … no.

'I've been told to tell you,' Candy said, 'that the old man is alive.' His voice was flat; he was apparently repeating the words verbatim. 'But he is wounded and requires medical attention. In order to ensure that you do as you are told, he will remain in that condition until after that wedding.'

I heaved in a breath, my fingernails curling into my hands and digging painfully into my flesh. He wasn't dead. Taylor wasn't dead.

Another lighter voice spoke up. 'And if there's even the faintest hint of a genie showing up, he will suffer more than you could ever imagine.'

I pushed myself up onto my elbows. A woman was watching me from behind another set of bars. I recognised her instantly: she was the guard I'd fooled with my Aifric Illusion. I guessed she was here to get payback. She smiled at me nastily. 'We're watching you twenty-four seven,' she said. 'Just to make sure you don't try anything.' She eyed me predatorily. 'Personally, I'm hoping you do. I could do with a little fun.' She cracked her knuckles. 'You should be glad you're in that cage.'

Candy scowled at her. 'Here,' he said, thrusting something under my chin. 'Drink.'

Grateful for the distraction, not to mention the liquid, I gulped at the water. It was brackish and foul-tasting but it was wet. The thought that it might be poisoned crossed my mind but Aifric could have already injected me with anything he wanted. Not only was I as weak as a kitten but there was no telling how long I'd been out for. I swung my head back to Candy, a question in my eyes.

'Two days,' he said. 'They gave you something to keep you under.'

I grimaced, drained the cup and forced myself up to a sitting position again. The world still wobbled around me but it was becoming more manageable.

'Has anyone else been down here?' I kept my eyes averted from the guard. She snorted as if amused but at least stayed quiet.

'They swap the guards every four hours,' Candy answered. He pursed his lips and shook his head to indicate that no one else had been to see us. Candy wasn't stupid; he'd know I was referring to Byron.

I wasn't sure whether to be relieved or dismayed that Byron probably didn't know what was going on. Somehow I doubted his Plan B had included this little scenario. I calculated: if I'd been comatose for two days, there was still plenty of time to find a way out. The wedding wasn't scheduled for another week at least. There was a whole lot I could do with seven days.

'The ceremony's been moved forward,' the guard said cheerfully, as if she could read my mind. I narrowed my eyes, wondering whether mind-reading was a Gift, then I relaxed. If she possessed that kind of magic, she'd have known instantly that I wasn't Aifric when I spoke to her at the Cruaich dungeons. She was just bloody canny.

'Tomorrow morning,' Candy answered, before I could ask. He wouldn't meet my eyes. This was as much of a disaster for him as it was for me. He had obviously worked out that everything was going tits up.

I grimaced. Well, shite. I wondered whether Aifric would create a sham trial first or simply dunk me in a well to check whether I floated. He had to know that I'd spill the beans if he gave me chance to speak. I tried to work through the possibilities but my mind felt too sluggish and slow.

Candy sighed loudly and lay down, putting his hands behind his head and gazing at the ceiling. The Sidhe guard continued to stare at me. It was so discomforting that in the end I did the same as Candy, lying back and looking up and wondering desperately if there was any chance I could find my way out of all this.

In the far corner of the room, barely visible through the shadows, a spider lurked. It was larger than your usual Scottish beastie and seemed to be having difficulty spinning its web. Silk spun out behind it, missing its invisible target. While I watched, the spider paused for one long moment as if it were giving up. Then it abruptly scuttled down the wall, travelling at what had to be an immense speed for its size. Maybe it had gone to get its buddies to help.

I closed my eyes, focusing on the throbbing pain in my skull and trying to will it away. When that didn't work, I searched within myself to see what magic I still had that I could make use of. There was definitely still a trickle of Apportation. Unhelpful. I could transport objects away from me but I couldn't transport anything to me. And I couldn't do anything with that eagle-eyed guard staring at me.

I could still call animals towards me. I pushed out, sensing some nearby rats. Ignoring the shudder that ran down my spine, I considered bringing them over. Maybe I'd get lucky and the guard would have a phobia. She'd run away screaming and I'd … what? Shamble slowly out of this cage and swim for it?

My big toe itched and I shook it absently. It didn't help. Muttering a curse, I glanced down. It was the damn spider, sitting right next to my big toe and staring at me with all of its glittering black eyes. Eurgh. I lifted my foot and shook it harder, sending the spider flying away from me. I supposed I should be grateful it wasn't like Debbie, the giant arachnid who'd been used in the Games last year. I paused. This cage we were in did look remarkably familiar. I supposed that until the wedding was official and Aifric could claim the Scrymgeour wealth for his own purposes, he had to make savings where he could.

Candy shifted restlessly next to me, muttering something unintelligible under his breath. He should have escaped when he had the chance, I thought sourly. All of us should have. I sighed. Then I felt my damned toe itch again.

The guard laughed. 'Looks like that creepy-crawly is the only friend you have left, Adair.' She hawked up a ball of phlegm and spat it noisily onto the floor. 'I guess the apple doesn't fall far from the tree after all.'

I glared at her. So we were back to that again, were we? That Gale Adair, my father, was a genocidal maniac? Why couldn't people see what was right in front of their faces? 'I'm not quite sure what you mean,' I said icily. 'My parents were heroes who died at the hands of your boss.'

'Ha!' she scoffed.

'You are a Moncrieffe, right? Don't you think it's strange that the Steward is locking up another Clan Chieftain? What about the police? Since when was Aifric Moncrieffe allowed to act like judge, jury and executioner?'

Rather than think about what I was saying, she looked at me as if I were toe fungus. 'You give the Sidhe a bad name.'

I laughed coldly. 'The Sidhe do that perfectly well without my help.'

'You've endangered everyone in the Highlands by your actions with the trolls. This whole country could be attacked by the Fomori demons and we'd all be vulnerable.'

'But this country has always been vulnerable to that. It's only the Sidhe who've had the liberty of hiding behind their magic borders. What about everyone else?'

Her lip curled. 'Because of you, Fomori demons attacked the MacQuarries.'

She was as blind as she was annoying. 'No, they didn't. It was Illusion magic. It was a Sidhe who was behind that. And Aifric Moncrieffe was pulling their strings as much as he is yours.'

She didn't seem to hear me. 'You're a thief and a murderer.'

'I'll allow the thief part but I've not hurt anyone.' I cast around, trying to think of a way to penetrate her thick skull. If I could get this woman to doubt Aifric and come over to my side, perhaps I'd have a sliver of a chance. So would Taylor.

My toe itched again. Irritated, I reached down to brush the bloody spider away once more. It was staring up at me and this time, one of its long – and remarkably hairy – legs was tapping against my skin as if it were impatient.

'I'm not listening to you,' the guard declared. 'The Steward said you'd try and turn me but I'm loyal.'

'To a fault,' I muttered in response. I was no longer interested in her, however.

The spider leapt off me and darted over Candy's shins back to the corner. My eyes followed it. I lay down to avoid appearing too obvious but made sure I tracked its every move. I really hoped I wasn't going crazy.

Once again, it tried to spin silk. Fine threads shot out and it leapt from one side of the cage to the other. This wasn't the perfect web of a normal spider, though; it looked more like a clumpy mess.

'Do you know the tale of Robert the Bruce?' I asked Candy.

'Sidhe bloke round the time of the Fissure, wasn't he?'

I nodded. 'Yep. There are quite a few famous stories about him.'

'Cave,' Candy grunted.

'Yeah. He hid out in one after his army was routed by the Fomori. He was convinced that all of Scotland was lost. Then he saw a spider.'

'If this is your way of telling me that you're not going to give up, then I got it,' drawled the guard. 'But remember that your friend's life is still hanging in the balance. Not that I suppose someone like you cares. You probably don't care about anyone.'

Whatever. I let her babble on. 'The spider,' I said to Candy, over the top of her voice, 'was trying to weave a web. The first time it failed. It tried again, and again it failed but it didn't give up. It kept on going and on the third attempt it finally succeeded. Because of that one little spider, Robert the Bruce decided not to yield. He pulled himself together for one more fight and he succeeded. The Highlands are free in part because of that, not because of magic but because of a spider. He could have had a genie with him but it wouldn't have made a difference because it was that spider that saved the country.'

As I watched, the spider halted in its attempts to spin its web and did what I could only describe as a flounce. I smiled. 'I hope Taylor's alright,' I half-whispered.

The spider stared at me again then twisted round and scarpered out through the gap in the bars. I tracked its movements until it was completely out of sight. Thanks, Bob, I said silently. It made a big difference knowing he was around. If everything really did fall into total shite, I could fall back on a wish. It was a last resort, and there was a part of me that was curious to see just how Aifric was going to play things tomorrow, but at least I knew I had a Plan B of my own.

***

I tried to stay awake for as long as I could, waiting for Bob the spider's return but my spirit was far more willing than my flesh. After an hour or two, despite my best efforts, I succumbed to unconsciousness again. In fact, I'd probably have stayed under for another forty-eight hours if a bucket of icy water hadn't been flung at me.

'Get up!'

Freaked out by my sudden awakening, I sprang to my feet. I shook off the freezing droplets and glared at my attacker. It was a different guard this time – a burly Moncrieffe Sidhe male. He took out some kind of truncheon and slammed it against the metal bars.

'Sort yourself out!' he screamed like a stereotypical drill sergeant. 'We are leaving!'

I rubbed the back of my neck. I still hurt all over but at least it was a dull ache rather than an all-encompassing pain that made it difficult to think. I straightened my wet clothes as best I could and glanced up to see if Bob was there. Unfortunately, there wasn't any sign of spiders or a genie. There was, however, a long length of web stretching from one side of the cage to the other. I squinted: it looked like a T followed by a squiggle. I couldn't work out for the life of me what the squiggle was though. T what? T bloody what?

Something smacked me in the face. More stunned than anything, I gasped. The new guard laughed. 'Put those on.' When I didn't move, he let out an impressive snarl and rattled the cage bars once again. I winced at the noise, bent down and picked up a pair of handcuffs. I considered refusing but it wouldn't help matters. I snapped them on and looked up again, still trying to work out what Bob's impenetrable message meant.

The guard unlocked the cage door and beckoned. 'Come on, then. This isn't summer camp. Get the hell out, scum!'

Scum? 'Surely you can come up with better invective than that,' I said, acting cheerful to throw him off his game. He glowered at me dumbly. 'Use your imagination,' I suggested, in a bid to help him along. He still didn't answer. Oh. 'A better insult,' I amended. 'Surely you can come up with a better insult.'

'Adair witch! Get the fuck out!'

Hmm. Not really better. I shrugged and shuffled forward. There were parts of my body which hurt that I hadn't realised existed before now. I supposed I could at least be certain that I wasn't dead.

'Hey!' Candy yelled. 'What about me?'

The guard ignored him. Damn it, I wanted Candy with me as much for my sake as for his. Safety in numbers. 'He needs to come too.'

The guard reached forward, grabbing me painfully by the shoulder in a bid to shove me along the corridor. Behind us, Candy gripped the bars of the cage. This wasn't the Cruaich dungeon – these bars were reinforced and no match even for a Wild Man. All the same, the metal creaked and shuddered. 'Let me out!' he roared.

'Look,' I said, biting my lip to take my mind off the rest of my pain. 'Tipsania Scrymgeour won't go ahead with the wedding until she sees him. You'll only have to come back later. It makes sense to bring him along now.'

The guard didn't pay me any attention but propelled me at speed through a maze of dark wooden corridors. I could still hear Candy shouting; it wasn't until I was dragged up a set of shaky stairs and taken out onto the deck that his voice finally faded away.

As good as it felt to get some fresh air into my lungs, I remained rigid with tension. Although the boat was busy with deckhands, the sky was still dark. Not just that, there was a fair wind gusting and repeatedly making my loose hair fly into my face. Cuffed as I was, I couldn't brush it away so, effectively blinded, I tripped and stumbled my way along.

I stretched out my senses. There had to be useful magic here that I could steal. The guy holding me was definitely Sidhe. I concentrated on pulling on the thready tendrils of his Gift but it was no use. It refused to come. Another strain of violent magic, then. With Morna dead, the MacQuarries corralled and Taylor seriously injured, maybe sticking to my pacifist guns wasn't such a good idea.

I was forced to stop, the guard's heavy hands pushing me downwards until I was on my knees. The good thing was that I was more sheltered from the wind and could see again; the bad thing was that I was eye-level with his groin.

He cupped himself. 'You like what you see? Right now, you're in the perfect position. We've got time. The Steward won't mind if I enjoy myself a bit first.'

I drew back my lips. 'Sure,' I said. 'I've still got teeth. This could be fun.'

His face twisted. Suddenly a surge of power sprang from him, striking me in the chest. Cold spread across my body, numbing me down to my arteries.

'Not so funny now, are ya?' he spat.

Someone shouted from behind and, distracted, he turned to talk to them. At the same moment, a merman strolled down the deck towards me, his large arms wrapped around a box entitled 'wedding favours'. He didn't glance at me as he went past but I could see his gills flapping rapidly at the back of his neck. If I hadn't appreciated how dire the situation was before, the sight of Brochan on a boat of all things would have hammered it home.

Brochan paused at the gangplank and shifted his burden, ostensibly to get a better grasp on it, as the guard returned his attention to me. He was holding a swathe of dark shapeless material.

'Black?' I enquired. 'I'm not sure that's an appropriate colour for a wedding. Before we go any further, could I get something to eat? Something sugary would be best. I'm feeling rather shaky.'

The guard's lip curled. He shook out the material and began to pull it down over my head.

'A boiled sweet would do!' I called out before the hood completely covered my face. 'Even just a barley sugar… I'm sure I saw some below deck.'

He cuffed me on the side of my head and I went reeling. I let out a muffled squeak and righted myself. Although the hood was claustrophobic, it was vital that I stayed calm. Brochan would have understood my message. It was me the Sidhe were worried about so the chances that there was a guard watching Candy now that I'd gone were slim. Brochan would have a good chance of freeing the Wild Man. We needed all the help we could get.

I was hauled up again and elbowed in the back. I stumbled forward, almost completely disorientated. Then I felt myself moving downwards, no doubt onto the gangplank. The wood under my feet felt unsteady and I could hear the sea lapping angrily against the side. I considered pitching to the side and falling in but, between the cuffs and the hood, there was too much that could go wrong. I told myself to act like a good girl. I could still find a way around Aifric's machinations.

I wished I knew more about Muck. I'd thought there would be time to research it properly before the wedding so any reading I'd done was scanty. I knew it was a tiny island – less than two and a half miles from end to end – and the native population reflected its size. Beyond that, we could have been landing on the moon for all I knew about the place. Its size meant we wouldn't have far to travel. Given how long it took me before my feet hit solid ground and I left the gangplank that was just as well.

I was jostled and shoved and yanked along. At least there was a proper tarmacked road so I didn't stumble as much. I sensed someone else join us, muttering a barely audible conversation to the guard as we shuffled towards wherever we were going. Then something scratched at the back of my neck and I felt the fabric of the hood shift. A moment later, Bob's weight settled in its usual spot behind my ear.

'Don't speak,' he warned in a low whisper. 'This is the first time they've been distracted. They're watching out for me and I have no desire to become genie kebab because of you, Uh Integrity.'

He was all heart. I exhaled and let out a soft murmur, simply to let him know that I understood.

'Good. Now listen. You know from my message about Taylor how he's doing. It's not looking good for him at all. He's a lost a lot of blood and I'm not sure he'll make it beyond the end of the day. I think there might be some organ damage. You need to prepare yourself for the worst.' He sighed. 'Humans are so delicate.'

Tears pricked at the back of my eyes. No. I was not going to let him die. Not if it killed me.

'Tipsania is here too. She's been locked in a room in the hotel. I can't get near the place. There are guards and magic barriers everywhere. Aifric Moncrieffe isn't taking any chances. Byron is somewhere in that building as well but he's got people round him constantly. I don't think he's a prisoner but his father's not leaving him alone. Angus has gone to see if he can sneak in but he's a lost cause. They both are.'

I hissed. Bob was taking far too much for granted – and he wasn't finished yet.

'Speck and Lexie are waiting offshore in a fishing boat they nicked in Mallaig. After I give them the signal, I'm going to count down from twenty. There will be an explosion. I can't do much about the handcuffs but I'll get this hood off. As soon as I reach one, you're going to run left. Just keep running. It's less than five hundred metres to the shore then a short swim. I'll make sure everyone is kept off your tail. After that, you'll be free and easy.'

He had to be kidding. I had never heard Bob sound so serious in all the time I'd known him but this had to be a joke. I was not going to run away and leave everyone else behind. I shook my head vigorously.

Bob tutted. 'Integrity,' he said, using my real name for emphasis. 'Byron and Tipsania can look after themselves. Aifric is not going to hurt them, no matter what happens.' That was probably true but I wasn't leaving. 'Taylor is dying,' Bob continued. He did his best to sound matter of fact but I heard his voice catch. 'I've spoken to him and he understands. All he wants is for you to get away safely. If you stay here, you will die alongside him. That much is a given. I need to start the countdown. We don't have much time.'

I shook my head. No chance.

'You're an idiot,' Bob told me. He didn't sound surprised. 'I should tell you then,' he said heavily, 'that over on the western side and far out to sea where they can stay undetected are about a thousand trolls. They commandeered an ancient ferry. If you die, they will attack. It'll be a bloodbath and most of the blood will be theirs. Leaving now is the safest option.'

Nope. Still not going to happen. The trolls' presence just meant I'd have to work harder at not corking it. I was not running away. It had been the best option for me when I'd been a kid but it wasn't the best option for me now.

Bob cursed. 'You're still not going to leave, are you?'

Got it in one. It was showdown time between Aifric and me. It was bound to happen sooner or later. I'd have preferred to have the upper hand or some element of surprise but I wasn't going to cry about it. I had to deal with this. My parents had named me warrior and I was going to war. Enough was enough.

'Integrity,' Bob said, sounding completely miserable, 'you still have a wish left. You could use it. But unless…' He sniffed and altered tack. 'It'll end badly. You know it'll end badly.'

I shrugged. Yeah, it would, but as much as Taylor's death would destroy me, I wouldn't subject him to the whims of a genie wish. Goodness only knows what might happen and he'd already made his feelings pretty clear when Morna died. I'd almost made that mistake then; I wouldn't do it again. But, regardless, the wish was there.

'This is all my fault. If I'd come with you to the MacQuarries…' Bob started. I growled. Aifric. This was Aifric's fault and no one else's. 'Please, Integrity,' he pleaded. 'Please escape.'

I straightened my shoulders and started to walk more quickly.

'Hey!' the guard barked. 'What's the rush? You keen to die, scum?'

Bob made one last ditch attempt. 'Integrity…'

'I'm going to face him,' I whispered. 'It's time.'

Chapter Fourteen

Two hours later, after spending the entire time in what at best guess from the smell and the plastic bowl was a portaloo, I was feeling less confident. It wasn't that I didn't think I could outsmart Aifric or that I was afraid of what pain I might have to go through, it was the waiting. I'd been adept at lying in wait for hours during my time as a thief if the situation called for it but I'd always known what I was waiting for. Now I didn't have a bloody clue what was going to happen.

Bob had left ages ago to inform the others that I wouldn't run away, so he was no help. All I could do was to cool my heels and turn over every possible eventuality in my mind. Few of them ended well. It was almost a relief when I heard the door unlock and the guard came to take me to my fate.

'Hey,' I yelled.

There was a grunt then he lifted up the front of the hood slightly to stare in my face. Unfortunately he got far too close and I caught a whiff of unpleasant halitosis but it was worth it to see the light outside. If Aifric was going to de-hood me, I didn't want to waste thirty seconds adjusting my sight while he chopped off my head.

'I bet your dentist always looks down in the mouth when you show up,' I quipped. The guard stared at me. 'You should lay off the tuna fish TicTacs,' I suggested.

His fat fingers bunched into a fist and I was sure he was going to punch me on my nose until another face appeared behind him. 'Not the face,' the second guard cautioned. 'The Steward don't want anyone feelin' sorry for her.'

The guard nodded and drove his hand into my stomach instead. He yanked the hood back over my face and dragged me out while I was still winded and gasping for air.

I counted steps for no other reason than it gave me something to do and kept my mind off the pain in my stomach. We didn't go far. At sixty-nine, where I'd have made another joke except it would have been lost on these two numbskulls, we stopped. I could hear Aifric's dulcet tones, although they were slightly muffled as if far away – or on the other side of a door.

'We live in dangerous times. While that doesn't mean we should stop living or be afraid of celebrating the simple, sincere love of two young people like dear Tipsy and my son, it does mean that there are actions which must be undertaken to keep us all safe. The Highlands of Scotland may be small in size but they are not small in stature. We need to do whatever is necessary to minimise the risk to our homes!'

There was a rumbling cheer which started small and got louder and louder. Aifric apparently had his audience in the palm of his hand. I tsked so loudly that I received a sharp kick in the shins.

'To that end,' he continued, 'it falls on me to perform some unpleasant but very necessary duties. I would hate to be accused of being underhand so these duties will take place in full view of all you good people. It pains me to do this but I have no choice. There is a Sidhe who stands accused of the most heinous crimes. I cannot pass judgment so I will leave it to you to hear the evidence and make the final verdict. Only that way will this be fair.'

I snorted. Fair? If he was being fair, I'd be in a proper court of law with a real defence. I had to admit that Aifric Moncrieffe certainly knew how to talk the talk. He was also leaving nothing to chance. No matter who was supposedly passing judgment on me for my 'crimes', whatever they were, I would be proclaimed guilty. But Aifric didn't hold all the cards.

I heard doors swing open and I was made to shuffle forward. There were several intakes of breath and low whispers. As yet, it appeared that no one knew my real identity.

'Who is that?' someone near me asked, as I fumbled ahead.

'None of the MacQuarries are here,' somebody else murmured. 'Do you think...?'

The voices fell away as I was told to stop and turn around. This wasn't the time to act up so I did as I was told, keeping my head bowed. My best shot right now seemed to be to act like an innocent, demure young woman. Maybe that way some of the more traditionally minded Sidhe would feel sympathy and veer to my side. You never knew.

There was movement beside me. I took a deep breath. 'Tonight, Matthew,' I intoned, 'I'm going to be...' I paused and the hood was whipped off my head. '...Integrity Adair.'

I was standing next to the altar of a church while a sea of wide-eyed, shocked faces stared at me. For a moment, I wished I still had my phone with me; a snapshot of this would win every photo competition hands down. Just about all the Sidhe I'd ever met was here – and a whole bunch of others whom I didn't recognise. Obviously the MacQuarries were absent and I couldn't spot Tipsania or Byron, but everyone else was here. And it was so quiet that I was sure that if I concentrated, I'd hear the hair standing up on the neck of the hirsute Fairlie Sidhe seated just in front of me.

Slack-jawed, Dorienne Darroch got to her feet then she sat down. Then she stood up again. She shook her head in amazement. I looked away from her and scanned the room. There were very few people here who seemed happy to see that I wasn't dead.

The Ochterlony Chieftain pointed a bony finger at Aifric. That was interesting. My mother was from that Clan, although she wasn't highly placed. They'd never made friendly overtures towards me but we were kin. 'You said she was dead.'

'Yes.' Aifric's expression was grave. 'She faked her own death. Unfortunately that's the least serious of her crimes.'

Wanker. I opened my mouth to argue but no words came out. It wasn't that I'd lost my voice, I'd forgotten how to speak. I couldn't make a sound. With narrowed eyes, I looked at Aifric. Yeah. There was a glint behind his sombre mask. On his orders, some bastard was doing something to prevent me from talking. I had to work out who.

'Unbelievable.' The Ochterlony Chieftain shook his head and sat down again. If I hadn't been sure about his feelings towards me before, I got an inclination now from his moue of distaste as he flicked his hands at me.

Malcolm Kincaid rose smoothly to his feet. I didn't need to wonder about his allegiance – I knew that he hated me. He also appeared less surprised at my resurrection than the others. Uh-oh. 'Well, this is a shock,' he said, his voice carrying across the congregation. 'I'll be very interested to hear what Miss Adair has to say for herself.'

If I could have killed him with a look, I might have. Last time I checked, I was still a bloody Chieftain and I still ranked alongside him. I tried to speak again, to no avail.

'If she has done the deeds of which you accuse her, however,' Kincaid continued, 'there is no doubt that she will lie. In fact, she has already obviously lied because she is standing there, living and breathing.'

Aifric rubbed his chin as if deep in thought. Were these idiot Sidhe falling for this act? 'Hmm, yes. I wonder if you would be so good...' he gestured towards the Kincaid Clan.

'It would be our pleasure. Several of my Clan members have Truth-Telling as a Gift.' Malcolm Kincaid nodded at Kirsty.

She blanched. 'Someone else.'

He seemed puzzled. So she'd kept the information that she no longer had her Gift from her own Chieftain. That was curious because Tipsania knew that she'd lost it. Before I could dwell on this little titbit, however, Kincaid pointed at an older woman. 'Molly then.'

Molly Kincaid inclined her head and stood up. Aifric beckoned her over. With obvious reluctance, she sidled past her compatriots and walked up the aisle, brushing past various flowers and ribbons.

'Let's try again, shall we?' Aifric said. He turned to me and asked in a sad voice, 'Did you fake your own death?'

I hissed and this time the sound tripped out of my mouth. 'Yes. But...' The rest of my sentence was ripped away from me. Apparently I wasn't going to be allowed to say much at all. That could prove troublesome.

There was a murmur from the watching Sidhe. This was beginning to feel like an episode of Jerry Springer. Aifric sighed loudly. 'This is very hard for me,' he declared. 'I took it upon myself to help Integrity. There were many among you who did not want her to visit the Cruaich grove and receive her true name but I trusted her enough to permit it. I was willing to take her in and treat her like one of my own family, despite her well-advertised past as a thief. You all know how close I was to her father and how difficult it was for me to accept what happened all those years ago.'

My mouth dropped open, so wide with disbelief that Brochan could probably have steered a container ship through it. Many heads nodded in agreement. Aifric was being incredibly canny here; his words were vague enough to avoid being outright lies but there was no doubt what he was implying. 'I have to face facts: Gale Adair was a dangerous man and his daughter is no different.'

I didn't hit people. I didn't hit people. I didn't hit people. But I trembled with bitter rage.

One of the Moncrieffes from Byron's stag party stood up. 'She let the Foinse escape! We've got less magic now because of her!' There was a chorus of angry mutters. It got louder and I felt as if I were being assailed with a wave of hatred from the crowd. Right now that was nothing compared to how I was feeling about Aifric, who held his hand up for quiet.

'That is true,' he said as if he begrudged admitting it. 'She did do that. And she has done even worse.' He turned to me again. 'Integrity Adair, how many times have you travelled across the Veil?'

The compulsion to remain silent was lifted from me once more. I was getting really tired of this. 'Technically four, although...' I ground my teeth as I lapsed into silence again. I searched the hundreds of Sidhe facing me, each face agog. Whoever was doing this would give themselves away. There had to be some kind of tell-tale movement.

Aifric raised his eyebrows at Molly Kincaid. She bobbed her head primly. 'She is telling the truth.'

I gazed across the gathered Sidhe. To say that they looked shocked would be an understatement. I forced myself to stop concentrating on how they felt and continued methodically searching for who was using their Gift to control my mouth. There were hundreds of them; I was going to need some luck. Scratch that. I was going to need a lot of luck.

'We all know,' Aifric said, 'that the Fomori have been causing us many problems lately.' He made an excellent effort at looking sad. 'The incursions they've made into the Highlands have had a devastating effect and I shall impart more tragic news concerning that in a moment.' He sighed. 'It was not clear before why they had decided to suddenly start broaching the Veil after years of peace.' His voice dropped. 'I think it is now. Tell me, Integrity, did they come here because of you?'

I snapped my eyes away from the crowd and stared at him. The fact was that he had *told* me they'd come to the Highlands looking for me, that they'd been afraid of the prophecy. On at least two occasions, I'd had proof of their motivation from my own eyes. 'It's complicated,' I began, as the magic lifted from me once more.

Aifric shook his head. 'Yes or no will suffice.'

Screw him. He was the one who had three dead Fomori demons bricked into a cavity in his study. I drew back my shoulders. 'No.' My voice rang out clear as a bell.

Molly Kincaid flinched. 'She's lying.'

I wanted to scream. The worst part was that this was Molly telling it as her Gift saw it. It wasn't the absolute truth – but there was enough of a lie in my answer for her Gift to tell her I was lying.

Chieftain MacBain rose slowly to her feet. Her face was white and pinched. 'Chieftain Adair,' she almost choked on the words, 'came to me to arrange for payment in return for passing through the Veil and retrieving Matthew's bones. If I had known she had ulterior motives

I would have prevented her. To be in league with those creatures…' Her horror was palpable.

I looked at her, using everything I had to impart silently that I had made no pact with the Fomori demons. Our alliance might be shaky but if I could just get her to see… It was no use; she'd already made up her mind.

'She really is just like her father,' someone murmured.

Catching the whisper, I glared at the offender. Yeah? I was just like him, I was just like him because I was a decent person who was being destroyed by Aifric Moncrieffe. Unfortunately for me, my simmering and obvious anger only created fear. Fear of me.

I looked from one face to another. No. No. No. No. Someone here was controlling me and I had to find out who. Not them. Or them. No. No. Maybe. Damn it. No.

'I have it on good authority,' Aifric intoned, 'that the Fomori are amassing an army. They are gathered on the other side of the Veil and are preparing to attack.'

For a moment his words barely registered then I stopped my panicked scan of the room and turned to him, gaping. The same Truth-Telling Gift which buzzed through Molly's body told me that he was speaking the truth. Things were worse than I thought.

'Whose Lands are closest to the Veil?' Aifric asked softly.

'Adair!' someone shouted.

He nodded grimly. 'Yes, Adair.'

Seriously? Now I was being damned because of geography? I threw my hands up in disgust but, because of the handcuffs, the gesture was lost on my audience although those on the front row did pull back as if they were scared that I'd attack them.

'You will have noticed,' Aifric continued, 'that the MacQuarries are not here. They were attacked only two days ago. There were…' he closed his eyes for a brief second as if in pain '…some deaths. Tipsania Scrymgeour's father, whom we know Integrity Adair despised, and Morna Carnegie.'

The entire Carnegie Clan jerked in horror. They weren't alone; Morna had been well liked by everyone. The Bull was dead as well but even this lot knew he had been an oaf. It was Morna's passing which caused the real dismay.

'Integrity,' Aifric said, looking me directly in the eyes, 'was her death a result of your actions?'

It seemed as if the congregation was holding its breath. That absolute bastard. He didn't know that by stealing her Gift, I had hastened her passing but he did know that I believed she would still be alive if I hadn't asked her to go to the MacQuarrie Lands. In that sense, she was indeed dead because of me. What answer could I give?

The Sidhe were growing agitated with my silence. 'Answer him!' several of the yelled. 'Say the words, you Adair bitch!'

Aifric knitted his fingers together. 'I'll ask again. Was Morna Carnegie's death a result of what you did?'

'Yes.' My voice was barely audible but it didn't matter. The room erupted and at least five Sidhe leapt out of their chairs and lunged towards me. Aifric blocked their path but they seemed determined to rip me to shreds. They were like a group of baying hounds – and they were baying for my blood. The noise was deafening. Aifric turned to face me, making sure no one else could see his expression. There was a glimmer of triumph in his eyes and a sly smile on his mouth. Then his face smoothed over into the calm façade of the benevolent Steward once again.

'People! Calm down! She will answer for her crimes in prison!'

There were shouts in response. 'No! She deserves to die!'

'Execute her!'

The call rippled round the room as if we were in a football stadium. At this stage, I wouldn't have been surprised if they started a Mexican wave. The chant rose and rose, 'Kill her. Kill her. Kill her.'

I straightened my shoulders. There was no sensible way out of this. I would have to rip the Gifts from as many of these Sidhe as possible and damn the consequences. I didn't know what I'd be getting but I'd have to pray to get at least some magic I could use – and that taking it and using it to serve me wouldn't send Taylor to his grave. I drew in a deep breath and prepared – then the doors of the church were flung open and a fireball was launched across everyone's heads, slamming into the wall just beyond Aifric's head. The chanting stopped immediately as Byron strode down the aisle, followed by Jamie and Angus.

'What the fuck is going on here?'

Aifric recovered from his shock in record time. 'Byron! You're supposed to be getting ready for your wedding.'

With his kilt swinging angrily from side to side and a crisp white shirt open at the neck, Byron marched up to his father until they were barely inches apart. 'What are you doing?'

If Aifric was concerned about his son's anger, he didn't show it. 'I didn't want to interrupt your preparations,' he said calmly. 'You shouldn't be worrying about all this.' I could see the cogs turning in his mind; he realised the situation was slipping away from him and he needed to bring it back under control. I held my breath. What was he going to do?

I jerked forward to try and warn Byron but Aifric's arm shot out and held me in place. 'Ladies and gentlemen, my son has always had a soft spot for Integrity. It would hurt him immeasurably to know of her crimes—'

'She hasn't committed any crimes,' Byron snarled. 'The only criminal here is you.'

A loud gasp reverberated around the room. Aifric's hand went to his mouth. 'Has she bewitched you? Son...'

Byron stepped away and glanced at me. The harsh light in his eyes softened for a heartbeat and then he re-focused and pointed at his father before addressing the congregation. 'Aifric Moncrieffe, the Steward of the Highlands and my father, killed Gale and Coira Adair and destroyed the Adair Clan.' Two old biddies in the second row clutched each other but everyone else seemed frozen. 'On several occasions he tried to murder Integrity Adair. Jamie's psychometry Gift will prove it. My father has plotted against all of us.' Byron held up the letter we'd discovered in the Fomori demon's pocket. 'This is a petition for peace from the Fomori demons. The three who brought it died at his hands.' He met his father's eyes. 'The only danger to the Highlands is you.' He gestured at Molly. 'Am I telling the truth?'

She squeaked and nodded. Aifric, however, merely tutted. 'You think you're telling the truth because this woman has manipulated you into believing her. We have proved that she is the evil one, not me. All of these people will back me up. In fact, even Integrity will back me up.'

From the corner of my eye, I saw Bob high above the heads of the stunned Sidhe. He was flapping his arms wildly in a panic. My stomach dropped. What now?

Byron exploded. 'Bullshit!'

Aifric drew back and gestured upwards. I saw Taylor on the balcony above us, propped up between two burly goons. His shirt was soaked in blood and I wasn't sure he was conscious. Byron, realising something was amiss, followed my gaze but Taylor and the two guards had already vanished. At the same time as Byron looked up, Aifric opened his palm, flashing a concealed blade. It wasn't me he was threatening, however, it was his own son.

The magic that prevented me from speaking was lifted abruptly. 'Speak, Integrity.' I didn't need to hear the warning tone in Aifric's voice to know what would happen if I didn't say what he wanted.

Rage spread through me, burning my body with more force than Byron's Pyrokinesis ever could and I trembled with the potential for violence. There wasn't anything Aifric wouldn't do to get his own way; he'd slaughter his own son right here in front of just about every Sidhe in Scotland if that was what it took.

'I'm the only thing keeping the Fomori demons at arm's length,' Aifric muttered. 'Without me they would swarm across this country and destroy us all. This isn't just about you and me. This is much, much bigger. Do the right thing.'

I sucked in a deep breath. Everything fell away and the large Sidhe congregation no longer existed. The walls of the church were nothing and even Byron ceased to exist. All I could hear was the thumping of my heart and all I could see was the intelligent evil glittering from Aifric's soul. That and the three strands of magic swirling inside him: Pyrokinesis, like Byron, Dowsing and Healing. I blinked and looked away.

Byron said something to me but it seemed as if it were from a long way off. I shook myself and focused on the rest of the Sidhe. Perhaps it was a result of the brute force of my anger; whatever the reason, I could now see all their Gifts too. Levitation here. Precognition there. With a clarity that I wouldn't have previously thought was possible, I could tell from looking at them what magic each person possessed. I stared at the man whose Gift was the ability to control another's body against their will. My eyes narrowed and I reached inside him and yanked it away, dragging it into myself and taking it all. I staggered back. The man let out a terrified scream and collapsed.

The sound was all it took to galvanise the Sidhe into action. Several yelled and surged forward once more. Aifric couldn't stop them this time and he probably didn't want to. All the same, he grabbed Byron and pulled him backwards. 'That was you,' he hissed in a low voice so others wouldn't hear. 'You burned down our own house. It wasn't an accident after all. You have betrayed me.'

'No, Father,' Byron replied. 'You have betrayed Scotland.'

Aifric threw out his arms, sending out plumes of fire across the church. 'Byron, no!' he yelled, immediately blaming his son for his own actions. 'Don't hurt these people!'

As I dodged a spark of lightning from a seething Fairlie Sidhe, the walls caught fire. All around us people shouted, pushing past one another in a bid to get to the door. A few with water-based Gifts tried to douse the fire but it had caught too quickly. The whole structure was doomed. The people around us screamed, scattered, stampeding towards the door to escape the flames.

'I killed my best friend and his entire Clan,' Aifric said, speaking the truth for the first time. 'Don't think I'll hesitate to kill my own son too if you continue to get in my way.' Molly Kincaid's mouth dropped open. She'd

---

heard his words and, unaware he'd been overheard, this time he wasn't masking his meaning.

I lunged forward, shoving her away to get her as far from Aifric as possible before he realised his error. 'Get out of here!' She turned and ran, only to be replaced by three Sidhe who were less afraid of the fire than the others. They came at me, their enraged and contorted faces obscured by the now billowing black smoke. 'You're not going to murder anyone else, bitch!'

Byron spun towards them and used Telekinesis to push them away before they could do any harm. As he turned his back, Aifric lunged for him. Most of the Sidhe wouldn't believe a word that came out of my mouth but Byron was a different matter and that made him a more dangerous opponent for Aifric.

I didn't waste any time – I needed this Gift anyway. I squeezed my eyes shut and reached out, separating Aifric's magic until I had what I needed. I snatched at the first strand and drew it away. Aifric gasped, feeling its absence. I ignored him and kept pulling. I needed it all. Aifric's knees buckled and he collapsed.

It was difficult to tell through the thick, choking smoke but it seemed as if everyone else had managed to escape.

'Integrity!' Byron yelled. 'We have to get out of here!'

That was stating the obvious. I tugged at Aifric's body. 'Help me.'

'Just leave him.'

I wiped my streaming eyes with the back of my hand. 'No. We're not murderers.' And, I added silently, he's still your father. You'll never recover if you do this.

I couldn't see Byron's expression but a moment later he was lifting his father and throwing him into a fireman's lift over his shoulder. Then, with his free hand, he grabbed mine and began to run, ploughing through the church and out to safety.

The bright morning seemed incongruous compared to the hell we'd left behind. Most of the others seemed to have moved a safe distance away. A few were still trying to put out the fire. There were still some pained grimaces in my direction.

A roar came from behind some small houses to the left and Candy appeared, carrying massive bundle of white fabric. It took me a moment to register that it was Tipsania. He bounded towards us, Brochan hot on his heels.

'Bob!' I yelled. 'Show them where the boat is!' There was a flash of blinding light and Bob appeared, bowing grandly in front of my face before taking off with the merman, the Wild Man and what could have been Little Bo Peep in his wake.

Byron lay his father on the ground. Aifric coughed, spluttered and rolled over to one side. I watched him for a brief moment; he'd be alright. 'Taylor!' I yelled, bending down and getting into his face. 'Where is Taylor?'

Aifric didn't answer and I cursed loudly. Was Taylor still alive?

There was a rumble as the timber roof of the church collapsed. Terrified that he was inside, I prepared to go back in if need be. Then I heard a shout from towards the back wall. With my cuffed hands in front of me, I ran as fast as I could.

Three bodies, Jamie and Angus standing over them. My heart in my mouth, I stumbled forward to Taylor's prone form. I was shaking all over. Tears were leaking down my cheeks; whether they were from the smoke or because I thought Taylor was dead, I couldn't have said.

'He's still breathing, Tegs,' Angus said. He didn't sound reassuring, despite his words. As I felt for my old mentor's pulse and registered his shallow, heaving breaths and the sallowness of his skin, I knew the reason why. This was like Morna all over again; Taylor was dying. This time, however, I could do something about it and it was all thanks to Aifric. The tragic irony wasn't lost on me.

I could only guess how the Gift of Healing worked. I ran my hands lightly across Taylor's body, trying not to let the gaping wound in his torso stop me doing what needed to be done. His eyes were closed and, even without any medical training, I knew that he was at death's door. Well, death could keep on knocking as far as I was concerned. Today, no one was going to answer.

I searched inside myself for the right magic and withdrew a delicate tendril. The last thing I wanted was to fill Taylor's body with power and cause an overload. While Angus and Jamie watched, confused and probably assuming I was saying my goodbyes, I let the magic out to do its work.

An invisible thread sneaked across and wrapped around Taylor's weak body. It bound him, spinning, working almost of its own volition. He moaned softly and Angus stiffened. I gnawed on my bottom lip, worried I was getting it wrong. Then I heard Byron's voice behind me. 'His cheeks.'

I jerked up my head. Byron was right: there was the faintest bloom of colour in Taylor's cheeks. Emboldened, I drew out another wisp of magic and pushed it towards Taylor. His eyelids fluttered open and he blinked a few times before he focused on me. 'Tegs,' he breathed.

'Shhh.'

'Let me go.'

'Ha! Fat chance. You're not going anywhere.'

He frowned as if puzzled and I grinned. 'Stop thinking about what you know and focus on what you feel.'

His white eyebrows creased together and he raised a hand to his stomach. 'It doesn't hurt.'

I nodded and pulled up his shirt. There was still a great deal of congealed blood but the wound had closed. I breathed once more.

Panic flared in Taylor's eyes. 'You didn't. Not Bob.'

I patted his cheek. 'No, you've got Aifric to thank for this.' I snorted. 'Although it's the least he could do.' Then I remembered that Byron was at my back and I faltered. I stood up and looked at Angus and Jamie. 'Thank you.'

Jamie nodded awkwardly and thrust his hands into his pockets. Angus reached out and wrapped me in a hug. I pulled him close, realising too late that there was a scowl on Byron's face. 'This isn't over yet,' he warned, angling his eyes away from us.

I nodded and pulled away. Byron was right. 'Speck and Lexie are in a boat off the shore. The others are already heading that way. Can you help Taylor get there?'

They nodded and picked him up. As they jogged away, I checked the other two bodies. Both seemed to have suffered from a series of right hooks and were out for the count; they'd have sore heads but they'd survive. I opened my mouth to say something about the state of their faces and then stopped. Taylor was alright and that was what counted for now.

I looked up. 'Here come the pitchforks,' I muttered. A mass of Sidhe were heading in our direction from the other side of the church. They seemed to have shaken off their shock and regrouped to confront us. Judging by the expressions on their faces, they weren't looking for white flags; they still wanted vengeance.

Byron looked at them. 'I can talk them round.'

I shook my head. 'Emotions are running too high. You were right earlier: too many of them are still on your father's side. And the evidence against me did look damning. We need to get out of here. Unless your Plan B…'

He grimaced. 'No. My Plan B was to use a Truth-Seeker like Molly Kincaid to help us.'

'Moncrieffe minds think alike,' I said before I could stop myself.

His jaw tightened. 'No. They don't.'

A small bunch of belligerent Sidhe peeled away from the main group and raced towards us. I counted at least three different violent Gifts among them. 'We don't want to hurt you, Byron!' one of them yelled. 'But your father was right. She's done something to warp your mind. She's trying to bring down our country!'

Bob popped up beside me holding a stick with a charred marshmallow on one end. He took a delicate lick and gazed at us. 'Some of those Sidhe are on your side, Uh Integrity. More than you'd think, especially after what you did in saving the Steward. Some are a bit doubtful. Many, however, still want to kill you. Crowd mentality prevails. Wanna wish?'

I considered. 'Nah. Let's run. When things calm down, maybe more sensible heads will prevail.' I thought about what Aifric had said. A Fomori army was preparing to cross the Veil; there wasn't time to worry about what was happening here – not any longer.

Bob nodded and tossed away the marshmallow. 'Amen to that.'

As the first Sidhe thundered towards us, we sprinted away. I was done talking anyway.

Chapter Fifteen

I'd never seen Brochan look so ill. In fact, when Speck and Lexie's tiny fishing boat pulled up alongside the massive ferry which held the trolls, he was so terrified that his hands seemed unable to release their grip on the side.

'You need to let go. We have to get away from here as quickly as possible,' I said, trying to be gentle.

Bob, now wearing tiny red Speedos as if he were auditioning for a part in *Baywatch*, opened his mouth to speak. I narrowed my eyes warningly and he pasted on a look of mock hurt and shrugged. 'I'm going to check on Taylor,' he declared and flew upwards onto the deck of the ferry.

'Just give me a minute,' the merman wheezed. Then he leaned over and threw up.

'Don't be a wuss, Brochan,' Speck said cheerfully.

Brochan pushed himself upright and gave Speck a look which would have felled the Sidhe on our tail. 'You have every phobia under the sun,' he growled. 'We pander to your fears all the time. I'd have thought, of all people, you would understand.'

Speck sniffed. 'When I'm scared you roll your eyes and tell me to get over it. You seem to think that approach works on me so why shouldn't it work on you?' He shrugged. 'Besides, I think Lexie is rubbing off on me. I don't feel half as jumpy as I used to.' Something splashed in the salty water beside him and he shrieked, leaping towards Brochan and cowering against him. 'What the hell was that? What was it? I'm allergic to shellfish! Don't get me started on jellyfish either! In fact…'

I held up my hand. 'Take a look behind you.' Brochan and Speck did as I asked. 'You see all those boats? The ones heading for us?' They nodded. 'They're full of magically endowed Sidhe who are hell-bent on seeing us dead. Get into the bloody ferry.'

Brochan and Speck exchanged looks. 'Someone got out of the wrong side of bed this morning.'

I sighed. 'Speck…'

He offered me a lopsided grin. 'Don't worry, Tegs. I've been practising.' He lifted up his chin and pointed towards the mini armada. 'Paneste.'

From out of nowhere, a wave between us and the Sidhe fleet began to swell, rising up in their direction. I licked my lips nervously. 'We don't want to drown them.'

'Don't we?' Brochan asked. Apparently I wasn't the only one becoming more blasé about hurting people.

Speck patted my arm. 'Don't worry. This is a warning shot.'

Unfortunately for us, the approaching Sidhe sent out their own warning shot in return. As the wave grew in size and threatened to engulf them, one of them slammed out their own Gift, making the wind pick up and smash the little fishing vessel against the ferry's starboard side. As the Sidhe yelled and tried to avoid the wave, there was a sound of splintering wood from our boat. We had seconds.

I ground my teeth. 'Get out.'

Brochan finally worked up the courage, reaching up for the flimsy rope ladder and pulling himself up. Speck followed on his heels and I took up the rear. Hands hauled me onto the deck and I spun round. The Sidhe were drenched and their boats had been pushed back some distance by the force of the wave but they were still standing.

'Sorley!' I screamed. 'Move this beast!'

Almost immediately, a foghorn sounded and the ferry shuddered, rolling away slowly then picking up speed. Several Sidhe tried to fling magic at us but the bolts of lightning and various other projectiles fell short.

'Shall I send out another wave?' Speck enquired.

I watched as we grew further apart. 'No. It's not their fault Aifric has a silver tongue. They're only doing what they think is right.'

I sensed rather than saw Byron come up behind me. 'You're more forgiving than I am.'

I sighed. 'It's not about forgiveness. It's about empathy.'

He ran a hand through his golden hair, which was damp with sea spray and curling more than it normally did. 'That didn't exactly go to plan.'

Speck smiled in commiseration. 'Well,' he began. 'We can always—'

Lexie appeared out of nowhere and grabbed his arm. 'Come with me,' she ordered.

'What? Why?'

She muttered something at him about male stupidity and dragged him away. Byron and I looked at each other. 'I'm sorry,' he said.

'None of this was your fault.'

'It was my plan.'

'Yeah,' I conceded. 'You'll need to work a bit harder next time. I think you've still got potential though.'

He didn't smile. 'Angus told me about Morna.'

I glanced away. 'Yeah.' I clenched my teeth together so tightly it hurt. 'I saved Taylor. I couldn't save Morna. She deserved better than that.' I shook my head, feeling the tears at the back of my throat. I pushed them away. If she'd seen me crying when there was still work to be done, Morna would have scolded me to hell and beyond.

Byron leaned forward and rested his forehead against mine. 'He'll still pay for what he's done. We'll work this out,' he promised.

'Yes,' I agreed. 'We will. Robert the Bruce didn't quit.'

'Eh?'

I smiled. 'Never mind.'

Byron drew back and watched me for a long moment. 'I saved you,' he said, eventually.

I blinked. 'Excuse me?'

'I saved you. In the church. If it wasn't for me, you'd be dead now.'

I crossed my arms. 'I had things under control.'

'Ha! It didn't look like it from where I was standing.'

I raised my eyebrows. 'Really? We're really going to do this? Because while you were primping and preening and getting ready for your *wedding*, I was kicked around and locked in a cage. You were probably enjoying chilled champagne and strawberries while I was working on a way to save Candy, Taylor and Tipsania.'

Byron pursed his mouth. 'Doesn't matter. I still rescued you.' He moved closer again. 'You needed me.'

'I did not!'

He smirked. 'You did. I understand it's hard for you to admit but you need a big, strong man like me around to save your skin from time to time.' He rocked forward on his toes. 'You owe me.'

'Screw you!'

He laughed. 'Funny. I was just thinking that would be the ideal payment.' He dropped his voice to a husky whisper. 'I'm picturing you lying on my bed in suspenders.' He paused. 'Nothing else.'

I glared. 'No chance.' I wrinkled my nose. 'Unless they're hot-pink suspenders.'

'Now you're talking.' Byron reached out, his thumb caressing my cheek. Heat flared up between us. Then someone cleared their throat right behind us.

'Chieftain?' It was Lyle or maybe it was Kirk; I still got those two trolls mixed up. 'What are your orders?'

Shite. I needed to come up with a plan that would keep us all alive. I gave Byron a last reluctant smile and gently kissed his cheek. He growled.

'Time to get to work,' I told him.

***

The ferry was huge. Goodness knows where Sorley and his buddies had boosted it from at such short notice. Sorley was doing well – I'd make a proper career thief of him yet. Everywhere I looked, trolls were doffing imaginary caps to me in deference as I walked by. Part of me smiled at the celebratory atmosphere; part of me was overtaken by foreboding about what was to come next.

'Is everyone here?' I asked the security-conscious troll.

'There are a hundred or so trolls back at your Lands keeping everything ticking over,' Sorley informed me. 'I can assure you that they will let no one in or out.' His small eyes grew distant and his fists bunched. I imagined that he was dreaming about the joy he would take in doling out punishments if any trolls disobeyed orders. Sorley wasn't their official leader but he might as well have been.

I nodded thoughtfully. 'I need another hundred at the MacQuarrie Lands.'

'No, it's too dangerous. We need to protect you.'

'Sorley, there are hundreds of trolls on this ferry. I think we're good. We can spare some.'

'Actually,' he sniffed, 'there are one thousand, two hundred and twenty-three.'

'Well, there you go then.' Guilt surged through me. 'We should have had them there from the outset.'

'We all decided it would have caused more problems than it solved. If the other Clans had noticed...'

I pushed back my hair. 'I know.' I sighed. 'But still...'

Sorley dropped his head. 'She was a good woman.'

I nodded. 'Yeah. Too good for the likes of us.'

We shared a glance. My heart ached at the thought of Morna and I was pretty certain I wasn't alone.

Sorley shook himself. 'We have set up perimeter guards around the deck.'

I raised an eyebrow. 'In case we're attacked by mermaids?'

He threw me a nasty look. 'Those Sidhe have all sorts of Gifts. They could send one of their water-Gifted dunderheads to assassinate you. Then there where would we be?'

'You'd be on a ferry in the Atlantic Ocean.'

The corners of his mouth tugged up.

'Actually,' Brochan said, 'we're technically in the Firth of Lorn, not the Atlantic Ocean. It's further west.' He scratched his gills. 'I wish I didn't know that kind of thing.' I patted his arm reassuringly. Considering where we were and what he'd just gone through, he was performing admirably.

'Fine,' Sorley huffed. 'As soon as we hit land, I'll send a group off.'

'They're our allies,' I reminded him. 'And they're in trouble because of me. They need protection.'

He gave a grudging nod. 'The rest of us should march on the Cruaich immediately. It'll take the Clans a while to sort themselves out. This is the best time to invade.'

'This isn't World of Warcraft. Besides, we have bigger things to worry about than the Sidhe.'

Taylor hobbled up, supported by Angus and Jamie. He was having some difficulty moving around but his eyes were alert and his skin had a ruddy glow which only good health and robust sea winds could provide. My heart lightened slightly. 'What is it, Tegs?' he asked quietly.

I sighed and told them what Aifric had said about the Fomori.

Angus's eyes were wide. 'You're sure he wasn't lying?'

'Positive. I took all of Kirsty's Truth-Telling Gift from her so the magic doesn't run out as it does when I steal smaller doses.'

Jamie exhaled. 'Bugger.'

'Yeah.'

A haggis rolled up to Sorley and started nuzzling his ankle. He reached down and scooped it up, cooing at it. Then he cleared his throat. 'Big deal. Let the Steward deal with them. The Adair borders are secure. We'll all be safe.' He glanced down at the haggis and affected a high-pitched tone of voice. 'Won't we? We'll be safe, won't we? Who's the cutest little...?' He stopped halfway through his sentence, seeming to realise what he was doing. He put the haggis back down on the floor and glared at us all. 'They're upset because of the Carnegie woman. I'm just being nice to them to stop them from annoying everyone else.'

I tipped my head to one side. 'You could have left them at home,' I pointed out.

Sorley's eyes shifted. 'I ... er...'

I smiled and returned to the topic in hand. 'I can't pretend the Fomori aren't there. I have to do something to get them to back down.'

Taylor glanced at me. 'But you won't fight them.'

'No,' I conceded.

He lifted his shoulders in defeat. 'Then what are you going to do? How are you going to stop them?'

I gazed at him. 'I'm open to suggestions.'

Byron burst in through the doors. 'You're not going to believe this,' he breathed, as giddy as a child. 'But I just saw the Foinse. It's here! The source of all magic is here on this ferry!' He shook his head in disbelief. 'Come, look.'

Jamie abandoned Taylor, dashed out the door and almost collided with Speck on his way in. 'Bloody hell! Who brought the Foinse here?'

Speck beamed. 'Me!'

Byron turned to stare at him. I threw up my hands. 'What if the Sidhe had caught up to us? It needs to be kept safe, Speck!'

'I thought we might need the extra magical boost. It helped me create that wave. You know, the one that allowed us to escape?' he added pointedly.

Out of the corner of my eye, I spotted Byron's expression flatten into an impenetrable mask. He folded his arms. Crapadoodle. 'You know it's here,' he said. It wasn't a question.

I scratched my neck. 'I do now,' I answered slowly.

'That wasn't what I meant.' He eyed me. Even Sorley seemed to think it was a good idea to back away. 'You've had the Foinse in your possession all this time and you didn't tell me?'

'It's not in my possession.' I wondered how I could extricate myself without pissing him off again. 'It's got free will. It chooses where to go.'

Speck jabbed his finger at me. 'Yes! If the Foinse hadn't wanted to come here, it wouldn't be here. So it's not my fault.'

I frowned at him and he grinned. I looked at Byron. 'And it's not like it's always been hanging around. It's only been with us since we got back the Adair Lands. It was there when we arrived.'

'That's true,' Taylor nodded.

'So what you're saying is that when I visited you there, the Foinse was there too?'

This wasn't going very well. 'Er, yes.'

'And you kept it a secret?'

'Byron, I…' I sighed. 'Yes, I kept it a secret.'

A muscle jerked in his jaw. He took a step towards me. 'Why shouldn't you tell a secret around a clock?' His voice was dangerously low.

'Excuse me?'

'You heard me.' He tapped his foot.

'Because, um, time will tell?'

Sorley's eyes turned from me to Byron and back again then his face cleared and he let out a loud guffaw.

'That's right,' Byron said silkily. 'And if it takes us until the end of time, I'm going to make sure that you trust me. You got that?'

'I've got it!' Shite. 'I mean, I do trust you. I just … forgot to tell you about the Foinse, that's all.'

'That's fine.' He stepped away.

Feeling hot and bothered, I rubbed my neck. I had completely lost track of what was going on. It was just as well that Bob took that moment to harangue us. He flashed into the room with a disdainful glance. 'You'll be relieved to know that we're safe. The Sidhe are no longer trying to pursue us.' He sniffed loudly. 'You're *welcome*.'

'Thank you, Bob.'

He zipped up to Byron. 'I didn't hear anything from you.' He wiggled his earlobe. 'I know you're broke but manners cost nothing.'

'Thank you, Bob.'

'Well,' the genie demurred, 'okay then.' He flew down, hovering at the edge of Byron's kilt. 'What do Scotsmen wear under these things? I've always wondered...'

Byron grabbed him before he could take a peek. 'Manners cost nothing,' he reminded him.

Bob pouted. 'Yeah, yeah.' He looked over his shoulder at me. 'I should tell you that Tipsy is throwing a tantrum up on the deck. Fergus, May and Candy are trying to calm her down but they're not having much luck.'

I pressed the base of my palms against my temples. 'Okay,' I said, 'okay.'

***

Bob hadn't been kidding about the tantrum part. Tipsania was marching up and down the slick boards, picking up everything that wasn't nailed down and throwing it away. 'I will wring his neck. I will pull out his fingernails one by one.' She grabbed a lifebelt and hurled it into the grey, churning sea. Mm. We might need those.

Candy stood to one side. 'It's better to let her run out of steam,' he advised.

'Steam?' Tipsania shrieked. 'I'll show you steam. I will ram a steaming hot poker right up his arse. Then you'll see steam.'

May shuffled up, Fergus following with a large golf umbrella in a bid to shield from the sun. 'Ip. Ee!' she squeaked.

'Not now, May!'

Byron said, 'That's a Fomori demon.'

Ah. 'Yes. Yes, it is. She's nice, though. Honest.'

'If it takes until the end of time, Integrity,' he reminded me.

'I wasn't keeping her a secret! She just never came up!'

He obviously didn't believe me. I gave up and focused on Tipsania instead. 'What's wrong?'

She stopped what she was doing and stared at me. 'What's wrong?' she shrieked. 'What's bloody wrong? You imbecile! You poor excuse for a Sidhe! You white-haired cretin!'

'I tried to warn you,' Candy rumbled.

'Tipsania,' I said, trying again. 'I know this has been tough on you. I'm really sorry about your dad. It's important to grieve but I'm not sure this is the best way to go about it.'

She put her hands on her hips and marched up to me. 'My dad was a wanker,' she said icily. 'I'm not happy he's dead and I'm certainly not happy about how it happened but that's not why I'm angry.'

Angry didn't begin to cover it. I wouldn't have been surprised if she'd turned green and ripped her way out of her sodden wedding dress.

'Aifric,' she said, spitting the name out with disgust. 'He's not dead.'

'No.'

'I want to kill him. Slowly.'

Bob began to applaud. 'Yes! You go, girl!'

Before I could say anything, Tipsania moved up until she was inches from my face. 'Do you know what he said to me? He said that if I didn't marry Byron, he would drag me to the altar himself and marry me. *He* would marry me! The nerve of the man!' I opened my mouth but she still wasn't finished. 'As if I would tie myself to someone like him! And look!' She grabbed my head and forced it down. 'Look at what I'm wearing! It's a monstrosity. Bows!' she spat. 'Nobody wears bows! I look like Cinderella. I'm not some servant playing dress up!'

Candy held up his hand like a wary school kid. 'I think you look pretty.'

She paused for a moment. 'You always think that! That's not the point! My wedding day is supposed to be the happiest day of my life. Now it's ruined!'

I was confused. 'You wanted to get married?'

'You don't understand anything!'

'Tipsania,' I said reasonably, 'Aifric can't touch you now. We're well away from him. You don't have to worry.'

She scowled at me ferociously. 'There's only one thing that will stop me worrying.' She stomped over to Candy. He looked rather frightened and I wasn't surprised. 'I want you to know,' she said, 'that I am not doing this just to take myself off the market and stop Aifric from forcing me into marriage with him or Byron or anyone else who comes along. I'm doing this because I love you. Got that?' The words flew out of her at a tremendous pace. She swallowed, smoothed her billowing dress down and forced herself to relax. Then she got down on one knee. 'Candy Carmichael. Will you marry me? If you don't say yes, I will cut off your bloody—'

'Yes.'

She blinked. 'Pardon?'

'Yes. I will marry you.'

'Well, that's alright then. I don't want this horrific excuse for a wedding dress to go to waste.' She clambered awkwardly to her feet and began kissing Candy. There was a lot of tongue action. Trying not to look at the way she was attacking his mouth, I coughed.

'Congratulations. But, er, we don't have a minister on board. You can't get married.'

Tipsania broke away and gazed at me scornfully. 'Idiot. How long do you think I've been planning my own wedding?' Apparently it was a rhetorical question because I wasn't given chance to reply. 'Since I was six years old! A ship's captain can marry someone.'

'She's right,' Angus said, butting in with a cheesy grin. Byron flashed him a glare but he didn't seem to notice.

'Who's the captain?' I asked. 'It's not me. I don't know anything about boats.'

Fergus pointed at Brochan. 'He's a merman. He should be captain.'

'Piss off.'

I thought about it. 'Sorley is the one who commandeered this ferry. Him and all the trolls. I guess that makes him captain.'

Tipsania paused for a moment. 'I'm to be married by a troll?'

I shrugged.

'Whatever. Let's get on with it.'

Candy beamed at her. 'I can't wait.'

'I love you,' she breathed. They began kissing again.

'True love,' I muttered. 'Oh well. I guess we're going to a wedding after all.'

***

The trolls worked quickly. They cleared out the canteen area and arranged themselves and us in formation. Someone managed to rustle up some cans of Irn Bru for a post-ceremony toast although we had to share them. I reckoned I got a thimbleful.

'This is the strangest wedding I've ever been to,' I said quietly to Byron as Sorley straightened the tie he'd borrowed from Taylor and mumbled to himself as he tried to remember his lines. The Foinse zipped overhead with one of Tipsania's lacy bows perched on top of it. Byron didn't answer. I turned to him and realised he was watching me closely. 'What?'

'Nothing,' he said. He licked his lips. 'Do you like weddings?'

'I like emotional weddings. The kind where even the cake is in tiers.'

'Ha,' he murmured. He put his arm round my waist and drew me close. I told myself sternly not to snuggle but it was a close-run thing.

Candy, looking rather nervous, took his spot. Then, while Bob produced a baby grand piano and began to tinkle out the wedding march, Tipsania made her grand entrance. The trolls acted suitably impressed, oohing and aahing at her dress. I decided now probably wasn't the time to tell her that she had a trail of seaweed knotted into some of the ribbons at the back.

'Dearly beloved,' Sorley shouted, causing half of the makeshift congregation to wince, 'we are gathered here today to witness the binding together in matrimony of this man and this woman.' From his ragged pocket, he produced a length of fabric. He wound it first around Tipsania's wrist then around Candy's, joining them together. As he continued, I stared at it.

'Join together,' I whispered. 'Of course.' I could have slapped myself for not thinking of it earlier. My ancestors at the Cruaich grove had given me the answer to all our problems and I'd been too stupid to see it.

Byron gave me a strange look. I grinned and leaned my head on his shoulder. The last few days had been amongst the worst in my life. Morna's face flashed into my mind; maybe it was just as well that we were all being kept busy, otherwise I'd have had to lock myself away in a dark room to deal with her loss. Aifric had so much to answer for. He would come after us again and next time he wouldn't waste time on fake trials, he'd move straight to the main event. I wasn't going to kill him though; I was better than that.

Candy and Tipsania leaned towards each other as they said their vows. I spotted Taylor wiping away a surreptitious tear, together with dozens of the supposedly hardened trolls who were watching. Tipsania looked radiant, all tantrums forgotten. And all of a sudden, there was a glimmer of real hope.

Chapter Sixteen

It wasn't difficult to drag Fergus and May into a corner during the post-ceremony celebrations. Fergus told me what he'd already gleaned about the Lowlands then we huddled together while May patiently answered the rest of my questions, with Fergus standing in as interpreter. A couple of times she seemed to falter and a shadow crossed her red eyes. On each occasion she stared hard at me and nodded to herself before telling me what I needed to know. When I had all the information, I asked her to open her mouth. I congratulated myself on not recoiling at the sight of the stub of her tongue that remained. Then, as Fergus gripped her hands tightly, I used Aifric's Gift.

It was the oddest sensation for both of us. May had obviously become accustomed to her condition because she looked as if she'd been given a humungous gobstopper. To suddenly have this thick fleshy thing shoved back into her mouth couldn't have been pleasant. She kept sticking it out and waggling it around. As for me, the act of growing new flesh was very different to healing Taylor's wounds. There had always been a strange connection between May and me, but now it felt more physical as if, somehow, we were tied together in ways I didn't understand. It went some way to explaining why the Gift of Healing wasn't used more often. Although I was filled with spreading warmth at the obvious success, I instinctively knew that using this Gift too regularly would invite insanity. The new connections that were formed each time between healer and healed would spread the magic user too thinly, both physically and emotionally. It was a sobering revelation.

May couldn't yet talk properly. The sensation of using an organ which she'd become so used to doing without meant that it was easier for her to continue communicating with Fergus through sign language. It didn't mean that she wasn't going to practise the 'new' sounds she could make, however. When I got up to leave, murmuring to Fergus about what I needed from him next, she clutched at his arm and beamed, her brow furrowed in deep concentration. 'Fer … gus.'

I pressed my lips together hard. It was difficult to say who was more jubilant, Fergus or May.

I turned to go, leaving them to enjoy her newfound skills. Fergus grabbed my arm. 'You should know,' he said, his eyes focusing on mine with an intensity I'd not seen from him before, 'her tongue wasn't removed as a punishment. It wasn't done to hurt her.'

'Then why?' I asked, my voice barely audible above the raucous cheering of the trolls around us.

He shrugged awkwardly. 'From what she's told me, it was some kind of parasite. It burrowed its way in and cutting out her tongue was the only way to get rid of it. Even then, she didn't think she was going to make it. Most demons affected in this way don't.'

'I assumed it was torture,' I said.

'So did I. But she keeps saying that the Fomori aren't as bad as we all think.'

We exchanged glances. I bit my lip, nodded and walked away. There was still a lot to do before the night was over.

***

We reconvened at the prow of the ferry. I checked my watch and gave a satisfied nod. Three in the morning. Many of the trolls were still on patrol but I reckoned we had a good five minutes before they'd swing round this way again.

Fergus had already worked out what was going to happen. He leaned nonchalantly against the side of the ship, a smile playing around his lips, while I outlined the plan. Byron remained impassive and I appreciated his silence until I'd finished talking. 'That's an even worse idea than planning a fake wedding,' he told me.

I was expecting this reaction. 'Right now, there's no alternative. Not unless letting an all-out war start is your idea of fun.' He looked irritated. I shrugged. 'I'm telling you all this because I'm not keeping any more secrets.'

Byron raised his eyebrows. 'Is that why Lexie, Speck, Brochan and Taylor are currently tucked in bed and not here?'

I met his eyes. 'Taylor almost died. And you're right, this is a really bad idea. It's risky and stupid and if he knew, Taylor would give me astronomical odds against the chance of success. If any of them was aware of what I'm about to do, they'd demand to come along but I'm not putting them in that kind of danger. I'd prefer not to put you in that kind of danger either. But for you,' I gestured helplessly, 'full disclosure.'

His response was quiet. 'Thank you. I appreciate that more than you know.'

'It would be good if you stayed behind—'

He growled. 'I'm coming.' As if that were the end of the matter, he looked at Fergus. 'Why him?'

'Because I promised he could come.'

'I'll volunteer to stay behind!' Bob piped up. 'I have no desire to sneak beyond the Veil. I don't want to die yet, I still have the new season of *Doctor Who* to watch.'

'Sorry. You don't get a choice.'

He gazed at me dolefully. It was a long time since he'd pretended that asking for wishes wouldn't have disastrous side-effects. I wasn't sure there would be much choice, however. I sighed heavily. Risk versus reward.

Heavy footsteps sounded along the deck, heading in our direction. I checked inside my bag one last time then closed it and swung it over my shoulder. I glanced at the three of them and they all nodded.

Byron turned his gaze towards the lifeboat hanging in readiness on the side of the ferry. Using Telekinesis, he lowered it silently down to the sea. Fergus let out a low whistle of approval. I scowled at him for making a noise then vaulted over the side and down into the boat. I didn't want to hide from the trolls but if they knew what I was up to, I'd end up with an army at my back. Reassuring as that might sound, it would only cause more problems than it would solve.

Byron released the lifeboat from the last of its moorings. The ferry chugged past us, its vast hull like some steel monster gliding through the night. That was it; we were on our own. I started the tiny starboard engine. We were fairly close to the coastline so it wouldn't take too long to reach land.

Fergus held up his hand. 'Wait.'

I glanced at him, askance, then I heard a soft splash. What the hell? May's unmistakable clawed hand curved round the lifeboat's edge and she hauled herself in. 'What?' I hissed. 'No! May, get back!'

'I think it's too late,' Fergus said drily. The ferry was already some distance away from us.

I glared at him. 'It's too dangerous.'

'She's the one person who can really help us. You know that.'

'We're putting her life at risk!'

'All our lives are at risk. She knows that and she wants to come.'

'You told her what we were doing.'

He gazed at me implacably. 'No secrets.'

A smile tugged at the corner of Byron's mouth. 'Can't argue with that.'

May gave me a cautious smile. 'In ... tegrity?' she asked, trying out the word.

I sighed. Crapadoodle. 'Fine. Let's go.'

Bob's bottom lip jutted out. 'Avast, me hearties,' he mumbled.

'Everything will be fine,' I told him. I injected as much confidence as I could into my voice. Sooner or later I was bound to start believing my own hype.

Bob crossed his arms and huffed. 'Remind me of that when Fomori demons are chewing on your heart.'

***

We made land shortly before dawn, pulling the small lifeboat onto a chilly, deserted beach before clambering over the dunes and jogging towards the Veil. I wasn't certain about our location but, when I saw the dark, lightning-filled wall of cloud looming ahead of us, I knew that my calculations had brought us close. From the expressions on my companions' faces, however, our proximity wasn't a cause for celebration. Each of them had good reason to be nervous.

'I never thought I'd say this, Uh Integrity,' Bob quavered, 'but I'd quite like a joke right about now.' He wrapped his arms around himself and shivered. 'It's not that I'm scared for me, you understand. It's you lot who will suffer. You need your minds taken off the horror that's about to come.'

May might not have understood Bob's words but she understood his tone of voice. She gave him a huge grin and stuck her thumbs up. He tutted.

'We should hold hands,' I said decisively.

Fergus raised his eyebrows. 'Are you looking to get close to me? Because I think I'm kind of spoken for.'

'Ha! No, but when I crossed with Angus he almost got lost in the Veil. It's safer if we hang on to each other.'

Byron's jaw tightened. 'I need to know. Are...?'

'No.' I touched his shoulder. 'We're just friends. I promise.'

He scanned my face then nodded. 'Okay.'

'That's it?'

'Trust works both ways.'

I patted my bag then Byron took my hand and squeezed. On my other side, I grabbed Fergus's hand while he took May's.

Bob squeaked, 'Byron? Can I hide under your kilt?'

Byron pointed downwards. 'Sporran.'

The genie's face was suddenly wreathed in smiles. He darted down towards the traditional leather purse and zoomed inside.

I took a deep breath. 'Let's do this. There's a prophecy that needs fulfilling.'

Byron grimaced. 'You know this could all be over in a matter of seconds. They're likely to slaughter you as soon as they catch sight of you.'

'Not if we play our cards right.' I had to believe that; there simply wasn't any other choice. 'Remember what I told you.' They all nodded. I licked my lips, wishing they weren't quite so dry. 'And on a count of three. One ... two ... three.'

Linked together, we stepped forward and plunged inside. Bob shrieked from the depths of Byron's sporran. I'd never had the comfort of so many others around me on previous occasions when I'd crossed over. Perhaps it was that, or perhaps it was the familiarity of the choking clouds and sense of impending doom, but I didn't feel scared. Adrenaline shot through me but there was also a pervasive feeling of calm, as if everything up until now had been leading to this point.

I held my breath and kept going, yanking on Fergus's hand when he started to falter. Then, when it seemed as if we could go no further, we were out the other side and breathing in the dark, dank air of the Lowlands. And there was indeed an entire army of Fomori demons facing us.

It was almost comical. As I stared at the long ranks of demons standing to attention, at first they didn't seem to notice our sudden appearance. Less than twenty feet separated us from the thousands of them. I sensed rather than saw when one pair of demon-slitted eyes landed on me. I turned my head and gazed at him as he gazed back at me, his shock swiftly transforming into abject horror. Good. That was what I'd been counting on. He reached across and hit his companion. One by one, the demons turned to look at us. Hello.

The ranks stretched lengthwise as far as I could see. I couldn't begin to guess how many of them there were but it was clearly too many for the Highlanders to cope with. If they attacked my homeland, it would be a bloodbath – and the demons would inevitably win. Armies, however, were prepared for armies; they weren't prepared to deal with a tiny group. A single person could stand against a tank; might and power weren't always about numbers. As far as the Fomori demons were concerned, I was the bogeyman; I was also the bogeyman who'd returned from the dead.

One of the demons who was made of sterner stuff than the others took a step forward. I calmly released Fergus and Byron's hands and reached into my bag. We had seconds before the Fomori recovered and charged.

The Foinse hummed as soon as my fingers brushed against it. The sound was reassuring, even though it felt hotter to the touch than normal. With slow, deliberate movements I drew it out and held it aloft, bathing us in its warm, silvered glow.

The nearest demons cowered, including the one who'd moved in our direction. It wasn't surprising; the Fomori lived in semi-darkness and these guys weren't swathed in the strange gloop I'd seen some demons wear when they crossed into our part of Scotland. That meant they hadn't planned any incursions until nightfall because they felt vulnerable to the light.

The Foinse didn't exude ultra-violet rays but the light which the source of magic cast was strange enough to create more fear and paranoia. Whatever the Draoidheachd looked like, it was either very different to this or it was kept well out of sight from the Lowland's citizens.

A peculiar rumble filled the air, growing louder and louder. I knew that sound. Next to me, Byron sucked in an alarmed breath. We'd been fortunate not to emerge in front of any of the winged demons but it was only a matter of time until they approached. It was now or never. 'Come on, baby,' I whispered. The Foinse hummed louder in response.

'I should tell you before you do this,' Byron said, his voice even and controlled. 'I love you.'

Magic crackled to my right as the Fomori prepared to attack and it prevented me from responding. I gave a tiny smile and then I threw the Foinse, using every ounce of my energy. Whatever sentient energy it possessed meant that it knew what it was doing; it somersaulted and kept low as it hurtled towards the Fomori ranks. They screamed and scattered.

The four of us began to run. Byron, Fergus and May veered to the right and I went left. The gap in the ranks created by the Foinse was greater than I'd hoped. While it danced and spun and held the Fomori at bay, I sprinted for all I was worth.

There was a whoosh of wind and my hair blew around my face. I grimaced. One of the flying demons was gunning for me and it was getting close. I zigzagged, trying to throw it off. The Foinse zipped towards me but I muttered and it curved off, heading away. The demon above me screeched in fury at my audacity in showing up then it flung a bolt of darkness towards me.

I had no way of knowing what sort of Gift this was. I could have paused, turned, and examined the demon but that was hardly likely to happen. Instead, I did what I could to speed away from the encroaching darkness.

My toe hit a rock that was jutting up out of the ground and I stumbled forward, forcing my body into a roll at the last moment. The demon screeched again and this time the call was taken up by the thousands at my back. I leapt to my feet, momentum propelling me forward. I clenched my fists to stop the trembling and glanced to my right. There were a couple of demons on the others' tails. I swallowed, my mouth dry. Another flying demon swooped down towards them, gaining on them.

'Adair!' I yelled, knowing the windless atmosphere would make my voice carry far across the grim moors.

The demon flipped its head and stared in my direction. The delay gave Byron, Fergus and May a chance. Byron lunged upwards, snatched the Foinse out of the air and bundled it inside his jacket. I smiled grimly. Before long, the darkness would swallow them up. Or so I hoped.

I yelled again. The thunder of thousands of feet slamming into the ground behind me would strike fear into anyone's heart. As long as they focused on me – the Adair – then I was happy. I took a deep breath, calling up my last traces of the Electrosurge Gift. There were raucous shouts behind me and I knew that the Fomori were preparing to throw every last scrap of magic they had at me. The element of surprise was well and truly over. My skin tingled. Work, I prayed. Please work.

The air ahead of me spat and crackled. Preparing for the pain, I tensed myself. Then I squeezed my eyes shut, drew out the last magic, and felt the power slam through me as if I'd been punched in the head by a giant. So that's what it feels like to be struck by lightning, I thought, as I spun in slow motion towards the ground. Shocking.

Chapter Seventeen

It was all about the illusion of control. When Aifric had me under lock and key, he'd grown over-confident because he thought he was in charge. This was effectively the same scenario: now the Fomori demons had the terrifying, monstrous Integrity Adair as a prisoner, especially after she'd electrocuted herself, they'd feel empowered. They'd hopefully be curious enough about me to delay their Highland invasion even if only for a day or two. Of course, there was the very real concern that they'd simply cut my throat and be done with me, but I'd removed the threat I presented by knocking myself out. The Fomori were supposed to be evil but how many people would execute an unarmed, unconscious young woman? Especially one they'd want to interrogate first? It had been a gamble but it was a gamble worth taking when you considered the alternatives. Still, when I woke up in even more pain than I had experienced at Aifric's hands, I was relieved that I'd woken up at all. I hoped that the others had escaped.

I'd wanted to find myself on Arthur's Seat, the same hill next to the old city of Edinburgh where Byron had been taken. Unfortunately, I wasn't there – in fact, I couldn't tell where I was other than that I was inside. Being blindfolded, trussed up and gagged had something to do with that. The Fomori weren't taking any chances.

I still had two of my five senses left. I couldn't hear anything but I could smell urine and vomit. Deciding that this situation simply wouldn't do, I shuffled on my back like an upturned turtle. It took some time but I made my way around the room, estimating it was about the size of a small bathroom. Or a prison cell. There was a metal bucket in one corner, which was where the godawful stench was coming from. I got as close as I could manage, retching once or twice. Given the danger of vomiting when I had a gag in my mouth, I needed to acclimatise pretty quickly.

I assumed that the Fomori demons didn't have an Ikea they could pop down to when they needed some cheap, disposable hardware. That meant the bucket had either been forged in a blacksmith's or it harked back to the pre-Fissure era. Either way, I hoped to find a sharp edge on it. Then all I needed was a little bit of friction.

Holding my breath, I figured that sight would help me more than anything else so I flipped onto my stomach and lowered the side of my head towards the bucket's rim. It took considerable effort – and numerous attempts – but I eventually pushed the blindfold upwards so that I could see. Only one eye was free and I probably looked like a jaunty pirate, but I felt buoyed by my success.

Sitting up, and scooting as far away from the offending bucket as possible, I took in my surroundings. It was indeed a small room but there were no bars so it wasn't a jail cell. There was a solid-looking oak door with a spyhole in the centre; thankfully, it was closed. No matter how hard I listened, I couldn't make out anyone on the other side but that didn't mean there wasn't someone there.

My head hurt and I felt weak and trembly. There were some grazes on my arms that hadn't been there before but other than that I seemed to be injury free. That boded very well for the future; as long as the Fomori weren't in a hurry to maim, torture or kill me, hope remained. I grinned. Hope always remained.

There were a number of ways that I could free myself from the rest of the restraints but the easiest and the quickest would be to use Apportation and simply magic away the ropes and bonds. I could even call any nearby rats and encourage them to gnaw through the bindings. But I wasn't Cinderella any more than Tipsania was, and I had serious doubts that I could make wild animals do my bidding. Besides, rats? Bleurgh. No, it made sense to conserve what magic I had. Alongside Kirsty Kincaid's Truth Gift, I now had Healing from Aifric and the ability to grow things from Morna. As I'd stolen those Gifts in their entirety, they were going to stay with me. The other magic I'd stolen from the Sidhe at the Cruaich was little more than a trickle now, even Illusion. I needed to be sparing.

With that in mind, I glanced at the bucket. There was a steel handle on one side of the rim which was attached by a nail. It wasn't very sturdy. It would take some doing – and no doubt more retching – but I reckoned I could use the sharp edge of the nail to saw my way through my bonds. Once my hands were free, I could unfasten everything else. It would take a lot of time but it wasn't as if I was going anywhere and it would give me ample opportunity to consider my next move.

In the end, it took me little more than an hour. I faced the door in case any demons appeared. My hands kept slipping and I almost knocked over the bucket on at least three occasions. Thankfully it stayed upright; the last thing I wanted was to be soaked by the contents of someone else's bladder and bowels.

Although the rope was wrapped tightly round my wrists and the knots were cleverly secured, it wasn't difficult to free myself. My thief background made it easier for me than it might have been for someone else, but the ease of the process gave me pause. I inspected the frayed edges of the rope; it wasn't very well made. I pursed my lips and considered. There was still no sound from outside and I seemed to be very much alone. I was beginning to wonder, however.

Shrugging, I loosened the gag. My mouth was unpleasantly dry and I'd have been tempted to sell Bob for a glass of water. I tried to work up some saliva and began to unknot the rope round my ankles. I didn't hurry; I had a feeling about what was going to happen once I was free. When I unwound the last loop and kicked the rope away there was a scuffle on the other side of the door and it swung open. Shite. Sometimes I hated being right.

The light was dim and the figure staring at me was difficult to make out. I tilted my head to one side and squinted. The Fomori demon spat on the ground and stepped inside. As his features grew clearer, I realised he wasn't looking at me with fear or apprehension. There wasn't any malevolence or sense of triumph in his gaze; he seemed simply curious. 'Adair.'

I decided that was a question. Staying on the ground to show that I was happy to remain subservient, I nodded. 'Yes.'

He grunted. In stilting, albeit grammatically accurate English, he asked, 'Why did you not use magic to free yourself?'

So it was a test. What would they have done if I'd had Teleportation as a Gift? Were they prepared for every eventuality? Given the neutrality of his expression, I thought the answer was probably yes.

I chose my words carefully, wanting to ingratiate myself without appearing manipulative or sneaky. 'One who relies on magic alone is a fool,' I said.

The demon rolled his tongue around his sharp, yellowing teeth. I suppressed a shudder and continued to look at him as if we were having an idle chat in a café.

He nodded. 'This will be interesting then.' He stretched out his bony arms and cracked his fingers one by one. I guessed I was supposed to be intimidated and I was. I was probably also supposed to ask why 'this' would be interesting but I wasn't going to give him the satisfaction.

If he was disappointed by my silence, it didn't show. He looked at me and I looked at him and absolutely nothing happened. It was like a bizarre staring contest. I was tempted to remain quiet and see if I could break him. Be good, Tegs, I told myself. This wasn't about my ego.

I licked my chapped lips. 'You speak English very well.'

The demon snorted. 'Yes. Our kind spent considerable resources learning Gaelic so we could communicate with your people.' He didn't crack a smile. 'Imagine our unbridled joy when we discovered that more spoke English than Gaelic.'

My eyebrows raised. Sarcasm? From a demon? 'Are you in charge here?' I asked.

'No.'

'Then,' I said, without irony, 'take me to your leader.'

'No.'

I scratched my head. Okay, then.

The demon gave a guttural noise and two more appeared and walked past him. They looked more nervous than him as they hauled me up by my armpits until I was face to face with their apparent boss, even if he wasn't *the* boss.

'We know of your prophecy,' the demon said.

'Prophecies are tricky things,' I returned. 'They often don't come true.'

He inclined his head and a length of straggly hair fell from his forehead. He tucked it behind his ear with one gnarled hand. 'You are correct. It is also true that to blame the individual for the words of a prophecy is to blame the tide for rising.'

I was starting to like this guy. 'So,' I said softly, 'there is no need for us to be at odds with each other.'

He smiled for the first time. 'There is plenty of need for that. Furthermore, the Fomori are not in the habit of taking chances, even if we are less bloodthirsty than our Sidhe neighbours.'

Less bloodthirsty? I'd seen compelling evidence to the contrary so that was an interesting statement. 'The prophecy is vague,' I pointed out. 'It could refer to anything.'

'Vague?' he asked.

'It means—'

'I know what the word means. There is nothing vague about the prophecy however.'

I was prepared to argue the point, even though the demons on either side of me had tightened their grip painfully. 'One Adair will save Scotland.' I shrugged. 'Or Alba, anyway. That could mean anything. Technically, the Lowlands are part of Scotland.' I leaned forward as much as I could. 'We are all Alba.'

'That is not what the prophecy says.' His lip curled. 'One Adair will destroy Alba.'

I shook my head vehemently. 'No! That's not the wording.'

'Yes, it is.' He regarded me calmly. 'Your own king confirmed it.'

I almost spat. Aifric. 'He is no king.'

'Whatever.' The demon flicked his hand dismissively. 'We are not monsters, regardless of what your kind may believe. But we will not take chances either.' For a brief moment, I saw sympathy flicker in his eyes. Then he gestured to the other two. 'Bring her.' He turned on his heel and left.

***

I was dragged through many narrow corridors. Given how vast this place was, together with the fact that it appeared to be made entirely of stone, there was only one answer: I was in Edinburgh Castle. That was both good and bad.

I kept my eyes peeled and my wits about me, trying to learn as much as I could during the uncomfortable journey. Other than a large number of closed doors and a lack of decoration, there was little I could work out. The silence, however, was gradually giving way to a strange sort of thunder. I'd never been past the Veil when the weather was anything but hot and muggy but it was possible that storms occurred.

Eventually I was taken up a winding flight of stairs. A female demon was waiting at the top; she glared at me with such ferocity that I thought she was going to kill me right then and there. Instead she unlocked the door next to her and I was shoved inside.

Shaking my head and rubbing the bruises on my arms, I looked around. The noise was deafening. It waxed and waned but it sounded too unnatural to be a storm. I still couldn't work out what it was.

'It's you!'

I jumped half out of my skin. From the shadowed corner of my latest holding pen came the tiny, familiar figure of a pixie. The last time I'd seen her, she was chained to a wooden pole on Arthur's Seat. Now she didn't look any the worse for wear for the experience; she was smiling so broadly, I wondered if her cheeks would split.

'You're here to save us,' she breathed. 'You came back.'

Uh-oh. I was here chancing my arm because I was out of other options and the Fomori army was on the verge of invading the Highlands. I was as much of a prisoner as she was, even if I had a plan or two up my sleeve. Taking the cautious route, I shook my head. 'If only,' I muttered.

She stared at me. 'You're right,' she said eventually. 'There's always someone listening.' She glanced round and raised her voice. 'You hear me? We're not imbeciles! We're not going to fall for your stupid plots!' I gaped at her. She turned her head and winked, then settled down in a heap on the floor.

'Where are we?'

'Castle, of course.'

I nodded. 'Yes, but…'

'Arena,' she said sourly. 'We're in the holding pen for the arena.'

Nausea rose in my stomach. That sounded… 'That's cheering, isn't it?'

The pixie nodded and my shoulders sank. So the arena was some kind of gladiatorial hell-pit. 'They think it makes them civilized,' she spat. I didn't need to ask who *they* were. 'Instead of killing us outright, they pretend to give us a way out. Win and you'll be freed.' She paused. 'As if. No one ever wins.'

'Execution as sport,' I whispered. Even Aifric wouldn't conceive something so horrific. No wonder the Fomori hadn't hurt me.

The door opened and the scowling female demon entered, carrying something on a tray. She thrust it at me and muttered a string of incomprehensible Fomori sentences.

'You're to take the food,' the pixie said. 'It'll help you in the arena.'

I blinked and stared. That was food? It looked like – fungus. The demon glared and yelled something. Helplessly, I took the tray.

'She doesn't like you,' the pixie offered.

'I kinda got that.'

'You killed her niece.'

I almost dropped the tray. 'Excuse me?'

She shrugged. 'That's what she says.'

I looked wide-eyed at the demon. I'd never killed anyone; I was never *going to* kill anyone. She spat at me and backed away, not taking her eyes from me until the door was closed again.

'The more dead Fomori the better,' the pixie said.

I didn't have a response to that. I huddled down with the tray, sniffing cautiously at the brown and grey lumps.

'We are lucky. They feed us well before the arena. They want us to be strong enough to give them a good show.'

I grinned, thinking she was making a joke then I realised she was being serious. Sobering up, I avoided looking at her, lifted the crude cup and took a sip. It was definitely water. It tasted even fouler than the stuff I'd been given when I'd been held at the Steward's pleasure. I tried not to think too hard about where it had come from and steeled myself to try the food. It helped that I was ravenously hungry.

I picked up the oddly carved spoon and gingerly tasted. It wasn't as bad as I'd feared – just mildly salty – but the texture was off-putting, something between the sludge that collects underneath drainpipes and wallpaper paste. I had serious doubts whether it had any nutritional value. Then again, the same could be said for my normal diet of Irn Bru and salt-and-vinegar crisps. One day I'd learn to eat my greens but apparently not today.

I forced down the lot. As soon as I put down the eating utensil, the door was opened again. I was expecting the same angry demon as before but this time it was a different face. Two different faces, in fact.

'Watch out,' the pixie muttered. 'This one can tell truth from lies.'

Interesting. That was at least one other Gift which had transferred to the Fomori.

The other demon, a pockmarked male with a sunken chest, kept his distance. He barked something at me. Unable to understand, I shook my head. He hissed and pointed at the pixie. She sighed. 'He wants to know how much magic you have,' she said.

Nonplussed, I frowned. 'Er … quite a bit?'

She translated for me. The demon glowered and clenched his fists. He shouted at her. 'How many magics,' she corrected.

'Oh. You mean how many Gifts?' I considered. I supposed I had just the one: stealing. I said as much, holding up a single finger for emphasis. The pixie translated.

The demon's eyes narrowed in suspicion. He stepped forward, his fist raised. His companion touched his arm and murmured something in his ear.

'She says you're telling the truth,' my cell-mate informed me.

At this, he scratched his head. He looked as if he'd been given a simple sum to complete that somehow wouldn't add up. He wrinkled his nose then lifted his knobbly shoulders. He yelled a few words, wheeled round and they both left.

I frowned after them. 'Didn't he want to know what my Gift … I mean, my magic … is?'

The pixie didn't seem to care. 'He already knows,' she replied carelessly. 'He told the others to make sure the arena fliers are overhead and at all the exits to stop you.'

'Stop me from what?'

She glanced at me as if I were slightly mad. 'Using your Gift.'

Now I was even more confused. Of course, they were under the impression that my Gift was something other than stealing. Last time I was here I'd used that strange dark cloud magic to make my escape. I'd used other magic too but, as far as the demons were concerned, that was the one they had evidence of because they'd seen me use it. Perhaps they thought Byron had created the Illusion of his body still in chains so he could fool them for long enough to run away. I couldn't see how some winged demons would make a difference against a heavy choking poisonous cloud, however. I didn't recollect it doing anything other than skimming the ground and rising up perhaps three or four metres. Some odd, nebulous thought tugged at the back of my mind, demanding attention. Unfortunately, before the idea was fully formed, it vanished again. Stupid synapses.

'What does the brain do when it sees its best friend?' I asked.

The pixie looked at me from under her eyelashes.

'Gives it a brain wave.' I smirked.

Instead of laughing, she looked dejected. 'You're not the one we've been waiting for at all.'

Everyone was a hater. 'Guess not,' I mumbled.

Outside, the arena crowd gave a roar. This time it was so loud I felt the vibrations beneath me. 'We're getting close,' she said. 'They're building up to the main event.'

I licked my lips. 'Us?'

'Yes.' She stared into the distance. 'I suppose I should be proud that they're putting me out there with you, even if you're not the saviour. They only hold these events twice a year so there are a lot of fights and executions to get through. I've been kept waiting for a long time.'

I put my arm round her little shoulders. Poor thing. She deserved better than my jokes. She deserved better than this. 'What did you do to end up here?' I asked softly, not really expecting a response.

The pixie answered, 'Stabbed three Fomori and drank their blood.' My mouth dropped open and I pulled away. She shrugged. 'I was really hungry.'

I leaned my head against the stone wall of my new prison. The illusion of control indeed.

Chapter Eighteen

The food, if you could call it that, was still sitting uncomfortably in the pit of my stomach when they came for us. I made a last stab at negotiation. 'Look,' I said reasonably, 'I have important information to impart. If you could take me to the guy in charge, I'm sure we can sort all this out.'

None of the many demons who were standing in the corridor and gawking at me answered.

'Or gal in charge,' I added. 'If you lot are all about equal rights and it's a woman who's the boss, that's great by me. I'll talk to her too.'

All I got was silence then one of the demons, somewhat younger than the others, stretched out an inquisitive finger and poked me. He snatched his hand back and cackled. The demon next to him looked at it in awe. I was tempted to lunge towards him and see what effect that had but I had to make sure that none of these demons saw me as a threat. Frankly, from what she'd told me, the threat was the tiny pixie by my side. She was about as far removed from Lexie as it was possible to get.

We were taken to an open doorway. Peering out, I saw row upon row of demons arranged round a large open area where we were no doubt meant to fight. Hoardings, with lethal-looking spikes poking out, were in place around the audience, presumably to protect them from the evil they were here to watch.

There weren't just Fomori in the crowd; I spotted various different races, including Sidhe. A frisson of fear ran down my spine; they were baying for my blood and I hadn't even done anything. They hated me because of what I *might* do, not because of anything I had done. I wanted to march out there with my hands on my hips and tell them they were being ridiculous. Not that they'd hear me; now we were almost at the arena, the noise was deafening.

The surface of the arena was covered in grey-coloured sand. Here and there were dark patches; I knew without getting close that they were blood. I hissed through my teeth. There had been a lot of variables to consider before I crossed into the Lowlands but I hadn't imagined anything like this.

There was a loud beating of wings. From this angle, it was difficult to see what was happening but the vast shadow of a winged Fomori was visible across the sand. I guessed he was someone important because the crowd immediately hushed. He began to speak, his harsh voice reverberating around the rickety stadium. He was the MC.

'Hammer time,' I whispered.

The pixie glanced at me. 'They don't let us have weapons,' she informed me. 'It's not meant to be a fair fight.'

I nodded; an explanation at this point would be far too complicated. And pointless. As the MC demon droned on, and the guards at my back bounced around in a buzz of excited anticipation, I raised and lowered myself on my toes and cricked my neck. I couldn't imagine just how shite things were about to get.

One of the demons shoved me hard in the small of my back, forcing me onto the arena floor. I stumbled forward, just catching myself from falling. The pixie followed. She might be a hardened killer but she was shaking. We both were.

I didn't know how many eyes were on us but it seemed like hundreds. Everyone was silent, which was more frightening than the thunderous cheering I'd heard before. I swung round, taking in every inch of the crowd. The air was filled with hovering demons, all of whose attention was fixed on me. I ignored them for now. If this was like a Roman gladiatorial venue, there would be an obvious spot for the very important demons. As I turned to my left, I saw them.

There was a dais, elevated a few metres above the rest of the audience no doubt to keep the elite from being splattered with all that pesky blood or to protect their delicate nostrils from the smell. The combined body odours of all these Lowlanders rivalled the bucket in the cell.

Without the night vision that I assumed everyone else enjoyed, it was difficult to make out much about the demon leaders. There were six seated figures that possessed the same wiry, skeletal bodies as the rest of the Fomori. Beyond that, I couldn't tell much more about them. I squinted, narrowing my eyes to see more, but it was a wasted effort.

There was a single harsh shout, which sounded like a heartfelt curse, from one of the audience members behind me. That yell opened the floodgates and they all began roaring and chanting again. Far too many tried to throw things. If the projectiles had been rotten eggs or squishy tomatoes that might have been okay but these were stones. With the force that they were being thrown, I'd only need to be hit once in the wrong place and I'd be a goner.

I bobbed and dodged. A small pebble glanced off my shoulder – it still bloody hurt. The pixie yelled, a figure of unmitigated fury. I had to admire her tenacity. She whirled round while I ducked yet another missile.

Just as I was starting to think we'd be stoned to death, a loud horn sounded. The stone hurling stopped and a loud cheer ran round the crowd. They began to stamp their feet, one after the other in perfect timing.

'Here it comes,' the pixie muttered.

There was a shudder from the other end of the arena and I saw a rusty-looking gate heave upwards. A furious bellow from the dark corridor beyond was followed by a snort. I licked my lips. 'What is that?'

The pixie's response was unequivocal. 'Monster.'

She wasn't wrong. The thing that emerged was something out of my worst nightmares. It had some of the features of a Fomori demon but it wasn't like any of the ones I'd seen before. For one thing, it seemed to be twice the size of the others. Its body was crisscrossed with scars, some gouged so deeply into its flesh that it was a wonder the wounds had ever healed. It was wearing a covering around its groin which I doubted had anything to do with modesty. It wore enormous boots, studded with sharp nails; its face, contorted into a snarl, spoke of darkness and pain.

Involuntarily, I stepped back and the crowd roared louder in delight. The pixie held her ground though her legs were shaking. I kept my focus on the creature advancing slowly towards us, one heavy foot after the other. The closer it got, the more the promise of vile murder glittering in its eyes became obvious.

One of the winged bastards above us dropped something on the sand in front of the monster's feet. It didn't even pause but bent down and scooped it up while it continued to stride in our direction. With a sinking feeling, I realised that it was a medieval flail – a spiked ball on the end of a heavy chain. It was far larger than anything I'd seen on television or in a museum and its weight didn't seem to bother the bastard. With as much effort as it would have taken me to wave a feather boa round my head, the monster began to swing. And still it advanced.

Suddenly it broke into a run, the flail spinning in the air with greater and greater speed. The pixie screamed, a sound not of terror but of a battle cry. She launched herself towards the monster and I had no choice but to throw myself after her. One swipe of that weapon and she'd be mincemeat.

I grabbed a hank of her hair and she yelled in pain as I threw her to one side and out of the demon's path. It bared its teeth in what was supposed to be a smile. By this point, I was barely aware of the screaming crowd.

The best thing I could do was to get rid of the flail. That was where the immediate danger lay. As my hefty opponent took his first shot and almost lopped off my head, I concentrated on the last trickle of Apportation magic I had left. There was very little there and, even as I pulled it out and concentrated it towards the weapon, I knew it would be touch and go. I clenched my fists and focused. The flail vanished from the creature's hands. While it stared down at its empty palms, I let out a quick breath of relief.

The creature snarled while the crowd booed their dismay then it barrelled towards me, using its whole body as a weapon. I ran, zigzagging away. It bellowed in frustration and turned from to me to the pixie, who was just getting back to her feet. Shite.

'Hey!' I yelled. 'Ugly boy! Get your arse over here!' I jumped up and down and waved.

It snorted and glanced back. Whatever it might look like, it wasn't stupid. It knew that I was trying to distract it and didn't veer off course. Before I could think of something to do, there was a sickening crunch of breaking bones as its fist connected with the pixie's body. She crumpled like a rag doll. The move was so sudden and completed with such brute force that I had no way of knowing whether she was alive or dead. Whatever state she was in, the demon decided he was no longer interested in her. He twisted back to face me and grinned, his tongue lolling out of his mouth in delighted anticipation.

I backed up again, unable to go much further because of the dangerous spikes surrounding the arena floor. In my peripheral vision, I caught a glint of metal as something flew down from the crowd behind me. A knife thudded into the sand by my feet. Huh; so not everyone was against me. I picked it up, gripping the smooth blade in my sweaty, clumsy fingers. There was a scuffle in the audience, no doubt because of whoever had tossed me this weapon. I didn't have time to worry about them; the demon was charging towards me again.

I took off, running away and following the ring of the arena round and round. I noted that the pixie was still breathing – that was something. The demon kept pace, hurtling behind me at full speed. When I felt it gaining on me, I switched direction and darted across the middle of the floor. It leapt high into the air, landing a foot or so away, then it kicked, catching me on my thigh as I spun away to avoid the blow.

I crashed in a shower of sand. I rolled, throwing myself into the movement to get away. When I thought I had enough momentum, I sprang back to my feet. The demon was already there in front of me and still grinning.

I raised my hand, the knife in front of me. For a second, the demon's smile faltered as I gazed from the blade to its stomach and back again. With a shrug, I tossed the knife away and crossed my arms.

It blinked then it hit me on the side of my head and I went flying. The force of the punch was strong enough to send me crashing into the ground several metres away. I climbed to my feet again and again the demon came after me. This time it went for a kick to my stomach. I was thrown onto my back, wheezing for air. I tried to spring up but my body wouldn't respond and I lay there, motionless, for several seconds. My opponent nudged me roughly and snarled. I knew what he wanted. He could have easily killed me by now but this was about more than ending my life; he was putting on a show.

I staggered up and faced him, stretching my arms out and waiting. He lunged and grabbed my hair and it felt like my scalp was tearing away from my skull. The pain was excruciating. He threw me in the air once more, sending me to the other side of the arena. I coughed, spitting blood. My vision was swimming but I got to my feet.

'Great plan, Tegs,' I muttered. 'You've really outdone yourself this time.' Then my knees buckled and I fell again.

The demon threw back his head and laughed. He started shouting at the watching crowd and they shouted back, delighted. I dropped my gaze; every iota of my strength was seeping away into the blood-soaked ground. I tried to push myself up again but I couldn't. Then I saw the pixie lying less than three feet away.

I crawled over to her, stretching out my hand. 'Heal,' I whispered, 'heal.' The magic flowed from my fingertips and almost immediately she stirred.

There was a roar from the demon as he realised I was up to something. He sprinted towards us. I swallowed. His figure blurred as I tried to focus on it but there was no doubt he was getting closer.

Then I blinked and he was gone.

I couldn't hear anything. There was a ringing in my ears and I didn't know if I was about to throw up or pass out. The pixie sat up and gaped at something above her head. Trying to clear my vision, I followed her gaze. Directly above us was the demon monster, impaled on one of the spikes.

I shook my head. 'What?'

The pixie stared. 'He tripped.' She started to laugh. 'He tripped.'

I frowned, my brain clouded by confusion as much as pain. I glanced to my other side. There, half embedded in the sand, was the flail. Apparently I'd had so little Apportation magic left that all I'd managed to do was transport it from his hands to the other side of the arena. The demon's foot must have caught on it. Now, instead of slamming my soul from here to kingdom come, the monster was skewered in its own playground.

Blood leaked from the wound in its stomach. It groaned, its hands slippery as it tried to slide away from the spike. I stumbled over and lay my hand on his shoulders. Once again, I called on Aifric's Gift as I pulled the limp body of the demon backwards. While he groaned, his weight shifted; he fell away from the spike and sprawled right on top of me. I gasped, writhing to get free. He clutched at what had been a mortal wound and stood up, looking at the blood on his hands.

'What the fuck have you done?' the pixie screamed. 'We had him. We could have won.'

I ignored her and watched the demon. I didn't have the energy to stand up again; the pain was too much. The demon scratched his head and looked away, glancing at something above. I rolled over. All six of the Fomori leaders were on their feet. The one on the end gestured to the demon. He nodded once and bent down towards me. I held my breath. Not again; I couldn't cope with another blow. Rather than slamming into me, however, he dragged me to my feet then half pulled, half dragged me across the arena.

Now what? The demon on the end, who was wearing a cloak round his shoulders, gazed at me. He leaned over to his companion and murmured and I realised it was the English-speaking Fomori from earlier.

There was only one question. 'Why?'

'It was right,' I gasped as another wave of agony rippled through me.

'He was going to kill you.'

I gave a short, humourless laugh. 'Who isn't trying to kill me?'

The demon leaned towards me, his face looming closer. 'Under our laws, if you won the battle we would have set you free. You had won. He was dying.'

I shrugged, almost immediately regretting it as I felt my knees shudder once more. Only my would-be executioner by my side was keeping me upright. 'I'm a pacifist.'

The demon frowned, still struggling to understand. 'A what?'

'I can't justify violence.'

His brow furrowed as he absorbed this. He murmured something to the boss man who stared at me, wide-eyed. Then he muttered something and his translator spoke again. 'That explains why you did not use the knife and why you did not attempt to fight back. It does not explain why you healed him. He was dying as a result of a clumsy accident, not by your hand.'

I licked my lips. I knew this was my one chance; there was no other way I could explain myself and get the chance to turn everything around. 'Standing by and not helping when I have the power to do so is the same as wielding a blade myself.' I squeezed my eyes shut. 'Forgive me. I'm not explaining myself very well. I don't feel too good.'

He regarded me quietly. 'Why do you not heal yourself?'

I started. It hadn't even occurred to me that I could do that. 'I…'

'You told us you had one type of magic. We assumed that was the ability to control the air, which we have already seen. You apparently did not lie. And yet we saw evidence of several different sorts of magic that cannot possibly be connected in the way that Levitation and the creation of clouds could be. You do not seem to fully understand some of this magic yourself. What is the truth?'

You could have heard a pin drop. I felt rather than saw every member of audience lean forward as if they were afraid to miss my answer. 'I steal,' I said simply. 'I am a thief and I can steal magic. That is my Gift.'

A twitch in his cheek was the only evidence he'd heard me. 'You could steal my magic from me?'

I nodded then I focused on the invisible swirl within him. 'You have the ability to teleport yourself,' I said. I smiled in understanding. 'And to learn any tongue should you so desire it.'

The demon rocked back and muttered quickly to the Fomori boss who gestured impatiently. The demon bowed in answer and looked back at me. 'Show me,' he demanded. 'Show me how this works.'

I had no idea whether I still had the strength for this. If he would give me a minute I could see if I could use my stolen Gift to heal myself but I didn't think that any delays would serve me well. Wasting no more time, I snatched and took a thread of his magic, drawing it into my own being.

He gasped, his hand reaching involuntarily to his chest. 'I can feel it.' He turned to his leader. 'It's gone. Not a lot, but I can feel that it's lessened slightly. She took my magic from me. I might not have noticed if I hadn't known what she was going to do.'

I tilted up my chin. 'Think on this,' I said in perfect Fomorian. 'I could have stolen teleportation and taken myself far from here but I did not. You can trust me. I am here to negotiate, not to fight, not to challenge, not to steal. Neither am I here to destroy Alba.' I met the leader's eyes. 'Deal with me.'

The watching crowed gasped. Unfortunately it barely registered with me because the energy it had taken to steal, not to mention how difficult it was to make my little speech, had almost done me in.

'Stop!' a female voice shouted. 'Leave her alone!'

May strode out from the far gates with Byron, Fergus – and presumably Bob – in her wake. I was sure I was still having issues with my vision because May never walked with that kind of confidence. Neither did she speak with that kind of authority.

She walked up to us, glaring at the huge demon who was holding me up and then addressing the Fomori leaders. 'She is not what you think she is.'

'You can talk,' someone burst out.

'I have a tongue.' May pointed at me. 'Thanks to her.'

I looked past her. The expression on Byron's face suggested that he didn't know whether to attack every single Fomori in the place for even thinking about hurting me or whether he should run over and cradle me in his arms like a wounded child. I was hoping for the latter. Fergus, meanwhile, had his mouth flattened and his face masked. There was a glittering rage in his eyes as he watched May, which didn't make sense.

'She isn't evil,' May continued. 'She isn't planning our downfall. With this one we can really negotiate.'

A thought poked through the clouds of pain and confusion in my mind. 'Wait,' I said suddenly. I looked at the English-speaking leader. 'Levitation. You said I could levitate. I only did that once though when—' I looked at May. 'You told them about that.'

She met my eyes. 'Yes. That was before I knew what you could really do.'

'So,' the other demon said, 'when you told us you only had one Gift and we knew you weren't lying, we assumed it was something to do with manipulating the air. We had never seen such a thing before. But,' he smiled slightly, 'we have never seen anyone who could steal magic before either.'

My eyes drifted back to May then to Fergus whose jaw remained tight with tension. 'May's a spy,' he spat, bitterness lacing every word. 'She's been working for the Fomori demons all along. She followed you across the Veil to watch you and report back. All along she's been manipulating us. May is no victim.'

His words penetrated my skull and I wobbled, agony nibbling at my body. Byron cursed and marched over, glaring at the monster demon who shrugged and passed me over. Byron wrapped his arms round me so I could lean back into his chest. 'You're alright,' he murmured into my ear. 'We're all still alright.'

And with that, I felt like I could let go. I'd been clinging to consciousness with every shred of my being; now Byron was at my back it was if my body decided of its own volition that I could relax. Voices continued but I closed my eyes and passed out. Later, my mind whispered. Later.

Chapter Nineteen

There was something on my nose. Even without opening my eyes, I was fairly sure as to what – or rather who – it was.

'I know you're awake, Uh Integrity,' came Bob's plaintive voice. 'Just how many times have you had a fainting fit in the last week? Should I start stocking up on smelling salts?'

My eyelids fluttered open. He was perched on the tip of my nose, staring fixedly at me. I pretended not to notice his relief and frowned. 'I have not had fainting fits,' I said in mock irritation. 'In fact, I think you'll find I've been in full control of my faculties.'

He peered at me. 'You have a concussion,' he declared.

I sat up, brushing him off. 'I'm fine.'

On the far side of the room, which didn't look all that different from the prison cells I'd been in, a door opened. Byron, looking tired and harassed, saw that I was awake and strode over. 'How are you?' he demanded. 'Where does it hurt?' His emerald eyes roved over me. 'What do you need?'

I smiled. 'Which question would you like me to answer first?'

His shoulders relaxed slightly although the concern in his expression didn't flicker. 'You looked like you were half dead in that arena,' he growled. 'What they did to you…'

I dismissed his worry. 'They had their reasons.' To appease him as much to rid myself of the pain that throbbed through my body, I sought out more of Aifric's

Healing Gift. Unsure how it worked, I pulled it out and told it to heal me. My body tingled, my blood hummed and a pleasant warmth spread through me, right down to my toes.

'Wow.' I shook my head in amazement. 'So that's what it feels like.'

'You should have done that at the start,' Byron chided.

I shrugged. 'It honestly didn't occur to me.'

'You're an idiot.'

I smiled at him. He smiled back.

'Jeez!' Bob said. 'Get a room!'

Byron didn't glance in his direction. 'We have a room. You should get out.'

Bob put his hands on hips and huffed. 'The nerve!'

'Actually,' I interrupted, albeit rather reluctantly, 'we have other things to do. Where are Fergus and May?'

Byron grimaced. 'Fergus is next door. We've not seen May since … well, you know.'

I nodded. She really was full of surprises. I stood up, declining Byron's offer of help, and looked down. I might have healed my wounds but I looked the worse for wear. My clothes were covered in blood, dirt and other things it was probably wise not to examine too closely.

'They don't know about Bob,' Byron said. 'But they have been more,' he pursed his lips, '*hospitable* than I would have expected. Your plan worked.'

I grimaced. I did almost die and we still had a long way to go before we could call this expedition a success. All the same, my optimism was coming back with considerable force.

***

We found Fergus slumped against a wall. It was the first time I'd ever seen the canny Bauchan look dejected. I knew I should probably keep my mouth shut but knowing it and doing it were different things. 'Why do spies avoid capitalisation?' I asked. He lifted doleful eyes to me. 'Because they like to keep things low key.'

A muscle jerked in his cheek. Other than that, there was no sign that he'd heard me. 'Too soon?' I sighed. 'You really shouldn't be upset about May. It's not the first time someone's lied and it won't be the last. Besides, did she really ever lie? I didn't ask her why she followed me across the Veil.'

'Well,' Bob piped up, 'that's because she didn't have a tongue so she couldn't tell you.'

I ignored him. 'She was doing what she thought was right. She's probably a hero to the Fomori demons. She thought she was risking her life to spy on someone who was supposedly the greatest threat to the existence of her race. We shouldn't be upset that she wasn't a helpless victim, we should admire her. In her position, I might well have done the same.' I watched him. 'And so far everything's turned out alright. She helped us, Fergus. She weighed up all the evidence and decided that we weren't monsters after all. She even fell in love.'

He blinked. I smiled and knelt beside him. 'Are you sure you're not annoyed because she fooled you and you're not used to that?' His eyes narrowed but I ploughed ahead regardless. 'Maybe,' I told him softly, 'you've met your match.' Fergus wasn't a fool and I could see him absorb my words.

There was a sharp knock on the door. We all stiffened and exchanged wary glances. Bob zipped over, burrowing into my collar to stay out of sight. Byron took a deep breath, walked over and opened it. As soon as he did, he was all but bowled over by a demon bustling in and shoving past him. My stomach tensed when I realised it was the furious female demon who'd been my guard down by the arena.

I put up my hands to ward her off but it was to no avail – she wasn't going to be stopped. She threw her thin arms around me and squeezed. 'Thank you! Thank you! What you did for May was more than I could have asked. If you need anything, you ask for me.'

'What is she saying?'

I translated for the others who seemed as taken aback as I was. I met Fergus's eyes meaningfully and he nodded, getting to his feet and picking up his bag. I pulled back from the demon. 'We would like to meet with your leaders now,' I told her in Fomori. Probably the sooner the better. The language Gift I'd acquired was only a tiny dose and it wouldn't last for long.

'Yes, yes!' she beamed and bowed, before nodding towards the door and heading out.

I looked at the others. 'This is where it really gets serious,' I warned.

'All for one,' Byron muttered.

Bob whispered into my ear. 'Screw that. If this goes tits up, you lot are on your own.'

I just laughed.

***

There was something unsettling about the sky always being dark. Part of me expected dawn to break at some point and for the sun to illuminate everything in golden brilliance, even though I knew it wouldn't. I itched to get back to the clean, fresh air of the Highlands. I was actually pleased when May's friend took us outside to a parapet rather than deeper into the bowels of the castle. The darkness was claustrophobic enough without being kept inside. No wonder the Fomori demons slept on the rooftops instead of inside the old buildings which remained from the pre-Fissure days.

The same six demons from the arena faced us, seated in a row. May stood to one side and her eyes immediately sought Fergus. Without turning, I couldn't tell what his reaction was. I cleared my throat. 'Thank you,' I said.

'For what?' asked the robed Fomori.

'For not killing us. For listening to what I have to say. For the chance to change all our futures.'

'The prophecy remains. You are still a threat.'

I lifted my chin. 'I don't believe I am.'

He knitted his fingers together. 'We shall see.'

I ran my eyes across them, seeking potential allies but their expressions were masked. Even May's expression was studiously blank. These guys would be fantastic at poker. I swallowed and began. 'Across the Veil, we have a fixed view of what you are like. It is a given that you are evil, that you are monsters who have no qualms about who you murder. Recent evidence bears this out. Your demons attacked one of our northern cities and there were several deaths. You have encroached onto our land and it rarely ends well.'

A couple of the demons stirred. The robed leader held up his hand to still them. 'We might say the same of your kind,' he replied mildly. 'You have made incursions into our territory. You have threatened us. We have nothing and yet you still seem to want to take that away.'

I nodded. 'You're referring to me? I've been here a few times.' I thought of the magical harp I'd used in the Games. 'On the first occasion I did steal something but I could argue that it didn't belong to you any more that it belonged to me. If it helps, I have stolen far more from the Sidhe than from you.'

'We do not just refer to you.'

I considered this. I didn't know of anyone else who'd been beyond the Veil who hadn't been with me. Then I frowned. 'Matthew MacBain.' It was a long time ago now but memories grew long and grudges extended beyond mere lifetimes.

The Fomori demon turned to one of his companions. They nodded and he looked back at me. 'That was the name we were given by one of your kind who dared to come to us. He said he was a treasure hunter. We do not like hunters.'

I kept my voice calm and level. 'What happened to him?'

'You see where we live, Adair. We do not have sun. Very little grows without light. We struggle to feed our people.' For a brief moment, I recognised sadness in his eyes then the mask fell again.

I considered the pixie and what she said she'd done. I was fairly certain I understood what had happened to Matthew MacBain and nausea churned in my stomach.

'I am not condoning what happened to him or to others who thought they could come here at will,' he continued. 'But understand that hunger will drive even the sanest person to depths they would never previously have considered.'

I inclined my head. 'It would be easy for me to stand here in judgment of those actions,' I told him. 'But I have never starved.'

'Do you have children?' he asked.

I shook my head.

'Then,' he said, 'you cannot understand what it is like to see your baby, your flesh and blood, wither in front of your eyes and to be unable to help them. That is the reality we live with here, every single day. Understand, Adair, we are a violent people but in this land, only the strong survive.'

'Why don't you leave?'

His answer was simple. 'We have nowhere else to go.'

'The one thing Scotland has,' I said, 'is land. If you had come to us...' Even as I said the words, I realised they were stupid.

The demon knew this too and he laughed harshly. 'Do you think we haven't done that? We tried every method possible of asking for aid. For a long time we were too proud then we were too desperate.'

My voice was quiet. 'Tell me.'

He sighed. 'We began with threats: help us or we will hurt you. More often than not we were beaten back by the Sidhe. Or we hurt the wrong people. You might think we are brutal but your people are brutal also.'

I knew what he meant. To the Sidhe, with their Clan Lands and magic and wealth, the rest of the country was disposable. However, from the departure of the trolls to the effect of the freed Foinse, that was changing. I knew it in my bones.

'We tried other tacks. We appealed to your leader and, initially, he appeared amenable. He told us we could barter, that he would provide aid. He also warned us that our entire race was in great peril.'

Byron didn't understand what was going on so I risked a glance in his direction. I gave him a reassuring smile but he remained on edge. 'That peril was me,' I said.

The demon nodded. 'Your Clan. He told us he would rid us of this immediate threat if we agreed to stay away and contact only him. He was,' he licked his lips, 'very persuasive.'

'Yeah.' My jaw clenched. 'He has that skill.'

Aifric could have done something; he could have helped them. He'd been in a position to change Scotland for the better and, because he wanted to remain the strongest leader in the land, he hadn't. Other Sidhe wouldn't have appreciated his actions and might have challenged him; equally, he might have been worried that uniting Scotland would make his position less meaningful and more diluted. And yet he had kept the Fomori sweet. He wanted to have them ready for his own sinister purposes.

'We sent delegations. Your Clan killed them.'

'Is that what he told you?'

The demon looked at me. 'Are you suggesting he was lying? It would be in your interests to suggest that was the case.'

'I spent most of my life believing my father was a genocidal maniac. I have no problem with believing that there were those in my Clan who were … less than noble.' I told him about the three dead demons Byron and I had discovered. 'You can get your Truth Teller. My story will not change.' I pointed at Byron. 'He will tell you the same.'

'We do not test our friends.'

I was taken aback. 'Am I a friend?'

He smiled toothlessly. 'Not yet.'

I considered this and hope flared through me. We were getting somewhere, we were really getting somewhere, but there was still a great to be said. I drew in a breath. 'What happened in Aberdeen…'

'Ah yes. A tragedy for all concerned.' He glanced down. 'Our situation is dire. We went to see if there were others we could negotiate with. As soon as your kind saw us, however…' His voice trailed off.

'They attacked,' I whispered. Byron himself had done so; he'd casually tossed a fireball into the back of a Fomori demon who'd pitched up in Perth. Fight first, ask questions later. We were all guilty of something.

'Yes. We tried other methods of communication but they were misunderstood.' He looked at me archly. 'Including by you.'

I frowned. 'What do you mean?'

'We knew that sooner or later someone would come looking for, what was his name? MacBan?'

'MacBain.'

'Ah, yes. We left a message for anyone who came.'

I closed my eyes. *Save us.* It was written in blood above his bones. I'd assumed it was a message from the Fomori's slaves but I was wrong. 'I'm sorry.'

He shrugged a bony shoulder. 'We should have been more explicit. We know our ancestors did your kind wrong when they first came here. They were afraid and they believed they needed to fight in order to stay. Our fathers sinned and we have been paying the price ever since. We know what you think of us; telling you the truth about our desperate situation would have invited disbelief. We were hoping for … investigation.'

'Because that way lies the truth,' I said.

He nodded. 'Indeed.'

'And the others? The ones who aren't Fomori?' I leaned forward. 'You don't even allow them names.'

'Names have power. They are powerless.'

My eyes narrowed. 'Yes, but—'

He held up a hand. 'It has been a point of contention for some time. We have struggles amongst our own kind – fights, violence, death. I'm sure you have noticed the scars.'

'I've seen the fights. I've seen your arena.'

'We have to keep the peace somehow. If we permit the others to have names, they will feel more empowered and there would be greater possibility of riot. There would be more death.'

'It's wrong.'

'Maybe.' He sighed. 'But things were not easy for us after the Fissure. We had to do something with the people from your side who remained. It was either kill them or find a way to keep them from hurting us further. I think we chose the more humane path.'

I wasn't convinced. 'It will have to change.'

He seemed amused. 'Or what?'

'There is no alternative. I am not threatening you, I'm here to help.'

The demon's amusement grew into laughter. 'You? How can you help? You're not the Sidhe leader. They've been trying to kill you as much as we have. We're not stupid, Adair, for all that you believe we are savages. May has told us enough.'

Out of the corner of my eye I noticed her flinch. Actually, I didn't think she'd told them everything. I swallowed. 'Bob,' I whispered.

He didn't waste his time burrowing out from his hiding place. The demons' jaws dropped as Bob glared at them, daring them to do something. 'He's a genie,' I said unnecessarily. 'And I have one wish left.'

The leader recovered first. 'It is unwise to ask a genie for anything.' He regarded me soberly. 'We have learnt this in the past.'

I nodded. 'It's true that there are always negative consequences but I'm sure we could put our heads together and think of a way to minimise the impact.'

He didn't move. 'What would you wish for?'

'How about a return to your homeland, wherever that is?'

'It is gone. It no longer exists in anything other than fairy tales.' He continued to watch Bob warily although he addressed me. 'Adair, we have lived here for three hundred years. *This* is our homeland.'

'There is always a way.'

Bob wasn't protesting much, which was uncharacteristic, and I didn't think it was because he was scared of the demons.

'You could wish for our demise. The prophecy—'

'Oh, to hell with the damned prophecy!' I snapped. 'It's worthless! It was probably made up in the first place. Even if it wasn't, most prophecies don't come true. Events don't stay fixed and people take different paths. You should ignore that kind of mumbo-jumbo. There's no future in prophecies.'

The demon's mouth twitched. Then, almost inconceivably, he started to giggle.

Bob glanced at me. 'These demons are even worse than I thought.'

I waited until the demon calmed down then walked to the edge of the parapet and gazed around. A lot of this place looked familiar; I could even see Arthur's Seat from here. I massaged my neck. I probably only had enough Language magic left in me for a few more sentences so I was going to make them count.

'I'll prove to you that we can work together,' I said. 'That we can be on the same side and things can change. That, with the right circumstances, your entire society can change.' I beckoned to them. May came over but the others were reluctant. I sighed. 'I couldn't throw you over the edge even if I wanted to.'

It took another moment but they got up and joined me. 'When I steal part of a Gift,' I said, 'it doesn't last for long. Eventually it runs out. When I steal all of a Gift, however, it's mine forever. And this,' I took a deep breath, 'is a Gift I'll have until I die.' I flicked out my hands, using everything that Morna had taught me. I really hoped this was going to work – with the dim light, it was possible there wouldn't be much of an impact. Work, I prayed. Bloody work. And then it did.

It started at the edges, down at the base of the castle. At first it was difficult to tell what it was but the demons had better eyesight than me in this dark land. They gasped. Byron stood beside me, placing an arm round my shoulder and sliding out Bob's letter opener from his sporran. He passed it to me and I carefully tucked it away. He didn't say anything; it was enough to know that he was beside me.

I continued my work as if I were merely rolling out a carpet. Grass unfurled, followed by flowers. I cast my power out towards Arthur's Seat. Screams reached my ears even from that far point as the people there were terrified by what was happening all around them. I didn't stop, though. My heart was racing, hammering out a beat against my ribcage and it was painful to breathe. To the east, I produced wheat; to the west, it was barley. I was hardly aware of the demons staggering as the scent of fresh, plant life rose into the air.

Then there was a loud crash and I stumbled.

A demon raced in from inside the castle. 'The Sidhe!' he yelled. 'They're here! They're attacking!'

The Fomori leader snapped his eyes to me. 'Bitch! You did this to distract us! You…' his words fell away as the last of the Language magic left me and Fomorian became incomprehensible once more. Another four demons burst through the door, each one dragging a captive: Lexie, Speck, Brochan and Taylor.

Bob shrieked and disappeared in a flash of light and I stared in dismay while all hell broke loose.

Chapter Twenty

Almost immediately we were rounded up and backed against the wall. Three Fomori stood in front of us, ready to cut our throats at the first command. Their weapons were unnecessary; I could see what magic swirled inside them and it made my veins run ice cold. 'Listen,' I began. 'We...'

The Fomori leader spun towards me with such force that I stopped. He barked something, no doubt along the lines of shut the hell up, then he turned to the messenger and spat out a question.

'This is no good,' I muttered. I had to understand what was going on.

I looked at the English-speaking Fomori. His brow was creased in a worried frown and he was poised for action. I hissed softly and then, as delicately as I could, reached out for his Language Gift once more. I tried to think of myself as a sneak thief and hoped he wouldn't notice what I was doing. Unfortunately, he was now so aware of my abilities that he sensed my magic grab almost instantly. His eyes narrowed and snapped towards me – but instead of a vengeful return attack he gave me a grim nod. Maybe, despite appearances, he was coming round to my side.

The messenger was explaining what had happened. 'We were unprepared,' he babbled. 'They didn't pass through the border, they came from the coast in boats and passed through the Veil there.'

Shite. I turned to Taylor and the others. 'How did you get here?' I asked urgently.

Lexie glared, tossing her blue hair. 'If you're pissed off that we're here, you should have told us what you were doing.'

'Lex!'

'By sea,' Brochan replied. 'We anchored in the middle of some dark, gloopy river and walked the rest of the way. That's why it took us so long to get here.'

The Clyde. Crapadoodle. 'The entire ship passed through the Veil?'

His mouth flattened and his gills twitched. 'It was not my idea. Nor was it fun.'

I stared at them all. This was important. 'Were you followed?'

For a moment no one answered. I repeated my question. 'Were you followed?'

Eventually, Speck nodded. 'Yes. But it's okay. We have a plan. We *wanted* them to come here.'

'You have a plan?' I shrieked. 'What kind of plan is going to resolve this?' Shite, shite and damn Aifric to shite. This was my fault: the Sidhe were here because I was. Aifric was worried about what I was up to. I curled my fingers into fists. Well, he should be worried.

'Where are they?' the Fomori leader asked the messenger.

'On the fringes of the city but they're moving in.'

'How many?'

Even in this dim light, I saw the messenger blanch. 'Thousands. It's as if every Sidhe in Scotland is here.'

He was probably right; apart from the MacQuarries, they'd all been gathered in one place. It would have been simple for Aifric to order all of them to arms. I shook my head. All my plots and plans were going to unravel and if it came to a direct confrontation between the Sidhe and all the Fomori ... a sickening chasm opened up in my chest. I wondered if the Fomori's version of the prophecy

– that I was going to destroy Alba – was about to come true.

Suddenly there was a mammoth roaring noise and the sky lit up with an orange hue. Byron lunged, throwing himself on top of me. I was knocked to the ground, disbelief and shock rippling through me. A heartbeat later, the castle was rocked. There were screams, followed by the sound of stones breaking off and falling far below.

'Pyrokinesis,' he said in my ear. 'The Sidhe are attacking.'

I pulled away from him, searching desperately for the Fomori. They'd been knocked off their feet by the impact but they were still conscious. The three who'd been in front of us, holding us in our place, scrambled towards their leader without thinking.

Fergus, a trickle of blood leaking from his forehead, pulled himself to his feet and wiped it away. 'It's a warning shot,' he said calmly. 'Or there would have been more. The Steward is sending a message.' He looked at May and said the same to her in Gaelic.

'Tegs,' Taylor whispered. 'We were caught as we came looking for you but we'd already found something else.'

I frowned at him, not sure what he meant. He unzipped his jacket a little and a faint golden glow appeared before he hastily zipped it up again. I gasped then clamped my hand over my mouth to muffle the sound. 'How did you know?'

'Know what?'

'That I needed the Draoidheachd?'

He turned his head to Speck. 'Told you that's what it was,' he said smugly. 'You owe me fifty quid.'

'Keep it hidden,' I told him. I looked at Byron, a question in my eyes.

He nodded, pointing to the bag by Fergus's feet. 'It's there.'

I drew in a shaky breath. Good. That was very good.

'May,' Fergus said. 'She knows we have it as well.'

I stiffened, glancing in her direction. After explaining the warning shot theory to the others, she was watching us, an intelligent gleam in her eyes. The tiniest smile crossed her lips and she turned away. 'She's not going to say anything. She knows what might be about to happen.'

Taylor frowned. 'Why would she say something? And what's about to happen?'

We had a lot of catching up to do but there wasn't time – the three Fomori had returned.

'Get up!'

We all got awkwardly to our feet.

'We should execute them now!' one of the others said.

My mouth was dry. The English-speaking Fomori murmured something into the boss-man's ear. He nodded. 'We can do that later. We can do that any time. But we might need them first.' He turned to the messenger. 'Get everyone in the city to safe ground. Not here – this will be the first point of attack. Get them to Arthur's Seat and tell them to be ready.'

The messenger didn't ask what they should be ready for. He bowed, whirled round and fled.

The air around us sizzled. At first, I thought it was simply from the tension but then, without further warning, an Ochterlony Sidhe flashed into existence right next to us. We barrelled towards him to stop him doing anything dangerous. He held up bare palms, however, and cleared his throat. 'I'm here to parley.'

The English-speaking demon stepped forward. 'You teleported here.'

The Sidhe inclined his head. He didn't look in our direction; he was wholly focused on the demons. 'Our leader, the esteemed Steward of the Highlands, Aifric Moncrieffe, is requesting safe passage to this castle to discuss current ... developments.' I almost snorted. Current developments? Is that what we were calling war these days?

There was a pause while this was translated. The Fomori leader scratched his chin. 'He is permitted to come with four others. None of them can be Sidhe.'

Again we had to wait for the translation, which was troublesome and time-consuming. I wondered how much had been lost in nuance over the years as a result. I promised myself that once all this was over I'd learn Fomori properly. I reckoned I was going to need it.

'Nine others,' the Sidhe shot back. 'And they must all be Sidhe. We need to know that he will be safe.'

'Are you suggesting that we would hurt him during the truce?'

'It's not only Fomori demons who are here,' the Ochterlony idiot responded. He still didn't look at us but we knew who he was referring to.

They bargained back and forth, eventually settling on five – a mix of Sidhe and others. Still unsmiling, the Ochterlony Sidhe bowed and vanished. 'You should have nicked Teleportation from him,' Taylor grumbled. 'We could do with being as far away from here as possible.'

At his words, I glanced at the English-speaking demon. His other Gift was Teleportation and he'd heard what Taylor had said but all he did was smile.

Byron squeezed my hand. 'I trust you with my life, Integrity. You need to make a decision and act now. If my father gets here, he'll do whatever's necessary to manipulate the situation. We won't last five seconds.'

I looked at the others. Every one of them met my eyes.

'I don't know what you're planning, Tegs,' Taylor said, 'but if anyone can find a way out of this, you can.'

Fergus nodded. 'We're dead anyway.'

Speck's hands were shaking. 'Did I ever tell you that I'm afraid of the dark? The sooner this happens, the better.'

Brochan rumbled in agreement and Lexie bobbed her head. Then, from out of nowhere, May spoke. Her Fomorian words were slightly stilted but she'd obviously mastered the art of speaking properly in record time. 'If your Steward demands your death, my king will grant it. He won't even think twice. The prophecy is still a danger, no matter what you say. Integrity, you must show him he can believe in you. And you have to do it now.'

Fergus sidled over to her; he didn't look at her but his arm brushed against hers in solidarity.

Strangely enough, I didn't feel nervous. This would either be our moment of glory or the moment when everything went to shite. It felt like my whole life had been leading up to this. I was going to succeed; I had to succeed. The fate of Scotland depended on me.

I cleared my throat. 'We haven't been properly introduced,' I said, my voice carrying across the air. 'I'm Integrity Adair.'

The demon leader looked at me. I had no clue as to what he was thinking but there was calculation in his red eyes. 'Names have power,' he said.

I sucked in a breath. 'My true name is—'

He interrupted me. 'I do not require or desire that sort of burden. I am Asbar.'

'It's nice to meet you.'

He blinked. I had the feeling I needed to get on with it or he'd get bored and fling me over the edge. 'I told you before that I can help you. I was telling the truth.'

There was a flash of light. The demons winced and shielded their eyes. 'Is it time?' Bob demanded. 'Are we getting ready to rock and roll? Because I gotta tell you, I've been thinking about this and I reckon it's a good idea after all. No other genie has tried something like this.' He nodded vigorously. 'They'll be singing my name for the next thousand years.' He looked round. 'Long after you lot are dust.'

'Thanks, Bob,' I muttered drily. I pointed at Fergus. He swallowed and reached for his bag, opened it and pulled out the Foinse. Its silver light cast a strange glow over us all. The demons gaped. Some were afraid, others were simply awestruck. 'This,' I said, with a dramatic flourish, 'is the Foinse, the source of all Highland magic.'

It hummed in response and pulled upwards from Fergus, flipping once and then spinning over to me. I smiled at it and reached out, brushing its warm surface with my fingertips. I gestured to Asbar. The Foinse seemed somewhat reluctant but even so it flew over and hovered in front of him. He stared at it in fascination. 'We have something similar,' he said, 'as I'm sure you already know.'

'The Draoidheachd. Yes.'

He didn't take his eyes from the Foinse. 'Your pronunciation is appalling.'

I wasn't going to get into an argument about the merits or otherwise of my Gaelic. 'What do you understand about it?'

'We keep it locked away. Looking at its light hurts us and we are wary of its capabilities. We would never permit it to get this close to us.'

I looked at Taylor who looked back, wide-eyed. He might not understand Asbar's words but he guessed the gist of them. 'Don't let go of it,' I warned him. 'Not yet.'

He nodded, unzipping his jacket once more and drawing out the golden sphere. At least three of the demons cried out.

'What is the meaning of this?' Asbar demanded. 'Where did you get it from?'

Taylor straightened, smiling casually even though I could see through the curve of his mouth to the fear beyond. 'We stole it.'

I grinned and added a quick translation. I received several furious snarls in response.

The nearest demon lunged for it. May, however, jumped in front and blocked his path. 'Wait,' she said clearly. 'Just wait.'

It was Byron's turn. 'My name is Byron Moncrieffe,' he said. His voice rang out confidently. 'I am the son of Aifric, the Steward of the Highlands. I have read enough history to know what happened during the Fissure.' He pointed to the Foinse that was still bobbing in front of Asbar's face and then to the Draoidheachd. 'When the Veil came down and Scotland separated, so did the magic. These two used to be one. They used to be together, just like Scotland was.'

Asbar looked at him. Oh. 'Sorry,' I muttered. 'He doesn't understand what you're saying. It sounded really good though.' I quickly translated.

Asbar drew himself up. 'What are you suggesting?'

I licked my lips. 'If we join the Foinse and the Draoidheachd together then,' I shot a glance at Byron, 'we think the Veil will collapse.' Every single demon froze; even Asbar seemed lost for words. I took a deep breath and continued. 'I might have used magic to create crops for you but we all know they won't survive for long without sunlight. Lose the Veil and I'm betting this land will return to what it once was.'

'Without adequate protection, sunlight will kill us.'

I nodded. 'But I still have one genie wish left.'

There were shouts from below the castle walls. Fergus edged over to have a look. 'It's Aifric,' he said grimly. 'He's here. Work quickly, Chieftain.'

I stared at Asbar. 'You don't need the Steward. We can end this right now without him.'

A Fomori demon spoke up. 'Don't forget the prophecy. She could wish for anything. She could wish for us to be destroyed! They'll take back the Lowlands and forget we ever existed!'

'She's not their queen,' another agreed. 'We should wait to hear what the other one has to say first.'

Asbar listened to them both and others chimed in with their own arguments. I tried to calculate how long it would take Aifric and his retinue to get up here. Minutes at best.

Byron leaned over. 'What's going on?'

'They're trying to decide,' I told him. 'Most don't seem to think it's a good idea. They don't trust us. They don't trust *me*.'

He gazed at me. 'Then you know what you have to do.' He was right. There was no point wasting any more time. Do or do not, as Yoda would say.

'Bob,' I whispered.

'Integrity,' he warned, using my real name for once. 'Think very carefully about this.' He was quivering in front of me.

I smiled. 'Don't worry, I already have.' I closed my eyes. I had lots of options but I knew which one was right. 'I wish for the Lowlanders to receive no ill effects from the sun.'

Bob's eyes welled up with tears but he held them back and bowed. 'Your wish is my command.'

All at once the demons stopped talking. 'Did you feel that?' one asked. 'My skin…' They turned towards me, realising something had happened. 'What has she done?'

'Get her!'

Byron stepped in front of me, using telekinesis to throw back the first furious advance. Asbar snatched out, attempting to grab the Foinse. It flew away, spiralling towards me. 'Now, Taylor,' I yelled. 'Release it now!'

His hands left the Draoidheachd and, for a moment, it hung in mid-air. Then it flipped and spun on a direct collision course with the Foinse.

Everything seemed to slow down. I heard Asbar shouting. Bolts of magic blasted out from everywhere as the Fomori tried to do something – anything – to stop what was about to happen but they were no match for the magics. I smiled serenely and stepped back. A sudden explosion of light blasted us backwards, Sidhe, Fomori and everyone else. A loud hum filled the air, musical and light – and, above all, triumphant.

The conjoined magic spun upwards, zipping vertically as if it wanted to reach the stars. Above our heads there was a shaft of light, as if the sun were piercing through dark storm clouds. The light grew and grew, bathing everything in gold. At first I heard screaming and then there was nothing but awe.

I was the first to stand up. I walked over to the castle wall and gazed out. The view was magnificent; instead of the dark, dim shadows, green land stretched in front of me. Whichever way I turned, all I could see was bright light and beauty. The Veil had gone. We were one.

Bob flitted up to my shoulder. I dragged my eyes away from the magnificent vista and spoke, my words heavy with dread. 'Go on then,' I said. 'What are the consequences? What's going to happen as a result of my wish?'

He pulled backwards, hovering away from me so I could see him properly. He took out a massive handkerchief and blew his nose. 'Bob,' I said, even more alarmed. 'Tell me. Is this going to hurt the Fomori?'

He wiped his eyes and threw the handkerchief to one side. Unfortunately it smacked Asbar on the nose. He hissed in disgust but he seemed to understand what I was asking of the genie. He watched us while the others gaped at the newly transformed Lowlands.

'There are no consequences.' Bob said, with a tremulous smile. 'Not for this.'

My brow furrowed. 'I don't understand.'

He nodded gravely. 'I know. No one ever does.' He leaned towards me. 'Why didn't you wish for the Fomori to be sent away? A bit of sunlight isn't going to stop all your problems. There still might be war.'

'Asbar said it himself,' I told him. 'This is their home now. For better or for worse. There's a Sidhe army out there preparing to meet them and…' I choked slightly. 'Things might yet become very bad. But this was the right thing to do.'

'There's your answer,' Bob said simply. 'Your wish was selfless. It won't solve your problems and they might still turn around and kill you. So might Aifric. But you used your wish to benefit them anyway. Most people suffer the consequences of their wishes because most people wish selfishly.'

Byron put his arm round my waist. 'You're saying the key is altruism? Why the hell didn't you tell us this before? It would have saved a lot of heartache.'

Bob rolled his eyes but Fergus understood. 'Because if you knew that to succeed you had to be selfless, it

---

would be almost impossible to be selfless. It wouldn't work. Your mind would trick you.'

Bob nodded. 'He's right.' He raised his voice. 'But I'm still the magnificent being around here. Not him.' Fergus just looked confused.

The English-speaking demon, who was listening in, murmured to Asbar. The Fomori leader stared at me. 'This is true?'

I pointed at the sun. 'You're not burning up yet.'

'No.' He gazed round in wonder then he walked over to me and held out his hand. 'You have saved Alba. And destroyed her too. We have a future now. All of us.'

'You fucking bitch! What have you done? You've doomed us all!'

I glanced over at Aifric's furious figure as he stood in the doorway and glared at me. Shite. It wasn't time to celebrate yet.

Chapter Twenty-One

'You cannot trust this woman!' Aifric bellowed at Asbar. 'The prophecy tells the truth! Look at what has happened! The sun will scorch your skin. Your children will burn and die. This is the end and *she* has caused it!'

'Father,' Byron said, 'shut up.'

Aifric stared at his son. Calculation flitted across his expression and then he spread out his palms pleadingly. 'Byron,' he said heavily, projecting himself as the voice of reason. 'I understand you have feelings for her. She is attractive in her way and power is always alluring. But she is a thief. I know the truth now. She stole my Gift from me. She ripped it from my very soul. That's the kind of person she is.'

Byron folded his arms. 'I know exactly what kind of person she is.'

'She's believes she's doing the right thing but by bringing down the Veil, she's brought about the destruction of the Fomori. And before the UV rays kill them, they will make a damned good attempt at killing us. Their armies were on our borders less than three days ago.'

'But,' Byron replied implacably, 'they're not there now.' He shook his head sadly. 'You have so much to answer for. What really happened to Clan Adair?'

'Gale Adair killed them.'

'No, he didn't.'

A muscle jerked in Aifric's cheek. The Sidhe, pixie and Bauchan, who'd been selected to come along, stared at each other. 'Fine,' Aifric spat. 'But you need to understand the harsh reality of life. The only person who was strong enough to keep the Highlands safe was me. I was bargaining with the Fomori. If it weren't for me, they would have invaded us long ago.' He glanced at Asbar. 'You know you were thinking about it.'

Listening to the translation, the Fomori leader shrugged. He didn't seem to care; he already had everything his heart desired and it had nothing to do with Aifric. 'It is true that we considered it. But we discarded the idea as too risky.'

I told Aifric what he'd said. The Steward of the Highlands could barely look at me. 'You see?' he said softly to his son. 'It was too risky because I made it too risky. Gale wanted us to adhere to the old traditions of term limits. He didn't think any one Chieftain should be Steward for too long. He clung to the old, outmoded ways without realising that experience is more important than length of service. I had that experience. He just wanted to take my place.'

Nothing I'd learned about my father suggested that was true. Other than offering my interpretative skills, however, I wasn't getting involved in this. Byron needed to do this for himself, otherwise he'd never find peace.

'So you killed an entire Clan?' he demanded. 'Because their Chieftain had a different political opinion to you?'

'Until Integrity Adair got involved, there wasn't a single Fomori demon incursion for twenty-six years,' Aifric said. 'What I did might have been brutal but we've had peace for that reason. Now we are on the brink of war.'

'On your orders,' Byron sneered. 'You are the one who is causing the problems. You could tell them to stand down but I already know that you won't.'

'They,' Aifric jabbed his finger at the Fomori, 'will come to us. If the sun doesn't kill them, they will invade our land – our land which is vulnerable because of Integrity Adair. They will attack us and kill us. There will never be peace while they roam free. They do not belong here!'

'They've been here for three hundred years. I'm not suggesting it's going to be easy; we have different standards and different morals. But I'm confident we can find a way. We will work together, Father, and we will live together. *That* is the future. Even if it weren't for them, the Sidhe are no longer the most powerful beings in Scotland.'

'Because,' Aifric spat, 'she let the Foinse go.'

'And we imprisoned it. And *she* has a name. Integrity. She's the woman I love and you need to start getting used to it.' For the briefest second I forgot to breathe.

Aifric was far from done. 'Just wait. Just wait and see how enjoyable life is when you're being told what to do by a warlock or one of those ... things.'

Speck frowned and started forward. I shook my head, warning him to stay out of this.

'It'll be an improvement on being told what to do by you,' Byron retorted. 'No more lies, no more manipulation. Scotland is free.'

'The sun...'

Byron turned to me. I nodded and slid out Bob's scimitar. 'This belongs to the genie,' I said softly. 'I used my last wish to arrange for their protection from the sun. No one is getting fried. Although,' I amended, 'they might get a nice tan.'

Asbar huffed. He'd had enough of all this to-ing and fro-ing. 'Let's just kill him. There are more important things to do.'

'No!' I said abruptly. He looked confused. For what would probably not be the last time, I tried to explain.

'We don't need to kill him. We don't need more violence.'

Despite not understanding my exchange with the Fomori leader, Aifric's entourage sensed the danger. One of them stepped forward and addressed Byron and me directly. 'If any harm comes to the Steward, the army has been ordered to attack.'

I grimaced. Aifric had thought of every eventuality. I appealed to Asbar once more. 'If you just…'

Aifric lunged towards me with such speed and suddenness that I wasn't prepared. Byron tried to shove him out of the way, a tiny fireball flickering at his fingertips, but it was too late; the Steward was holding Bob's scimitar and backing away.

'Don't even think about it, son,' he hissed. 'I've got the power now. With this letter-opener and with a genie at my beck and call, I can make all of this right. I can keep all of us safe.' He glared at me. 'You think you're so powerful. Integrity Adair, the woman who has it all. You're just a child,' he sneered. 'You're no one. If it wasn't for your Gift and your ability to steal magic from others, you'd still be hiding under a rock with your criminal friends. Well, let's see what happens when I have that power instead.' He held up the blade. 'I wish for the Gift of Stealing, just like hers.'

Bob flew up, his expression utterly miserable. He looked at me helplessly but I knew he didn't have a choice. 'Your wish is my command,' he whispered.

Aifric's eyes widened then he threw back his head and laughed. 'I can feel it! I can feel it flooding through me. I can take any magic I want.' He strode towards me. 'And I'm going to take yours.'

'Father…'

It was too late, Aifric was already doing it. He reached inside me and ripped out all the magic contained there. He took back his Gift of Healing, he took Morna's Gift of Growth and Kirsty's Gift of Truth-Telling. He took the trickles of Animal Calling and Electrosurge. He took it all. I felt like my insides had been sucked out, like someone had reached to me and taken my heart. My legs gave away and I fell.

I heard Byron cry out and rush towards me. Blood thumped in my ears. Taylor was at my side, then Lexie and Brochan and Speck and Bob and May and Fergus. They were all there. Even Asbar started towards me. I was dimly aware of Aifric cackling loudly and dancing, pirouetting around the castle top.

'The power!' he yelled. 'It's consuming me! I will be unstoppable!' He spun and cheered.

'Wait,' I whispered. Nobody heard me. I tried again. 'He's taken too much in one go. He's not used to it and he's going crazy with the adrenaline and the rush.'

Bob floated in front of my eyes. He winked at me, as aware of the consequences of the wish as I was. I lifted my head while Aifric jumped up and down. 'I'm going to take it all,' he roared. 'All the magic in Scotland will be mine. I'll take Scotland and then I'll move to England. The world will be mine for the taking. I'll...' his eyes widened. 'Shit.'

In his glee he hadn't paid attention to where he was going. He was too close to the edge and the wall designed to hold people back wasn't high enough. He was already toppling to one side. His hands flailed. 'Help me!' he screamed. 'Help...' I caught a glimpse of self-awareness and terror in his writhing eyes as he tipped over the edge. '...me....'

I closed my eyes. A second later there was a thump as his body landed far below. Bob zipped over and looked down. 'It's not a letter opener!' he shouted. 'It's a scimitar!' He frowned for a moment then turned to us and shrugged. 'I don't think he heard me.'

'The army,' I whispered.

The group who'd come with Aifric stared at the spot where he'd disappeared then turned and ran, disappearing through the door through which they'd entered. They wouldn't get far but that might not matter. Any Sidhe Farsensers would have already realised that Aifric was dead. 'We have to do something,' I gasped.

Asbar snapped out brusque orders, telling the others to muster their forces and meet the Sidhe face on. 'No, no, no,' I whispered. 'No.'

Over my head, I heard Fergus shout. With Byron's help, I struggled up. 'I need to see,' I said. 'What's going on?'

He pointed. 'There,' he said quietly. 'There they are.'

He was right, they were all there. The Sidhe were amassing and, even though I couldn't see any expressions from this distance, I knew they were ready for the fight. Fomori demons came spilling out from the castle gates below and from Arthur's Seat to the side. It wouldn't matter who won, this would be a massacre on both sides.

'Relax,' Fergus said.

'How can I relax? Hundreds, thousands are going to die and I can't do anything to st—' I paused. 'What's that?' A cloud of dust was approaching the Sidhe army at a tremendous speed. I gaped.

'I told you we had a plan,' Speck said. He wagged his finger at me. 'You should have more faith, Chieftain.'

'Are those trolls?' Asbar asked, blinking out in shock. Everyone around me beamed and nodded. 'Are they being led by a very large man and a woman in a strange white dress?'

Lexie gave Taylor a high-five. I shook my head. 'But won't the Sidhe…'

'Wait,' Byron cautioned.

I blinked and stared. The trolls weren't alone; the MacQuarries were behind them. So much for their promise to stay within the safety of their Lands. Next to them stood a towering group that couldn't be mistaken for anything other than Wild Men.

'Candy came through,' Brochan said. He raised his eyebrows at Speck. 'And so did your lot.'

My mouth was dry. Hundreds and hundreds of warlocks were encircling the group.

'The Foinse is free,' Speck said simply. 'Now we have more magic than the Sidhe. The Clan-Less aren't powerless any more.'

'We stand with Clan Adair!' they screamed, their combined voices as loud as if they were standing next to us.

Tipsania raised her hand. Whether reluctantly or not, the entire Scrymgeour Clan pulled away, crossing the divide and joining her. There was a pause and then, when she dropped her arm, they all bellowed, 'We stand with Clan Adair!'

Byron smiled grimly. 'You're not the only one who's been working hard to make things better.'

A smaller figure appeared from the middle of the Sidhe. The army of trolls came to a halt and Tipsania walked forward, her head held high and with the confident deportment of a Chieftain, and met the other figure halfway. I squinted. 'Is that…?'

'Kirsty Kincaid.' Byron grinned. 'She must have done what she promised.'

'Which was?'

'To usurp her own Chieftain and take the reins of her Clan. They're one of the top four, you know. The others are conditioned to listen to her.'

I watched in shock. Molly Kincaid's tiny figure joined them and she shouted something to the mass of waiting Sidhe. From this distance, her words were indistinct but I had a good idea of what she was saying. In fact, she was still talking when Jamie Moncrieffe strode up to her.

'I told you I wasn't twiddling my thumbs while you were dead,' Byron chided me. 'I wasn't just learning how to pick locks. Obviously not all of this is down to me but I've helped smooth the way.' He sounded rightly proud. 'They were taken in by my father's words but now they're seeing the light.'

Literally and figuratively. I stared while the entire Kincaid Clan moved, effectively switching sides. They took up places next to the MacQuarries. 'We stand with Clan Adair!'

At Jamie's behest, at least three-quarters of the Moncrieffes did the same, then the Carnegies followed. Their Chieftain was a canny woman: she knew which way the wind was blowing and she knew what it would take to survive. With the Veil gone, the smart move was to fall back and, whether she liked me or not, she was smart. Others peeled off and followed. Each time they did, the call was the same.

'We stand with Clan Adair!'
'We stand with Clan Adair!'
'We stand with Clan Adair!'

I pressed my lips together, my vision blurry with tears. 'Three days ago, they wanted me dead.'

'And now the Steward is dead instead,' Fergus murmured. 'People gravitate to where the power is. Some would have followed you anyway. Others will follow you because you're the one who's now in control. There will be plenty who are praying that you fail but unless you do, they'll keep quiet. They'll do whatever's necessary to keep themselves safe.'

Crowd mentality indeed. Fickle freaks. Taylor took my hand, squeezing it hard. 'The Adairs are never going to be forgotten now,' he said quietly.

Bit by bit, the original Sidhe army was decimated. Plenty still remained but their ranks were in tatters. Even though I knew that I'd have their unmitigated hatred for a generation, all I could do was gape.

'The Fomori are still approaching,' Fergus warned.

My heart pounded. I turned to Asbar and gestured helplessly. 'Call them off. We've helped you.' I smiled at Speck. 'There was a plan.' He grinned back and doffed an imaginary cap. Then I pointed at the brilliant blue sky and gave Asbar another meaningful look. 'You're free now. All of us are free now.'

He stared at the dappled shadows around us which highlighted the now-golden sunshine. Even the Fomori army below us kept craning their necks upwards as if to check that the sun was still there. This wasn't the day for fighting. It might be the end of Scotland as we knew it but it was also the beginning of our country. The Fomori king knew it as much as I did.

Bob beamed. 'I can go tell them we're all friends now.' He glanced at Asbar and addressed him in Fomorian. 'If that suits you? Are we friends?'

Asbar blinked rapidly before turning to me questioningly. 'There is a lot that needs to change,' he said.

I nodded. 'On both our sides. We will need to talk and draw up agreements.' My voice hardened. 'We will not accept violence.'

He rubbed his chin. 'It will not be easy.'

'Nothing good ever is.' I glanced at Byron with the tiniest of smiles.

Asbar held out his hand. 'You have proved yourself,' he said simply. 'You have honour. You have...' he looked at the green expanse stretching out from the castle and faltered for a moment '...changed our world. We will change with it.' His voice hardened 'We will *have* to change with it. So, yes, I suppose we are friends. You may go ... Bob. I shall send other messengers too. Just in case.'

The little genie fist pumped the air, choosing not to hear the last of Asbar's words. 'Bob the genie saves the world! The prophecy was all wrong. It's me who's the saviour.' With that, he zipped away.

I glanced down at the masses of people. Bob was going to be disappointed. The combined glowing swirl of Foinse and the Draoidheachd was already there, drawing enough attention to itself to distract anyone who had considered getting blood on their hands. We were going to have to come up with a better name for it now.

Byron pulled me to him and wrapped his arms round me. 'I'm sorry about your dad,' I told him.

He sighed. He wasn't grieving yet but he would. 'Yeah. He did it to himself in the end, though. I'm sorry he took all your magic.'

I grinned into his shoulder. He'd only taken what I'd already stolen. Because he had wished for the Gift of Theft from Bob, he hadn't taken that from me with the rest of the magic. I wasn't quite as bereft as Byron thought.

'I'll get over it,' I told him. My smile grew. Maybe I'd keep this one secret for a little while longer. Just for fun.

Far below us, the Fomori army stopped their advance. As the remainder of those loyal to Aifric dropped their shoulders and slunk to the side, the front ranks of the Sidhe, trolls, warlocks and Wild Men walked forward cautiously to greet their opponents. There were no smiles but the threat of violence had diminished. Nobody actually wanted to die. We'd been brought up to hate them and they'd been brought up to hate us. It would take a long time before we achieved real peace and I knew things wouldn't smooth themselves out just because I, Bob, Asbar and a few others said we were okay now. Revolutions might happen overnight but real change took far longer. We'd get there though; we were Scotland, after all.

'If the prophecy really is coming true,' I said slowly, mulling it over, 'then that kind of makes me *The* Highlander. You know what that means.'

The others groaned behind me. 'What?' Byron asked, humouring me. Yeah, he'd get tired of that pretty soon. I'd have to milk it while I could.

I drew back and met his eyes. 'There can be only pun.'

***

A few days later, I was back at the same spot, gazing at Edinburgh and the land beyond. There had been skirmishes and fights and a lot of traded insults but some Highlanders and Lowlanders were beginning to integrate. It helped that the trolls were glaring at anyone who dared to think about breaching the peace. I was under the impression that they were absolutely delighted.

Bob flitted up, landing on the parapet in front of me. 'Penny for your thoughts,' he said.

I gave him a smile. 'I was just wondering what my parents would have made of all this and if they'd be pleased that the Highlands and Lowlands are back together again. If they'd be happy that we're going to co-exist with the Fomori demons or if they'd be terrified that we'd never find a way to get along.'

'If they're anything like you, Uh Integrity, they'd be thrilled. They'd be so proud of you. I know because I'm a magnificent all-knowing being with powers you can only dream of.'

I laughed slightly. 'If you say so.' I glanced round. 'Where's Byron?'

Bob sobered up. 'Looking after his father's remains.'

I bit my lip and nodded. Aifric might have been a bastard but he was still Byron's father. Byron was going to be very mixed up about his feelings but he was a decent, good man and I knew he would grieve. 'I'm surprised you're still here,' I said to Bob. 'I thought you'd already be off looking for a new target. Those wishes ain't gonna wish themselves.'

Bob toed the stone. 'I thought I might hang around here for a while, if it's alright with you.'

He didn't look up so he didn't see my happy grin. 'It's very alright with me.'

Bob suddenly beamed. 'Really?'

'Really.'

He leapt up into the air and somersaulted. 'Great! I need your help then. All you have to do is to sneak my scimitar into Brochan's pocket. You're a thief, you can do it without him noticing. I think the big merman and I could have a lot of fun together.'

I watched him and he deflated slightly. 'You're not going to do it, are you?'

'Nope.'

'Uh Integrity! You're just no fun.'

I smiled and gazed down the hill. If I squinted, I could make out May and Fergus. It looked as if she was introducing him to a group of Fomori demons. I shook my head in amusement. The Bauchan would end up running the entire country if we weren't careful.

'They make a good couple, don't they?' Bob beamed.

'Yeah,' I nodded. 'They really do.'

'So when are you going to do it?'

I glanced at him. 'Do what?'

'Duh! You know what. You and Byron. When are you going to tie the knot? Get hitched? Walk down the aisle? Take the plunge? Get yoked? Say I do?'

'It's early days yet. Anyway, I think we've had enough excitement for a lifetime.'

He arched an eyebrow. 'You think your wedding will be exciting? It'll be the most monotonous and boring day I could imagine. It'll be you and Byron gazing googly-eyed at each other and going all soppy.' He made vomit noises.

'Then why are you bringing it up?'

Bob straightened. 'Because he's the one.'

I loved Byron. But to say he was the one? That seemed rather … definite. 'I don't know that.'

'Yes, you do,' Bob said, not unkindly. 'You're not *that* stupid, Uh Integrity. You know what love is.'

'Perhaps. But too many women think that a wedding is good just because it has a nice ring to it.'

'I could kill you with my thumb, you know.'

My grin widened. 'Go ahead. Give it a shot.'

He tutted. 'Be serious, please. Is Byron perfect?'

'No. Although,' I amended, 'he might be perfect for me.'

Bob grabbed my little finger and gave it a tight hug. 'Lust projects. Lust sees perfection where none exists. You know Byron has faults and you know he's not perfect. He knows you're not perfect. You're stubborn and hard-headed and you have a criminal past, not to mention that your jokes are possibly the worst ones in the universe.' He held up his tiny hand. 'Don't interrupt me, I'm on a roll. Love isn't about possession. It's not about filling an empty void within yourself. I see you when you look at him. You want the best for him. You don't idealise him. You know he still has a spoilt streak. You know he still has untapped potential but you want him to realise that for himself. You think your feelings for him are complicated but they're really not. There are no secrets. No ulterior motives. No joking around or kidding yourselves. You're willing to accept each other as you truly are. That's why you should get married.'

I stared dumbly at him. For the first time in my life I might have regretted making a stupid joke before giving Bob a chance to speak. The genie clearly had hidden depths I didn't know about.

'Plus,' he added, 'I have always wanted to be a bridesmaid. None of that ugly dress shite though. I want to be beautiful. And I want fabulous wedding favours. Also, the chance to ridicule you because you're wearing a giant white meringue.'

I flicked him away. 'Get lost.' I rather liked the idea of proposing to Byron. Maybe I'd consider it but I wasn't wearing white. Hot pink all the way.

'Yeah, yeah.' He glanced behind my shoulder. 'Speak of the devil.'

I turned round and spotted Byron. We smiled at each other, the rest of the world fading away until I barely noticed when Bob vanished, no doubt off to do more mischief.

'Hey,' I said eventually, when it became clear that we'd probably just stand there and grin at each other all day. 'Did you manage to sort out, uh, your father?'

'Yes. I've arranged for him to be taken back to the Moncrieffe Lands. His body will be safe from desecration there. And it's important that we don't just pretend he didn't exist. Like it or not, he's part of our story now.' He slipped his hand into mine. 'If he'd seen in you what I see in you, he would have yielded long before.' I gave him a questioning look. Byron shrugged. 'You're a fighter. No matter how bad the going is, you never give up. When things are dark and it seems like there's no way out, you find the exit. You're a true warrior, Integrity.'

'Layoch,' I whispered. I smiled. 'That's my true name.' Byron's mouth dropped open slightly. 'I told you I would trust you.'

His eyes gleamed. 'I'm Buaidh. It translates as victory.' He watched me carefully; a shiver ran down my body. 'I've not been victorious yet though.' He swallowed. Then I realised his hands were shaking.

Alarmed, I stared at him. 'What's wrong?'

'I've heard about this place down near England. I thought maybe we should go and pay it a visit.'

'Why? Are there problems there? Has there been fighting of some kind?' I gnawed on my bottom lip. 'I know there are going to be difficulties but I thought we'd have at least a bit of breathing space first. Surely none of us have got that far down the country yet.' Something else suddenly occurred to me. 'It's not the English, is it? That's all we need.'

'It's not that. And it's not a problem. It's just that there's an old blacksmith's there which used to be very famous. I remember reading old stories about it in my school history books. Of course, it fell out of use after the Fissure.'

'A blacksmith?' I was thoroughly confused. 'Are you getting some horses?'

'Uh, no. Bob reminded me about it. It's called Gretna Green. I know it might not seem like the right time but…' He scratched his neck. 'This is harder than I thought it would be. Maybe you think we ought to spend more time together first. But when you know, you know.'

Know what? I was thoroughly confused now. I'd seen Byron in a lot of different situations and I didn't think I'd ever seen him look so scared.

From out of nowhere, Bob reappeared. 'What are you doing?' he screeched. 'I've already softened her up for you. Just say the words!'

Byron ignored him. Still holding my hands, he got down on one knee and gazed up at me.

My mouth dropped. Hang on a minute…

Thank you so much for reading Last Wish and sticking by Integrity to the end!

I truly hope you enjoyed it. It would mean a huge amount if you could review – any and all feedback is so very, very welcome and hugely important for independent authors like myself.

Acknowledgments

There are so many people without whom this book, and indeed series, wouldn't have been possible and who I can't possibly thank enough. Any omissions here are entirely my own fault.

First and foremost, to Karen Holmes for her superlative editing – not to mention her ability to keep me buoyed up when I'm sure what I've written isn't worth the paper. To Clarissa Yeo and her always wonderful cover art. To Saskia Maarleveld for her wonderful audio narration, as well as all the fabulous folks over at Tantor. To the Women of Urban Fantasy for keeping me sane. To Barbara Hall, Yvanca Wensing and Luma Zetani for their invaluable beta reading.

To Marlowe, Scout, Lara and Mavis for giving me (mostly) peace to write when I've needed it.

To the Taylors Education Group for their unwitting inspiration for Integrity.

To Adrianna, the most perfect PA I could ever wish for.

To my family for their continued and unstinting support.

Finally, to Malaysia. It's been seven and a half years and, as I write this, I'm surrounded by boxes and crates and suitcases as I prepare to return to the UK. The tropical weather, the amazing food and, above all, the warm, kind people have made this such an inspiring adventure. Terima Kasih from the bottom of my heart.

Helen xxx

About the author

After teaching English literature in the UK, Japan and Malaysia, Helen Harper left behind the world of education following the worldwide success of her Blood Destiny series of books. She is a professional member of the Alliance of Independent Authors and writes full time, thanking her lucky stars every day that's she lucky enough to do so!

Helen has always been a book lover, devouring science fiction and fantasy tales when she was a child growing up in Scotland.

She currently lives in Devon in the UK with far too many cats – not to mention the dragons, fairies, demons, wizards and vampires that seem to keep appearing from nowhere.

Helen Harper

Made in the USA
Monee, IL
26 March 2020